D0721915

The Life Story of Jayber Crow, Barber,

of the Port William Membership,

as Written by Himself

Also by Wendell Berry

JAYBER CROW

A Novel by Wendell Berry

COUNTERPOINT
WASHINGTON, D.C.

This book is a work of fiction. Nothing is in it that has not been imagined.

The final two chapters of this book have been published by the *Temenos
Academy Review* (Kathleen Raine, ed., London).

Library of Congress Cataloging-in-Publication Data
Berry, Wendell, 1934–
Jayber Crow : the life story of Jayber Crow, barber, of the Port William
membership, as written by himself : a novel / by Wendell Berry.
p.   cm.
ISBN 1-58243-029-2 (alk. paper)
1. Port William (Ky.: Imaginary place)—Fiction. 2. Kentucky—Fiction.
3. Barbers—Fiction. 4. Orphans—Fiction. I. Title
PS3552.E75 J39 2000
813'54—dc21   00-035889

FIRST PRINTING

Jacket and text design by David Bullen

Printed in the United States of America on acid-free paper
that meets the American National Standards Institute z39-48 Standard.

COUNTERPOINT
P.O. Box 65793
Washington, D.C. 20035-5793

Counterpoint is a member of the Perseus Books Group.

10   9   8   7   6   5   4   3   2

Virginia Berry
1907–1997
Requiescat in pace

ACKNOWLEDGMENTS

A publisher's job is to provide a writer with encouragement, correction, amusement, and (of course) publication. For all of these things, and for kindness and friendship, I thank the people at Counterpoint Press: Heather McLeod, Trish Hoard, John McLeod, and Jack Shoemaker.

For typing my manuscript in various drafts, I thank Tanya and David Charlton and Tanya Berry. For reading the book and giving indispensable advice, I am indebted to the aforementioned two Tanyas, Ross Feld, Maurice Telleen, Don Wallis, and Donald Hall. Carole McCurdy copyedited the manuscript; I am grateful for her vigilance and her gift for marginal conversation.

NOTICE
Persons attempting to find a "text" in this book will be prosecuted; persons attempting to find a "subtext" in it will be banished; persons attempting to explain, interpret, explicate, analyze, deconstruct, or otherwise "understand" it will be exiled to a desert island in the company only of other explainers.

BY ORDER OF THE AUTHOR

Contents

Magnanimous Despair alone
Could show me so divine a thing . . .

Part I

1

The Barber in Port William

I never put up a barber pole or a sign or even gave my shop a name. I didn't have to. The building was already called "the barbershop." That was its name because that had been its name for nobody knew how long. Port William had little written history. Its history was its living memory of itself, which passed over the years like a moving beam of light. It had a beginning that it had forgotten, and would have an end that it did not yet know. It *seemed* to have been there forever. After I had been there a while, the shop began to be called Jayber Crow's, or just Jayber's. "Well, I'm going down to Jayber's," people would say, as if it had been clearly marked on some map, though it was so only in their minds. I never had a telephone, so I was not even in the book.

From 1937 until 1969, I was "the barber" in Port William. The shop was at the bottom of the swag in the midst of the town. The road came up the river from Hargrave; about a mile from Port William it climbed the hill onto the upland, made a couple of dips and turns, passed the graveyard and the houses opposite, passed the church and the bank and the handful of business places, went by my shop and the garage down in the swag, and then rose up again, going by more houses; at the top of the rise it passed the school, and then it hurried on. Except for the law, and the local habit of stopping in vehicles to talk in the middle of the road, car drivers from elsewhere have never seen much reason to slow down when they go through Port William. I still am the Port William barber, the only one it has got—though since 1969 I have not been in town.

When I came there and set up shop in January of 1937, the place was maybe better off than I have seen it since. Thirty-seven was a Depression year, and I don't ask you to believe that the place was flourishing. But it was at least thrifty. People didn't waste anything they knew how to save; they couldn't afford much new stuff, and so they hung on to what they had. There were a lot of patched clothes in those days. But all the commercial places in town were still occupied and doing business. The people of the town still belonged to it economically as well as in other ways. And we still had a doctor, "old" Dr. Markman, who was not then as old as he was going to be.

Except for Saturdays, when I would sometimes be at it from breakfast until midnight or after, the haircutting trade in Port William was, as you might say, intermittent. When I had no customer, I would climb into the chair myself and talk to whoever was loafing, or if the place was empty I would read or take a nap. A barber chair is an excellent place to read or sleep. It tilts back and has a footrest and a headrest. Or (since you can't loaf or read or nap all the time) I would keep an eye on the town. If the weather was bad, I would stand at the window and look; if it was good, I would carry a chair out and sit under the sugar tree at the edge of the road.

I always tried to keep faith with my customers—to keep faith, that is, with the random possibility that at almost any moment one or another of them *might* take a notion to come in for a haircut or a shave, or would need a place to sit. And to tell the truth, I generally had need of the coins that wandered about in Port William pants pockets, and yearned to add them to my collection in the cigar box on the backbar.

I kept faith, but I confess that I kept it somewhat irregularly. Sometimes, when my clients were absent, I would be moved to stray about. My predecessor had left me a little cardboard sign with a clock face and drooping metal hands that declared invariably: BACK AT 6:30. When I left, it would always be a good while before six-thirty, and so I had plenty of time. If I got back before the promised minute, I counted it much to my credit. I might walk up to see who would be loafing along the street or in the stores. From there I might stroll out the road and into the woods on the bluffs above the river. Or I might just cross the road to Mr. Milo Settle's garage, a place of often interesting work and sometimes ferocious political debates instigated by Mr. Settle's chief assistant, Portly Jones, who had opinions he was willing to die for. If I wanted no company, I walked in the other direction, up the rise, past the schoolhouse, and out into the country that way. Sometimes I might take off a whole day to go fishing with Burley Coulter or one of the Rowanberrys—always taking care to get back before six-thirty. Of course, if I didn't leave until *after* six-thirty in the evening, I had all night to get back. And since nobody was apt to want a haircut at six-thirty in the morning, I could stay away until the next evening. My clock said I would be back at six-thirty, but it didn't say what day. And sooner or later, until the last time, I always got back.

Port William repaid watching. I was always on the lookout for what would be revealed. Sometimes nothing would be, but sometimes I beheld astonishing sights.

One hot summer afternoon, for instance, I saw Grover Gibbs passing along in front of Mr. Settle's garage with a plumber's helper over his shoulder. He saw, sticking out from beneath an automobile, Portly Jones's sweat-shiny big bald head, to the top of which, with a smooth and forceful underhanded thrust, he affixed the suction cup. Portly then enacted a sort of seizure in which, with his feet and left hand, he tried to hurry out from under the car, while with his right hand he tried unsuccessfully to detach the plumber's helper. It appeared that he was trying to drag himself out by the head. He didn't get out very fast. Meanwhile his assailant walked on up the street a ways and then turned and walked casually back to see the results of his inspiration. He walked with his hands innocently folded behind the bib of his overalls, a disinterested look in his eyes, his face rather tensely drawn around a small hole between his lips, through which he was whistling a tune. He allowed himself to be confronted by Portly, looking perhaps like a unicorn with a red face.

"Grover," he said, "who done this? If it was you, I'll *kill* you."

Grover said nothing, but solemnly, still whistling, tried to help Portly remove his horn, which they were able to do only by boring a hole in the cup to relieve the suction.

"It completely ruined my plunger," Grover told me later, "but of course I couldn't've claimed it anyhow."

And on an early morning, when I was almost the only one awake, I saw Fielding Berlew in the middle of the road, dancing to "The Ballad of Rose McInnis," which he sang with deep feeling and tears in his eyes. He had spent the night in a lonely vigil in town—"three-thirds drunk," as he would say—owing to his failure to see eye to eye with his wife. He danced with his arms held out like wings, in slow steps round and round, as gracefully as it could be done by a drunk man in a pair of gum boots. All of a sudden a trailer truck popped over the rise. It began to shudder and buck and weave; there was a great howling and hissing of brakes and the tires shrieked on the blacktop. Only when the front bumper was virtually touching Fee's thigh did the driver manage to bring the truck to a standstill and then collapse with relief and thanksgiving. Fee, who had taken no notice of the late commotion, continued to dance and sing. The driver then reconcentrated his forces and blew the horn, a long exasperated bleat that disparaged Port William and all it stood for. Fee thereupon took notice. He stopped dancing, and then as an afterthought he stopped singing. He regarded the driver. He regarded the truck. He looked down upon it, insofar as a small man can look down upon a thing towering many feet above his head. He looked back at the driver. He said, "Get that sonvabitch out of the road—before I *kick* it out of the road."

Another morning, a fine Saturday in the late fall, I got a little break between customers and went up to Lathrop's for the makings of a quick lunch. Some of the boys had started a baseball game in the empty lot next to the church. Shorty Sowers, the banker's son, was on his way to the church to take his violin lesson from Mrs. Alexander, the preacher's wife. As he was going by, a batter struck out. Shorty seized his fiddle by the neck and stepped up to the rock they were using as home plate. He told the pitcher, "Show me what you got!"

I came out of Lathrop's just in time to hear that, to see the pitch, and then Shorty's little pop fly to third base.

"After that," he said, "I knew her by the crack."

Yet another sight I used to see—one that was more or less regular during the year or two that he lived after I came to Port William—was Uncle

Ab Rowanberry shuffling by, carrying a rifle, a lantern, and a sack containing a chamber pot, a cowbell, a corn knife, and a long leather purse tied with a rag string. He would be on his way between daughters. He had five daughters all living in the neighborhood, and he stayed a while with each in turn, leaving each before he wore out his welcome. "Company is like snow," he said. "The longer it stays, the worse it looks." Since one of the daughters and her family now occupied the home place, Uncle Ab carried with him all his worldly possessions, the terms of his independence and self-respect: the rifle with which he provided a little meat for the table and with which he could defend himself if attacked, the corn knife in case he needed it, the lantern and chamber pot to preserve his dignity when he had to get up at night, the cowbell to ring if he fell down and couldn't get up, and his own hands with which he worked at whatever small tasks he was still able to do. He was something of the old life of the place. I observed him carefully and have remembered him always.

Other things too were revealed to me that were not so quickly ended. Poor old ramshackledy Fee Berlew, of all people and in his later years, was the only man I ever had to (so to speak) throw out of my shop. His nephew, visiting at Christmas, had slipped him a pint of whiskey, a dangerous item to have lying about in Mrs. Berlew's house. Fee undertook to preserve it from all harm in the shortest possible time, with the result that shortly after supper he found himself unable to see eye to eye with Mrs. Berlew. He came, of course, to my shop for such shelter and comfort as I could give. But his condition by then was just awful. He was completely sodden, bewildered, half-crazy, and full of the foulest kind of indignation. I could neither quiet him down nor, finally, put up with him. And so I helped him out the door, not being all that happy to do so on a cold night.

But he didn't go away. He pecked on the front window, put his face close to the glass, and reviled me. He called me a "clabber-headed stray," an "orphan three days shy of a bastard," a "damned low-down hair barber"—and meaner names. This delighted the several big boys who were passing the time with me that evening, but it did not put more joy into my life.

And then the next morning here came Fee the first thing, easing his head in through the door as though expecting me to cut it off with my razor. He had overnight achieved that state of sobriety in which, racked by pain and sorrow, he wished to be unconscious or perhaps dead. When he finally looked up at me his little red eyes filled with tears.

"Jayber," he said, "Could you forgive an old son of a bitch?"

"I could," I said. "Yes, I can. I do."

Maybe because I had been a good while in school myself, and had liked it and not liked it, and had finally failed out of it, the Port William School was a place I observed with a kind of fascination. The school had eight grades. If it had taught the grades all the way through high school, maybe it wouldn't have interested me so much. The future presses hard upon a high school, and somehow qualifies and diminishes it. The students in a high school begin courtships; the *next* generation begins to assert its claims; people begin to think of what they will do when they get out. But the Port William School, grades one through eight, seemed to house the community's almost pure potential, little reduced by any intention on the part of the students themselves. They were there in varying degrees by interest or endurance, but not by purpose. And always, interested or not, they were there somewhat under protest. The children in the lower grades, I believe, thought that school would go on more or less forever, interrupted at dependable intervals by recess and lunch, Christmas and summer. By the time they got to grades seven and eight, they knew that it would end and they would leave, but they thought they would leave only to go to the high school down at Hargrave, and their heads were full of innocent illusions about what they would do there.

I liked best the school as it was when I first knew it, when it served only the town and the immediate neighborhood, when the students got there on foot. Then the neighborhood seemed more freestanding and self-enclosed than it ever did again after consolidation. The town contained the school, and the school, for a while at least, contained the children.

To walk up past the school while it was in session was like coming near a sleeping large animal. You could hear the enclosed murmurs and rustlings of an intense inward life, belonging, it seemed, to another world, whose absence from the town made *it* seem otherworldly. While the children were in school, the town seemed abnormally quiet. The quiet, by midafternoon, would sometimes seem almost entranced.

And so I loved especially the time of day when school let out. What the will of the neighborhood had managed to pen up all day in something like order would all of a sudden burst loose and stream out both ways along the road. A rout of children would pour from the schoolhouse down into the quiet town—a cataract of motions and sounds: voices calling, shouting, singing, laughing, teasing, arguing; boys running, dancing about, hitting each other, sometimes fighting in earnest; girls switching their dresstails and hair in mock disdain and condemnation of the behavior of the boys. And often you would hear a boy's voice chanting above the rest: "School's out! School's out! Teacher wore my britches out!" Or something on the order of *"Hey, booger-nose!"*

At such a moment, to the best of my memory, I first took actual notice of Mattie Chatham—or Mattie Keith, as she was then.

It was a spring afternoon, warm. I was standing in the open door of the shop, leaning against the jamb, watching. Mattie was walking arm-in-arm with two other girls, Thelma Settle and Althie Gibbs. I suppose Mattie was to spend that night at Thelma's or Althie's house, for ordinarily she would have gone in the other direction; her home was down in the river bottom, a mile and a half from town by the children's shortcut over the bluff.

They had crossed the road to be out of the crowd, and they were telling each other things and giggling. They were "older girls" by then, feeling themselves so, and yet unable to maintain the dignity that they felt their status required. This failure made whatever they were giggling about even funnier. They were being silly, each one tugging in a different direction, so that they had trouble even staying on the walk. They were not aware of me until they were almost even with my door, and then they looked up and saw me—a tall, lean, baldish man, almost twice their age, smiling down upon them from the threshold. This sight, so incongruent with all they had on their minds, increased their merriment. They looked up at me, raised the pitch and volume of their laughter, and ran past. But I *saw* Mattie Keith then, and after that I would be aware of her. Seeing her as she was then, I might have seen (had I thought to look) the woman she was to be. Or is it because I knew the woman that I see her now so clearly as a child?

She was a pretty girl, and I was moved by her prettiness. Her hair was brown at the verge of red, and curly. Her face was still a little freckled. But it was her eyes that most impressed me. They were nearly black and had a liquid luster. The brief, laughing look that she had given me made me feel extraordinarily seen, as if after that I might be visible in the dark.

2

Goforth

The afternoon of my first memory of Mattie Keith (Mattie Chatham, as she was to be) would have been, I believe, in the spring of 1939, when I had been "in business" in Port William a little more than two years.

If you have lived in Port William a little more than two years, you are still, by Port William standards, a stranger, liable to have your name mispronounced. Crow was not a familiar name in this part of the country, and so for a long time a lot of people here called me Cray, a name that was familiar. And though I was only twenty-two when I came to the town, many of the same ones would call me "Mr. Cray" to acknowledge that they did not know me well. My rightful first name is Jonah, but I had not gone by that name since I was ten years old. I had been called simply J., and that was the way I signed myself. Once my customers took me to themselves, they called me Jaybird, and then Jayber. Thus I became, and have remained, a possession of Port William.

I was, in fact, a native as well as a newcomer, for I was born at Goforth, over on Katy's Branch, on August 3, 1914—and so lived one day in the world before the beginning of total war. You could say that Goforth was somewhat farther from Port William then than it is now; all that connected them then was a wagon road, imperfectly rocked, wondrously crooked, and bedeviled by mud holes. Goforth had its own church and school and store, but people from over there came to Port William to bank and vote and buy the things they could not buy at Goforth.

I don't remember when I did not know Port William, the town and the neighborhood. My relation to that place, my being in it and my absences from it, is the story of my life. That story has surprised me almost every day—but now, in the year 1986, so near the end, it seems not surprising at all but only a little strange, as if it all has happened to somebody I don't yet quite know. Certainly, all of it has happened to somebody younger.

My mother was Iona Quail, and through her I am related to the Cotmans, the Thigpens, and the Proudfoots. Her mother died fairly young, and because of that, perhaps, when she was too young my mother married a boy from somewhere across the river—"from off," as we said. He came courting her afoot every Saturday night, walking six miles (so I've heard) to where he borrowed a johnboat opposite the mouth of Katy's Branch, rowed across the river and up the creek to the first riffle, and then walked the rest of the way to the starveling little hillside farm above Goforth. The marriage was a have-to case. I was not thought of until too late, and this was something I seem to have known almost from birth. Around here it is hard for an interesting secret to stay a secret.

My father, whose given name was Luther, was by trade a blacksmith. His people could, or would, do nothing for him. My grandfather Quail, having only the one child, helped his new son-in-law to set up a little shop, with forge and anvil, across the road from Goforth Church, and to gather up some sticks of furniture for the house adjoining.

I have in memory only a few scattered pictures of my early lost life at Goforth. I remember sitting in my mother's lap in the rocking chair beside the kitchen stove, and the sound of her voice singing in time to the beat of the rockers. I remember that in winter we lived mostly in the kitchen, for the kitchen was the only room with a stove. I remember my father's shop, which I loved. I remember the plows and sleds that took shape there in the light of the open doorway. I remember my father bent over a horse's hoof held between his knees. I remember the ringing of the anvil and the screech of hot metal in the slack tub. I remember walking from house to shop, holding my mother's hand. I remember a hound named Stump and a horse named Joe and a cow named Bell. These and other things seem clear when they are off on the outer verges of my mind, but then, when I try to see them straight, they grow misty and fade away under the burden of questions. What did that kitchen actually look like? What was the song my mother sang as we rocked by the stove? I can remember my father's stance and movements at his work, but I might as well never have seen his face. We lived, I know, a life with very little margin. We were not hungry or cold, but we had nothing to spare.

My first clear memories are of the terrible winter of 1917 and 1918. It was not terrible for me, at least not at first. For me, I suppose, life went on for a while as it always had. But I knew that the grown-ups thought it a terrible winter. There was, to start with, a war going on over across the sea—an idea as strange to me as if it had been going on over across the sky. I had no clear understanding of what a war was, but I knew that it killed people and that my elders feared it. I imagined people shooting one another in a darkness that covered everything.

And then snow fell until it was deep, and then it drifted and froze, and the cattle and horses wandered loose about the country, walking over the tops of the fences. The river froze and then a thaw came and it rained, and the river rose out of its banks. Great ice gorges formed that sheared off or uprooted the shore trees and wrecked steamboats and barges. People had never seen anything like that ice. No flood that they had known even resembled it. The ice groaned and ground and creaked. When it broke loose, nothing—nothing!—could stand against it. It crushed or tore loose and carried away everything it came to. It broke steel cables as if they were cobwebs. That was a legendary winter; nobody who lived through it ever forgot it. I have shorn many a whitened head that preserved inside it the memory of that winter as clear as yesterday.

And then that winter became terrible for me by more than hearsay, for both of my young parents fell ill and died only a few hours apart in late February of 1918. I don't know how I learned that this had happened. It seemed to me that they just disappeared into the welter of that time: a war off somewhere in the dark world; a river of ice off somewhere, breaking trees and boats; sickness off somewhere, and then in the house; and then death there in the house, and everything changed. I remember a crowd of troubled people in the house. I remember crouching beside the woodbox behind the kitchen stove while several people offered to pick me up and comfort me, and I would not look up.

And then an old woman I knew as Aunt Cordie gathered me up without asking and sat down in the rocking chair and held me and let me cry. She had on a coarse black sweater over a black dress that reached to her shoetops and a black hat with little white and blue flowers on it there in the dead of winter. I can remember how she seemed to be trying to enclose me entirely in her arms.

"God love his heart!" she said. "Othy, we're going to take him home."

3

Squires Landing

And that was what they did. There really was nobody else to do it, but she treated me like a prize she had won. Uncle Othy too. They had had three children of their own, and all three had died as children. I suppose Aunt Cordie and Uncle Othy had a store of affection laid away that they now brought out and applied to me. Later I would know how blessed I had been.

Aunt Cordie had been born Cordelia Quail, my grandfather Quail's sister. She married Otha Dagget, she liked to say, "because he could whistle so pretty." They lived where they had always lived: over on the river at Squires Landing, two miles and a little more from Goforth, and about four miles from Port William. I remember my life at Squires Landing from the first day.

By the time I came, the worst of that winter was over. The river was back in its banks and free of ice. But the shores that once had been lined with trees were now bare mud, except for here and there a broken stump, and here and there a big tree that had managed somehow to survive, though scarred and splintered by the ice. And in the bottoms were still great heaped-up jagged piles of ice that would not entirely melt away until summer. Where the ice gorge had passed, the shores of the river looked scoured and bitten and lifeless. Years later, when I saw pictures of the battlefields of World War I, I would be reminded of the Kentucky River valley in the late winter of 1918. But to me, then, that dead and shattered landscape looked only as it seemed it ought to look after the death of my parents and the loss of our old life at Goforth.

For a while after I came to Squires Landing, I would stay as close to Aunt Cordie as I could. I tried to keep her not just in sight but in reach. When she moved, I moved. "Be careful now, Cordie," Uncle Othy would say. "Don't tramp on the boy."

And she herself told me once, "I was like an old hen with one pore forlorn little chick."

I remember too how spring came, just when I thought it might stay winter forever, at first in little touches and strokes of green lighting up the bare mud like candle flames, and then it covered the whole place with a light pelt of shadowy grass blades and leaves. And I remember how, as the days and the winds passed over, the foliage shifted and sang.

I began to feel at home.

I will tell one story that was often told during that winter and spring. I heard it many times from several people, then and since, and I have thought of it many times.

There was a shantyboatman named Emmet Edge who had his boat tied up at the end of a big bottom upriver, where some of the Thigpens were living. The morning the ice gorge broke up, the Thigpens were in their stripping room with a good fire going, getting the tobacco ready for market. They heard somebody in a pair of gum boots—*thwock! thwock! thwock!*—coming as fast as he could step. There was a knock on the door, too loud, as if the knocker expected the ones inside to be asleep.

One of them slid back the latch, and old man Edge stepped in among them, not bothering to pull the door to behind him. His eyes were wide open and his face as white as his hair. At first he didn't say anything but just stood looking at them as if he couldn't decide they were real.

"Well," one of them said, "what's the matter, Mr. Emmet?"

And then he told his tale.

He had been expecting the ice to go, and had been awake most of two nights. The second night, he sat holding a pan in his hands between his knees, the way the old shantyboatmen used to do when the river was changing, so that if they went to sleep they would drop the pan and the clatter would wake them up. What he expected to do when the ice went, maybe he didn't know himself.

And then it went. When he felt the boat heave, snapping its lines like sewing threads, he knew there wasn't anything for him to do except get ashore, if he could.

He barely made it, scrambling through the great mill of broken and breaking ice, sliding and grabbing and falling and getting up again, until finally, having given himself up for dead, he got solid ground under his feet.

"So, boys," Emmet Edge said, "I very nearly was a goner, and my boat is gone for certain."

But the Thigpens—who had not had the wits scared out of them—said, well, maybe so, but they thought they at least ought to go back and have a look.

So they all walked back across the bottom to the place on the now-unrecognizable shore where Emmet Edge thought he had left his boat.

And there the boat was, sitting perfectly level atop a great heap of ice, just like the Ark on Mount Ararat. Not even a dish was broken. Emmet Edge hewed some proper steps into the hill of ice, moved back into his boat, and lived there while the spring warmth brought it gently down again onto the Thigpens' last year's cornfield, where it landed toward the end of May.

The Daggets kept the store at the landing and had a farm of a dozen or so acres—a shelf of bottomland and a scrap of hillside—on which they grew a little tobacco crop and a garden, and kept a horse, a milk cow, meat hogs, and flocks of chickens, turkeys, guineas, and geese. The life of that place had an amplitude I had not known before.

Squires Landing was just below the mouth of Squires Branch, a steep small stream that dried up in summer but after a hard rain tumbled furiously down over its course of heaped and shifting rocks. The house stood well up the hillside, overlooking the confluence of branch and river. Behind it were the henhouse, smokehouse, coal shed, and privy. Tucked in under the slope, down near the branch, was a small barn, where Uncle

Othy housed his crop and sheltered his animals. The store stood on a narrow bench below the house and above the road. Below the road and the patch of bottom where the garden was, the river was always coming down and passing by and going on.

The river moved me strangely, and I loved it from the day I first laid eyes on it. When Aunt Cordie made me stay inside because of the weather, I would stand at the window and look upstream and downstream and across. The river was a barrier and yet a connection. I felt, a long time before I knew, that the river had shaped the land. The whole country leaned toward the river. All the streams flowed to it. It flowed by, and yet it stayed. It brought things and carried them away. I did not know where it flowed from or to, but I knew that it flowed a great distance through the opening it had made. The current told me that.

So did the boats. There were little landings like ours every few miles, and there was a fairly steady traffic of steam or gasoline packets that carried freight and passengers and livestock, and of towboats shoving barges loaded with coal or lumber. I remember the *Hanover,* the *Revonah,* the *White Dove,* the *Richard Roe,* the *Falls City,* and the *Dot.* The goods that Uncle Othy sold in his store all came by the river. The boats would whistle three times, pull in to shore, let down their plank, unload whatever cargo was directed to Squires Landing, load on whatever freight or creatures were outbound, and be gone quicker than you could believe, up or down. It was wonderful the way the river and the banks and the whole valley would be quiet, preoccupied with the lights and shadows and the regular business of a summer morning, and then you would hear that whistle, and all of a sudden there would be this commotion: the sound of a big engine, a bell ringing, shouts, blocks creaking as the plank was lowered, cattle bawling, pigs squealing, men cursing, the roustabouts chanting as they passed bags or boxes from hand to hand. I liked to watch them pen the fat hogs at the banktop and then force them across the gangplank onto the boat. You would hear some fancy language from the captain then, especially if a shoat got loose. Boat captains were the chief tyrants of the world in those days. They thought you could say anything to anybody from a pilothouse, and the black men who were loading or unloading the boat just had to grin and look away.

Often, forgetting Uncle Othy's instructions and warning, I would venture as far into the thick of it as I could go, dodging here and there for a better look, for I wanted to see everything; I wanted to penetrate the wonder. I would be in the way and sometimes in danger. And then Uncle Othy would see me, and under the eyes of the experienced and worldly men of the boat, he would be embarrassed by me. He would speak to me then as he never did at other times: "Damn it to hell, boy, *get* out of the way! I *told* you! Damned boy ain't no more than half weaned, and here he is in the way of working men." He would be trying to get me thoroughly cussed before the captain could get a chance to do it.

There would often be passengers too, getting on or getting off, accompanied sometimes by valises or trunks. I could never get enough of watching them. They had, to me, the enchantment of distance about them. They would be going to or coming from Frankfort or Hargrave, Cincinnati or Louisville, or places farther away—places, all of them, that were only names to me, but names that seemed palpable and rich, like coins in the hand.

And so I came along in time to know the end of the age of steamboating. I would learn later that there had been other ages of the river that I had arrived too late to know but that I could read about and learn to imagine. There was at first the age when no people were here, and I have sometimes felt at night that absence grow present to my mind, that long silence in which no human name was spoken or given, and the nameless river made no sound of any human tongue. And then there was the Indian age when names were called here that have never been spoken in the present language of Port William. Then came the short ages of us white people, the ages of the dugout, the flatboat, the keelboat, the log raft, the steamboat. And I have lived on now into the age of the diesel towboat and recreational boating and water-skiing. And yet it is hard to look at the river in its calm, just after daylight or just before dark, and believe that history has happened to it. The river, the river itself, leaves marks but bears none. It is only water flowing in a path that other water has worn.

Or is that other water really "other," or is it the same water always running, flowing always toward the gathering of all waters, and always rising and returning again, and again flowing? I knew this river first when

I was a little boy, and I know it now when I am an old man once again living beside it—almost seventy years!—and always when I have watched it
I have been entranced and mystified. What is it? Is it the worn trough of
itself that is a feature of the land and is marked on maps, or is it the water
flowing? Or is it the land itself that over time is shaped and reshaped by
the flowing water, and is caught by no map?

The surface of the quieted river, as I thought in those old days at
Squires Landing, as I think now, is like a window looking into another
world that is like this one except that it is quiet. Its quietness makes it
seem perfect. The ripples are like the slats of a blind or a shutter through
which we see imperfectly what is perfect. Though that other world can
be seen only momentarily, it looks everlasting. As the ripples become
more agitated, the window darkens and the other world is hidden. As I
did not know then but know now, the surface of the river is like a living
soul, which is easy to disturb, is often disturbed, but, growing calm,
shows what it was, is, and will be.

As close to the river and involved in its traffic as we were, you would
think that sometime or other we would have traveled on it, but we never
did. The world of travelers was another world to us, and it charmed us
no end. We talked a great deal of what we had seen come and go on the
boats. And there was the *Princess,* a showboat that would tie up at the
landing once or twice a summer. The calliope would play, drawing the
people down off the ridges and out of the hollows; there would be a
night when we would all sit wide-eyed in the presence of a world entirely
unlike our own; and then it would go cranking off upriver in the morning and our life would go on as before.

Though it verged on the world of flow and travel, Squires Landing
was a world in place. We were too busy to go anywhere. Besides the
landing and the store, we had to look after the farm and the garden and
the many branches of Aunt Cordie's housekeeping. Aunt Cordie was
always surrounded by food that was growing or getting fat, or being
gathered or canned or cured or dried or cooked. We ate very little from
the store, which stocked mostly the things people couldn't raise: salt and
flour and New Orleans molasses in barrels, pepper, cloves, nutmeg,
vanilla, coffee, cheese, cloth in bolts, hardware, coal, harness, and so on.

And Uncle Othy bought eggs and cream and old hens and other produce that the housewives brought in when they came to buy.

As everywhere, people would come in to pass the time, whether they bought anything or not. When Uncle Othy had to be busy in his crop, Aunt Cordie and I went down and kept the store. When Aunt Cordie and I went wandering off to gather wild greens or berries, Uncle Othy kept an eye on the house. We really didn't go much of anywhere except up to Port William to church on Sunday morning. We could easier have gone to Goforth Church, but that was Methodist. Port William, anyhow, was our town.

Our nearest neighbors were Put Woolfork and his family on the upriver side, and on the downriver side Arch and Ada Thripple and their grown daughters, Wanda and Bernice.

We hardly ever saw Put Woolfork's womenfolk or children, but we saw Put every day. Aunt Cordie would say, "Now, that Put. He puts them all to work over there—I know he does—and then he comes over here to where he won't even have to see them working. He's got little enough sense to think he's smart."

And Uncle Othy would always answer, "I reckon I go to all the sweat and worry of keeping store just to provide Put Woolfork a place to set down."

Put didn't often buy anything. Neither he nor any of his family ever came to our house, and we never went over to theirs. "I see enough of him as 'tis," Aunt Cordie said.

But we often walked across the hillside to the Thripples' to sit till bedtime, or they walked over to sit with us. Aunt Cordie taught me to call them Aunt Ada and Uncle Arch, and I did. She also insisted that I call their daughters Miss Wanda and Miss Bernice, and I did that too, but only in Aunt Cordie's presence.

The Thripples were good, industrious people like Aunt Cordie and Uncle Othy. They took care of themselves, were good neighbors, and I never heard them speak an envious word. Uncle Arch farmed about fifty acres, mostly hillside with a narrow strip of bottom. He stayed busy all the time, though he didn't hurry much; he never had a lot to say, and was in most ways quiet. But he had one oddity that interested everybody and that nobody could account for. The old man was famous all over the

Port William community for the noise he made working a team. Days would go by sometimes and we would hear not a whisper from over there, and then Uncle Arch would hitch up Dick and Bob and go to work, and then you could hear him all over the valley. He just ranted and rared.

And I remember this:

The only neighbors we had across the river—the only ones we ever saw—were an elderly black couple, Ben and Ellie Fewclothes. The story was that Uncle Ben had wandered into our part of the country from somewhere down south when he was a young man, with nothing of his own but the ragged clothes he was wearing. They called him Ben Fewclothes and perhaps because he needed a new one, he took the name. He and Aunt Ellie had a farm in the big bottom over there—about thirty acres or so, bordering on a slue. It was good land, and they made a pretty self-sufficient thing of it, the way all the farming people did then, or tried to. I called them Uncle Ben and Aunt Ellie. You might be thinking by now that I had a lot of aunts and uncles, but that was just the courtesy of those days; children were not allowed to go around first-naming older people.

Uncle Ben would come over occasionally, but not often. He didn't fish much, at least not in the river, and didn't own a boat. But Aunt Ellie was a regular customer at the store, and whenever she came over she and Aunt Cordie would sit down together and visit and talk a while. Aunt Ellie conducted herself very consciously as a lady—was precise and careful always in her manners and her speech. Every Saturday morning she would come down the dug steps in the bank with a basket of eggs, a bucket of cream, and sometimes two or three old hens with their legs tied. Without much raising her voice, she would call out, "Mister Dagget! Mister Dagget!" And Uncle Othy would go in the boat and set her over the river to do her weekly dealing. After I got big enough, one of my favorite duties was to go along to help.

When we got to the far side, I would step up into the bow of the johnboat, and while Uncle Othy held the boat steady against the bank I would help Aunt Ellie to step in and situate herself and her bucket and basket and whatever else she had brought. She would always say, "Well! Thank you, honey!" And then I would go back to my seat in the stern, and Uncle Othy would row us across. When we got to the landing on our side, I would go forward and help Aunt Ellie get ashore. And she would say again, "Well! Thank you, honey!"

We were bringing Aunt Ellie across one fine Saturday morning in June. The river was as still almost as glass; it was quiet all around, except for Uncle Arch Thripple who was up on his hillside plowing tobacco with old Dick. Uncle Arch was ripping as usual:

"*Get* up, Dick! Haw! Haw! Whoa! Get over *haw!* Get up! *Gee,* Dick, damn you to hell! Whooooa! *Haw!* Get up, Dick!"

And Aunt Ellie, perhaps unable to resist, looking neither at Uncle Othy nor at me but speaking in her precise way as if to the swallows flying over the water, said, "Seem like Mistah Thripple having trouble with his Dick this mo'ning!"

I caught it—I was old enough by then—and was about to laugh, but Uncle Othy looked quickly at me and said, "Sh!"

From start to finish, I was pretty much Aunt Cordie's boy. When she spoke of me to other people, she always called me "my boy," tenderly and proudly, for I was her helper. She was on in years and somewhat slowed, but she was seldom idle. We went steadily from one thing to another, from can see to can't see, and then on by lamplight, and I helped her with everything: keeping up the fires, maintaining the lamps, cooking, cleaning fish, dressing poultry, washing the dishes, washing the clothes, cleaning the house, working in the garden, putting up food for winter. Aunt Cordie was good company and always kind, but she saw to it that I did my work right. The best part of my education, and surely the most useful part, came from her.

When Aunt Cordie didn't need me, I would go down and hang about in the store and listen to the talk. For there was always talk. "More talk than business," Uncle Othy would say. But perhaps he liked the talk as well as the business; at least he always took part, and he was seldom alone. Sometimes he would let me help a little in the store, or would recruit me for some farming job that required more than two hands. But Uncle Othy was persnickety in his ways and hard to please; I liked better to work with Aunt Cordie.

I was Jonah Crow in those days. When I thought of myself, I thought, "I am Jonah Crow." A pretty name. I imagined that my mother had loved the sound of it. I was Jonah Crow entirely.

Aunt Cordie had several pet names for me. When she used my right name, she pronounced it with an air of preciseness, as if to show respect for my great namesake.

Uncle Othy said "Jony" for the same reason that he said "sody" and "asafedity" and "Indiany." But when he was calling me down, he said "Jon-ah" with a heavy stress on the second syllable. "Jon-*ah*, get out of that, *sir!*"

It has been a many a day since I thought of myself as Jonah Crow. To me, it seems that Jonah Crow was a small boy who once lived at Squires Landing with Aunt Cordie and Uncle Othy Dagget for several years. In those years, the only change seemed to be that from one Christmas to the next the boy grew a little taller.

And now, a long time past the time of that boy, I live again beside the river, a mile and a half downstream from Squires Landing, maybe two and a half from Goforth, having traveled so far, by a considerable wandering and winding about, in only seventy-two years.

Back there at the beginning, as I see now, my life was all time and almost no memory. Though I knew early of death, it still seemed to be something that happened only to other people, and I stood in an unending river of time that would go on making the same changes and the same returns forever.

And now, nearing the end, I see that my life is almost entirely memory and very little time. Toward the end of my life at Squires Landing I began to understand that whenever death happened, it happened to me. That is knowledge that takes a long time to wear in. Finally it wears in. Finally I realized and fully accepted that one day I would belong entirely to memory, and it would then not be my memory that I belonged to, and I went over to Goforth to see if there was any room left beside my parents' graves. I learned that there was room for one more; if it belonged to anybody, it belonged to me. I went down to the Tacker Funeral Home at Hargrave and made my arrangements.

Some days, sitting here on my porch over the river, my memory seems to enclose me entirely; I wander back in my reckoning among all of my own that have lived and died until I no longer remember where I am. And then I lift my head and look about me at the river and the valley, the great, unearned beauty of this place, and I feel the memoryless joy of a man just risen from the grave.

What I liked best to do with Uncle Othy was go along with him in the boat or the buggy. He loved to fish and to eat fish, and so we would often be on the river, the first and last thing of the day, to run a trotline or raise a net. I loved to be out there in the early mornings and the late evenings, for then the river would seem spellbound, we and it caught in the same spell. It would be quiet, beckoning us into the presence of things. Uncle Othy would feel adventurous at those times and was easy to get along with. He took care to teach me to fish and to handle the boat.

Except for our trip to church on Sunday morning, our only regular use for the buggy was to take groceries to Dark Tom Cotman. After he was struck blind, Tom Cotman said, "I'm dark," and ever afterward that was what they called him: Dark Tom.

To get to his place, we would follow the river road—it was just a track in those days, with gates to open as you went along—across the branch and up past Woolforks' and over the Willow Run bridge. After a little more than a mile, where the river came in closest to the hill and there was no bottomland at all, Dark Tom's house stood on the hillside, looking right down at the river.

A long wire had been anchored in the river and stretched tight to a post in the yard. For wash water, when his well was low, Dark Tom hooked a weighted bucket onto the wire, let it slide down into the river, and hauled it up again by a rope tied to the bail. Other wires led from the back porch to the privy, the coal pile, and the barn where he milked his cow and fed his hens and fattened his hog. When he got beyond the wires, he felt his way along with a stick. Sometimes he would feel his way clear down to the landing and spend half a day talking. When he got drunk, he said, he got around by falling: "I've surveyed the whole geography hereabouts in man-lengths." He had been in the Spanish-American War, and had a pension. The neighbors, of course, helped him out, but he did pretty well on his own.

He sent his list one day, as he usually did, by somebody coming down to the landing. Uncle Othy boxed up his order, and that evening we took it up to him in the buggy. Dark Tom was in the kitchen, frying corn batter cakes on a griddle. Uncle Othy set the box down inside the door and then stood, leaning against the jamb, and talked a while with Dark Tom. I didn't hear what they said because I was too taken up with what was happening there in the kitchen. It is another of those moments long past that is as present to my mind as if it is still happening.

Dark Tom was frying the batter cakes one at a time, feeling at the edges with the spatula to tell when to turn them. When they were done, he laid them on a plate on the seat of a chair at the end of the stove. His black-and-brown-spotted foxhound, Old Ed, was sitting by the chair, and every time Dark Tom laid down a batter cake Old Ed promptly ate it, all in one bite, and then sat and licked his chops until Dark Tom laid down another batter cake. I should have said something, I suppose, but I didn't think of it. At the time, and for years afterward, I thought that Old Ed was eating Dark Tom's supper, taking advantage of his blindness, and that Dark Tom and Uncle Othy were too occupied by their talk to notice. Later it occurred to me to wonder if that was merely Dark Tom's way of feeding his dog. It is a question with me still, and the answer has altogether disappeared from the world.

That would have been in the summer of 1923. Though of course none of us knew it, Uncle Othy was then living the last of his days in this world. One afternoon Put Woolfork found him lying in the mud down on the riverbank, where he had gone to bail out his boat after a hard rain. Put hollered for us, and Aunt Cordie sent me running across the hill to the Thripples'. Put and the whole Thripple family helped us to get Uncle Othy up the hill to the house and into bed, and then stayed and watched with us. Uncle Othy died just a little while after dark.

And that left Aunt Cordie and me to keep things going there on the place and at the store. We were not, I believe, anyways near equal to the job. The neighbors, especially the Thripples, were always coming over to help us with something. Uncle Arch took over the crop on the halves, but that still left us a lot of work. And we missed Uncle Othy. We were always needing him to help with something or tell us something, but we missed him just for his own sake too. We needed to hear him say, "Hurry along with them biscuits, Cordie, for I got things that needs a-seeing to," or, "If you can't do it, son, quit and get out of the way. Don't send a boy to do a man's work."

It was a time under a shadow, and yet I remember being happy, for I had responsibilities then, and I knew that I was useful. I took charge of the milking and the care of the animals, and at the store I had the hang of things better than Aunt Cordie did. I had been watching Uncle Othy for years, and I knew how much he stocked of this and that and how he arranged things. And since I had been going to school some, up at the mouth of Willow Run, I could keep track of the figures.

I could see that Aunt Cordie was grieving, and yet she took care to be a good companion to me. She praised my work, calling me "my boy," and told me stories, and would sit with me by the hour after supper, playing Rook or Old Maid. We were, in a way, playmates.

And then toward the end of the next summer I saw her begin to fail. She got so she couldn't remember things. And she would have to rest two or three times coming up from the store to the house.

One day, standing in the kitchen door, she called loudly, "Oh, Othy! Oh, Othy!"

I said, "Aunt Cordie, Uncle Othy ain't here."

And she said just as nicely, as if I had put her mind at rest, "Well, I reckon that's why he don't answer."

Sometimes she would look at me with a worry in her eyes that I didn't understand until later, and she would say, "I don't know. Honey, I just don't know." She meant she didn't know what would become of me after she was gone.

One evening when the wind blew up the river with the first cold edge of fall, she stopped to rest as we were coming up from the store. She turned and looked north, the way the wind was coming.

"It's got a chill in it," I said. "We'll need a fire tonight." I remember I was looking forward to the fire, the good warmth.

But she said, "Child, I just don't know if I can endure another winter."

I can see now that she had given up. She had searched inside herself, looking for some sign that she still desired to live, and had found none. She wanted to live for me, maybe, but not for herself.

One morning I woke up and realized that it was daylight already and

I had heard not a sound. Though there was frost on the ground, I didn't even wait to put on my shoes but just barefooted it over to the Thripples'.

Aunt Cordie had died in her sleep, an easy way to go. I am thankful.

I was a little past ten years old, and I was the survivor already of two stories completely ended.

4

The Good Shepherd

Telling a story is like reaching into a granary full of wheat and drawing out a handful. There is always more to tell than can be told. As almost any barber can testify, there is also more than needs to be told, and more than anybody wants to hear. The story of the next dozen years of my life could be made long, but I want to be careful to offer you only the proper handful—just enough to describe the course that carried me away from the Port William neighborhood and then twelve years later brought me back again to the proper end of my life, to the love of my life, Mattie Chatham.

Aunt Cordie, departing, left behind her the problem of me. What, as she had wondered, was going to become of me? I could not stay on at the landing by myself, though of course that is what I wanted to do. I remember arguing, to the forces of seniority and authority who had to decide what was to become of me, that staying on was what I *could* do, that I was well able to do so. But of course I was only a child trying to call back a lost world.

By then I had no living relative, or none who was known to me. The people around Squires Landing were poor, scratching a living from hillside patches as hard-worn as their clothes. The Thripples were old. And there are several good and pressing reasons why people are not eager to take in a ten-year-old boy they are no kin to. There was no Aunt Cordie to come to my rescue this time. I had used up my allotted supply of Aunt Cordies. There had been one, when I needed her the most, and that was all.

I don't mean to say that one was not enough—one was enough and more—but only that there was no second. And so I went out of the hands of love, which certainly included charity as we know it, into the hands of charity as we know it, which included love only as it might.

I was sent away to a church orphanage called The Good Shepherd up in the central part of the state. It was a beautiful place, that orphanage. The superintendent's home and office were in a fine old brick house set well back from the road in a lawn shaded by big trees. Behind it, scattered over a broad hilltop, were the dormitories, the dining hall, the school building, and the gymnasium. When I lit there, I felt so far away from home that I might as well have been in another world.

My first memory is of the long driveway sweeping up among the trees to the superintendent's house. And then, immediately, I remember meeting face to face, across the top of a large desk, the superintendent himself, Brother Whitespade, one of the crossest of Christians, who said in a big, pretty voice, "Ah! This will be Mr. Crow."

Brother Whitespade's desk was as wide as a field. It was as wide maybe as an ocean. For a minute or two I didn't think I could see across it. And then I could see Brother Whitespade over there, looking at me pointedly through a pair of steel-rimmed eyeglasses and smiling in a way that gave me no comfort. His stare was the most concentrated part of him. Otherwise he was a soft man with a smooth face, wavy hair, and a tight collar. But all that he was seemed to be gathered up in his eyes and pointed across that wide desk at me.

I knew all of a sudden that I was facing a man who was filled with power, and that I had no power, none. I could not have told you this then, for the knowledge did not come to me in words. It came into me as a hollow place that opened slowly and ached under my breastbone. I knew that I had come there by no thought of my own. I was a long way removed from any thought of my own. I had no thought.

I was who? A little somebody who could have been anybody, looking across that wide desk at Brother Whitespade. I knew that I could not even leave until he told me to go.

"Jonah Crow," he said, looking at a paper on his desk. And then he looked back at me. "Mr. Crow, since I believe you have not yet found your way to Nineveh, I will call you J."

And I saw him write in large, curving strokes my name as it was to be: "J. Crow."

I remember waking up in my dormitory room the first several mornings, for maybe a minute or two not knowing where I was, and then knowing. I would recognize the chest of drawers, the two chairs, the table, the two iron cots, the other boy still asleep. And I would be filled with a strange objectless fear, as if in the twinkling of an eye I had been changed not only into another world but into another body. Shrunken by fear, I lay on my back and looked straight up at the ceiling, waiting for something to move.

When the wake-up bell sounded over the hilltop and the other boy stirred in his bed and this new world began to assemble itself in small motions and sounds, the fear left me. I would know then that I would make it until night, when again in the narrow cot in the dark room I would cover my head and, in despair of anything else to do, go immediately to sleep.

I thought at first that Brother Whitespade, by changing my name to J., had made me a special case. But I soon found out that all of us orphans— who were called "students"—were known by the initial letters of our first names along with our last names. My roommate, for example, was T. Warnick. If the institution had received a second Warnick by the name, say, of Thomas Robert, he would have to be called R. Warnick. If he had had no middle name, he would have been assigned an initial arbitrarily: N. Warnick or P. Warnick, whatever Brother Whitespade chose. The girls too all were named by the same method. We were thus not quite nameless, but also not quite named. The effect was curious. For a while anyhow, and for how long a while it would be hard to say, we all acted on the assumption that we were no longer the persons we had been—which for all practical purposes was the correct assumption. We became in some way faceless to ourselves and to one another. You would discover, for example, that E. Lawler's original first name was Elizabeth. But she would not *look* like Elizabeth Lawler; she would not look precisely like E. Lawler, either. I remember walking around saying my name to myself—"Jonah Crow, Jonah Crow"—until it seemed that it could never have belonged to me or to anybody else.

At Squires Landing everything seemed to be held close in mind—in my mind or in some older or larger mind that my mind belonged to. The world was present when I shut my eyes, just as it was present when I opened them. At The Good Shepherd I entered for the first time a divided world—divided both from me and within itself. It was divided from me because it did not seem to be present unless I watched it. Within itself, it was divided between an ideal world of order, as prescribed and demanded by the institution, which was embodied most formidably by Brother Whitespade, and a real world of disorder, which we students brought in with us as a sort of infection. Though of course I could not sort it all out until afterward—not, really, until after I had come back to Port William—I know now that order was thought to emanate from the institution, and disorder from nature. Order was of the soul, whose claims the institution represented. Disorder was of the body, which was us.

We stood in line for meals, for our thrice-daily entrances into the school building, for church, for almost anything that required going through a door. There were daily inspections of our rooms. There were nightly bed checks. There were supervised study halls and recreation periods. We were all assigned jobs that were necessary to our own feeding and shelter, and of course our work was closely supervised. We all, I think, had the feeling that we were being watched, not by God, which was the endlessly repeated warning, but by Brother Whitespade and his faculty, who evidently lusted to know all that we least wanted to tell. And to these ever-watching eyes we reacted in ways peculiar to ourselves. Some lived lives of flagrant indifference or transparency, seeming to have no secrets that they wanted to keep. Others, like me, developed inward lives of the intensest privacy.

But whether we were loud or quiet, sociable or solitary, we were constantly involved in sins against the institutional order. We lived within a net of rules tightly strung between ourselves and the supposed disorder and wickedness of the world. But the meshes were always a little too wide; the net could never quite become a wall. There was leakage in both directions. Not all of us, maybe, but anyhow most of us boys were forever crossing back and forth between constraint and upheaval. And so we seemed forever involved in some form of punishment: gathering demerits, receiving hard licks on the seat of our pants, losing little privileges that seemed to have been given for the purpose of being revoked.

You will get the impression that I am looking back very critically at my old home and school, and I acknowledge that I am. But I mean to be critical only within measure. It is true that I dislike the life of institutions and organizations, and I am slow to trust people who willingly live such a life. This is not a prejudice, but a considered judgment, one that The Good Shepherd taught me to make, and so I acknowledge a considerable debt to that institution. But when, to be fair, I ask myself what I would do if confronted with a hundred or so orphan children of two sexes and diverse ages and characters all to be raised and educated together, then I remain a critic, but I can't say with confidence that I would do better.

As a matter of fact, leaving all my criticisms in place, I can say that I have kept some fine memories of my years at The Good Shepherd. I remember getting up early to walk among the trees on the front lawn while the light was fresh and the dew undried and the official forces still asleep. And when I stood in line before going into the dining hall or the school building I could see, off on the horizon, a good old brick farmhouse with trees and brick outbuildings. It was all well proportioned and laid out. Especially in the sunlight of early morning or late afternoon, it looked to me like a vision of Paradise. And I like to remember myself standing in my fixed and appointed place, always a little lonely and a little homesick, watched and under suspicion, looking over at that beautiful house at the point of the meeting of earth and sky. I would let my mind go there and make itself at home.

Although I can't say that I liked school, when I wanted to be I was a good enough student. I liked learning, especially the learning that could be got by reading. I made fair grades, but I and my teachers knew that I could have done better. I was, they said, like a good horse who would not work; I was a disappointment to them; I was wasting my God-given talents. And this gave me, I believe, the only self-determining power I had: I could withhold this single thing that was mine that I knew they wanted. I had ways of not allowing myself to be fully present in the classroom, even though I was physically confined there. I looked out the windows. A window opening on nothing but the blank sky was endlessly attractive to me; if I watched long enough, a bird or a cloud would appear within the frame, and I watched with patience. A window that looked out into a tree was a source of inexpressible happiness, for it permitted me to observe the foraging of the birds and the life history of leaves. When my attention was called back into the room, as sooner or later it always would be, I let my mind wander. I found out that I could not willfully place my mind elsewhere, but that, if I let it loose from what it was expected to be doing, it would *go* elsewhere. "J. Crow," they would say, "I am not out there in that tree," or "J. Crow, would you honor us by paying attention to this problem up here on the blackboard?"

And I would say "Yes, ma'am" or "Yes, sir," as if only too happy to have their help in dealing with my waywardness.

If the classroom was not my natural habitat, the library pretty much was. The library was a long room across the back of Brother Whitespade's house. There were lots of windows along the east wall, and comfortable chairs in front of the windows, tables here and there, and several tall cases of books. The books had mainly been donated, I think, and some of them practically nobody would have wanted to read, but there were some good ones too. The librarian was a nice lady named Mrs. Eades, who was hospitable and quiet and kind. Now and then our teachers would send us to the library on some project or other, but there were times too when we were free just to go: Saturday mornings, and every night between supper and study hall.

Back in a corner between a bookcase and one of the east windows, there was a small table where I liked to sit and read. It was one of the best places in the world to be on a rainy Sunday afternoon in the winter. And I like to remember sitting there on a bright Saturday morning in the spring, with the window open and the sun shining in and the spirea bushes in bloom outside. At first I read books about horses and dogs, because I wanted a horse and a dog. And then I read several books about a boy named William Greenhill, an orphan like me, and then *The Swiss Family Robinson* and *The Boy's King Arthur*. I read the stories of Tom Sawyer and Huckleberry Finn, two more orphans, and Rip Van Winkle, and David Copperfield, another orphan.

One day I found in a trash can the hinder part of a little anthology of American poems. The cover and a lot of pages had been torn away, so that my copy began:

> *Keeping time, time, time,*
> *In a sort of Runic rhyme,*
> *To the tintinnabulation that so musically wells*
> *From the bells, bells, bells, bells,*
> *Bells, bells, bells . . .*

I thought *tintinnabulation* was the finest word I had ever seen. I kept that piece of a book with me until I came back to Port William. I still have it.

In my last years of high school I read Thomas Paine's *The Crisis* and "Self-Reliance" by Ralph Waldo Emerson and *Walden* by Henry David Thoreau, a book that made me want to live in a cabin in the woods. I drew a picture of the cabin I wanted to live in, and drew the floor plan, and made a list of the furniture and dishes and utensils and other things I would need.

I don't remember exactly when, but I started copying out passages that I liked into a tablet. And then I started making what I thought were improvements on the things I copied; I was uneasy about that, not being sure it was right. Also I kept a list of words I especially liked: *independent*, I remember, was one, and then *tintinnabulation* and *self-reliant* and *free* and *outside*. There got to be a good many.

Among the books in the library were two large blue volumes containing photographs of World War I. And so at last I saw what had been going on over across the sea in that winter of 1917 and 18 when I had heard the rumors of war and imagined people shooting one another in darkness. I studied those pages by the hour, for the battlefields did look as though they had been passed over by something vast and pitiless, as our riverbanks at home had looked, scoured by the ice.

After I quit waking up afraid, feeling that I might be nowhere, I began getting used to the place. I began to take for granted that I was some-where, and somewhere that I knew, but I never quite felt that I was somewhere I wanted to be. Where I wanted to be, always, day in and day out, year in and year out, was Squires Landing and all that fall of country between Port William up on the ridge and the river between Sand Ripple and Willow Run. When I heard or read the word *home,* that patch of country was what I thought of. *Home* was one of the words I wrote in my tablet.

Lying in bed in the dark before I went to sleep, I would picture myself coming up the hill to the house at Squires Landing. I would go around the house to the back, the way we always did, and up onto the porch and through the kitchen door. I would go through the house slowly, room by room, looking at everything: the kitchen table with three places set and covered with a cloth, the skillet and the pots and the kettle on the stove, Aunt Cordie's chair in the living room, her little stand table, her Bible lying on the table by the good Aladdin lamp, the beds in the bedrooms, the quilts on the beds, the rag rugs on the floors, the cracks in the wall-paper, Uncle Othy's whetrock on the mantelpiece and his old straw hat on its nail over the washstand. I liked especially to return to my own bed-room, which was the eastward one, the brightest of the two rooms up-stairs. When I went in, it would be early in the morning, in summer; the room would be clean-swept, full of light and moving air, the shadows of the curtains swaying on the floor.

I would wander into the store and on down to the garden and the riverbank and back up by the coal tipple. It seemed to me that I could remember even the leaves and the grass blades and the little rocks in the paths. It would all be so real to me that I would think I couldn't stand it if I didn't just get up and go back.

But always in these imaginings I would be the only one there. For some reason, I could never make myself remember Aunt Cordie or Uncle Othy. I could remember them only by being reminded of them. I never knew when this would happen, but when I was reminded they would just all of a sudden appear to me as they had been on a certain day—Uncle Othy rowing the boat, Aunt Cordie walking down to the garden, using her hoe as a walking stick—and then I would see them plain.

Sometimes when I wasn't trying to think about it, one of the old times would come over me entirely, and I could remember sitting in Aunt Cordie's lap while she rocked me and sang, "Old Crammy was dead and lay in her grave." Or I would hear Uncle Othy spelling *woodpecker*: "Wee-w-double-o-d-sockeedledypeck-e-double-ek-ek-r."

Of course, what I wasn't telling myself, and maybe was trying not to know (though I did know), was that at Squires Landing, and Goforth too, things were already changed. The things I was remembering were gone from everywhere except my mind.

I would remember these rememberings after I went back to be the barber in Port William, for of course one of the first things I did after I had settled in was go to look again at both of my old homes. In my dreams of remembrance, I had failed to reckon not only with the certainty of change under any circumstances, but also with the new circumstances of automobiles and improved roads. Already the only surviving blacksmith shops were those in the towns. My father's shop, which had opened right onto the Katy's Branch road, had been torn down when the road was widened. And our house had burned. There was nothing there even to recognize—just a patch of weeds and tree sprouts with a chimney sticking up in the middle.

At Squires Landing the buildings and all were still in place, but were not cared for as they had been when Aunt Cordie and Uncle Othy were alive. The landing and the little farm still provided a living for the family that lived there, but you could see that the days of such enterprises were numbered. Goods were being trucked into the country by then, not brought by the river, and the stores at the river landings and crossroads were losing out to the bigger ones in Port William, just as, in another ten years, the stores in Port William would begin losing out to yet bigger ones in Hargrave or Louisville.

And so there would always be more to remember that could no longer be seen. This is one of the things I can tell you that I have learned: our life here is in some way marginal to our own doings, and our doings are marginal to the greater forces that are always at work. Our history is always returning to a little patch of weeds and saplings with an old chimney sticking up by itself. And I can tell you a further thing that I have learned, and here I look ahead to the resting of my case: I love the house that belonged to the chimney, holding it bright in memory, and I love the saplings and the weeds.

I have all this in mind again now, as I remember myself remembering in my first years at The Good Shepherd. I was just a scantling boy, scared and out of place and (as I now see) odd. Not just lonely, but solitary, living as much as I could in secret, looking about, seeing much, revealing little. I was being preserved by the forces of charity in an institution, and at the same time I was preserving in myself a country and a life, steadfastly remembered, to which I secretly reserved my affection and my entire loyalty. I belonged, even defiantly, to what I remembered, and not to the place where I was. My not belonging to the institution, I suppose, is the reason I remember the next thing I must tell about.

For a while after they had come to The Good Shepherd, the newcomers were known as "newboys" and "newgirls." This status of newness we sooner or later simply wore our way out of. Eventually we would not be new anymore, but familiars having names (of a sort) and local histories.

Eventually I also was no longer new. I was J. Crow to my classmates, and they were names to me. We remembered each other from the past. But having been once a newboy myself, I remained aware of the other newboys and newgirls when they came in. I was not helpful to them, I am ashamed to say; I was too secretive and shy and sly for that. But I was always aware of them. They drew my sympathy, and I watched them.

I remember a little girl, the E. Lawler I mentioned before, who came to The Good Shepherd when she was about seven years old. She was a slight, brown-haired, sad-looking, lonesome-looking girl whose clothes did not fit. She looked accidental or unexpected, and seemed to be without expectation, and resigned, and so quiet that even in my selfishness I wished I knew of a way to help her.

I watched her all the time. When her class went out to play, she did not take part but only stood back and watched the other girls. She always wore a dress that sagged and brown cotton stockings that were always wrinkled. She was waiting. I did not understand that she was waiting, but she was. And then one day as her classmates were joining hands to play some sort of game, one of the girls broke the circle. She held out her hand to the newcomer to beckon her in. And E. Lawler ran into the circle and joined hands with the others.

I wrote *E. Lawler* in my tablet so that I would not forget her.

5

The Call

One thing you would sooner or later realize about The Good Shepherd was that it had no neighbors. Like (I think) most institutions, it was turned inward, trying to be a world in itself. It stood at the edge of the little town of Canefield, which it looked upon as a threat to its morals. In his many chapel talks and sermons, Brother Whitespade suffered over the possibility that some of the Canefield merchants might sell cigarettes to The Good Shepherd children for some of the tiny allowance of spending money we received, and over the possibly regrettable results of mixing between our older girls and boys and the older boys and girls of Canefield, who had not had the advantage of orphanhood and the moral instruction of Brother Whitespade.

And so The Good Shepherd, officially, was enclosed within itself. When we went out among the fleshpots of Canefield, as when we went anywhere, we went in groups carefully chaperoned. And outside influences were handpicked by Brother Whitespade. Remembering, as always, the free and casual comings and goings at Squires Landing, I wrote *neighbor* down in my tablet.

As a part of the general effort to protect us from outside influences, The Good Shepherd had its own barbershop—a chair and mirror and little backbar in a room in the basement of the boys' dormitory. The barber, a friendly man named Clark, came in the afternoon two days a week, and so kept us boys respectably shorn. One of my jobs, after I reached the responsible age of twelve, was to be the barber's assistant. I swept the floor and shined the mirror and kept things in order. And then, because I longed for knowledge, Barber Clark showed me how to care for the equipment. He taught me how to clean and oil the clippers, and how to hone and strop a razor. By little stages, as I got older and taller, he taught me to cut hair and even to give a shave, letting me practice on him, good and brave man that he was. I got so I was good at it and liked to do it.

Because The Good Shepherd tried so hard to be a world unto itself, the students, especially the older ones, naturally hungered for the world outside. Among the high-school boys, whose hunger and boldness were greatest, there were always escape artists who stuffed their beds and stole away at night to visit town girls, to buy cigarettes, to purchase such as they could afford of the wares of the bootleggers in the hollow below town. They would sometimes get caught, of course, and would get punished, and of course would try their luck again. Not everybody went in for this, but for the ones who did it was a sort of guerrilla warfare. They would not have been easy in their minds if there was something they could have got away with if they had not got away with it.

My own temptation was not to go into the town at night but to escape into the countryside in the daytime. It was a fine, lovely part of the world—excellent, rolling farmland, with old ashes and oaks in the pastures, divided by streams with trees along the banks and patches of woods along the steeper slopes of the valley sides. As long as the weather was cold, I stood confinement pretty well, but as soon as the weather warmed and the buds began to swell on the water maples, I would begin to itch and ache to get out. I wanted room. I wanted to follow paths or streambanks a while just to see where they would take me. And from the time I was about thirteen, there would be times—Saturday mornings or Sunday afternoons or between classes and supper—when I would just go.

Over the ridge beyond The Good Shepherd there was a sizable stream, Dowd's Fork, that at one place ran by a big, shelving outcrop of limestone. Sometimes a whole band of us boys would disappear from official notice and go over there to swim. We would have two or three hours of outlawry: swimming, diving out of the overhanging trees, and then sitting around in our birthday suits, smoking cigars that we bought at a little general store by the railroad bridge.

But even more I liked to go by myself, to begin just with whatever whim or disgruntlement or longing got me started, and walk without reference to anything but my own interest or curiosity until it came time to turn back. If nobody was around, I looked into barns and corncribs. I followed paths and the courses of streams. If I got hot, I would take a swim. One cold, bright, windy March day I came upon an abandoned house where several farmhands had built a fire on the hearth and were loafing and talking, the ground being too wet to plow. They let me warm myself at their fire and were nice to me. Sometimes I would take a book and climb into a tree along Dowd's Fork and read all afternoon. These excursions were worth whatever punishment I received if I got caught.

Sometimes, of course, I got caught. One fall afternoon, after the frosts had killed the summer foliage, I put a fishing line in my pocket and stole off toward Dowd's Fork. I was almost out of sight when for some reason I looked back, and I saw Brother Whitespade standing, facing in my direction, at the back of the library. I immediately pitched myself onto the ground, hoping he couldn't see that far, but thinking that, if he could, the dead weed stalks would hide me while I crawled into better cover. But when I raised my head to peep around, Brother Whitespade was coming straight toward me, wading through the weeds, raising his knees high. I put my head down and crawled faster, but when I looked again he was still coming straight toward me. And only then, and much too late, I realized that I was wearing (of all things!) a bright red sweater.

When I was about fourteen, I think it was, I joined a few of the nighttime escapades—maybe just to declare to myself whose side I was on. But that did not last, for at about the same time a more serious matter began to occupy me of a night. How it came about I am not quite sure, but I began to suspect that I might be called to preach. My suspicion may have been no more than fear, for with all my heart I disliked the idea of becoming a preacher. But for as long as I could remember, I had been hearing preachers tell in sermons how they had received "the call"; this was often the theme of Brother Whitespade and the many visiting preachers who spoke at The Good Shepherd. Not one of those men had ever suggested that a person could be "called" to anything but "full-time Christian service," by which they meant either the ministry or "the mission field." The finest thing they could imagine was that an orphan boy, having been rescued by the charity of the church, should repay his debt by accepting "the call." What was so frightening to me about this call was that once it came to you, it was final; there was no arguing with it. You fell blind off your horse, and then you did what the call told you to do. I knew too well that when another Jonah had refused the call to preach he was permitted to change his mind in the belly of a great fish.

This possibility of being called began to keep me awake of a night. I had heard no voice, but probably because I was starting to respond at about that time to the distant calling of girls, I could not shake the notion that I was being called by *something* that I knew nothing about.

I knew the story of the boy Samuel, how he was called in the night by a voice speaking his name. I could imagine, so clearly that I could almost hear it, a voice calling out of the darkness: "J. Crow." And then I thought maybe the voice *had* called, and that I had almost but not quite heard it. One night I got out of bed and went to the window. The sky over the treetops was full of stars. Whispering so as not to waken my roommate, I said, "Speak, Lord; for thy servant heareth." And then, so help me, I heard the silence that stretched all the way from the ground underneath my window to the farthest stars, and the hair stood up on my head, and a shiver came into me that did not pass away for a long time.

Though I knew that actually I had heard no voice, I could not dismiss the possibility that it had spoken and I had failed to hear it because of some deficiency in me or something wrong that I had done. My fearful uncertainty lasted for months. As the siren song of girls became ever stronger in my mind, I wondered if maybe that was the trouble. Finally I reasoned that in dealing with God you had better give Him the benefit of the doubt. I decided that I had better accept the call that had not come, just in case it had come and I had missed it. This was in the late summer before my final year at The Good Shepherd. I went to Brother Whitespade and told him I was pretty sure that I had received the call.

I did not at all foresee the benefits that followed. It turned out that I was the first, in Brother Whitespade's several years at The Good Shepherd, who had been even pretty sure of having received the call. By my declaration, without intending to at all, I set the stage for well-paying hypocrisy and self-deception. Brother Whitespade was delighted with me. I had fulfilled his fondest dream. The once-lost lamb now proposed to become a shepherd. All of a sudden, with me, he no longer kept up the appearance of displeased and distant authority that he used to protect himself from everybody who might try to take advantage of him. Now he showed himself to me as just a man who thought too well of himself but wanted to be kind, who was too sure of a lot of things but also a little lonely. He began to treat me almost as a friend.

For his sake and my own, I am ashamed to tell you this, or even to remember it. For the truth is that I had not changed very much, if any. I did not become a better student or a tamer one, or less troublesome or troubled, or less inclined to wander away through any opening that presented itself. But now I had a reputation with Brother Whitespade, and therefore with the other official people, that was a perfect camouflage for what I had been and continued to be. Once I had the reputation, so long as I continued to talk up to it, I did not have to *live* up to it.

I continued to hold my professed intention to become a preacher, and I did as well as I could all the special tasks that were now assigned to me because of my professed intention. One of these was to speak from time to time in chapel, which Brother Whitespade thought would be good practice for me. For my first talk—hypocrite and fool that I was—I took my text from I Samuel 3, the story of the young Samuel and the voice of God.

I will add, to be fair to myself, that there was in all this a speck of sincerity. By then I had heard the Bible read quite a lot and had read it some myself. I liked the stories of Adam and Eve, Noah, Abraham, Ruth, King David, and Daniel. I was truly moved by the story of Jesus, and had read every verse of the Gospels for myself. I can't say that all of those stories had made any noticeable change in me, but I had them in mind and sometimes I thought about them. And sometimes I imagined things about being a preacher that appealed to me. I thought that if I became a preacher, I would have learned a great deal during my education, and I would spend a lot of my time reading. I liked those thoughts, and also the thought that I would live in a nice town with shady streets and be well-loved and admired by my congregation.

But the thought that I liked most was that I would have a wife. In the spring of my second year of high school, a copper-haired girl named N. (for Nan) O'Callahan and I had stepped into the shadow of the spirea bushes by the library and had given each other a kiss that was the strongest thing that had happened to me since Aunt Cordie died and I came to The Good Shepherd. It was as if the world, leaving me upright, had turned itself upside down above my head and poured over me rivers and oceans of warm water. After that, it was clear to me that if I became a preacher I was going to need a wife. And so I imagined a wife with red hair like Nan O'Callahan's. When I began to imagine her, I ceased entirely to imagine the nice town and the church and the congregation and the reading of books. I imagined my wife and me coming home from the grocery store late in the afternoon, our arms loaded with sacks of groceries—for at The Good Shepherd we were always a little hungry. I imagined us sitting at our kitchen table, eating a big supper that always ended with a cherry pie like Aunt Cordie used to make, with sugar glazed on the strips of the top crust. And then I imagined us together in the parsonage bedroom, enacting scenes that could have been enacted nowhere in the world but in the imagination of a lonely, ignorant boy.

Thus confused and hopeful and self-deluded, I emerged from The Good Shepherd with a scholarship and a job waiting tables at a small denominational college in Pigeonville, about forty miles away.

And Nan O'Callahan? She was gone long before I was. Our kiss in the shadow of the spirea was, in fact, a farewell kiss. She was going away to live with some relatives she didn't know, and she didn't want to leave without a trace. She wanted to think that somebody would miss her. And so that kiss passed between us, that moment of my sudden immersion in her welcoming warmth, living moisture, and good smell.

"Remember me, J. Crow," she said. She gave me no address, probably not knowing what her address would be, and I never saw her after she left. But how could I forget her?

6

Pigeonville

And so I became a "pre-ministerial student" at Pigeonville College, beginning a curriculum of courses designed to prepare me for the pulpit, and waiting tables three times a day in a girls' dormitory, which set me enough at cross purposes even without all the questions I had ahead of me that I had not yet even thought of.

And for a while, though I believe I felt the influence of my unthought questions, I continued not to think of them. One reason was that I had to get over another big change. It took me a while to deal in my mind with the knowledge that my life at The Good Shepherd had ended, that I would not go back, that I probably would not see again the people I had known there.

Now I had a new place and new people to learn about. All the circumstances and rules were new to me. I had more freedom now and I had to feel my way into it, see which barriers had fallen and which still were up. I had this feeling for freedom, you see, that I had carefully and quietly nourished for eight years at The Good Shepherd. I couldn't be satisfied until I knew the boundaries and where the openings were, if any.

But at this school I not only learned what the rules were but even willingly kept them. As long as we did what was expected of us and kept the rules, we boys at least could come and go pretty much as we pleased.

There was less reason to break rules because there were not so many of them, but also I didn't want to be punished. I didn't want to get crosswise with anybody who had authority to punish me; I had had enough of that at The Good Shepherd. I didn't want ever again to stand in front of the desk of somebody who had more power than I had. If all that required was keeping a few rules that I didn't much object to, then I would keep the rules.

Beyond that, I was more conscious than before that I was a beneficiary. I wanted to be worthy of my scholarship. If I came to look unworthy in other people's eyes, I was afraid I would look unworthy in my own.

I worked harder in my classes at Pigeonville than I had at The Good Shepherd, but not a lot harder. I did the assignments and made tolerable grades, but I knew I could have done better. I was working against what I was now beginning to understand as a limitation of character. You can judge for yourself how much of a fault it was that I had what seemed an inborn dislike for doing anything that somebody else told me to do. And it wasn't an ordinary dislike, either. There were lengths beyond which I just could not make myself go. When I reached this limit, the thought of approval or praise, let alone a better grade, did not even tempt me.

Pigeonville College had a much better library than The Good Shepherd, of course, and I spent a lot of my time there, reading in books and magazines. I'd had the idea, once, that if I could get the chance before I died I would read all the good books there were. Now I began to see that I wasn't apt to make it. This disappointed me, for I really wanted to read them all. But it consoled me in a way too; I could see that if I got them all read and had no more surprises in that line, I would have been sorry.

For a while, anyhow, I had a pretty good life there at Pigeonville. I went to class and studied and read and waited my tables and did other odd jobs as they came up. The times were hard, but my tuition, room, and meals cost me nothing. And I never missed a chance to earn a little money. The word got around that I was a willing worker, and I did all kinds of hand-and-back jobs that earned me a dime here, a quarter there: mopped floors, washed windows, dug holes, mowed yards. I had never had any money of my own, or hardly enough to notice, and now it meant everything to me to have some. And once I made it, I kept it. Except for my clothes and books, I spent just nearly nothing. I would let the coins rattle in my pocket until I got enough to change into a bill, and then I would put the bill into my shoe, or poke it through a little hole in the lining of my jacket. I was as tight as a tick in those days, and would as soon have thrown my money away as trust it to a bank. You can bet I took care where I hung up my jacket or took off my shoes.

Here is the way I was in those days. My life just filled out into all the freedom it was allowed, like water seeking its level. My private life—my *secret* life, I might as well say, though really I had no secrets worth keeping—achieved length and breadth and height. After the first year, I asked for and was given a small single room, and in that way got shed of my roommate. I now had money that I had earned myself; I now had a few possessions that I had bought with my own money. These few things that were mine I cherished with a steady small exultation that was also mine. At night, shut in my little room with all my worldly possessions, I felt like a worm in an apple.

I had no social life to speak of—no friends, really. Working three times every day in a big dining room full of girls caused me to do some thinking, naturally. From time to time I thought about asking one girl or another to go out, but I never did. To tell the truth, at The Good Shepherd I had fallen into the habit of keeping myself to myself. I was shy and always full of thoughts and had no great craving for company. Whenever a teacher or anybody took up my old name and started using it, I would say, "Call me J."

But finally the questions I had not thought of caught up with me, and had to be thought of, and had to be asked. Pigeonville was scrupulous about being religious. You couldn't have got hired to teach there if you weren't a member of the denomination, and most of the students were there because it was a church school. Several of the teachers—the ones I was most likely to have—were ordained preachers. You could say that the place had a pious atmosphere. It was an atmosphere that I finally had to think about, and when I thought about it I had to admit that I could not get comfortable in it; I could not breathe a full breath in it. Though I didn't get out into the country as often as I used to—because I was busier and because Pigeonville was a bigger town than Canefield and harder to get out of—the atmosphere at the college always made me long for the open countryside and flowing streams. My on-the-side life as an odd-

jobs man took me out into better air, and I was more and more consciously grateful for that.

I wish I could give you the right description of that atmosphere. It
was soapy and paperish and shut-in and a little stale. It didn't smell of
anything bodily or earthly. A little whiff of tobacco smoke would have
done wonders for it. The main thing was that it made me feel excluded
from it, even while I was in it.

And then one day I asked myself, "How is it going to suit you to be called
Brother Crow?" I walked around a while, saying over and over to myself,
"Brother Crow, Brother Crow, Brother Crow." It did not seem to be referring to me. I imagined hospitable, nice people saying to me before Sunday dinner, "Brother Crow, would you express our thanks?" And then I
couldn't imagine myself.

I took to studying the ones of my teachers who were also preachers,
and also the preachers who came to speak in chapel and at various exer-
cises. In most of them I saw the old division of body and soul that I had
known at The Good Shepherd. The same rift ran through everything at
Pigeonville College; the only difference was that I was able to see it more
clearly, and to wonder at it. Everything bad was laid on the body, and
everything good was credited to the soul. It scared me a little when I realized that I saw it the other way around. If the soul and body really were
divided, then it seemed to me that all the worst sins—hatred and anger
and self-righteousness and even greed and lust—came from the soul. But
these preachers I'm talking about all thought that the soul could do no
wrong, but always had its face washed and its pants on and was in agony
over having to associate with the flesh and the world. And yet these same
people believed in the resurrection of the body.

Although I was shaken, maybe I could have clamped my mouth shut
and gone ahead. But about then I began to get into different trouble and
more serious. You might call it doctrinal trouble.

The trouble started because I began to doubt the main rock of the
faith, which was that the Bible was true in every word. "I reckon there
ain't a scratch of a pen in it but what is true," Uncle Othy used to say, but
he spoke as of a distant wonder, and was not much concerned. The pious
men of The Good Shepherd and Pigeonville were concerned. They had

staked their immortal souls on the infallible truth of every pen scratch
from "In the beginning" to "Amen." But I had read all of it by then, and I
could see that it changed. And if it changed, how could all of it be true?

For instance, there is a big difference between the old tribespeople's
coldhearted ferocity against their enemies and Jesus' preaching of forgiveness and of love for your enemies. And there is a big difference again
between Jesus' unqualified command, "Love your enemies," and Paul
the Apostle's "If it be possible, as much as lieth in you, live peaceably
with all men," which amounts to permission *not* to live peaceably with
all men. And what about the verse in the same chapter saying that we
should do good to our enemy, "for in doing so thou shalt heap coals of
fire on his head?" Where did Jesus ever see doing good as a form of
revenge? I saw the Bible as pretty much slanting upward until it got to
Jesus, who forgave even the ones who were killing Him while they were
killing Him, and then slanting down again when it got to St. Paul. I was
truly moved by the stories of Jesus in the Gospels. I could imagine them.
The Nativity in the Gospel of Luke and the Resurrection in the Gospel
of John I could just shut my eyes and *see*. I could imagine everything
until I got to the letters of Paul.

Questions all of a sudden were clanging in my mind like Edgar Allan
Poe's brazen alarum bells. I still believed in the divinity and the teachings
of Jesus and was determined to follow my purpose of preaching the
Gospel—when I preached, I thought, I would just not mention the parts
that gave me trouble—but it got so I couldn't open a Bible without setting off a great jangling and wrangling of questions that almost deaf-
ened me.

If we are to understand the Bible as literally true, why are we permitted to hate our enemies? If Jesus meant what He said when He said we
should love our enemies, how can Christians go to war? Why, since He
told us to pray in secret, do we continue to pray in public? Is an insincere
or vain public prayer not a violation of the third commandment? And
what about our bodies that always seemed to come off so badly in every
contest with our soul? Did Jesus put on our flesh so that we might
despise it?

But the worst day of all was when it hit me that Jesus' own most fer-
vent prayer was refused: "Father, if thou be willing, remove this cup

from me: nevertheless not my will, but thine, be done." I must have read that verse or heard it a hundred times before without seeing or hearing. Maybe I didn't want to see it. But then one day I saw it. It just knocked me in the head. *This,* I thought, is what is meant by "thy will be done" in the Lord's Prayer, which I had prayed time and again without thinking about it. It means that your will and God's will may not be the same. It means there's a good possibility that you won't get what you pray for. It means that in spite of your prayers you are going to suffer. It means you may be crucified.

After Jesus' terrible prayer at Gethsemane, an angel came to Him and gave Him strength, but did not remove the cup.

Before that time I may have had my doubts about public prayers, but I had listened to them complacently enough, even when they were for the football team. I had prayed my own private prayers complacently enough, asking for things I wanted, even though I knew well already that a lot of things I wanted I was not going to get, no matter how much I prayed for them. (Though I hadn't got around to thinking about it, I already knew that I had been glad to have some things I had got that I had never thought to want, let alone pray for.)

But now I was unsure *what* it would be proper to pray for, or how to pray for it. After you have said "thy will be done," what more can be said? And where do you find the strength to pray "thy will be done" after you see what it means?

And what did these questions do to my understanding of all the prayers I had ever heard and prayed? And what did they do to the possibility that I could stand before a congregation—*my* congregation, who would believe that I knew what I was doing—and pray for favorable weather, a good harvest, the recovery of the sick and the strayed, victory in war? Does prayer change God's mind? If God's mind can be changed by the wants and wishes of us mere humans, as if deferring to our better judgment, what is the point of praying to Him at all? And what are we to think when two good people pray for opposite things—as when two devout mothers of soldiers on opposite sides pray for the safety of their sons, or for victory?

Does God want us to cross the abyss between Him and us? If we can't—and it looked to me like we can't—will He help us? Or does He want us to fall into the abyss? Are there some things He wants us to learn that we can't learn except by falling into the abyss? Is that why the Jonah of old, who could not say "thy will be done," had to lie three days and three nights in the dark in the belly of the great fish?

"Father, remove this cup from me," I prayed. And there I stopped. For how would I know what God's will was, even provided I could have the strength to submit to it? I knew a lot of hearsay about God speaking to people in plain English, but He never had (He never has) spoken so to me.

By then I wasn't just asking questions; I was being changed by them. I was being changed by my prayers, which dwindled down nearer and nearer to silence, which weren't confrontations with God but with the difficulty—in my own mind, or in the human lot—of knowing what or how to pray. Lying awake at night, I could feel myself being changed—into what, I had no idea. It was worse than wondering if I had received the call. I wasn't just a student or a going-to-be preacher anymore. I was a lost traveler wandering in the woods, needing to be on my way somewhere but not knowing where.

I went to my professors with my questions, starting with the easiest questions and the talkiest professors. I don't think about them much anymore. I don't hold anything against them. They were decent enough men, according to their lights. The problem was that they'd had no doubts. They had not asked the questions that I was asking and so of course they could not answer them. They told me I needed to have more faith; I needed to believe; I needed to pray; I needed to give up my questioning, which was a sign of weakness of faith.

Those men could go on all day about the sins of the flesh or the amount of water needed for baptism or whether you could go to Heaven without being baptized or who could or couldn't go to Heaven, but they couldn't say why, if we're to take some of the Bible literally, we don't take all of it literally, or why we kill our enemies, or why we pray standing in the synagogues and in the corners of the streets that we may be seen of men.

That I should give up my questioning was good enough advice, which I would have been glad enough to take, except that my questioning would not give me up. It kept at me. Sometimes it seemed to me that people I walked by in the street must be able to hear the dingdonging in my head.

And so finally, late one afternoon, I went to the professor I was afraid to go to, old Dr. Ardmire. I was afraid to go to him because I knew he was going to tell me the truth. Dr. Ardmire was a feared man. He was a master of the Greek New Testament, a hard student and a hard teacher. We believed that he had never given but one A in his life. The number of students in his class in New Testament Greek, which he taught every fall, varied from maybe twenty to maybe three or four, as the horror died away and was renewed. He was known, behind his back, as Old Grit.

I knocked at his open door and waited until he read to a stopping place and looked up from his book.

"Come in, Mr. *J.* Crow." He didn't like it that I went by my initial.

I went in.

He said, "Have a seat, please."

I sat down.

Customarily, when I came to see him I would be bringing work that he had required me to talk with him about. That day I was empty-handed.

Seeing that I was, he said, "What have you got in mind?"

"Well," I said, "I've got a lot of questions."

He said, "Perhaps you would like to say what they are?"

"Well, for instance," I said, "if Jesus said for us to love our enemies— and He did say that, didn't He?—how can it ever be right to *kill* our enemies? And if He said not to pray in public, how come we're all the time praying in public? And if Jesus' own prayer in the garden wasn't granted, what is there for us to pray, except 'thy will be done,' which there's no use in praying because it will be done anyhow?"

I sort of ran down. He didn't say anything. He was looking straight at me. And then I realized that he wasn't looking at me the way he usually did. I seemed to see way back in his eyes a little gleam of light. It was a light of kindness and (as I now think) of amusement.

He said, "Have you any more?"

"Well, for instance," I said, for it had just occurred to me, "suppose you prayed for something and you got it, how do you know *how* you got it? How do you know you didn't get it because you were going to get it

whether you prayed for it or not? So how do you know it does any good
to pray? You would need proof, wouldn't you?"

He nodded.

"But there's no way to get any proof."

He shook his head. We looked at each other.

He said, "Do you have any answers?"

"No," I said. I was concentrating so hard, looking at him, you could
have nailed my foot to the floor and I wouldn't have felt it.

"So," I said, "I reckon what it all comes down to is, how can I preach if
I don't have any answers?"

"Yes, Mr. Crow," he said. "How can you?" He was not one of your
frying-size chickens.

"I don't believe I can," I said, and I felt my skin turn cold, for I had not
even thought that until then.

He said, "No, I don't believe you can." And we sat there and looked
at each other again while he waited for me to see the next thing, so he
wouldn't have to tell me: I oughtn't to waste any time resigning my scholarship and leaving Pigeonville. I saw it soon enough.

I said, "Well," for now I was ashamed, "I had this feeling maybe I had
been called."

"And you may have been right. But not to what you thought. Not to
what you think. You have been given questions to which you cannot be
given answers. You will have to live them out—perhaps a little at a time."

"And how long is that going to take?"

"I don't know. As long as you live, perhaps."

"That could be a long time."

"I will tell you a further mystery," he said. "It may take longer."

He held out his hand to me and I shook it. As I started to leave, it came
to me that of all the teachers I'd had in school he was the kindest, and I
turned around. I was going to thank him, but he had gone back to his
book.

7

The Great World

It was enough to make your head swim. There I went, walking away from Dr. Ardmire's office down the empty corridor late in the afternoon, and once again all my life so far was behind me. I had a feeling of strangeness and a feeling of being free; I had no more obligations, no more fear of failure, for failure had already come and, in a way, had gone. My questions were still with me, but for the time being anyhow they weren't crying out to be answered. I wasn't yet as free as I was going to become, but I knew that I was freer than I had ever been before. More than anything, I was glad to be free of being a preacher. It has always taken me a long time to think of something to say, and then more often than not I say it to myself. I would have had no business trying to preach a sermon three times a week.

And then, even before I got out of the building, and without any intention on my part, the thought of Nan O'Callahan returned to me. But she didn't come to mind this time as "Sister Crow," the entirely supposed preacher's wife of my hopeless daydreams. She came as herself, comely, weighty, fragrant, and warm.

That was in the early spring of 1935, just as the jonquils were starting to bloom. I brought my involvements at Pigeonville to an end with a few short farewells. What had happened seemed not to have happened to me so much as to the world, which seemed all of a sudden to have got a lot bigger.

Since I couldn't stay where I was, I had to think of someplace else. I could have gone in one direction as easily as another, and so I went to Lexington, which was the nearest city. I had never lived in a city, and I thought I would like to try one. I had my several pieces of folding money in the lining of my jacket and in my shoe, but they weren't enough to go far. Pretty soon I was going to need a job; I thought Lexington would be the place for that. I trusted my willingness; I didn't aim to be any kind of crook, but short of that I would do whatever anybody would pay me for. I had in the back of my mind the idea that I would take courses at the university and sooner or later graduate. If I was freer than I had ever been in my life, I was not yet entirely free, for I still hung on to an idea that had been set deep in me by all my schooling so far: I was a bright boy and I ought to make something out of myself—if not a minister of the Gospel, then something else that would be (I had by now actually thought this) a cut or two above my humble origins.

I owned a few books and a few clothes, a razor, a toothbrush, and a comb. I packed it all into a smallish cardboard box bound with several wraps of cord to make it easy to carry, and just after daylight I set off for Lexington afoot. It made me happy to have all my belongings in a box that I could carry with one hand and walk wherever I wanted to go. I thought, "I could go anywhere. I could go to the North or the West. I could just put one foot in front of the other until I would see places and things I have never imagined."

But after I walked four or five miles, a man driving a truck loaded with fat hogs stopped and gave me a ride, much to the relief of my feet.

I climbed into the cab, which was neat as a pin, set my box on the floorboard, and said thank you to the driver.

"You entirely welcome," he said. "Entahrly" was the way he said it.

He seemed to wait for me to say something else. When I didn't, he said, "Well, are you traveling or going somewheres?"

He was studying me out of the corner of his eye as he watched the road, and I eased my hand down to where I could feel the little sheaf of bills inside my jacket lining and held them tight. I knew there were people in this world who would cut your throat for a quarter.

But he didn't look like that kind. He was a small, neat man with eyebrows that were too bushy and ears that were too big for the rest of him. His chin stuck out, when he wanted it to, as though he used it for pushing open doors. His clothes and shoes were nearly spotless, which you wouldn't expect of a man hauling hogs. He was smoking a pipe. After my walk in the frosty morning air, that warm cab fragrant with pipe smoke was welcoming to me.

I said, "I'm heading over about Lexington."

And then, when I offered no more, he said, "Well, have you got a name?"

"J.," I said.

He stuck his hand out. "Sam Hanks."

I could have laughed, if I had let myself, or just as easily have cried. I knew who Sam Hanks was. He was the main livestock and tobacco hauler in Port William. He was the nephew of Miss Minnie Proudfoot who lived on Cotman Ridge above Goforth. All in a pang I remembered seeing his truck in front of my father's shop with a set of new racks, which I suppose my father had made. He had stopped by the store at Squires Landing a many a time.

It was a touchous moment. I felt like I was on top of a tall pole, ready to fall off. I could have told him who I was and he would have known. And yet it was too much. I had been ten years gone, and I had no thought of ever going back. To have identified myself to him would have been like raising the dead. I didn't have the heart. Also (as I was proud to think) who I was was my own business.

I shook his hand and said, "Where you from, Mr. Hanks?"

"Port William. Ever heard of it?"

"No," I said. "Are you a right smart ways from home?"

"Not too far," he said. "But usually I run to Louisville more than Lexington. Lately, though, I been coming up here some. People down home get tired of giving their stock away at Louisville, so they try giving it away in Lexington."

"Do you raise stock yourself?" I asked, because in fact I couldn't remember.

He drew on his pipe a little. "No. There's plenty of people to do that— and borrow money and pay interest, like as not, for the privilege." He said "privi-lege," in a way I remembered.

"No," he said, "I'm just the man that hauls it to where they can give it away. Me, I ain't aiming to owe anybody anything. I am an independent man, and take my hat off to nobody."

That was Sam Hanks—an independent man indeed, as stubborn as independent, and almost absolutely principled. In the time to come I would know him well. He was a man quiet enough, inclined, like most Port Williamites, to keep his own vital concerns to himself, but he could be goaded into a kind of eloquence. What goaded him invariably was the suggestion that there was any human under Heaven to whom Sam Hanks ought to take off his hat.

His great enemy—and frequent client—was John T. McCallum. John T. did not goad Sam Hanks in order to enjoy his eloquence; their differences were profound and sincere. John T. was full of the spirit of patriotism and progress and he venerated public figures; he was therefore deeply affronted by Sam Hanks and could not resist the thought that Sam might be brought to see things in the proper way. In later years, when the two of them would converge in my shop, they always worked their way sooner or later to some version of the same conversation.

John T., for instance, would itch until he had to invite Sam Hanks to go with him to hear the governor speak from the courthouse porch in Hargrave.

And Sam Hanks would reply, *"Hell, no!"*

"Well, why not?"

"Because he ain't got anything to say that I want to hear."

"Well, he's your elected governor."

"He may be the elected governor of Kentucky, but he ain't the elected governor of *me*."

"And I reckon the elected president of the United States ain't the president of you, either."

"The Old Marster elected me president of myself."

"What are you? Some kind of a communist or something?"

"I'm Sam Hanks and a grown man."

On that morning in 1935 I had not yet heard Sam Hanks on the subject of his own independence, freedom, and dignity. But if he had proceeded to enlighten me I would not have been surprised, for you could see that he had his ways. Something about him told you that he was easily offended. And something about him made you feel that you would not like to be the one to do it.

He looked slantwise down at my box, and then looked me over again in a way that made me realize I didn't look as neat as he did and my clothes weren't as good. In the college I would have looked like a poor student. Out on the road with my box, as I all of a sudden knew, I looked like a bum.

He said, "You got folks there at Lexington, I reckon." He was a true son of Port William, where, as Art Rowanberry used to say, people don't have what you would call their own business.

"No," I said.

He said, "Well, are you from around here somewheres, or are you from somewheres else?"

And then I lied: "We been living over about Bell's Fork."

"And now you're hellbent for the big city."

"I'm going to try it a lick or two and see what it's like."

"Well," he said, "let me put it this way. What are you aiming to do when you get there?"

"Work," I said.

"What at?"

"I don't know."

"*Hunh!*" he said. "Do you think the country nowadays is full of people out at night with lanterns, looking for boys to pay wages to?"

"No," I said. But he was making me uneasy. I was beginning to feel silly, and needing to give myself the dignity at least of desperation. With an ease that startled me I lied again: "Well, Mam's sick, and we're living with Grandpap, and he ain't able. So I reckon it's up to me."

"Are you the only boy?"

"I'm the only chick in the nest."

"The only one!" he said. "Well, there comes a time when we got it to do. And when that time comes, my opinion, we ought to do it."

"That's right," I said.

He took a little time then to revive the fire in his pipe, and then he said, "Fine country."

"The finest," I said. It was too. Even in that lean time there was good stock everywhere. The ewe flocks were just coming out onto the green wheat and barley fields with their young lambs.

We rode and looked a while, and then Sam Hanks said, "Do you *know* anybody in Lexington?"

"No, sir," I said. "I don't know anybody."

He took a slow, thoughtful draft on his pipe. "Now, where I'm going to is the stockyards," he said. "But if I was you, I wouldn't hang around there. You don't want to be no drover in no damned stockyards. A young man like you needs a *future*."

"Yessir," I said. "I appreciate your advice."

We were coming into Lexington then. He was dealing with the traffic and the lights. He had put the pipe in his pocket.

"Not bossing you," he said, "but if I was you, which I know I ain't, I'd go over about the trotting track. You being a country boy and all, you could make your way there, maybe."

We got to the stockyards. He drove in, turned, and backed up to a chute.

When we got out we could hear the bawling and bleating and squealing in the yards, and the drovers shouting.

I raised my hand. I was going to call "Much obliged!" to Sam Hanks and go my way, but he was coming toward me around the front of the truck. He hooked me by a quick thrust of two fingers into a pocket of my jacket, as if to hold me while he spoke his mind. He pointed.

"The trotting track is yonder," he said, raising his voice over the clamor of the yards. "You'll find it. You won't have any trouble. Good luck to you. There's bastards in this world that would cut your throat for a quarter."

And then I did say, "Much obliged," and walked away in the direction he had pointed.

I was already several blocks away when I put my hand into my jacket pocket and felt paper. It was a new five-dollar bill that never had been folded but once.

And so the first money I made on my entrance into the great world was liar's wages. It didn't make me feel a bit better. But I didn't go back.

Sam Hanks had probably already unloaded and started home. I was stuck with my lie, and I was going to be stuck with it for some time to come.

Maybe because I was ashamed, I took Sam Hanks's advice and headed for the trotting track. As he had said, it wasn't hard to find. He may have been wrong about the future it offered, but I did like it better than the stockyards. At the trotting track the animals—which were mostly horses, with a dog or a goat or a pet rooster thrown in here and there—weren't all crowded together into pens but lived one to a place in stalls that were roomy and dry and light and well bedded. In fact, the horses lived better than a lot of people, including some of the grooms and stable hands who took care of them. They were worth more money than a lot of people, and they had the best grain and hay and straw; they never wanted for shelter or medical care or new shoes, and they were attended to like kings and queens. The horses were royalty at the trotting track, and their needs came first.

The drivers and trainers, you could say, were the princes—or anyhow the best of them were. They amounted to something; they were the ones who *knew*, and when they spoke the others listened. Below them were the grooms and stable hands. The trotting track was an orderly little world, ordered by the force of one idea: the idea of a paramount trotting or pacing horse that would stride down to the wire, not just in front of every other horse in the race but in front of every other horse that ever had raced up to that time. Everybody in that world was set in motion by this one idea.

It seemed wrong to me that some horses should fare better than some people in that time when so many went without enough to eat or wear, or even without a tight roof over their heads. And yet I too for a time came under the spell of the idea of the supreme horse. And some of the actual horses were wonderful. They had speed and courage and spirit and beauty. I remember several that just to see them standing in their harness like lords of the world could send a chill over you from head to foot.

I'm sure that the "future" Sam Hanks spoke of was there for some. And maybe, if I had been destined to it or called to it strongly enough, it might have been there for me. But my future, as it turned out, proved to be elsewhere. I hadn't even glimpsed it yet. I had imagined no future. Who she was who would have my heart to own I had not imagined.

With Sam Hanks's five-dollar bill added to the several others that made my savings, I had a pretty good little nest egg, for the times, and I protected it like the Holy Grail. Nobody needed to tell me that the world I was in now was not the world of the college, where I'd had my scholarship and a sure job and, you might say, connections. The world I was in now could fix a man mighty quick to where he would need more than I had saved just to keep living. Suppose I got sick or broke a bone. So I made a law for myself that I wouldn't spend a cent of my savings unless I absolutely had to, but would live on present earnings only.

It was far from easy. There were plenty of people who needed work as much as I did, or more. There were considerably more than a pair of hands for every handle. And at the trotting track it helped if you were known. Of course, I wasn't known. I could have turned up from anywhere, and I didn't know a soul. All I could do was hang around and look willing. If a hand was needed on the handle of a fork and I was there and nobody else was, then I would earn a nickel or a dime cleaning out a stall. I carried buckets of water. I ran—and I mean ran—for coffee and sandwiches. Whenever I caught the scent of a small coin looking to change pockets, I tried my best to furnish the pocket. "*I'll* do it!" I'd say. "Let *me* do it!"

And in that way I got to be recognized a little. It got so that when some odd job needed doing, somebody would jerk his head in my direction and say, "*He'll* do it! Let *him* do it!"

But if you've never tried it, you'd be surprised how long it takes to make a dollar out of nickel-and-diming at little jobs that come just now and then. It was a good thing for me that you could get a pretty good meal (if you weren't particular where you got it) for a quarter. I was a long way from what you would call steady employment. However willing I was, I was a long way from working for anybody in particular. And hard to tell how long it would have been before anybody would have let me actually touch a horse.

I was lucky that spring was coming, for it was clear right away that present earnings might keep me clothed a little on the decent side of nakedness, and fed a little short of full, but they were not going to buy me a place to sleep. And so, lost and ignorant as I was, I made a good discovery. There were drivers and regular hands who, if they saw you still hanging around after dark, would let you go up in a loft and sleep in the hay. They would always make you turn out your pockets to see that you had no matches, and then they would say, "Boy, if anybody asks you, I didn't tell you you could sleep up there. I don't know a *thing* about it."

And then I made another good discovery. I liked those nights of sleeping in the hay. I still like to remember them. If I could I would find an old horse blanket—a cooling blanket was best—and double it and lay it down on the hay and pile a forkful or two of hay on top of it, and then just burrow in. That was fine when the nights were cold. When they were warm, I could just lie down anywhere on a pile of hay, or even in the bedding on the floor of an empty stall. Aside from eating and keeping warm, I didn't have anything on my mind, and I slept good.

After the human stir had quieted down, and the stable hands had quit talking and laughing or shooting craps, I loved to lie there in the dark, listening to the horses eating their hay or shifting about in the bedding. Now and again I'd hear a snort or a dog barking, and off in the distance the sounds of traffic and trains. I always went to sleep before I thought I would. The next thing I knew, roosters would be crowing and horses nickering, and though it would still be dark the horsemen would be up and busy, putting the morning ration into the troughs and fresh hay in the mangers. They were fanatical about feeding times. You could set your watch by them, if you had one. I would lie still a little while just to enjoy the sounds, and then I would get up too, to be on hand for little jobs and maybe a few scraps of somebody else's breakfast. As I said, I didn't have any cares except for a few necessities, and I felt industrious and alert and on the lookout in those days.

It was hard to keep my box of personal things either safely in sight or well hidden, but that got easier. And I wore my old jacket with my money in the lining like it was my skin. I almost never took it off.

"Boy," somebody was always saying, after the weather began to warm up, "ain't you hot in that jacket?"

And even if the sweat was running down my nose and dripping off, I would say, "I ain't hot!"

For bathing and shaving, I would wait until after dark and borrow a water bucket, or slip into a public restroom.

I went on in that hand-to-mouth, day-to-day fashion until well into

June without looking forward or back and without any plans at all. And then everything changed, by surprise.

One of my problems, living on present earnings, was that my hair kept growing. People were beginning to say, "Boy, when you going to get you a hairnet?" And one or two even started calling me "girlie." It was beginning to interfere with business.

So I decided I'd have to sacrifice one day's eating money to a proper haircut. Not far from the track was a sort of run-down barbershop on a run-down street. When I got there not long after dinnertime I was the only customer. I climbed into the chair and told the old barber to civilize my mop.

He hadn't even shaved was the kind of barber he was. As he started in on me, he started talking, as barbers generally will. He waved his comb toward a second chair that sat idle, covered with a cloth, and said that he and another barber had once stayed busy there all day every day with hardly time to sweep up the cut hair. And he went on to name all the famous horsemen who had been his customers, and he was telling me a number of things that various ones of them had told him.

Maybe I was a good listener, or maybe he hadn't had a customer for several days, but he went on and on with his talk about how good the times had been there in the shop back in the old days, stopping now and then to let fly a streak of ambeer at a spittoon under the backbar.

He went on so much that finally I got to feeling dishonest, sitting there listening and not saying anything. So I said, "Well, what happened?"

He said, "What do you mean what happened?"

"There's surely been a comedown," I said. "It don't look like you say it used to."

He hadn't been working very fast, and now he slowed down even more. He took another wild shot at the spittoon. "Well," he said, "the other fellow died."

"Well, what about you?" I said. "You're still among us."

He didn't say anything for a while. He seemed to be refining his work, leaning way back to keep his bifocals homed in, and cutting little snips just here and there.

"Verily," he said. "I ain't sober all the time anymore."

And then for a longer time he didn't say anything but seemed to be thinking, or maybe he was embarrassed by his confession. Maybe he was just snipping his scissors in the air over the top of my head.

Finally he spat and cleared his throat. "You don't know a barber looking for a job, I don't reckon, do you?"

"Yessir," I said. "Me."

He quit work entirely then and came around in front of the chair and stood there with his scissors in one hand and his comb in the other, looking at me, with his face all bristly and the white whiskers around his mouth stained with ambeer.

Finally he said in a low voice, "Hunh!"

He was brisk about his work after that. He brushed off the loose hair, shaved around my ears, and whisked away the neckcloth.

I had no more than stood up and was reaching into my pocket to pay him when he climbed into the chair.

"Suppose you just give me a haircut," he said, "and let's see."

He needed a haircut as badly as I needed to give him one, and I didn't hesitate. I flipped the neckcloth out over his lap, pinned it around his neck, and went to work. It had been a long time since I had barbered anybody, but I took my time and was careful. After I had cut his hair, without either of us saying a word I put in the headrest, tilted him back, lathered his face, and gave him a shave. He turned out not a bad-looking fellow, and a good deal younger than I had thought.

He got up and looked at himself this way and that in the mirror while I stood holding out my coins.

When he had seen enough, he said, "Turnabout's fair play. Keep your money." And then he said, "When can you start?"

We struck a deal. He would furnish shop and equipment, and I could keep half of whatever I earned. I said all right, but what if I wanted to take a couple of courses in school? He said he would keep things going while I was gone, if I wasn't gone too much, and if I would do the same for him. I said all right, if he wasn't gone too much, and we shook. He was Skinner Hawes, he said, from down about Sweet Home, and I don't know to this day if Skinner was his real name or not.

Maybe a lot of people could say the same—I think they could; the squeak between living and not living is pretty tight—but I have had a lucky life. That is to say that I *know* I've been lucky. Beyond that, the question is if I have not been also blessed, as I believe I have—and, beyond that, even called. Surely I was called to be, for one thing, a barber. All my real opportunities have been to be a barber, as you'll see, and being a barber has made other opportunities. I have had the life I have had because I kept on being a barber, you might say, in spite of my intentions to the contrary.

Now I have had most of the life I am going to have, and I can see what it has been. I can remember those early years when it seemed to me I was cut completely adrift, and times when, looking back at earlier times, it seemed I had been wandering in the dark woods of error. But now it looks to me as though I was following a path that was laid out for me, unbroken, and maybe even as straight as possible, from one end to the other, and I have this feeling, which never leaves me anymore, that I have been *led*. I will leave you to judge the truth of that for yourself; as Dr. Ardmire and I agreed, there is no proof.

Anyhow, I told Skinner Hawes that I could start right then. There was little enough work to be done—one haircut all afternoon—but I put in the time cleaning the place up. Skinner had fallen into the habit of putting things just anywhere and then letting them lie until he wanted them again, if he could find them. The only dusting that had been accomplished there in a long time had been done by the seats of the customers' pants. The big front window was about as transparent as an old bedsheet.

So I carried out a big pile of old newspapers and *Police Gazettes* and dusted everything and washed the windows and mirrors and swept the floor and mopped it. When quitting time came I went back to the trotting track and retrieved my box of possessions from where I had hidden it. On the way back I invested my haircut fund in a pretty good supper.

For two or three nights I slept on the floor of the shop, and then I found a poor old widow lady in a poor old house with a room to rent for the little that I thought I could afford. The room was just a little longer and wider than I was. It had an iron cot, a table, and a chair, and a few nails driven into the wall for hanging things up. It was the first room I'd ever had in my own right, paid for by me, with my own door that I could shut and lock. As long as the rent was paid, it was my room, and I liked the feeling. I came and went through a side door. The landlady was a nice woman who would have taken me to raise, as the fellow says, if she had seen enough of me. But even when I was there I was never much in sight and made no commotion. I could have been a mouse in the wall.

At the shop, I saw right away that we would have to do something to stir up business. Skinner's old customers had fallen away, partly, I thought, because they didn't like the way he and the shop looked. Cleaning up the shop and keeping Skinner shorn and shaved would help, I thought, but we'd have to get the word out. So I got some paper and lettered out a few little signs. They said: SKINNER'S BARBERSHOP. 2 CHAIRS AT YOUR SERVICE. GOOD PRICES. PLENTY OF SITTING ROOM. And then I listed our "special prices" for the next two weeks, knocking a nickel off of everything. I didn't even ask Skinner; I just did it. And then I tacked up my signs on some trees and barn doors over at the trotting track, and I advertised a little too by word of mouth.

All that I had done didn't amount to much, really, but it seemed to help. The place looked better, and people began to drift in from the trotting track and other places, either to loaf or to get a shave or a haircut. We made them feel welcome, whether they were loafers or customers, hoping that the loafers would become customers, which sooner or later they mostly did. It wasn't long until we had enough regular customers to keep us going.

They were a mixed lot, I will have to say. We had people from the shops and stores in the neighborhood, people who lived nearby — decent-enough working people, most of them. We also had several second-string touts and gamblers from over at the track, a pimp or two, and maybe worse than that. I was pleased, for it seemed to me that I was getting a good look at city life and hearing talk and learning things I probably couldn't have learned anyplace else. And I did learn a good deal. For a barber, I never was very talkative. Mainly I listened. At Skinner's Barbershop I heard people taking things for granted that I had never even imagined before. And I mean several *kinds* of people, talking about several kinds of things. But we never did get any of the famous horsemen Skinner continued to brag that he had barbered in the old days.

We were doing all right. I don't mean to say we were getting rich, but we were getting the things we needed and paying for them. I was eating

my meals with the comforting thought that in several hours I was almost
certainly going to eat again. And I had gone back to saving my money. I
would go to the bank to change my small bills into bigger ones, so as not
to accumulate too big a wad in my jacket lining or my shoes. But I never
opened an account. I knew I was being reckless with my money, risking
losing it or having it stolen or burnt up, but it was my money and I didn't
trust anybody to take care of it but me. A bank account just didn't appeal
to me. I was too standoffish and sly. I never deposited a dime in a bank
until about three years after I set up shop in Port William. And even now
I like to have a few bills stuck here and there, where only I know where
they are.

I assumed that since I didn't have the religion of Pigeonville College I
didn't have any religion at all. That seemed a big load off my mind. I felt
as light as a kite. Anybody who had been to The Good Shepherd and
Pigeonville College knew very well what was forbidden and what was
not. I was well acquainted with the unforbidden, but now that I was
accumulating a little money I invested some in the forbidden. Wherever
I could locate the forbidden—and with our clientele, it wasn't hard—I
went and tried it. Wherever the sirens sang, I went ashore. Wherever
I heard the suck of whirlpools and the waters gnashing on the rocks, I
rowed hard to get there. It's a little bit of a wonder that I didn't get cast
up from the depths in several pieces, or at least contract a foul disease.

Why I didn't, I think, was stinginess and my wish to read books. I
never shirked or shorted my work, and I never was free with my money.
I found that I could experience the forbidden just as well on a tight
budget, probably, as by squandering every cent I had saved. This was
another of my good discoveries. I didn't settle on any final terms with
the forbidden. I just floated in and floated out. I was a cut-rate prodigal.

When the fall semester started at the university in the middle of September, I did what I had told Skinner Hawes I was going to do. I went
over and paid the tuition fee and signed up for two courses. Looking
back now, I can see how noncommittal and stealthy I had become. The
official forces were there, seeing to the process of registration, and with
them I was like a fox at night, passing through with as little commotion
as possible. I can sort of see myself as I must have been that day, looking
about for fear I would run into somebody who had known me before,

filling out the papers with false information or as near none as possible. I said that my name was J. Crow, that I was from Diehard, Kentucky, that I planned on becoming a schoolteacher. Parents? None. Religion? None. National origin? Diehard. Race? Lost. Sex? Yes.

I didn't come clean about anything, really. What I wanted were courses in book-reading, and I wasn't particular which. Once I got over there in the actual presence of the classroom buildings and the library, it seemed to me that I hungered and thirsted to hear somebody talk about books who knew more about them than I did. I didn't *mean* I wanted to be a schoolteacher. I just made that my pretense to be there, for I had never heard that anybody ever went to a university just to read books. There had to be a real reason—namely, something you wanted to do later. Anyhow, I never took any courses in the college of education. I signed up for literature courses.

And I thoroughly liked them. I could say I loved them. When the time came I would leave the shop and walk across to the campus and through the between-classes mobs of students to McVey Hall and climb the steps up to the classrooms and sit down. I would get there a little early if I could. I would stroll past the professors' offices full of books and look in at the doors, and then wait in my seat in the classroom while the students sorted themselves out of the passing crowd and came in and took their seats. And then the professor would come in and call the roll and begin talking. This was what I longed for. I just sat and took it in. Even though I couldn't quite make myself care whether I passed the courses or not, I took notes like everybody else. I remembered everything I read and heard. Maybe I was lucky, but for the courses I took I had professors who knew what they were talking about and loved to talk about it, and it seemed wonderful to me. I answered questions if I was asked, but I asked no questions. The professors were pretty aloof, like the university itself, and I was as aloof from them as they were from me.

I read in the textbooks that were assigned, and I also went to the library and checked out the books the professors talked about or recommended, and read them. Or read at them—some were dull. At the shop when I didn't have a customer, I would climb into the chair myself and read. That caused some curious looks and some comment, but Skinner would jerk his head in my direction and say, "He's taking courses. He's

going to become a gentleman and a scholar. Verily, I expect to see him
walk in here someday and tell me he's a professor." That took care of
that, and I let it go.

I read in my room at night, when I wasn't out prowling. And some
nights I went over to the library and read there. The library had beautiful rooms lined with books, and tables for reading and writing. And
there was a perfectly lovely room called the Browsing Room, with shelf
upon shelf of books, and several tall windows looking out into the trees,
and easy chairs with reading lamps, and sofas. It was far and away the
finest, most comfortable room I had ever seen in my life, and I loved to
sit in it. If you were there on a Sunday afternoon you could sometimes
steal a splendid nap on one of the sofas.

After The Good Shepherd and Pigeonville, the university was a big relief to me. Unless you were a girl, nobody cared much what you did. Nobody was going to call you in for a talking-to across the top of a desk—
or, rather, they might invite you or "require" you, but they couldn't *make*
you come in if you didn't want to, and they knew it, and mostly I think
they didn't care if you came in or not. If you failed your courses, you disappeared back into the outside world again, and they would see you no
more.

The university was in some ways the opposite of The Good Shepherd. The Good Shepherd looked upon the outside world as a threat to
its conventional wisdom. The university looked upon itself as a threat to
the conventional wisdom of the outside world. According to it, it not
only knew more than ordinary people but was more advanced and had a
better idea of the world of the future.

Otherwise, the university and The Good Shepherd were a lot alike.
That was another of my discoveries. It was a slow discovery and not one
I enjoyed—I was a long time figuring it out. Every one of the educa-
tional institutions that I had been in had been hard at work trying to be a
world unto itself. The Good Shepherd and Pigeonville College were trying to be the world of the past. The university was trying to be the world
of the future, and maybe it has had a good deal to do with the world as it
has turned out to be, but this has not been as big an improvement as the
university expected. The university thought of itself as a place of freedom for thought and study and experimentation, and maybe it was, in a

way. But it was an island too, a floating or a flying island. It was preparing people from the world of the past for the world of the future, and what was missing was the world of the present, where every body was living its small, short, surprising, miserable, wonderful, blessed, damaged, only life.

I was going along and going along, led by this love I had of reading books and pushed by the feeling, left over from my earlier teachers, that I ought to make something out of myself and rise above my humble origins. I was attending my classes, doing the reading, taking the tests—even making good grades, though I pretty much didn't care whether they were good or not. But aside from my declaration that I wanted to be a teacher, I had made no "career preparation" at all. I wasn't taking required courses. I had a "faculty advisor" whose name I had never spoken and could not remember. I had not been in ROTC; I had not taken hygiene or physical education or a science. I had taken a course in which we had read some of Dante in English, and it made me wish I knew his Italian, but I had never enrolled in a course in any foreign language. I was not preparing for any career or life that the university recommended or that I could imagine. I tried to imagine myself as a teacher, but I had no more success at that than I'd had at imagining myself as a preacher—though, as before, I sort of dreamed of a salary and a wife. The future was coming to me, but I had not so much as lifted a foot to go to it. Maybe my failure at Pigeonville carried over into my time at the university, like an infection. Maybe my character was leading me astray. Maybe I was called to what I had not thought, as Professor Ardmire had said.

Along in the fall of 1936, after the weather got cold, about the time I finished figuring out that all the institutions I had known were islands, the whole weight of my unimagined, unlooked-for life came down on me, and I hit the bottom—or anyhow I hit what felt mighty like the bottom. For the first time, maybe, since my early days at The Good Shepherd, I felt just awfully lonesome. I felt sad beyond the thought or memory of happiness. Maybe I had felt those feelings before, but before I could stop them. Now I couldn't stop them. It got so that whenever I was by myself I would think again and again of myself running barefoot over the frozen grass the morning Aunt Cordie died, and I would cry.

When I was crying I would be hearing in my mind Aunt Cordie's voice saying, "I don't know. Honey, I just don't know."

One of the sights in Lexington in those days was an old Negro man, wearing a tall silk hat and a swallowtail coat, who walked all day up and down the sidewalk in front of some not-so-good houses close to the university. He had a certain length of the walk that he walked. When he got to the end of his walk in one direction he would make a low, graceful bow and turn gracefully and walk in the other direction. He walked back and forth, back and forth, day after day. I thought of him too.

Or I didn't exactly *think*, of him or of myself or Aunt Cordie either. Maybe I wasn't thinking then at all. It was just that when I wasn't working or reading or going to class, or when I couldn't sleep, these images would come into my mind. I would see myself running or the old man walking, or I would hear Aunt Cordie's voice and I would cry.

By the time I had got to Lexington, I was so convinced of the temporariness of any stay I would ever make in this world that I hadn't formed any ties at all. At the trotting track and at the shop, I made acquaintances, but I didn't make any friends. At the university I came and went almost without speaking to anybody. Maybe I did and have forgot, but I don't remember eating a meal with another soul during the year and about ten months I stayed in Lexington. For a long time I liked it that way. I enjoyed coming and going without telling or explaining, being free. I enjoyed listening without talking. I enjoyed being wherever I was without being noticed. But then when the dark change came over my mind, I was in a fix. My solitariness turned into loneliness. When I was alone those images moved and Aunt Cordie's voice sounded in my mind, and I couldn't stop them. What I had thought was the bottom kept getting lower in little jerks. When I cried it was getting harder to stop.

The memories of my days at Squires Landing—which I had once been able to walk about in, in my mind—had shrunk and drawn away. That old life had come to be like a little painted picture at the bottom of a well, and the well was getting deeper. The picture that I had inside me was more real than anything outside, and yet it was getting ever smaller and farther away and harder to call back. That, I guess, is why I got so sad. I was living, but I was not living my life. So far as I could see, I was going nowhere. And now, more and more, I seemed also to have come from nowhere. Without a loved life to live, I was becoming more and more a theoretical person, as if I might have been a figment of institutional self-justification: a theoretical ignorant person from the sticks, who one day would go to a theoretical somewhere and make a theoretical something of himself—the implication being that until he became that something he would be nothing.

I kept attending classes until the Christmas vacation began, and I kept on working, but I could see that I had come to another end. I had completely lost the feeling that I should make something of myself. Aunt Cordie's voice troubled my mind, but it told me I didn't look down on my humble origins and didn't yearn to rise above them. It took me a long time to see what was happening to me then. I have known no sudden revelations. No stroke of light has ever knocked me blind to the ground. But I know now that even then, in my hopelessness and sorrow, I began a motion of the heart toward my origins. Far from rising above them, I was longing to sink into them until I would know the fundamental things. I needed to know the original first chapter of the world. I had no past that I could go back to and no future that I could imagine, no family, no friends, and no plans. I was as free as a falling stone or a floating chip— freer, for I had no direction at all.

When classes took up again after Christmas, I made up my mind not to go back.

Skinner said, "I thought you was going to school."

I said, "I reckon not."

I had a customer, and Skinner was sitting in his chair, reading a newspaper somebody had left. When I said "I reckon not," he lowered the paper and looked at me, waiting for me to explain. I didn't explain.

Finally he said, "Mmmm-*mnh!* Verily, I'll be damned if ever *I* seen anything like it."

Maybe because not going back to my classes was in a way doing something, another image began moving in my mind. I could see myself getting out of Sam Hanks's truck at the stockyards, and I could see him coming around to face me. When he hooked his two fingers into my jacket pocket, I could feel the pull. More than I ever had before, I felt ashamed of my lie and wanted to undo it. I thought for a while of sending the money back, care of the postmaster at Port William. And then, without deciding not to, I didn't.

One morning in the latter part of January, in 1937, instead of going to the shop, I packed my belongings into the same box I had brought with me from Pigeonville, leaving out what wouldn't fit in, and laid a full week's rent along with my key on the table in my room. I walked out of town as easily and freely as one of the old beat-down gamblers who would show up and hang around the shop for a few weeks or months and then be gone. I thought of taking leave of Skinner Hawes and my old landlady—but what for? To be asked for an explanation that I didn't have?

I headed westward, for Louisville. I knew that along the rivers the waters were rising.

8

The Gathering Waters

Because, to save money, I had got around in Lexington purely by walking, I had invested in a raincoat and rainhat and also a good pair of overshoes. On the journey I began from Lexington, the Friday morning of January 22, I figure my rain gear paid for itself and turned a profit. The coat was made of a stiff fabric coated with rubber, and it had big pockets that I could reach all the way through to carry my box first with one hand and then the other. It must have been made for a fat man. Even though I was wearing my jacket under it, there was plenty of room in it for me and my box too. The hat was made of the same stuff and had a broad brim to shed the rain down past the collar of the coat. If I didn't sweat, I could stay dry in any kind of weather.

When I left Lexington early that morning, I was not sweating. The day was cold and wet. It had been raining, and it was still raining. It was going to rain. The rain fell steady and pretty hard, and there was no place you could think of where it wasn't raining. It was the kind of winter day that makes you forget that the weather was ever any different, and you feel like it has been winter all the way back to Adam. The people walking along the streets, the horses drawing the freight wagons, even the trucks and cars, all seemed resigned and slow, as if they were determined to keep going without hope.

I can't say that I was full of hope myself, but I was full of excitement. By the time I had taken just a few steps, I could feel that I was leaving behind the little closed spaces of my room and Skinner's Barbershop and the university, and was out in the wide world. I welcomed even the cold and the wet, and was glad when I went past the edge of town and there were farms on both sides of the road. I didn't feel sad and lonely any-more but just alert. I don't think I had even begun to have an idea where I was going, but wherever it was, that was where I wanted to go.

For the time being, I had in mind just to go and see the risen waters. Though I had never been to Louisville, the flood in Louisville had been a big thing in the newspapers, and I was going there to see it. From there, I thought, I would just let my way branch off wherever it would. I walked on the right-hand side of the road, not asking for a ride but in a position to take one if one was offered. My agreement with myself was that if I was going to go, I ought to be willing to go by my own means, which is to say by foot. I did get several rides, but not a one of them took me far. It is about twenty-five miles from Lexington to Frankfort, and I would guess I walked better than half that distance. But the trip itself turned out to be a good deal longer than twenty-five miles.

The first fellow who gave me a lift said the water was already over the road I was following. He said I ought to try the Leestown Pike, and he let me out at a side road that would take me across. After I got to the Leestown Pike I walked a long time toward Frankfort before I got to a sign saying that road was closed. And so I had to double back to another side road that took me across to Versailles. It was afternoon by the time I got there, and I had walked and ridden a long way and was still fifteen miles from Frankfort. I found a little eating joint there where I got two hamburgers and drank several glasses of water, and then I set off again.

The talk in the eating place and with the people who gave me rides was all of the flood. The Kentucky River had risen six inches an hour at Frankfort during the night and was still rising an inch an hour, which would be two feet a day. I had lived for my whole childhood, you might say, in sight of that river. I knew what a two-foot rise meant, once the river was out of its banks. For every inch it rose the water would widen by feet. And all along, as I was making my way back to it again, I got more and more excited. As I imagined the water rising in the river valley,

I seemed to feel it rising in me. That feeling was my old life coming back to me, though I hadn't the words or even a thought for it. As in those first weeks at The Good Shepherd when I had longed to go home, I now longed to see the waters.

By the time I got to Frankfort, dark was coming and the rain was turning to sleet. As soon as I was past the edge of town, a long time before I saw the river, the turmoil of the flood was right there to be seen. The streets were crowded with traffic and people walking—people needing shelter, people trying to help the people needing shelter, people going home from work or going about their usual business, and a lot of sightseers too. You couldn't tell which was which, except that a lot of the walkers and riders were carrying things, like me, and I guessed they were the ones whose houses had been flooded.

I was tired by then and my hands were sore from carrying my box. But I was anxious too, for I knew that to get to Louisville I was going to have to cross the river, and I didn't know where.

I started asking people, "Where's the bridge?"

The first one I asked seemed not to hear me at all. He just hurried on by, staring straight ahead, with his shoulders hunched and his hands shoved down in his pockets.

And then I asked a woman, who said, "Lord God, honey, *I* don't know!"

And then I asked a man who seemed to know where he was. He smiled as people sometimes do when you have revealed your ignorance and said, "Which bridge?" raising in my mind for the first time the possibility that there was more than one.

I said, "The closest one."

"That would be the St. Clair Street Bridge. I think you can still get across." And he told me how to go.

But by then night had altogether fallen. The lights scattered along the streets and the headlights of the passing traffic glaring on the puddled water and glancing off the falling sleet were more confusing to me than the darkness. I kept having to ask for directions.

A long time before I got to the bridge I could hear the river, the great sort of hushing roar it makes when the currents are shoving and swirling along, sucking around the trunks of trees, and the tree branches are shaking and clashing. The air was full of the fear of it—the waters rising and the sleet falling and the sky altogether dark above the little human lights that were winking and flashing and darting about. It was exactly what Aunt Cordie could make you imagine when she was in one of her end-of-the-world moods—the signs being fulfilled, and the dreadful horsemen about to make their way across the earth.

When I got to the bridge, the entrance was barricaded with long trestles. I started around the end of one of them and this big sort of elderly policeman stepped right in front of me.

"Son," he said, "you can't go over there."

I said, "Why not?"

We were right in each other's faces, yelling to be heard above the crashing of the waters.

He said, "Hell fire, boy! Don't you know nothing? This bridge is liable to go any minute. They've lassoed a big barn right up the river yonder and tied it up to some trees. If that barn breaks loose and hits this bridge, she's a *goner*, and you too if you're on it."

And then I said something that I had never thought of saying, that I didn't even know was the truth until I remembered myself saying it. Right then I only felt all of a sudden so lonely and homesick I could barely talk. I said, "I've got to get to my people down the river."

He said, "Your *people!* Where?"

"Squires Landing!" I said, and then, thinking he probably had never heard of that place, I said, "Port William!"

Maybe he had heard of Port William. I don't know. Maybe he wasn't much of a policeman. Some troublesome kindness was working in him—you could see it. He said, "Son, I didn't see you come, and I didn't see you go." He turned his back and went into shadows.

In a few steps I was out of sight and beyond all the street sounds. Out there on the bridge, I was closed in by the many-stranded sound of the river. It was like a living element. It was like a big crowd shouting. And above or within the uproar of the water, I could hear the sleet hissing down. I could feel the river throbbing in the bridge. I can't say that I was not afraid, but it seemed the fear was not in me but in the air, like the sound of the river. It seemed to be something I had gone into and could not expect to get out of easily or very soon. It didn't make me want to run.

When I got out about to the middle of the span, I stopped and looked upstream over the rail. A strengthless, shapeless cloud of light that in the daytime would have seemed a shadow hovered over the river. Without trying exactly to see anything, but sort of just letting myself see, I could make out the troubled surface of the water and the shapes of things moving swiftly down—great rafts of drift, barrels, bottles, sawlogs, whole trees, pieces of furniture. I even saw what looked to be the gable of a house, with what might have been a cat perched on top. Everything came turning in the currents, into sight and then out of sight almost faster than I could believe. Along what had been the shores I could see the trees shaking and battering their limbs together. And the waves and swirls of the water caught the human lights of the town and flung them hither and yon.

And this is what it was like—the words were just right there in my mind, and I knew they were true: "the earth was without form, and void; and darkness was upon the face of the deep. And the Spirit of God moved upon the face of the waters." I'm not sure that I can tell you what was happening to me then, or that I know even now. At the time I surely wasn't trying to tell myself. But after all my years of reading in that book and hearing it read and believing and disbelieving it, I seemed to have wandered my way back to the beginning—not just of the book, but of the world—and all the rest was yet to come. I felt knowledge crawl over my skin.

I went on across the bridge then, and felt myself let back down onto solid ground out of the shuddering darkness. Into my own misery too, for the cold had gotten into my clothes by then and I was shivering. The sleet had piled up on the roads and walks nearly ankle deep. The light gleamed and glared on the surfaces of everything, and glanced on the little grains of ice as they fell. And even where it fell into the light, the sleet was like a cold and bitter darkness falling out of the sky. It only then really hit me that I was alone and in need and helpless, and didn't know where to go. Water was already well over some of the streets. In places you could hear the currents slurring around lightpoles and the corners of buildings.

It took me a long time to make my way up to what I could feel was high ground. I had pretty certain knowledge of where the bridge and the main course of the river were, but that was all. I had never been in that place before. I didn't even know anyplace I could ask for directions *to*. And instinct wasn't helping me a bit. I kept turning in to the wrong streets, where I would walk a little way and pretty soon hear again the sound of water flowing, or hear the sleet sizzling down onto a patch of dead water, and then I would turn back and cast out a little wider.

When you are in a fix like that, it is always easy to see where you made your mistake. I could see plainly where I had made mine. I had been so anxious first to get to the river, and then to get across, that I had never even wondered how I would find shelter for the night. I wished mightily that I had stopped while I was still out in the country and found a good dry loft full of hay to nestle down into. And since I was wishing, I wished that when I was in Versailles at dinnertime, poking away those two hamburgers, I had looked ahead to supper. It would have been easy then to buy a few slices of cheese or a can of sardines and some crackers and stick them into my pocket. But where I was now, everything that looked like an eating place or a grocery store was shut tight. I was getting so cold and tired and hungry that it got easy to imagine that the few hurrying people I met and passed in the streets would see that I needed help and would help me. And then I imagined that they were cold and tired and hungry themselves, and I wished that I could help *them*. I hadn't imagined yet that I might just out-and-out *ask* for help. My old habit of aloofness and solitude was too binding—though afterward I realized that my imagination hadn't been all that far from changing. I wasn't all that far from saying "Help me."

But what happened was I finally blundered into a long, broad street where I met another policeman. He took a look at me and the bulge of my box under my raincoat, and said, "Buddy, are you looking for a place to go?"

When I unclenched my jaws to say, "Yes," my teeth chopped it into about seven syllables.

He just took hold of my shoulder and turned me toward a big domed building looming up at the end of the street, and pointed. "Up there," he said.

It was, of all places, the capitol. I recognized the shape of it from pictures. I had never seen it before, of course. Really, I had never thought of it before, let alone expected to go there. And it was such an immense, imposing building. The closer I got, the more it seemed that nobody ought to go there who did not have somebody walking in front, blowing a trumpet. But I was a boy in need of a direction, and I went ahead.

Several other people—two or three families, it looked like—got to the door at the same time I did. They were sort of shuffling in, taking their turn, and I shuffled in behind them. Now that warmth was at hand, I realized that my feet were as numb as two rocks; I couldn't feel the floor.

The big hallway seemed full of people, children and grown-ups and old people, some laughing, some crying, some just standing and staring, some with suitcases or bundles, some well dressed, some without even enough clothes, some so grateful to be alive they didn't care whether they had enough clothes or not. I found a place to stand and set my box down between my feet and just stood there with the others. They all seemed to be waiting, and none of them seemed to know what they were waiting for. We were a sorry-looking bunch, all of us, dripping and shifting our feet and glancing about, and the great building with its high, shining walls and gleaming floor seemed not at all to have been expecting the likes of us. It was prepared for something altogether different from these cast-up people trying to quiet their babies and hold on to their children and keep track of the few possessions they had managed to save from the river, talking or listening as they told one another what had happened to them. Refugees is what they were, and ever since, when I have read of the refugees of war or other calamities, I have thought of them.

I was a refugee too, I suppose, but of a different kind. Just to look, you couldn't have told me from the others, but inwardly I knew the difference and I tried not to be in their way. I hadn't lost anything I wanted to keep. I hadn't carried all the downstairs furniture upstairs and then fled away, or stepped off a porch roof into a boat with a baby in my arms, or turned all the livestock out to save themselves if they could. And I wasn't waiting either, really. I was on my way. My mind had changed as completely as if I had never thought of going to Louisville. I was on my way home, as surely as if I had a home to be on the way to. And to my surprise, I might add, for not a one of my teachers had ever suggested such a possibility. I suppose that in my freedom, when it came, I pointed to Port William as a compass needle points north.

Or maybe the needle was the five-dollar bill that Sam Hanks trusted to me on the basis of a lie.

What I was feeling mainly was pure relief. I stood a little apart from the others in that warm air, breathing it in and out, feeling the life ache back into my feet and hands, looking at the people and the strange luxurious light of that place.

And then gradually it came clear to me that we weren't just a helpless, aimless mob of strays, but people were there who were in charge of us— people setting up cots, moving about, asking if anybody was sick or hurt, giving help where it was needed. And then it came to me that I was smelling food. I looked around a little and saw that several smiling ladies were handing out bowls of soup and pieces of bread.

As I knew I wasn't exactly in the same fix as the other people, I didn't go to the table in any kind of rush but waited until I could go without getting in front of anybody. Especially I didn't want to push in ahead of any of the children. But when the way got clear, I went. I got my bowl and my spoon and my piece of bread and went off to the side again and sat on my box and leaned my back against the wall. I stuck my nose into the steam rising off of that hot soup and let my heart rejoice.

Pretty soon people began putting their children to bed. And the grown-ups who had no children were finding places for themselves. I didn't take one of the cots, but found a little nook behind a statue of a man of another time and folded up my raincoat for a pillow and lay down on the floor with my back to the crowd and my box between me and the wall.

I was thoroughly tired, and I didn't exactly lie awake, but I didn't exactly sleep either. As soon as I shut my eyes I could see the river again, only now I seemed to see it up and down its whole length. Where just a little while before people had been breathing and eating and going about in their old everyday lives, now I could see the currents come riding in, at first picking up straws and dead leaves and little sticks, and then boards and pieces of firewood and whole logs, and then maybe the henhouse or the barn or the house itself. As if the mountains had melted and were flowing to the sea, the water rose and filled all the airy spaces of rooms and stalls and fields and woods, carrying away everything that would float, casting up the people and scattering them, scattering or drowning their animals and poultry flocks. The whole world, it seemed, was cast adrift, riding the currents, whirled about in eddies, the old life submerged and gone, the new not yet come.

And I knew that the Spirit that had gone forth to shape the world and make it live was still alive in it. I just had no doubt. I could see that I lived in the created world, and it was still being created. I would be part of it forever. There was no escape. The Spirit that made it was *in* it, shaping it and reshaping it, sometimes lying at rest, sometimes standing up and shaking itself, like a muddy horse, and letting the pieces fly. I had almost no sooner broke my leash than I had hit the wall.

In a funny way, it was hard for me to get up and leave that place. Finding such a shelter on such a night had probably saved my life, and I had this feeling that I oughtn't to leave until I found somebody to thank. I felt sort of captured by gratitude. And too, after coming in with them out of the cold darkness and passing the night with them, I felt a belonging with those people as though they were kin to me. But it seemed I had already received all the help I had a right to. I didn't want to stay until all the people woke up and the good women came back and started serving breakfast.

I'm an early riser. I come wide awake right out of sleep, and generally know the time within maybe five or ten minutes. When I stood up and made sure of my box and unrolled my raincoat, the place seemed unearthly quiet. Only two or three of the men had wakened and were sitting and smoking on the edges of their cots—farmers, I imagined, with no chores to do *that* morning, and they were worrying about their places and their animals. All the others were asleep, and I remember how small and still and tender they looked. If I could have done it, I would have liked to tiptoe around and just lay my hand on each one.

I put on my raincoat carefully to keep from making a noise and put my hat on. One of the wakeful men looked at me and nodded and I nodded back. And then I picked up my box and eased away.

The rest of my journey might have gone better if I had had a map.

Back in those days, filling stations gave away road maps, but they were meant for people who drove cars. I didn't know how they would feel about giving a map to somebody on foot, and I didn't ask. On the other hand, maybe a map wouldn't have helped me much.

The main trouble, as you would expect, was the high water. I have been watching the stages of this river for most of my life. I know how easy it is to suppose that you can sight a line across the valley floor and know everywhere the water will be when it gets to that line, and I can tell you that most of the time you will be wrong. It is almost impossible to sight a *level* line, to begin with. And then it is almost impossible to imagine how perfectly the river seeks its level and fulfills itself. In the time of a big flood, a road that you think of as an upland road may get to the bottom of a hill and all of a sudden disappear under water where the river has backed up into a creek valley for several miles. And of course there is never any telling when a hard rain will put a creek over a road, even if it is well above the level of the flood.

I was traveling by instinct again, and having a hard time of it. My instinct was to keep turning toward the river as I made my way downstream, going in a direction generally northwest, the way the river flowed, but always nudging northward or northeastward so as not to go too far astray.

But of course I did go astray. North of Frankfort the country is rougher than what I had come through the first day, the ridges narrow, the hollows steeper and more frequent, and the roads hellaciously crooked. I didn't know the names of the roads or where they went. Almost nobody I asked knew where Port William was, let alone Squires Landing. Whenever I asked directions or caught a ride with somebody who asked where I was going, I would just say, "I'm trying to get down the river." I got a lot of bad advice. People either didn't know the way or were guessing, or they were mistaken about where the roads were blocked. I traveled by going wrong and then going right and then going wrong again, lost most of the time in the web of backroads, walking and occasionally catching rides, and sometimes even trying shortcuts through fields and woods. It is only forty-some miles from Frankfort to Port William, but it took me better than two days, and hard to tell how many miles, to get there.

Luckily for me, in that day and time that country was still full of little hillside farms, where I could get a drink of water from a clean spring or barn cistern and find a hayloft I could creep into at night. And at a lot of the crossroads there were little stores where you could get a cheese or baloney sandwich or a can of sardines and a few crackers, along with as much advice as you wanted about almost anything, and always a good fire to sit and eat beside. On this part of my trip I used my head and kept some rations in my pockets, just in case. That turned out to be a better idea than I thought, for I had forgot it was Saturday and the next day the stores were mostly closed. Aside from being more or less lost all the time, the biggest problem I had was finding a dry place to set down my box when I wanted to rest. It rained nearly all the time. There wasn't a scrap of dry ground anywhere that wasn't under a roof. I made up my mind that if ever I went traveling again—which, as it has happened, I never have—I would not carry my things in a cardboard box.

By the third day—the day known as Black Sunday, because then the sky and the rivers did their worst—I had pretty much used up my feeling of excitement and adventure. I was getting tired and sore-footed, and my hands hurt so from carrying my box that I was always shifting it from one hand to the other and watching for a barn or shed where I could set it down for a minute or two. When the rain and sleet quit I would carry the box on my shoulder, and that would be a relief for a while, but mostly the rain and sleet didn't quit. Mostly it poured down, and the visible world was just a few acres around me. I settled down to my journey like it was just a hard job of work that I had to do. For long stretches sometimes I would walk looking straight down at my feet, so that while I walked along it seemed that I was staying in place and the world was turning backward beneath me like a big wheel. When I looked up again I would see that I had come a considerable way since I had looked the last time, and that would be a pleasure.

I walked most of that Sunday afternoon, none of the few passersby ever offering me a ride, and by the time the sun must have been going down, I felt that I was getting close to the Port William country, though in fact I had not the least idea where I was. I was somewhere on earth under the falling rain, somewhere I had never been before. Pretty soon I spied a barn close to the road and not too close to a house. It was feeding

time. I watched from a row of trees along a rock fence while the farmer
fed and watered a pen full of shoats and led several mule colts out to
drink. When he had finished and gone away, the light was failing. I went
quiet and easy over to the barn and let myself in. The loft was full of
excellent, fragrant timothy hay. I ate a can of sardines, saving half of my
crackers and two slices of cheese for breakfast, made myself a good bed
in the hay, and slept like a dead man.

I don't believe I moved, or even dreamed, until morning. After I opened
my eyes, I didn't move. Until I could see daylight through the cracks in
the wall, I just lay still, feeling rested and at peace, thinking, "Now I am
close. Today I will be there." I said those words in my mind, and as I said
them, I was moved. I had been gone for twelve years, and it had been a
long time since I had thought of myself as being "gone." But now, as if
all of a sudden, I was going back. And being so close was not just something I thought I knew. It was a feeling I felt. It was such a feeling, maybe,
as brings birds back to their nests, or foxes to their holes. I had not
thought of going back for years, not since I got over my homesickness at
The Good Shepherd. From then until Friday night, I had never thought
of going back, and this was only Monday morning, and yet this feeling
came over me that I had strayed back onto the right path of my life. It
was as if in all my years of wandering, even when I had been the most
uncertain or lost, I had been crossing back and forth across my path as if
now and again I had seen a sign, "J. CROW'S PATH," but without an arrow.
I was telling myself, "It won't be the way you remember it. Things will
be changed. People will have died. Trees will have fallen." And yet, lying
there in my hay burrow in the dark loft, my body still seeming asleep and
my mind wide awake with the thought that I was now close by, I was
happy. When the first light came, I slipped away.

It had stopped raining. Maybe the worst was over, I thought, but
the clouds were still low. It was a gray, drippy morning. With the rain
stopped, I could see that the road was leading out along the crest of the
ridge toward the river valley, and pretty soon I could see the backwater
lying over the bottoms on the far side. And then the road went into the
woods and down the hillside, and soon I could hear the river. I knew
pretty well what that meant—before long, if I wanted to follow that

road, I was going to have to swim. But I had had my fill of backtracking, and anyhow I was anxious to see if I could tell where I was. So I followed the road on down until it went under water, and then cut downstream along the hillside through a weedy pasture and a gullied tobacco patch.

And then I came to a little farmstead—a house, a barn, a corncrib, a henhouse, a smokehouse, a privy—perched on the slope with the woods behind it and water now right up to the floor of the house. I called, but everybody was gone. The hill went up too steeply behind the house to leave room for a back porch, but there was a side porch off the kitchen and a well nearby. I had pumped a drink and stepped across water from the well top onto the porch before I realized that I knew where I was. I don't remember figuring it out. It just all of a sudden came over me, so that in one breath I was lost and a stranger, and in the next I was found.

I was at Dark Tom Cotman's place, where I had watched Old Ed eating the batter cakes. Dark Tom, it seemed, was gone—dead, I supposed—and a family was living there. A rusty tricycle was sitting by the smokehouse, and one little pink sock was hanging on the clothesline. The man of the house seemed to be a fisherman as well as a farmer, for there was a good dip net hanging under the eave of the smokehouse, along with some snooded hooks for a trotline. And so they had a boat to get away in. When I looked in through the window-light in the kitchen door I saw that the room was bare except for the cooking stove, and I imagined that they had carried all the furniture upstairs before they left.

They had forgot a little table that stood on the porch right beside the kitchen door. A water bucket and washpan were on the table, and soap in a dish, and a little mirror fastened to the wall above. The sight of the mirror reminded me that for three days I had not thought about how I looked. When I peeped into the glass, I saw somebody it seemed I was not very well acquainted with. Since the year I had begun to grow whiskers, I don't think I had ever gone three days without shaving. My face was as dirty as my hands.

The first thing I did, though, was eat the rest of my cheese and crackers. I sat on the porch, with water all around me, taking in the sights and eating my breakfast, eating slowly again because the supply was short. While I ate, a little flock of Dominecker chickens stood at the edge of the water and watched me. The house was on the outside of a bend. For a little way in front of the house the water was quiet, flowing slowly along without a sound, almost without a wrinkle on its surface. But out beyond and maybe a hundred yards upstream, the current came rattling full-force through the tops of the trees along what had been the shore. It sucked and swirled straight toward me as if about to carry off the yard fence, and then it swerved away and went out of sight beyond the corner of the house. The river was carrying a tremendous freight of drift—tree limbs and trees and all manner of human things such as bottles and buckets and barrels. I saw a johnboat go past, turned upside down, and a privy and just the four legs of a table sticking up, and a dead cow. I saw a fodder shock go by with several chickens riding on it. It was possible to imagine a couple of happy endings to that story, but neither one was likely. Chickens in that fix pretty certainly were not going to die of thirst.

I was sitting not six inches above the surface of the water, and you can't be that close to a flood and not feel the size and power of it and also a kind of fascination. If you let yourself, you could sit for hours and watch it, just to see the next thing that would float by. And also you feel a little yen for a boat, and you imagine putting your boat right into the current and letting it carry you away. I could see a line of dead grass blades and leaves and little twigs rising up and floating along the edge of the water, and I knew it was still rising. And in fact it would rise another foot before it crested at about noon the next day.

When I had eaten and then watched the water until I began to get cold, I stirred about, looking for something dry enough to burn. I hoped for something worthless, but all I found was a pile of kindling already split and a rick of firewood in the barn. So then I had to take some care to justify myself. I figured that if it was my wood and a stranger came along in such a time, I wouldn't begrudge him a few sticks.

I carried the wood and kindling out to a place well away from the buildings and started a fire. When the fire was going good, I pumped a bucket of water and set it over the fire to heat. I carried my hot water back to the wash table on the porch. I gave myself a pretty good bath and a shave, and dug a change of clothes out of my box, and then went over and stood by the fire until I was warm. It was good to be clean and warm and dry, and the fire cheered me up.

But I had to admit that I had come to another jumping-off place. I was back again in my native country. I knew exactly where I was. But what was I going to do? Suppose I made my way on down to Squires Landing. I couldn't just walk up to the door and announce to whoever in the world might be living there that I had come home. I still belonged to it in a way, but it didn't any longer belong to me. And even supposing that I wanted to go to Squires Landing, which wasn't far as the crow flies, I would have had to go I didn't know how far around the backwater in Willow Run to get there. And if I wanted to see Port William again, supposing I did, I would have to get around the backwater in Willow Run *and* Katy's Branch. Furthermore, I didn't have anything to eat and before long I was going to be hungrier than I was already. So I had to think again.

I knew that if I went back by the road, as I had come, it would be a long way before I would be able to buy something to eat. Also, I couldn't find that I had even the smallest wish to go back the way I had come. I decided that I did want to see Port William again. Beyond that, I didn't know what I would want. From where I was I could follow the water's edge downstream and then into the Willow Run valley. When I got around the backwater there, I could cross Cotman Ridge and come down into Goforth. There was, I supposed, still a store at Goforth where I could buy something to eat—if Goforth was still above water. I had a long, hard walk ahead of me, and the best I could do was just start out and put one foot in front of the other until I got to Goforth. Or somewhere.

So I washed the soot off the bottom of the water bucket, and turned it and the washpan upside down on the wash table, and weighted the whole business with rocks so it wouldn't float away. There was corn in the crib, and I shelled what I thought would be a two or three days' supply for the chickens that had been watching me ever since I got there. And then I shouldered my box and went on.

I was in woods, thickety in places, soon after I left the house. It was impossible to hurry there, and so I settled myself into patience. There was plenty to look at, and I picked my way along, staying close to the water because I was thrilled in a way by the sight of it and its nearness and by the difference it made. The sound of it, so close, was almost too much, so that I also had to resist a little urge to get away from it. The air was full of a hundred different sounds of pouring and of tree branches beating together, and my mind got full of those sounds. I was going along, not listening but just hearing, not looking but just seeing, not thinking anymore of where I was trying to go or even of how I was going to find something to eat, just setting one foot in front of the other.

And then, still following the edge of the water, I slowly turned away from the swift current and the uproar into the Willow Run valley, where the backwater lay as quiet as a pond—or rather a lake; it was wide enough—over open fields that last summer had been in pasture and crops. Everything was so still there, and the river's commotion so near, that it seemed you could hear and feel the silence. And then I saw something that made me stop.

Maybe fifty or sixty yards out on the water a man was standing in a boat. When I first saw him, he was just standing there with his back to me, he and the boat and the water all so still that I could see the gleaming line where boat and water touched. He was right where the muddy backwater from the river met the clearer water from Willow Run. Presently the man leaned and lifted a jug into the boat, and then he began to draw in a rope that was tied to the ear of the jug. I saw that he was raising a long slatted basket, which he hauled to the surface and rolled over into the boat. He did this gracefully, wasting not a motion, moving confidently and rapidly. There were several fish in the basket, and he placed them carefully into a half-barrel filled with water.

There came a time when I knew he had seen me, though he had not looked right at me. He went on about his business, and I continued to watch him from my place among the trees at the edge of the water. He looked to be forty or a little past. He was broad in the shoulders and strongly built. He wore a canvas hunting coat, much creased and stained, and a felt hat that no longer remembered the shape it had when it was new.

When he had let the basket back down into the water and had laid it again into its place, he tossed out the jug. And then he walked back to the middle seat, sat down, and looked straight at me. "Hello!" he said. He did not raise his voice, and in the quiet I heard him as well as if I had been in the boat with him.

I knew him then. He had fought in that dark war that had been so fearful to me only to hear about when I was a child. Sometimes when he was out hunting he had stopped by the store at Squires Landing for a bite to eat to keep from going home. I had changed far more than he had, and I knew he could not know me.

I said "Hello!"

He was no longer looking at me, but at the water and the trees and the general state of things. He took out a sack of tobacco and began to make a cigarette, not ceasing at the same time to look about.

I felt called upon to continue the conversation, and so I said, "Some flood!"

He lit his cigarette. "I'd say it's a right good one," he said. "But then what did we expect?"

He hadn't looked back at me. I couldn't think of an answer to his question, and he sat there at ease, smoking and continuing his casual study of the day and the weather.

Finally I said, "Wouldn't you be Burley Coulter?"

He looked straighter at me than he had before. "Well, I reckon I ought to know you, but I sho don't."

"My name is Jonah Crow. They call me J."

"Well!"

"I was born at the blacksmith shop at Goforth and lived a while at Squires Landing."

"Aw! You're the one that lived with Uncle Othy and Aunt Cordie. You went away when you was just a little bit of a boy—after Aunt Cordie died."

"And here I am back, passing through again. I'm trying to get to Port William."

He gave a little laugh. "Well, I reckon you can get there, if you don't mind a lot of winding about."

"Well," I said, "I've *been* winding about."

"Or," he said, "I could set you down below Katy's Branch, and then all you'd have to do would be climb the hill."

"That would be fine," I said.

He was thinking again and didn't answer.

After he had thought, he said, "Well, well. I remember you. I sure do. And what's your line of work, Mr. Crow?"

"I'm a barber."

He had a further thought, then, that amused him. "Now, I reckon you work in one of them big fancy shops—in Louisville, I imagine—with fans in the ceiling and a shoeshine stand and a pretty woman that files fingernails."

"Not hardly," I said. "At present, I'm out of a job."

"Well, now! Ain't that a coincident! Or did you know? They're fresh out of a barber at Port William."

I heard him, and then all of a sudden I was afraid. I said, "How come?"

"Aw," he said. "Barber Horsefield. I don't reckon you knew him."

"No."

"Well, he pulled out—I reckon it was ten days or two weeks ago."

I said again, "How come?"

"Well, he had a big family, and Port William will starve a barber with a big family, if he won't raise anything to eat, and Barber Horsefield didn't believe in raising anything that don't grow by itself, like babies and hair and subjects of conversation."

"The shop's for sale?"

"Oh, I *imagine* it is."

Then it was my turn to look about at the state of things and think.

He tossed away the butt of his cigarette as if he had all of a sudden remembered his manners. He rowed over to where I was, spun the john-boat around like a top, and pushed its stern right up to my feet.

"If you're going to Port William, get in."

I set my box in, gave the boat a little shove away from the shore, and stepped in myself.

"Well," I said.

"Well, what?"

"Well, I would like to take a look at that shop."

He only nodded to show that he had heard. He was looking over his shoulder, rowing carefully to get the boat through a winding way among the treetops and out into the river.

When we were free of the trees, he set the boat right in the channel and down we went, just booming along. Not far below the mouth of Willow Run we passed by Squires Landing. Having kept it so clearly in my mind for so long, I saw it now in the strangeness of time. It was a floating world, I thought, a falling world, a floating world rising and falling. All the buildings were still there, changed by whatever had happened during the last twelve years, and by the flood that had risen up to the foundation of the store and had carried a good-sized barn into the road in front of the house. But it seemed to me that even if everything had been changed, I would have recognized it by the look of the sky.

9

Barber Horsefield's Successor

So far, what I have told you about Burley Coulter is what I saw and heard that day. Why he was where he was when I found him, I learned only after a while. I don't mean for you to believe that even barbers ever know the whole story. But it's a fact that knowledge comes to barbers, just as stray cats come to milking barns. If you are a barber and you stay in one place long enough, eventually you will know the outlines of a lot of stories, and you will see how the bits and pieces of knowledge fit in. Anything you know about, there is a fair chance you will sooner or later know more about. You will never get the outlines filled in completely, but as I say, knowledge will come. You don't have to ask. In fact, I have been pretty scrupulous about not asking. If a matter is none of my business, I ask nothing and tell nothing. And yet I am amazed at what I have come to know, and how much.

I know, for instance, that on that January morning Burley had three baskets in the backwater in Willow Run valley, not just the one I saw him raise. He had started out on Friday morning, about when I left Lexington. He had known that people in the bottoms and on the lower slopes of the valleys would be in trouble and needing help. But also—and I know this just from knowing him—the rising water called out something young and wild in him, and he couldn't stay away from it. He had hunted all over the country and knew everybody, and so he worked his way upstream in the deadwater and the eddies close to shore, looking in at the farmsteads that were reachable at that stage by boat, and helping where help was needed. At night, because he was liked and welcomed almost everywhere, he stayed wherever he had got to when dark fell. He worked with other boatmen along the shores of the river and in the valleys, first of Katy's Branch and then of Willow Run.

By noon on Black Sunday, everything had been done that could be done. Everything was safe that could be made safe. Burley, who had spent the night before at the house of his old hunting and fishing partner, Loyd Thigpen, well above the water on one of the slopes of Willow Run, was there again, eating a splendid meal featuring pork sausage, hot biscuits, and gravy. Loyd Thigpen, though he was getting on in years, was as answerable to the excitement of the time as Burley was, and they had been in the boat together for the past day and a half.

"Compliments on your vittles, Mrs. Thigpen," Burley said as he buttered his seventh and eighth biscuits and reached for the pitcher of sorghum molasses.

"They do very well," said Loyd Thigpen, knowing his man, "but don't it ever come over you at a time like this that you'd enjoy to have a good mess of feesh?"

"Well," Burley said, "being as it's up and we can't help it, we might as well fish."

They agreed that they would put out Loyd's fish baskets that afternoon, Burley would take what fish he found in them on his way home the next morning, and after that Loyd would raise them for himself.

And so when I came upon him that Monday morning, Burley was ready to raise the third basket, but for the moment was standing there so quietly just to warm his hands in his pockets and enjoy himself, afloat in the flooded world.

While we were going down the river we didn't say anything. Keeping his own direction out there in the confusion of currents took all of Burley's attention, and I had plenty to look at and think about on my own. Among other things, I was wondering where and how we were going to get ashore. But at a certain place, Burley pulled us out of the channel and through an opening among the tops of the shore trees. And then we were in the woods. As the slope of the hillside rose under us, the tops of the trees rose over us, and it was clear going among the trunks of some fairly big elms and box elders and water maples and sycamores and a few walnut and ash.

Burley rowed by the gable and roof of what looked to be a camp house. He said, "It don't look like it now, but I slept there Thursday night."

The hillside was steep in that place. Not far behind the house, Burley pulled up beside a sort of wooden cage, only the top of which was visible above the water. He put the fish he had caught into the cage, saving out and stringing two nice catfish that weighed about five pounds apiece. Then he rowed to shore.

"From here," he said, "we got to walk or fly."

He laid his oars in the bottom of the boat, picked up the two fish, and stepped ashore. When he had got out, I followed, carrying my box.

He tied the boat to a tree and started up the slope toward the road, which wasn't far. He hadn't looked at me again.

I said, "Much obliged for the lift, Mr. Coulter."

He said, walking on, "Burley. Burley. Mr. Coulter's my daddy."

I followed him on up to the road. When we got up there onto comfortable footing, he stopped and turned to me. He looked me over, from top to toe and from toe to top, and then he grinned at me, remembering, I think, that I had been "winding about" for three days.

He said, "How was it you got here?"

"Well," I said, "by enacting my ignorance of geography—which is to say, by being lost the better part of three days."

He enjoyed that. "Afoot?" he said.

"I got a few rides, but most of the time I was walking, I guess."

"And in all that rain!"

"I've got a good raincoat," I said.

He looked me over again and said, "In fact you do."

He started on again. I was uncertain whether to come with him or not, until he said, walking along, carrying the fish, "What did you eat?"

I told him more or less what, as I hurried to catch up.

He said, "Are you hungry?"

"I could eat," I said.

He said, "Well. Come on."

We left the road presently and went through a stand of big trees and then up along a little stream—Coulter Branch, as I would learn—that was coming down a lot faster than we were going up. After a longish climb we left the hollow and angled across a hillside pasture to a weather-boarded double log farmhouse right on the point of the ridge, from where we could look back over the woods and down to the flooded river. We went to the back of the house and up onto the porch.

Before we got to the kitchen door, it opened. Burley's mother, Zelma, a determined-looking woman with her white hair in a bun, stood there with her hand on the knob. She was wearing a clean apron over a long dark blue dress with long sleeves.

"Burley Coulter!" she said. "I had given you up for drowned!" She was both aggrieved and half joking, as if she had worried about him too often to have worried too much. But she said, "Come here and let me see."

He went obediently to her, grinning. She pressed the sleeve of his coat to assure herself that his own arm was actually inside, and he bent and gave her a loud kiss.

He made a little gesture with the fish.

"Oh, Lord!" she said, pleased. "More fish to fry!" And then she looked at me.

Burley said, "You remember that boy Aunt Cordie and Uncle Othy Dagget took to live with them? This is him."

"Well, honey, I didn't know you! Lord, how long has Aunt Cordie been dead? It was when?"

"Nineteen twenty-four," I said.

"Well," Burley said, "he needs to be brought in and wrung out and hung up to dry. He's been rambling around in the rain for three days."

"My land!" she said. "Come in, honey!"

Burley had started out to a three-legged table leaning against the cellar wall, where he cleaned his fish. An old yellow tomcat was sitting on the table, eyeing the fish and licking his chops.

Burley called back to his mother, "He's a barber." And then he said, "He's hungry. Me too."

I stepped through the door and set down my box. Mrs. Coulter showed me where to put my coat and hat and overshoes, and where to wash. She started stirring about at the stove, building up the fire, sliding various cooking vessels over to the heat, putting a pan of biscuits into the oven to warm.

"Dave and Jarrat and the boys already ate and went back," she said.

She set two places at the table and brought out a pitcher of buttermilk.

"You never know," she said, "when to expect that Burley Coulter to show up. Or disappear, either. When he does show up, you can expect he'll be hungry. But as like as not he'll bring something to cook. So maybe it all evens up. Somewhere."

She seemed at first to be talking to me, and then only to herself. But when she had set the pitcher down she turned and looked at me.

"I don't remember your name," she said, "but you're welcome."

"Jonah Crow," I said.

She drew a chair out from the table to bring it closer to the stove. "Come and get warm," she said. "Sit down."

Mrs. Coulter fed us a wonderful big dinner, lamenting all the time that she hadn't had much to fix and that all of it was warmed over, until Burley diverted her by telling about the flood—how high the water was, and who had had to move out, and so forth.

"Well," she kept saying, clearly proud of him and happy to be in possession of so much firsthand news, "did ever anybody hear the like!"

When we had eaten every bite we could hold, washed down with several cups of hot coffee, and pushed our chairs back and rested for a few minutes in the warmth, Burley said, "I reckon you want to go see that shop."

I said, "I reckon I do."

So we got back into our wraps and I picked up my box and thanked Mrs. Coulter. We walked out a long lane on the backbone of the ridge and then took the road to town.

When we passed the schoolhouse and came down into the swag, Burley walked up to the front of a small weatherboarded building, gave it a pat with the flat of his hand, and said, "Here she is."

It was a two-story building, one room of about twelve by twenty-four

feet over the top of another, the upper story reached by an outside stairway. It was as plain a structure as you could imagine, all rectangles, with
a false front and a brick chimney poked up through the middle. And it
was ungainly, too narrow for its height. The whole thing was slung a little askew like an old dog half-minded to lie down, and it was badly in
need of paint. It was clearly several steps down from Skinner Hawes's
establishment, let alone the University of Kentucky, but in twelve years I
had not seen anything I wanted so much.

Burley was leaning to one of the front windows with his hands cupped
around his eyes. "She's ready for business," he said. "Barber chair, setting
chairs, stove—everything it needs, except a barber and some loafers."

I looked in the other window and saw that it was true. There were
maybe a dozen chairs lined up along one wall. Some of the chairs were
the wire-backed kind, some were hickory-bottomed. There was a big
heating stove with a register in the ceiling over it to let warm air rise into
the upstairs room. And the barber chair was one of the good old-
fashioned ones, porcelain and polished metal and leather, well-worn but
fine as a throne. Behind it there was a narrow little backbar, just a shelf
painted white like the walls and ceiling. Above the backbar was a good-
sized mirror and another, not matching, was on the opposite wall. The
room was walled and ceiled just as it was floored, with six-inch tongue-
and-groove boards nailed across the studs and joists, making it look
longer than it actually was. The finish on the floor was simply wear, the
treading of many feet for a long time, so that it was brighter in some
spots than in others.

"Yessir!" Burley said, seeing a vision. "Why, a single man with a place
like this would be *fixed*. He'd have his dwelling place and his place of
business right together. And look a-here."

He led me around to the side of the building where the stairs went up.
Grinning, he pointed up to the little landing at the top. "A man could set
up there of an evening," he said, "and rock and look out."

We climbed up and looked through the door glass into the upstairs
room, which was completely empty.

From the landing or stoop or what you may call it, we could see the
remainder of the property. The lot was twenty or so feet wide, giving
room for a sort of driveway on the side where the stairs were. Below us

we could see where coal had been piled. When he left, Barber Horsefield had taken everything but the black stain on the ground. Behind the building the lot continued back maybe a hundred and fifty feet to a brushy fencerow that divided that part of town from a large sheep pasture. In one of the back corners there was a privy under a good-sized wild cherry tree.

Burley went down first and turned to face me at the bottom of the stairs. He pinched my sleeve and gave a little pull. "What do you think about it?"

It was clear that he wanted me to buy the shop, but at the time I had no idea of his reason. Had he bought the shop himself from Barber Horsefield, and was wanting to sell it at a profit? Was he anxious to redeem his own vision of the good life a man could live in such a place? Or, maybe, did he like me?

I hoped so. But I said, "Well, what will you take for it?"

He laughed. "Oh, it ain't mine. I don't own anything I can't carry or that won't follow me when I whistle."

"Well, who owns it?"

"The bank, so I hear. They took it to clear Barber Horsefield's note. My opinion, Barber Horsefield got the best of the deal."

"Where's the bank?"

"It's up the street yonder, but I believe it's shut by now."

I said, "Aw!" in a way that showed my disappointment more than I meant it to.

"But what we can do, we can go see Mat Feltner. He's on the board."

We went up the road then, past the poolroom and three stores and the Independent Farmers Bank and the post office and the church, and around to the back of a large house that was actually a farmhouse at one of the corners of the town. In Port William only strangers and preachers and traveling salesmen ever went to anybody's front door. Burley knocked at the kitchen door and stood back with his hands inside the bib of his overalls.

A quick-stepping woman with a kind face opened the door, saw who was there, and said, "Why, hello, Burley."

Burley took off his hat and I hurried to do the same.

"Howdy, Mrs. Feltner. We was wondering if Mat's around."

"He just came in." She turned and called back into the house: "Mat!" And then she opened the door wider. "You all come in."

"Aw, we'll just wait here," Burley said.

She shut the door, and then pretty soon it was opened by a man who looked too young to have white hair.

"Hello, boys. Come in."

"Aw, Mat, our feet's muddy." Burley had put his hat back on and his hands were again behind his bib.

"No, they're not," the man said. "Come on in."

He held the door open for us and we stepped inside. Mat Feltner glanced at me and saw that he didn't know me, and then looked at Burley. "What have you got on your mind?"

And then Burley, as if preparing to auction me off, told him who I was, how I had come, where I was when he had found me, what my trade was, how he had showed me Barber Horsefield's old shop, and how I liked it and wanted to ask about buying it. "He thinks it's just the ideal place for a young fellow to settle down and take hold."

Mr. Feltner—who would not be "Mat" to me for a long time—turned to me and stuck out his hand. "Mr. Crow, I'm Mat Feltner. I'm glad to know you. I knew your mother's people. I remember the Daggets very well."

There was nothing glancing or sidling about the way he looked at you. He looked right through your eyes, right into you, as a man looks at you who is willing for you to look right into him.

When we had shaken hands and he had given me that look, he pulled chairs back from the kitchen table. "Sit down."

We sat down. He studied me for a minute again, and then he said, "You're not married, Mr. Crow? You've got no family responsibilities?"

"No, sir."

He laughed a little and glanced at Burley. "A single man might make it." But he was serious when he looked back at me. "And you've got experience as a barber?"

"Yes, sir." I told him my experience.

He sat, looking out the window, and I knew he was deciding whether or not to ask me why, if I had had a job, I was now looking for one. And

I sat there trying to think, and failing, thinking only that whatever I would say was probably going to be a surprise to me.

He decided not to ask. He looked back at me and studied me up and down. We had come to the dare.

He said, "Three hundred dollars'll buy the shop and whatever's in it. We'll need a third of the money down, the shop for collateral." He went on to set out all the terms of the loan, fair enough, but very strict in what he would expect of me.

When he had finished the room was quiet. You will appreciate the tenderness of my situation if I remind you that I had managed to live for years without being *known* to anybody. And that day two men who knew who and where I had come from had looked at me face-on, as I had not been looked at since I was a child. And now there I sat with about a hundred and twenty dollars in bills in my shoe and in the lining of my jacket and, as I remember, thirty-five cents in my pocket.

I was not, as they now say, "mentally prepared." My face turned red to the eyeballs—I could feel the heat radiating from it. Both men were watching me, waiting to hear if I wanted the shop on the proposed terms, and to see if I could come up with the money.

"I'll take it," I said. I worked a tight little roll of bills tied with string out through the hole in the lining of my jacket. And then I took off my overshoe and shoe and got the rest. I laid a fifty-dollar bill and two twenties and a ten on the table in front of Mr. Feltner.

It was a funny moment; a time would come when even I would think so. But that day it was hard. I felt revealed, as if to buy the shop I had had to take off all my clothes. But Burley and Mr. Feltner never allowed the least twitch or touch of amusement to show even in their eyes. They sat there as if not a man in Port William had ever paid for anything without taking off his shoe.

When I had given the money and leaned down again to put on my shoe and overshoe, I heard Mr. Feltner say, "*Yes*sir. All right."

He went to get a piece of paper and wrote out a little contract, which we both signed, by which he agreed to sell and I to buy a property known as "the barbershop," on the terms he had offered and "in consideration of $100 in hand paid." He gave me the keys.

As soon as we left Mr. Feltner, Burley went his way, saying he imagined he would see me before long.

I carried my box down to the shop, let myself in, and took possession of my property by going first into one room and then the other and walking from window to window, looking out. And then I went into my backyard and spent a good while walking up and down and looking and stopping to think. I thought I would have a garden.

You can imagine, though, that becoming so quickly and surprisingly a propertied man ready to "settle down and take hold" required a long thought, and that I didn't finish thinking it that day, or for many days afterward.

Dark was falling by the time I got myself up to Jasper Lathrop's store and made another supper of cheese and crackers.

Why I didn't think until too late of buying or borrowing a few sticks of wood or lumps of coal to burn that night in the stove, I don't know. Up until then, my foresight ran more to saving what I already had than to providing what I would need. But maybe I had already had too much to think about for one day.

Anyhow, I spent that night in the barber chair, wearing all the clothes I had and several sheets of a newspaper, and by daylight I was cold enough.

Burley Coulter and Mat Feltner proved good friends to me from the start. They didn't just get me started and then leave me to fare the best I could. By their knowing where I could buy or borrow the things I needed, I soon had my shop and household put together and going. For the shop I had to purchase clippers and scissors and combs (I already owned a good straight razor, mug, brush, hone, and strop). I bought talcum powder and tonic and lotion, which looked very professional on my backbar, and two neckcloths and half a dozen towels. And Jasper Lathrop gave me a new cigar box that I used to collect my earnings and to keep my change-making money. For the room upstairs, I soon had a cot, a table, a chair, a little oil stove that I could cook on, some bedclothes, and a few dishes and cooking utensils. Most of that was used stuff that Burley found for me cheap, or that Mat and Margaret Feltner loaned or gave me.

I felt at home. For a long time I didn't have any more to ask for. When I didn't have customers or loafers to deal with, I spent my time cleaning and recleaning the place and fixing it up.

I learned people's names. Some of my customers I remembered from my old life at Squires Landing, but I didn't need to explain much or renew acquaintance. The town took care of that. In no more than two days the town and practically all the countryside knew that I had come and who I was and where I had got my start. And yet, with few exceptions, people were cautious, calling me "Mr. Cray" and waiting for me to reveal myself as I might do only by staying long enough. Which suited me. I knew, or was soon reminded, that most of them were not necessarily eager to know things by names that they did not already use. Until I read the deed, for example, I did not know that Barber Horsefield was in fact Peter A. Haussfeldt.

But I had been at work only a week or so when a man came in to whom I did need to explain myself. Sam Hanks.

He was my second customer that afternoon. The first was John T. McCallum, who was so fastidious that he liked a weekly haircut and so tight that he would drive from his farm down near Hargrave all the way up to Port William to save a dime.

John T. was in the chair when Sam Hanks, back from his morning run to the stockyards in Louisville, pushed open the door and came in, his pipe clenched in his teeth as if he expected to be picked up and swung by it.

He took a chair and he and John T. began a conversation, pretty much ignoring me. This I was already used to. The Port Williamites took me for granted, as I suppose they had taken for granted Barber Horsefield and all his predecessors. The growth of hair called forth the barbershop. The barbershop called forth the barber. I was there as expectably as the furniture and the stove, as the town itself and the river down at the foot of the hill.

John T. wanted to know about livestock prices, and Sam Hanks told him at some length. They spoke of last year's lamb market, and of the prospects for this year's. And then they got onto the subject of the flood, which had been costly for John T., much of whose farm lay in the river bottoms. The talk went the way I love it, so quiet and unhurried I could hear the dampened fire fluttering in the stove.

And then John T. said easily and philosophically, as if to conclude that part of the conversation: "Well, they say we won't have such another flood for a long time to come."

Sam Hanks did not move, and yet he seemed to spring upward onto a higher level of being, like a bird dog coming to a point. *"They!* They who?"

"Why, the experts!" John T. said, already offended, his voice becoming chirpy. "The ones that *predicts* such things!"

"Predict!" said Sam Hanks. "How do they know?"

"Because they know! They're smart men. Not like me and you."

"How," said Sam Hanks, "do they know what's not going to happen when the time it's supposed to not happen in hasn't come yet?"

"By being smarter than you and me both, and this fellow here throwed in."

This was a generous acknowledgment of my presence, and I had to smile. I had finished his haircut but he was still sitting in the chair.

"I don't believe in noooo prediction," Sam Hanks said.

They then had a perfectly fierce argument on the issue of the general predictability of earthly phenomena. After maybe half an hour, it wore out way short of compromise, John T. contending that everything was predictable by the smarter people (who, if not yet smart enough, soon would be) and Sam Hanks that nothing was or ever would be predictable by anybody.

John T. finally let it go, shaking his head in what appeared to be pity. "Damned if I don't believe you'd argue the world is flat."

"It *is!*" said Sam Hanks without missing a beat. "Except Old Marster had to tilt it this way and that to drain the waters off."

"I got to go, I got to go," John T. chanted, finally descending from the chair. He paid me without looking at me, put on his coat and hat, and started out. "I got work to do and I can't be long about it."

Sam Hanks, betraying by no sign that he had been enjoying himself, waited until the door shut behind John T. and then knocked out his pipe on the leg of the stove, hung up his cap, climbed into the chair, and came to rest with a sigh. "Short," he said.

The remainders of his and John T.'s rippit seemed still to be floating in the air like ashes or snowflakes. I was nearly done cutting his hair before I felt the quiet again and could think of what to say.

I said, "Mr. Hanks, I'm sure you remember that you did me a big favor a couple of years ago."

He said, "I'm sure I don't, young man."

So I had to tell him the story of our ride into Lexington, of his good advice, and of my later discovery of the new five-dollar bill in my jacket pocket.

I was in the midst of confessing my lie and acknowledging my right identity—which he undoubtedly already knew—when he said, "Son, you've got the wrong man."

He not only denied that he remembered what I remembered, he denied that he had hauled a load of hogs to Lexington that year. He didn't remember when he ever had hauled a load of hogs to Lexington.

He handed me a dollar bill. I took a five from under my cigar box, where I had it waiting for him, and wrapped his change in it. He stripped the coins out of the bill with his thumb as if hulling peas and laid the bill down onto the backbar.

"Son," he said, going out, "I already *got* five dollars."

Part II

10

A Little Worter Dranking Party

One of the early signs of my acceptance into at least a part of Port William society was the following letter, folded once and stuck under the shop door in the dead of night:

> Come to a little worter dranking party Sat night at the Grandstand.
> Whatever you want to delute your worter with will be fine.

I did not then recognize the handwriting as that of my friend Burley Coulter. Had I done so, I might also have recognized at least one of the misspellings as the work of Burley's conscientious sense of humor. "Worter," as I would know later, was quoted from a famous letter-to-the-teacher written by Oma Wages on behalf of her daughter, who during her three years in the eighth grade had come to be known by the boys as "Topheavy":

> Please let Bobra Sue be excuse when she akses. She cant hole her worter.

That Burley wrote anonymously, making no attempt to disguise either his hand or his manner, was a joke on anonymity and on himself, his way of laying by a little something to laugh about at a later time.

This was the spring of 1937. I received (or found) my invitation on the morning of a warm day just after the leaves had fairly opened. Early May, I suspect it was. At that time I had never been to the Grandstand, though, from overhearing, I knew where and approximately what it was. It was not, in fact, a grandstand at all. It was a spot in the woods on the very rim of the cut that let the road descend the valley side on its way downriver to Hargrave. "The Grandstand" was just the name of the spot. A number of the men and grown boys of the neighborhood went there for a certain freedom that the town did not publicly countenance. It was a place where water could be unguardedly diluted, or done without, where talk could proceed without fear of interruption by anybody who would mind. No preacher or teacher or woman or public official or anybody self-consciously respectable would be there. If you were there, your presence was taken to indicate that you would not mind. The primary sport at the Grandstand was the card game known as tonk, but dice also had been known to gallop there, and it was an ideal sitting place for foxhunters, for it looked and listened right into the river valley; you could hear a pack of running hounds for miles. Maybe two or three times a year, on good nights of spring or fall, a water-drinking party would be announced by grapevine, and on these occasions, beyond the usual pastimes, the featured event would be a supper of fried fish or wild game or hen soup. Emptied of the little society that gathered and dissolved there from time to time, the Grandstand was just another place in the woods. Nothing was there but trees and rocks and a burnt spot on the ground.

When I read the invitation I felt both flattered (a little honored, to tell the truth) and curious. At that time in Port William there would be a crowd in town every Saturday night, and I would be busy until late. It may have been ten o'clock on that particular night before I had shorn and shaved my way to the far side of the final customer and the last talkers had gone, still talking, out the door and up the street. I put on my cap and jacket then and turned off the light.

The crowd of shoppers and talkers had nearly all dispersed. The town was growing quiet. Jasper Lathrop was locking up his store. The night was clear, with a big moon. I could see my way along the road as well nearly as if it had been daylight. I could hear whippoorwills, and somewhere not too far off a mockingbird.

At a place just before the road came to the vertical wall of the cut, where maybe half a dozen cars were parked along the roadside, I began looking for the path I supposed would be there, and soon found it. Already I could hear voices above me, and not long after I passed into the shadow of the woods I could see the light of a fire glancing on the undersides of the leaves. So now maybe you can imagine it: the moon hanging all alone out in the sky, its light pouring down over everything and filling the valley, and under the moonlight the woods, making a darkness, and within the darkness a little room of firelight, and within the firelight several men talking, some standing, some sitting on stools of piled rocks or on logs, some sitting or squatting or kneeling around a spot swept clear of leaves where they were playing cards, and all around you could hear the whippoorwills. Nearly everybody there had a coal oil lantern, most of them unlit to save oil. One of the two or three that were lighted hung from a low limb to illuminate the card game.

When I came into the light, the place fell silent and everybody looked at me. A great embarrassment came over me and I stopped; it seemed a place where you did not belong unless you had been there before. I recognized Rufus Brightleaf, Portly Jones's brother Wisely, the Ellis known simply as Big, Roy Overhold, and River Bill Thacker. Grover Gibbs, who was jack-of-all-trades, was bending over the fire, lifting the last frying of catfish and corn pone out of the grease. They all looked at me, and I gave a silly little wave.

And then from off at the edge of the dark I heard Burley Coulter: "Come in, Mr. Crow, come in!"

And then, as I glanced around, the others acknowledged me: "Mr. Cray"—"Mr. Cray." One of the younger ones said, "Hello, J. You got your scissors?"

And then a little swirl of talk passed among them:

"What? You want a haircut?"

"Give *me* a haircut."

"In the dark?"

"In the dark he cuts it *all*. Ears too."

"When he barbers in the dark, he don't charge extra for ears," said a man playing cards with his back to me.

They laughed.

And so I was there.

"Here," Burley said, handing me a tin plate and leading me by the sleeve of my jacket toward the fire.

There were two sizable pans on rocks, close enough to the fire to stay warm. One held several pieces of fish and the other corn pones. I put a piece of fish and a corn pone on my plate.

"Here," Burley said again, and took my plate and heaped it up and handed it back. "Come on," he said. "Over here."

I followed him back to where he had come from: the trunk of a blown-down red oak out on the edge of the firelight and close to the drop-off where the hill had been blasted to make way for the road. We sat looking right out into the moonlight with the valley all silvery below us. Besides Burley and me, there were four others—Martin Rowanberry from down on Sand Ripple; Webster Page, a man of about seventy, a serious fox-hunter who lived at Goforth; Uncle Isham Quail, who had come with Mr. Page; and Julep Smallwood from town—all of us sitting spaced apart along the tree trunk.

It was good fish, fried crisp, and the corn pone was just right too, crusty, and salty enough. I ate with my pocketknife until the food cooled a little, and then with my fingers.

Nobody said anything. Our purpose evidently was to listen, but I did not yet know for what. Mr. Page smoked his pipe and looked out over the valley at nothing, not even the moon. Julep Smallwood sat watching the rest of us while pretending not to. The others sat with their heads down, their elbows on their knees, their hands clasped together.

"Well, the earth just swallowed him up," Uncle Isham said finally. "Or he went off into thin air."

"He went up Sand Ripple and lost them, I'd rather think, just about at the mouth of the Cattle Pen branch," said Martin Rowanberry.

"He went through your hog lot and they lost him there," Webster Page said, "and then he ran up the branch. Rounder'll piece it together. Give him a little time."

"He's done out-roundered Rounder," Uncle Isham said.

Before I thought, I said, "Who?"

"The fox," Burley said. And then, as if suddenly remembering me and his manners, he said, "Here. Hold on."

He groped a moment in the shadows behind him and drew out a half-gallon glass jug, its mouth stopped with a corncob. He withdrew the cob and held out the jug to me.

"That fish'll dry you out," he said. "See if this won't moisten your swallow."

I took a taste—it was a local product, as innocent of water as the inmost coal of the fire, but also mellow and fragrant—and then I took three swallows, for the fish surely was drying me out.

"Did you hear what it said?" Burley asked me. "It said, 'Good-good-good.'"

He tilted the jug to his own lips and it said, "Good-good."

He handed it past me to Mart Rowanberry, who tilted it, and it said, "Good-good."

Mart handed it to Uncle Isham, and it said, "Good."

Uncle Isham handed it to Webster Page, and it said, "Good."

Mr. Page handed it to Julep Smallwood, who had been watching it as a cat watches a mouse, and it said, "Good-good-good-good-good."

And then—without Burley needing to say anything, I noticed—the jug traveled back along the row of us, and Burley stoppered it and set it down again.

We listened some more. After a while we heard a bass voice lift out of the shadows way up the valley. I did not yet understand that the voice was saying, "Fooox!" But that was what it said. It said so again: "Foooox!"

"Rounder," said Webster Page.

By the time the hound's voice made its announcement a third time it was joined by a higher, brighter voice that said excitedly, "Yes! Fooox!"

Mr. Page said, "Gail."

And then the whole pack opened—six or eight hounds altogether, it sounded like. They hesitated briefly again when the fox doubled back in the running water of the branch up Cattle Pen, and then came on. Their voices faded as they went deeper behind the hill, crossing the Sand Ripple valley, and then grew gradually clearer. As they came into the river valley and turned more or less in our direction, they were running close to the fox and very fast, their voices rising into the moonlight like a string of pennants. The men on the log spoke in one-word sentences, naming places and hounds, as the cry moved down the river valley—swiftly across the open lands, slower and with more trouble in the woods—and passed below us and went on.

From time to time Burley would fish the jug up out of the shadow, offer it first to me, for I was his guest, then drink himself, and pass it down along the tree to where Julep Smallwood sat at the root. The jug invariably pronounced its longest benediction upon Julep Smallwood. "Good-good-good-good," it would say. And again, "Good-good-good-good-good."

Julep had straddled the tree and was riding it like a man on a bucking horse, watching always with pretended indifference for the jug to appear and begin another journey toward him. When he saw Burley lean back and reach into the shadow, Julep glowed like a firefly.

Julep Smallwood, as his comrades told one another amusedly and somewhat resentfully in endless speculation on the matter, was not an alcoholic. He had not even an honest entitlement to be called a drunk. If Julep had drunk only the liquor he paid for, he would have been dry as a preacher. He would have crackled when he walked, as Burley Coulter would now and again inform him. Julep's addiction was to *free* liquor, namely other people's. When other people's was available, he drank of it merely all he could hold. Julep, as Grover Gibbs attested upon oath, was one of those rare fellows who could drink himself drunk and then continue on to drink himself sober. He was as partial to other people's food as to their whiskey, but it was an article of belief generally sworn to that he could drink *way* more than he could eat. His favorite Bible verse was, "Drink no longer water, but use a little wine for thy stomach's sake and thine often infirmities"—which he quoted frequently when he was sober and able to propose and believe that he drank in moderation, since on the average he did, and in a tone conveying a certain self-pity for his often infirmities and the cruel scarcity in Port William of the sanctioned remedy.

And here I must confess that, having never drunk a drop in my life that I had not paid for myself, I too was somewhat under the spell of Burley's hospitality. I loved to hear what that jug had to say for itself; when it said it was "good-good-good," I believed it. Presently I observed that the moon had become abashed and uncertain of its position out there in the fathomless sky.

Julep Smallwood called out to Burley, making his voice arch over the rest of us who were on the log: "Oh, Burley!"

Burley was wearing a big grin, signifying that he understood perfectly and enjoyed deeply the whole complexity of Julep's thirst, the course of the fox race now again out of hearing, and the embarrassment of the unsteadied moon. After a longish while, he said, "What?"

"Ohhhh, Burley!"

"What?"

"Do you still know where we are?"

After due consideration, Burley said, "Where else would we be? Right here!"

"Where's here?"

"Here on this log."

"Where's this log?"

"Why, it's right here at the Grandstand."

"Well, where's the Grandstand, old Burley Coulter, old bud?"

"Why it's right here beside Port William."

"Where's Port William?"

"In Kentucky."

"Where's Kentucky?"

"In the United States of America *and* the republic for which it stands."

"Where's the United States?"

"*In* the world *indivisible*."

"Where's the world?"

"*In* the universe."

"Where's the universe?"

Burley's grin now included the universe, with liberty and justice for all. "I dog if I heard 'em say."

He said this in a tone of deference and fair-mindedness, as if to acknowledge the likelihood that at some time in his youth somebody had told him the whereabouts of the universe but he had not been listening or it had slipped his mind.

The jug again passed along the row of us as if obedient merely to the course of nature.

Shortly after that I noticed that Burley was gone. Just gone. He had stood up with his unlit lantern and stepped beyond us into the moonlit, shadowy woods. For a moment I was astonished at how quickly and surpassingly free he was, even from that party at the Grandstand, which I had thought was pretty free.

The next thing I noticed (or that I remember) was Webster Page standing up beneath the two moons and blowing his fox horn. The hounds must have faltered or run the fox to his hole somewhere nearby, for they were soon among us. Mr. Page and Uncle Isham and Martin Rowanberry lit their lanterns and made their way amidst the hounds down the path to the road.

Julep then gathered up the jug, which seemed to have come into his sole possession, and, carrying it like a doll in both arms, walking as if each of his legs was a little shorter than the other, went over by the fire, where Wisely Jones and Rufus Brightleaf and Roy Overhold and Big Ellis were still playing cards. Grover Gibbs and River Bill Thacker were watching and talking with the players, who by now appeared to be playing in a sort of hypnotic trance, as if they might go on from one more hand to one more hand forever.

Seeing that Julep had appropriated Burley's jug, Grover and River Bill offered me a drink, which I refused with thanks, having apparently retained one final grain of sense. But somebody had thought to bring a jug of water, and I helped myself eagerly to that, remarking as I set down the jug that I could see now that it had been, in fact, a water-drinking party. And all agreed, saying solemnly that every drop they had drunk all night had been drunk in honor of water.

The fire was putting out a pleasant warmth. I stretched myself on the dead leaves nearby, thinking to watch the game and take part in the conversation from a more comfortable position. I heard Grover Gibbs resume a tale that he evidently had been in the midst of:

"Anyhow, them two gentlemens just stood up right there and went at it. They had the hellovest fight that ever you seen."

"Call the law!" Julep Smallwood cried urgently up into the moonlight, but Grover did not even look toward him, if he heard him at all.

"Until finally that little 'un—he must have been a science man—he drawed back and hit that big 'un one lick right in the googler, and he went over like a plank. *That* put the quietus on him."

"Looord, increase his pain!" said Julep Smallwood.

And then the quietus came upon me, and I slept.

When I woke up it was well on in the morning. The sun was high, and except for the birds singing, the world seemed to have stopped. There was not the least breeze, and the cardplayers were sitting still with their heads up. They held their hands of cards in front of them but they were not looking at their cards. They were listening. I lay without moving and listened also. I could see that now there were only five of us, Grover Gibbs and Bill Thacker and Julep Smallwood having straggled away.

After a moment, Roy Overhold got up and tiptoed over to where he could see down into the road. And then quietly and seriously he began to climb a small sugar tree that branched nearly to the ground. He went up in a hurry and the other three came in quick succession right behind him.

What had wakened me, what they had heard, was Cecelia Overhold, Roy's wife, slamming her car door down beside the road. For just a moment after Roy and Wisely and Rufus and Big Ellis had gone up as high as they could go in the tree, it was absolutely quiet again.

And then I saw Cecelia Overhold coming up the path. She was wearing a sort of baggy hat tilted stylishly over her right ear, a nicely tailored broadcloth coat with a fur collar, and stockings and high heels. And she was walking like the Divine Wrath itself. She was a beautiful woman still, in those days, really something to look at. But I did not regard her with extreme pleasure that morning. I just shut my eyes and lay still. Why I didn't get up and run, I can't tell you, any more than I can tell you why Roy and the others had not run. We were all involved, I think, in a form of self-induced mental retardation.

Lying there with my eyes shut, filled with alarm and the recognition of catastrophe, I fully expected her to come right up and kick me. I was tensed for the blow. But she paid no attention to me at all, either because she didn't see me or because she thought me unworthy of attention; she was capable of that. I heard her gathering up the scattered cards and throwing them onto what was left of the fire. She picked up a piece of a limb and knocked loose the hanging lantern and sent it flying. She battered all the tin plates. And then I heard her breaking the jugs and bottles that were lying around. She even broke the water jug. The fury of battle was on her.

When I heard her walking over toward the sugar tree I opened my eyes. I have never beheld such a spectacle in all the time since. Roy Overhold was at the very top of the tree; Wisely Jones was under him, and under him was Rufus Brightleaf, and under him was Big Ellis. They all gazed downward like treed coons, and then they gazed upward as if hoping to find that the tree continued into the sky like Jack's bean stalk. The tree looked like a totem pole that had come to life and sprouted branches and leaves. And down at the foot was that beautiful outraged woman, looking up, with her fists on her hips.

She said, "Come down from there, you Sunday cardplaying sons of bitches!"

The only one up there with any conceivable reason to come down was Roy, and since he was at the top, he could not come down unless the others would come down first. Big Ellis would have had the honor of being first to accept her invitation, and he declined. Nobody came down. Nobody said a word.

And then Cecelia looked over at me and saw that I was watching. Our eyes met for a second and a chill passed over me.

"What are *you* looking at, you bald-headed *thing?*"

Well, in fact I was getting bald, but I had been telling myself that it wasn't very noticeable. I hate to admit my vanity, but what she said hurt my feelings probably worse than anything else she could have done.

What else she could have done, and did do, was pick up a smallish rock all jaggedy and crusty with fossils and throw it at me. It hit me square in the mouth.

After that, I played dead (which wasn't hard). Even after she went away and I heard her start her car and turn it around, I lay still with my eyes shut, tasting blood and feeling my broken tooth with the end of my tongue.

It was a while too before the others came down out of the tree. It was as though Cecelia had run us not out of the place but out of the day, and it took some time and thought for us to get back in.

And when we finally gathered ourselves together again among the ruins, we were changed. It had been a beautiful night and now it was a splendid day, but embarrassment and sorrow had come over us.

Everybody knew that Cecelia and Roy Overhold were each other's all, and that for both of them their all was varyingly either too much or not enough. Both of them were good people, as people go, and they had a nice farm, but they were living out the terms of a failure that was long and slow. I don't claim to understand it. I only know, from what I had seen already and what I saw later, that they would go along together quietly enough for a while, and then one night (it would always be at night) they would come face to face again with their old failure, each with needs that the other could not fill, and nothing they could do for each other that would not make things worse. Maybe it was childlessness that caused it. Maybe it was just one of those inescapable errors that people sometimes make. When Roy would turn up at my shop after dark or at some nighttime gathering of the men, I would know that he had come in from failure and despair that he could not escape but hoped at least to get off his mind for a while.

So we stood there, not knowing either how to stay or how to go, and felt the weight of that failure. We felt sorry for Roy, who was a quiet, smiling, unhappy man, and sorry for Cecelia, who was a beautiful, unhappy woman, and sorry we could think of nothing to say that would help.

And then Roy seemed to realize that if anybody was going to say something it would have to be him. He said, "Well, boys, if we've got anyplace to get, I reckon we had better get."

And so we too straggled off in our various directions.

That worter dranking party turned out to be one of the most famous social events in the history of Port William. It started some things that kept happening, and continued some things that were already happening and that went on happening afterward. And in true Port William style, it had achieved its full renown by bedtime Sunday night.

The preeminent topic, of course, was the dramatic entrance upon the scene of Cecelia Overhold, and what she had done and what she had said. You could no more have kept that quiet than you could have prevented thunder from following lightning.

But also Bill Thacker, walking home over the Katy's Branch bridge, blundered into the railing and mistook it for his yard gate. Finding that he could not unfasten it, he climbed over and fell fifteen feet into a field that Webster Page had plowed for corn. Fortunately, the backwater had just withdrawn from the bottom at that place, and instead of breaking his neck Bill only made a deep impression in about a foot and a half of mud. The mud was so soft and comfortable that he took a good nap before he got up. This story would have been hard to learn except that Bill Thacker himself thought so highly of it that he walked to town the next Saturday afternoon to tell it on himself.

And Julep Smallwood, to put a good face on things, had started home at the crack of dawn. But he made the trip in slow, difficult stages, being often obliged (as he said) to lie down. At Sunday school time he was standing by no means far enough from the church, as stupefied as Lot's wife.

And that was the moment that I happened to make my own entrance into town. I did not know the time; I did not see the talkers standing in the churchyard before it was too late to stop or go back. I went on by, pretending not to see, and keeping to the far side of the road. It was not a situation in which a bachelor barber newly come to town would prefer to be seen with a bloody lip and his clothes all covered with wood ashes and dead leaves.

11

An Invisible Web

Ernest Finley used to say, at about the time I returned, "In Port William we don't distinguish the masses from the classes." And in a way that was true. People did freely mingle in the gathering places of the town. Even Joe Banion, the last black man ever to live in Port William, was a participant and subject in the town's ever-continuing conversation about itself. People loved and befriended one another and were loved and befriended, talked with and about one another, quarrelled with and resented and sometimes fought one another, all pretty much without thought of "special privilege." The only one in my time who might have been accused of putting on airs was Cecelia Overhold, and in her younger days even Cecelia didn't do it all the time.

And yet certain lines were drawn that weren't much spoken of or much noticed. You would be aware of them only if they were overstepped or if you came into the town as an outsider. I could see, for instance, that Joe Banion was treated pretty much as an equal in talk and in work and in other ways, but also that he never sat down with white people indoors. The white people, who called him "Nigger Joe" to identify him among the several other Joes who lived around, never did so to his face.

I pretty soon found out too that several lines were drawn around a bachelor barber who was known to take part in social events such as the

Little Worter Dranking Party at the Grandstand. The barbershop, for one thing, was a precinct strictly masculine except on Saturday mornings, when mothers with small sons would bring them in for haircuts. At other times, the small boys would be brought in by their fathers and you would have been just as likely to find women in the poolroom. This was not my rule; it was just what the arrangement was and, I suppose, had always been. Anyhow, as the barber of the town, I was pretty effectively divided from its womanly life. I mingled a little, of course, when I went into the stores, and also when I would go out in the mornings and evenings with my buckets to get water at the town pump across the road.

As the barber I was placed also within economic limits that were generally recognized. The shop, as I had been told at the start, and as I had to agree, would not support a man with family responsibilities; it might support a bachelor, if he was careful. The barber lived on what would nowadays be called a "renewable resource" and so would never be out of work, if he could keep going on what his customers could reasonably be charged, but the resource itself was limited.

At times it could be severely limited. I nearly went under, for instance, in the first full month I was in Port William. Almost nobody came to the shop—for a haircut, that is; I had plenty of talkers—and I couldn't imagine what was the matter until I learned that a lot of the people thought it unlucky or unhealthy to get a haircut in February. My income varied also according to the weather, the stages of farmwork, and the state of the local economy. What I had, Grover Gibbs said, was a full-time part-time job.

Such jobs were not highly esteemed. One day I made the mistake, while cutting Mr. Milo Settle's hair, of referring to my "line of work."

"Boy," said Mr. Settle, "you ain't got what I call a *job*. You got what I call a *position*."

When I set up in Port William I was going on twenty-three years old. I was what I would prefer to call not-pretty, which is to say balding, long of face and frame, without resemblance to any movie actor or electable politician. Also I was a man of limited means and prospects, and a bachelor. By "bachelor" I mean, as was generally meant, a man old enough to be married who was not married and who had no visible chance to get married. A bachelor was, by nature, under suspicion. The women did not turn their backs as I passed along the street; they were, in fact, polite and friendly enough, as a rule. And I did learn (a little too late) to pursue my bachelor's aims and satisfactions with some discretion. But nobody ever told me pointedly or even casually that any eligible maiden was a good cook. I was not held up as an example to the young.

And so, in a society that was in some ways classless, I was in a class by myself. I was soon identified as a man who now and again wouldn't mind to take a drink, or join a nighttime party of fox or coon hunters, or attend a water-drinking party at the Grandstand or a roadhouse dance.

The biggest disadvantage, maybe, was that I remained a sort of by-stander a lot longer than I remained a stranger. They were calling me "Jayber" a long time before I was *involved*. Most people treated me well from the start, and some a lot better than well. But it only takes one or two, like Cecelia Overhold, to keep you reminded of how you fit in. So far as she ever let me see, Cecelia never looked straight at me again in her life. I got so that when I met her in the street I would tip my hat to her, if I was wearing one; if not, I would make a little bow. She always went by without looking at me, her head tilted to indicate not that she did not see me but that she had *already* seen me, and once was enough.

As for advantages, they were there right from the start, and there were several of them.

One was, I felt at home. There is more to this than I can explain. I just *felt* at home. After I got to Port William, I didn't feel any longer that I needed to look around to see if there was someplace I would like better. I quit wondering what I was going to make of myself. A lot of my doubts and questions were settled. You could say, I guess, that I was glad at last to be classified. I was not a preacher or a teacher or a student or a traveler. I was Port William's bachelor barber, and a number of satisfactions were available to me as the perquisites of that office.

Burley Coulter was correct, for instance, about the goodness of having your dwelling place and your place of business right together. When I came down the stairs and into the shop I was "at work." When I went back upstairs I was "at home." This was handy in a lot of ways. The stove that heated the shop heated my bedroom–living–room–bathroom–kitchen (my "efficiency apartment") upstairs. Often, in the winter, while

I was at work (which included loafing and talking) in the shop, I would have a pot of beans or soup or stew simmering on the stove.

People respected the difference. The shop was a public place, but the upstairs room was private. I've had people in the shop or down there banging on the door all hours of the day and night, for Port William never went altogether to sleep, but I expect I could count on my fingers the number of times anybody ever came to the door upstairs. And most of those times it was Burley Coulter, who, up there, would be mannerly and reserved, very formal—as opposed to his behavior in the shop where, like nearly everybody, he felt at home.

My occupancy of the ramshackle little building seemed to give him immense satisfaction, as if he had foreseen it all in a dream and was amazed that it had come to pass. He didn't harp on the subject, but if it came up he enjoyed talking about it. And he made occasions to review my situation and accomplishments.

One day he came in and walked all around the shop, looking at everything in it and out every window. He then sat down and rubbed his hands together. "Yessir," he said, "it's fine. You got your working and your living right here together."

And then the others took it up:

"Yessir, it's hard to tell whether he's working or living."

"Especially when he's working, it's hard to tell if he's living."

"When he's working it's hard to tell if he's alive."

And so on.

Burley Coulter himself was one of the best perquisites of my office. Burley was nineteen years older than I was, old enough to have been my father, and in fact he was the same age my father would have been if he had lived. He was the most interesting man I ever knew. He was in his way an adventurer. And something worthy of notice was always going on in his head. I found him to be a surprising man, unpredictable, and at the same time always true to himself and recognizable in what he did. I had lived in Port William several years before I realized that Burley was proud of me for being a reader of books; he was not himself a devoted reader, but he thought it was excellent that I should be. It must have been 1940 or 1941 when he first came all the way into my upstairs room and saw my books in my little bookcase.

"Do you read in them?"

"Yes," I said.

He gave the shelves a long study, not reading the titles, apparently just assaying in his mind the number and weight of the books, their varying sizes and colors, the printing on their spines. And then he nodded his approval and said, "Well, that's all right."

I knew him for forty years, about, and saw him endure the times and suffer the changes, and we were always friends.

Among the other perquisites of my office, I might as well say, were all my customers. I remembered a surprising number of them from the days when, for one reason or another, they would turn up at Uncle Othy's store at Squires Landing. And a surprising number of them sooner or later acknowledged that they had taken notice of me back in those old days. I liked them varyingly; some I didn't like at all. But all of them have been interesting to me; some I have liked and some I have loved. I have raked my comb over scalps that were dirty both above and beneath. I have lowered the ears of good men and bad, smart and stupid, young and old, kind and mean; of men who have killed other men (think of that) and of men who have been killed (think of *that*). I cut the hair of Tom Coulter and Virgil Feltner and Jimmy Chatham and a good many more who went away to the various wars and never came back, or came back dead.

I became, over the years, a pretty good student of family traits: the shapes of heads, ears, noses, hands, and so forth. This was sometimes funny, as when I would get a suspicion of a kinship that was, you might say, unauthorized. But it was moving too, after a while, to realize that under my very hands a generation had grown up and another passed away.

My most difficult times were the early hours of Saturday when the parents would bring in the littlest boys. You talk about a trial—it would come when a young mother would bring her first child for his first haircut. At best it was like shooting at a moving target. At worst the boy would be a high-principled little fellow who found haircuts to be against his religion, and whose mother was jumping half out of her chair all the time, saying things like "Be still, sugar—Mr. Crow's not going to *hurt* you."

About as bad were some of the old men. They would forget they had faces until their beard began to itch, and then would come in for a shave. They were good-mannered old men who thought that when they were in company they ought to have something to say and that they ought to look at the people they were talking to. While I shaved them they would talk and look around as if I was not even present, let alone working around their ears and noses and throats with a straight razor.

But I must say I always liked having the old ones around. I sort of had a way of collecting them. There was a long string of them who made a regular sitting place of my shop after they got too old to work; some came in every Saturday and some came in every day, depending on how close by they lived. Some of them were outlandish enough, like the one everybody called Old Man Profet who, when he talked, breathed fiercely through his false teeth, which he took out, he said, only to sleep and to eat. Mr. Profet was inclined toward boasting and self-dramatization and belief in whatever he said. To hear him recount the exploits of his youth (in love, work, and strife) with the wind whistling in and out between his gritted teeth, you would think yourself in the presence of some dethroned old warrior king.

Uncle Stanley Gibbs, Grover's father, had no teeth at all and talked like a bubbling spring, and would say anything at all—*anything*—that he thought of. And sometimes he said, as Grover put it, "things that he nor nobody else ever thought of."

"Did you know," said Uncle Stanley, "that they cut a rock out of old Mrs. Shoals's apparatix as big as a hen egg?"

"No," I said. "I did not."

"Well, they did."

Mr. Wayne Thripple, on the other hand, never said much at all. He was a loose-skinned old fellow who just sat and stared ahead, glassy-eyed, as if about to go to sleep, but he never went to sleep. He spent a lot of time clearing his throat, loudly. *"Humh!"* he would say. "Unnnh uh-*hum!* Uh-hum! Hmmmmh! Uh-hum, uh-hum, uh-hum! Uh-*hum*-ahum!"

But there were also men such as Uncle Isham Quail and Old Jack Beechum and, later, Athey Keith and Mat Feltner, intelligent men who knew things that were surpassingly interesting to me. They were rememberers, carrying in their living thoughts all the history that such places as

Port William ever have. I listened to them with all my ears and have tried to remember what they said, though from remembering what I remember I know that much is lost. Things went to the grave with them that will never be known again.

Uncle Marce Catlett would ride in on horseback to get a haircut and a shave the first thing every other Saturday afternoon, hitching his mare to the sugar tree in front of my door. There came a time when I would have to help him off and back onto the mare. Uncle Dave Coulter, Burley's father, always walked in, to save his horse. Neither of them ever loafed.

I came to feel a tenderness for them all. This was something new to me. It gave me a curious pleasure to touch them, to help them in and out of the chair, to shave their weather-toughened old faces. They had known hard use, nearly all of them. You could tell it by the way they held themselves and moved. Most of all you could tell it by their hands, which were shaped by wear and often by the twists and swellings of arthritis. They had used their hands forgetfully, as hooks and pliers and hammers, and in every kind of weather. The backs of their hands showed a network of little scars where they had been cut, nicked, thornstuck, pinched, punctured, scraped, and burned. Their faces told that they had suffered things they did not talk about. Every one of them had a good knife in his pocket, sharp, the blades whetted narrow and concave, the horn of the handle worn smooth. The oldest ones spoke, like Uncle Othy, the old broad speech of the place; they said "ahrn" and "fahr" and "tard" for "iron" and "fire" and "tired"; they said "yorn" for "yours," "cheer" for "chair," "deesh" for "dish," "dreen" for "drain," "slide" for "sled," and "juberous" for "dubious." I loved to listen to them, for they spoke my native tongue.

Among the best things that could happen (and that happened less and less often as time went on) were the nights when we would have music. I never quite knew how these came about. In my early days in the shop and on for a good many years, Bill Mixter and his brother and his sons had a band that would go about playing at square dances and such. Maybe there would be times when they would be in need of a place to gather and play. Maybe they had taken notice of my habit of keeping the shop open at night as long as anybody was there.

Anyhow, there would be a night now and then when they would wander in, one after another, a little past a decent bedtime, carrying their instruments. Maybe Burley Coulter would take down his old fiddle and come too. They never said that they had come to play; the instruments seemed just to be along by accident.

They would come in and sit down as people did who had come in to loaf, and the conversation would begin about as usual.

"Good evening to you, Jayber."

"Good evening to you, Bill."

"Well, what do you reckon you been up to?"

"Oh, no good, as usual."

If I had no customer, as I probably would not have at that hour of the night, I would climb into the seat of my profession and make myself comfortable.

They would greet me and one another as they came in. They took chairs, sat down, commented on the weather and other events, smoked maybe.

And then one or another of them would pick up his fiddle or guitar or banjo (you could never tell who it would be) and begin to tune it, plucking at the strings individually and listening. And then another would begin, and another. It was done almost bashfully, as if they feared that the silence might not welcome their music. Little sequences of notes would be picked out randomly here and there. (Their instruments just happened to be in their hands. The power of music-making had overtaken them by surprise, and they had to grow used to it.)

Finally Bill Mixter would lower his head, lay his bow upon the strings, and draw out the first notes of a tune, and the others would come in behind him. The music, while it lasted, brought a new world into being. They would play some tunes they had learned off the radio, but their knowledge was far older than that and they played too the music that was native to the place, or that the people of the place were native to. Just the names of the tunes were a kind of music; they call back the music to my mind still, after so many years: "Sand Riffle," "Last Gold Dollar," "Billy in the Low Ground," "Gate to Go Through," and a lot of others. "A fiddle, now, is an atmospheric thing," said Burley Coulter. The music was another element filling the room and pouring out through the cracks. When at last they'd had their fill and had gone away, the shop felt empty, the silence larger than before.

But you could not be where I was without experiencing many such transformations. One of your customers, one of your neighbors (let us say), is a man known to be more or less a fool, a big talker, and one day he comes into your shop and you have heard and you see that he is dying even as he is standing there looking at you, and you can see in his eyes that (whether or not he admits it) he knows it, and all of a sudden everything is changed. You seem no longer to be standing together in the center of time. Now you are on time's edge, looking off into eternity. And this man, your foolish neighbor, your friend and brother, has shed somehow the laughter that has followed him through the world, and has assumed the dignity and the strangeness of a traveler departing forever.

The generation that was old and dying when I settled in Port William had memories that went back to the Civil War. And now my own generation, that calls back to the First World War, is old and dying. And gray hair is growing on heads that had just looked over tabletops at the time of World War II. I can see how we grow up like crops of wheat and are harvested and carried away.

But as the year warmed in 1937, I was a young man. I hardly knew what I knew, let alone what I was going to learn. In March, Burley Coulter brought his breaking plow in to the blacksmith shop and, in passing, plowed my garden. It broke beautifully. There was, as Burley said, nothing wrong with it. The dark soil rolled off the moldboard and fell to pieces. In the early mornings and late evenings, and in the intervals between customers, I brought to life the useful things Aunt Cordie had taught me and became a gardener. I worked and manured the ground, and on Good Friday planted potatoes, onions, peas, salad stuff, and set out some cabbage plants. It was lovely, then, to see the green things sprigging up in my long, straight rows. The garden took up nearly all the space between the shop and the privy out by the back fence, a hundred and fifty feet or so, and was only about eighteen feet wide. Depending on how I spaced them, I could have seven or eight rows.

I became a sort of garden fanatic, and I am not over it yet. You can take a few seed peas, dry and dead, and sow them in a little furrow, and they will sprout into a row of pea vines and bear more peas—it may not be a miracle, but that is a matter of opinion. When the days were lengthening and getting warmer and the sun was shining, I would be back in my garden all the time, working or just looking. When it was warm and I could leave the back door open, I could hear when anybody came into the shop, and I would go in, accomplish the necessary haircut or shave or conversation, and come back out again as soon as I was alone. I knew better than to expect a visible difference in an hour, but I looked anyhow.

Another new thing that happened to me after I came back to Port William was the feeling of loss. I began to live in my losses. When I was taken away from Squires Landing and put into The Good Shepherd, I think I was more or less taken away from my grief. I was just lifted up out of it, like a caught fish. The loss of all my life and all the places and people I had known I felt then as homesickness. After I got over my homesickness and learned in my fashion to live and get along at The Good Shepherd, I learned to think of myself as myself. The past was gone. I was unattached. I could put my whole life in a smallish cardboard box and carry it in my hand.

But when I recognized Burley Coulter on the water that morning and told him who I was, and he remembered me from that lost and gone and given-up old time and then introduced me to people as the boy Aunt Cordie and Uncle Othy took to raise—well, that changed me. After all those years of keeping myself aloof and alone, I began to feel tugs from the outside. I felt my life branching and forking out into the known world. In a way, I was almost sorry. It was as though I knew without exactly knowing, or felt, or smelled in the air, the already accomplished fact that nothing would ever be simple for me again. I never again would be able to put my life in a box and carry it away.

The place itself and its conversation surrounded me with reminders. Aunt Cordie and Uncle Othy and the Thripples and Put Woolfork and Dark Tom Cotman and Emmet Edge and Aunt Ellie and Uncle Ben Fewclothes—all the people of that early world I once thought would last forever, and then thought I had left forever—were always coming back to mind because of something I saw or heard. They would turn up in the conversation in my shop. They returned to my dreams. In my comings and goings I crossed their tracks, and my own earlier ones, many times a day, weaving an invisible web that was as real as the ground it was woven over, and as I went about I would feel my losses and my debts.

In those days I was always sticking money here and there for safe-keeping. I stuck Sam Hanks's unrepayable five-dollar bill into a book where I would have it to use if I had to use it, but where as long as I might keep it I would always know it from any other five-dollar bill. I kept it to remind me that there are some accounts that cannot be settled.

With that in mind, I watched for the first warm Sunday morning. When it came, I left town early. I followed the road along the ridgetops, and down into the Katy's Branch valley and up the other side, and then across the fields and down through the woods until I came to the open hillside above Squires Landing. Just at the woods' edge, where I could look down at the house and the store and the other buildings, I found a good sitting place and leaned my back against a tree.

I sat there a long time. I looked at everything and remembered it, and let my memories come back and take place. I don't believe I was exactly thinking; my mind was too crowded and too everywhere touched. What would come, came. The child I had been came and made his motions, out and about and around, down to the store, down to the garden, down to the barn, up to the house, up to the henhouse, across the river in Uncle Othy's johnboat, up the river in the buggy, over to the Thripples, up to Port William on Sunday morning, down to the river to see the steamboats land and unload and load, up into the woods—weaving over the ground a web of ways, as present and as passing as the spiders' webs in the grass that catch the dew early in the morning. All my steps had made the place a world and made me at home in it, and then I had gone, just as Aunt Cordie and Uncle Othy had been at home and then had gone.

And like a shadow within a shadow, the time before my time came to me. I was old enough by then to know and believe that the old had once been young. Once, Aunt Cordie had been Cordie Quail, a pretty girl. There had been a day when Uncle Othy and Aunt Cordie had come there, young, just married, to begin their life at the landing, to have their pleasures and to endure what had to be endured. There had been a time before they came, and a time before that. And always, from a time before anybody knew of time, the river had been there. From my sitting place where the woods stood up at the edge of the pasture, I could see the river, risen a little, swift and muddy from the spring rains, coming down the mile-long reach above the Willow Run bend, swerving through the bend and coming on down past the landing, carrying its load of drift. And I saw how all-of-a-piece it was, how never-ending—always coming, always there, always going.

When I was filled with knowledge and could not hold any more, I went back over the ridge and down to Katy's Branch and up along the creek road to Goforth. I went to the site of my parents' house—*our* house—now gone, and my father's shop, gone, the place overgrown with young box elders and elms and cedars and redbuds and all manner of weeds and vines. I pressed in amongst the tangle and stood by the still-standing chimney and thought, "This is my home itself, where I began." I thought of my young parents, Iona and Luther. My few memories of that place came to me, and I felt the presence of memories I could not remember. I remembered so plainly that I could *hear* the sound of a hammer shaping metal on an anvil, the hammer blows muted at first on the heat-softened iron and then ringing clearer as it cooled and hardened.

The sunlight now lay over the valley perfectly still. I went over to the graveyard beside the church and found them under the old cedars: Uncle Othy and Aunt Cordie, Iona and Luther, and round about were Quails and Cotmans, Proudfoots and Thigpens, my mother's and Aunt Cordie's people. I am finding it a little hard to say that I felt them resting there, but I did. I felt their completeness as whatever they had been in the world.

I knew I had come there out of kindness, theirs and mine. The grief that came to me then was nothing like the grief I had felt for myself alone, at the end of my stay in Lexington. This grief had something in it of generosity, some nearness to joy. In a strange way it added to me what I had lost. I saw that, for me, this country would always be populated with presences and absences, presences of absences, the living and the dead. The world as it is would always be a reminder of the world that was, and of the world that is to come.

12

The Gay Bird's Heel

If you could do it, I suppose, it would be a good idea to live your life in a straight line—starting, say, in the Dark Wood of Error, and proceeding by logical steps through Hell and Purgatory and into Heaven. Or you could take the King's Highway past appropriately named dangers, toils, and snares, and finally cross the River of Death and enter the Celestial City. But that is not the way I have done it, so far. I am a pilgrim, but my pilgrimage has been wandering and unmarked. Often what has looked like a straight line to me has been a circle or a doubling back. I have been in the Dark Wood of Error any number of times. I have known something of Hell, Purgatory, and Heaven, but not always in that order. The names of many snares and dangers have been made known to me, but I have seen them only in looking back. Often I have not known where I was going until I was already there. I have had my share of desires and goals, but my life has come to me or I have gone to it mainly by way of mistakes and surprises. Often I have received better than I have deserved. Often my fairest hopes have rested on bad mistakes. I am an ignorant pilgrim, crossing a dark valley. And yet for a long time, looking back, I have been unable to shake off the feeling that I have been led—make of that what you will.

I will call back now and lay in a row some passages of my early knowledge of Mattie Keith, who was to be Mattie Chatham.

I have mentioned my first memory of her, when she came giggling down past my shop with Thelma Settle and Althie Gibbs and they saw me and ran away. After that, I was aware of her. She would have been only fourteen years old, and I had no extraordinary affection for her in those days. But anybody who saw her then, I think, would have seen that she was a standout—a neat, bright, pretty, clear-spirited girl with all her feeling right there in her eyes—and would have hoped, as most of us do for things that are young and fine, that the world would treat her kindly.

From time to time I would see her pass the shop with Thelma or Althie or some of the other girls her age, as she was drawn more and more into the social life of the town's young people. You could see that the other girls looked up to her and that she treated them generously and was in no way stuck-up. The girls would call out to her and she always answered with a good openhearted smile.

And then it came about that sometimes, and then often, when I would see her go by she would be walking with Troy Chatham, and he would be requiring her attention with his talk, which he always accompanied with gestures of his hands and eloquent facial expressions and much dancing and prancing about. He was in her grade, though about a year older, I think, and was as attractive in his way as she was in hers. He was handsome and as athletic as a fox. It was easy to know why she walked with him and listened to him and gave him her smile. They were about equally beautiful and they recognized each other. They had picked each other out.

It is a serious fault in a man to dislike a boy, but I have to confess that I never liked Troy Chatham. Even before he began keeping company with Mattie Keith, I disliked him, you might say, in his own right. He was the kind of boy who always assumes that people are watching him with admiration. He had reason for assuming so, but that in itself made me unwilling to give him the credit he expected. He was a show-off; with the other boys, he was a braggart and a bully. He was not making up for any felt inferiority, either. His faults, if he knew them, never laid heavy on his mind.

One Saturday morning Mattie came into the shop with Althie Gibbs to bring Althie's four-year-old brother for a haircut. They were being very motherly and dutiful with the little boy. Because of that, maybe, both girls left behind the schoolbooks they had brought with them. I suppose they didn't remember where they had left the books, because nobody thought to come back for them until Monday. I laid them on the backbar to have them out of the way.

When the shop had cleared that night and I was putting the place in order, I picked up one of the books to look at it. It was Mattie's American history book, and various ones of her classmates had written things on the flyleaves and endpapers. Althie, for instance, had written:

> When you get married and have twins
> Don't call on me for safety pins.
> Love from
> your friend forever,
> Althie Gibbs

But what most struck my notice was an inscription written in a flourishing hand smack in the middle of the front flyleaf by Troy Chatham. He had used up fully half the page, first by writing big and then by drawing a scalloped border around what he had written. It said:

> Remember me and bear in mind
> That a gay bird's heel sticks out behind.
> You know who

I did know who, and in the way of the knowing bystander I took offense. Troy Chatham's inscription was a claim; beyond anything it actually said, it announced that he felt entitled to a lot of room in the mind and life of Mattie Keith. It bothered me in particular that, having claimed her, he did not sign his name.

Where I found his name was in Mattie's reader. On the flyleaf, in her hand, was written:

> If my love's name you wish to see
> Look on page 63.

On page sixty-three, the inscription said:

> But if there you fail to find
> Look on page 109.

On the hundred-and-ninth page, in the same penciled script, she had written his name:

> Troy Lafayette Chatham

It seemed to me, as I looked at the three words of his name inscribed in pencil in her hand, that I could imagine the overturning, all-including love that such a girl could feel for such a boy. Though I believed she was mistaken, I felt the power and freshness and fragrance and the innocence of such love. And then I grew ashamed of my intrusion and put her books away.

I am reluctant to say that the die was already cast, but it was. ("You watch 'em," Elton Penn used to say. "They don't change much.") Mattie remained all that she at first appeared to be, subtracting only freshness and innocence. Althie was *(is)* Mattie's friend forever—the best of the Gibbses by far. She was a plain, strong-bodied, undaunted girl with green eyes full of intelligence and humor, who no sooner finished raising her younger sisters and brothers than she began a family of her own. And Troy Chatham had correctly named himself—a gay bird with a good bit more heel than he had in view.

When their class left Port William and entered the high school down at Hargrave, Troy became almost immediately a basketball prospect that everybody was watching, and after a year or two he became a star. And Mattie continued, I knew, to belong to him. As for his belonging to her, I had my doubts, and I was not the only one.

Mattie's parents were Athey and Della Keith. They lived on a good, large river-bottom farm in the bend between Sand Ripple and Katy's Branch. If you looked northward from the Coulter ridges, you would be looking right across the Keith place. It had been the Keith place for generations. The upper end of the boundary crossed the Coulter Branch and took in a fine stand of timber on the upriver side. Della and Athey Keith had married late, and Mattie was their only child.

Athey was a regular customer of mine. He was a good farmer, a man who liked farming and liked his farm. You didn't see him in town a lot. He didn't much take to crowds. If the shop was full when he came in, he would have little to say and would leave as soon as he paid me. If he was the only customer—and I think he tried to come when the shop would be uncrowded—he would sometimes linger to talk. I got to know him; pretty soon we became friends. That he did not approve of Troy Chatham was not something he ever said, so far as I heard, in his life. I believe that he would not have said it, except, for a time, within the walls of his own house. Later, after a particular day, I am fairly certain that he never spoke of it again to anybody.

I knew of his disapproval not from anything that he said but from what, in certain circumstances, he did not say. If he was in the shop, for instance, and the talk turned to basketball and the prowess of Troy Chatham, Athey said simply nothing. He would not so much as look in the direction of the conversation. The Hargrave basketball team and Troy Chatham's excellence as a player did not matter to Athey Keith. They were not the point. I knew that he had subtracted Troy Chatham's talent as a basketball player from Troy Chatham, and had found not enough left over. I knew too that Della agreed with him. They didn't tell me this. Nobody did. You don't need to be *told* some things. You can sometimes tell more by a man's silence and the set of his head than by what he says. By such signs you can tell, for instance, what he thinks of his wife; there is a kind of conversation about women and marriage that I never heard Athey take part in, ever. And you can tell what his wife thinks of him.

Nor did I ever say or give any sign to Athey that I concurred in his judgment of Troy Chatham. It was not my business. "It is none of your business," I kept telling myself. But by that time, the limits of my business notwithstanding, and however secretly, I was involved.

That I was involved became clear to me one spring afternoon in about 1941. Six or eight of the boys were playing basketball on the cinder-covered lot in front of the blacksmith shop. They had put up a hoop there, and the packed cinders made it a good place to play. A little crowd had gathered to watch the game—Mattie and Althie among them. They must have been on an errand of some kind for Althie's mother, for each of them was carrying a bushel basket; Mattie was holding hers by both handles in front of her. She was wearing a simple short-sleeved cotton dress, a white dress with little flowers on it. Her hair was tied back a little away from her ears with a ribbon. She was perfect.

The two teams were made up of any boys who wanted to play, boys of all sizes and abilities, no two of them as good as Troy Chatham, who was putting on a show. He could do just about anything with a basketball, and he was doing all of it, outthinking and outmoving the other players, trying difficult shots and making them, leaping and running. He was just beautiful and graceful to see. But also he was using his skill to impress the watchers and to make fools of the other players.

I was beginning to be uncomfortable with the thought that he would take my presence there as a tribute to him, and I was starting to leave. About then somebody fed him a pass as he came running in for a shot. He took the pass, faked at the goal, and then, leaping, dropped a perfect over-the-head shot into Mattie's basket. It was the most beautiful thing he had done, and yet it was proprietary and aggressive, a kind of violence.

"*Oh,* Troy Chatham!" Mattie said, and dumped the ball out onto the ground.

You could see nevertheless that she was pleased.

And I thought, "Why, you impudent son of a bitch!"

13

A Period of Darkness

You would need to draw a very big map of the world in order to make Port William visible upon it. In the actual scale of a state highway map, Port William would be smaller than the dot that locates it. In the eyes of the powers that be, we Port Williamites live and move and have our being within a black period about the size of the one that ends a sentence. It would be a considerable overstatement to say that before making their decisions the leaders of the world do not consult the citizens of Port William. Thousands of leaders of our state and nation, entire administrations, corporate board meetings, university sessions, synods and councils of the church have come and gone without hearing or pronouncing the name of Port William. And how many such invisible, nameless, powerless little places are there in this world? All the world, as a matter of fact, is a mosaic of little places invisible to the powers that be. And in the eyes of the powers that be all these invisible places do not add up to a visible place. They add up to words and numbers.

A town such as Port William in this age of the world is like a man on an icy slope, working hard to stay in place and yet slowly sliding downhill. It has to contend not just with the local mortality, depravity, ignorance, natural deficiencies, and weather but also with what I suppose we might as well call The News. The obliviousness of Port William in high places unfortunately is not reciprocated. The names of the mighty are known in Port William; the news of their influence is variously brought. In modern times much of the doing of the mighty has been the undoing of Port William and its kind. Sometimes Port William is persuaded to approve and support its own undoing. But it knows always that a decision unfeelingly made in the capitols can be here a blow felt, a wound received.

The News intensified—it concentrated the air like a whirlwind—as World War II was cooking up. The war did not make Port William more visible, except to itself; to itself, it became extraordinarily visible. We looked around us, seeing everything as eligible to be lost.

The Monday after Pearl Harbor, my usually cheerful next-door neighbor, Miss Gladdie Finn, was crying as she hung out her wash in the backyard.

"Oh, Mr. Crow," she said when I came out for a bucket of coal, "have you heard about the terrible war that has started?"

I said, "Yes, ma'am, I've heard."

"I tell you," she said, "I don't think much of these wars." She was crying the way a woman cries who is no longer surprised to be crying.

And I knew why. Her son had been killed in the First World War, and now the coming of this new one had put her back into the midst of her loss.

I said, as consolingly as I could, "Well, Miss Gladdie, maybe it won't last long. Maybe it'll be all right."

But she said, "Oh, honey, boys will be killed."

That brought it home to me. I thought the rest of the day of my childish fear of that first great war, and remembered the pictures of the dead lying all askew in the muddy trenches.

Miss Gladdie had been a widow for a long time. She had never remarried. She remained true to the two men she often referred to lovingly by name, Forrest Senior and Forrest Junior. She lived alone on little checks that came in the mail, and from her henhouse and garden, always busy trying to keep body and soul and her infirm old house together. She was a woman of sorrows and might have been excused for seeming so. And yet I rarely saw her when she didn't have a smile and a cheerful word. Now and then when I saw she needed help—a lift with something heavy, say—I would go over and help her. She would let me help her and thank me kindly, if I came, but she was very particular about not asking. "Honey, I hate to bother you," she would say.

And I liked her. She was the last one to practice what had been an old Port William custom of trading household things. When she got tired of some of her stuff, she would gather it into her apron and hike off among the neighbors to trade for stuff that they were tired of.

She was the heroine of a famous story. One time before the war, before her losses, she and Maxie Settle and Dora Cotman were sitting on her back porch hulling peas when Thig Cotman came up in one of his fits. He cursed and ranted, damning them and everybody he knew and himself into the bargain, and demanded to know what Miss Dora had done with his razor, for he wanted to cut his throat with it. And poor Miss Dora, who had hidden the razor for fear that he would cut his throat with it, just sat with her head down until Miss Gladdie said, "Thig, Forrest Senior's got a razor. He would never let you shave with it, but if you wanted to cut your throat with it I'm sure that would be all right."

You could see, still, that she was the woman who had said that. She was a woman who loved her hen flock and her garden and her flowers. Every day, from early spring to late fall, she made a little wander around her house and yard to see what was coming up or getting ready to bloom or blooming. She was always bringing home some plant or seed or root or "sticking it in the ground" to see if it would grow. And within all else she was, she was keeper and protector of the grief by which she cherished what she had lost.

I thought a good deal about Forrest Junior and wondered where he was buried and if anybody even knew where. I imagined that soldiers who are killed in war just disappear from the places where they are killed. Their deaths may be remembered by the comrades who saw them die, if the comrades live to remember. Their deaths will not be remembered *where* they happened. They will not be remembered in the halls of the government. Where do dead soldiers die who are killed in battle? They die at home—in Port William and thousands of other little darkened places, in thousands upon thousands of houses like Miss Gladdie's where The News comes, and everything on the tables and shelves is all of a sudden a relic and a reminder forever.

And yet, as I knew already and would learn again and again, when these blows fall into life, life contains them somehow and keeps on going. After her grief at the onset of the new war, Miss Gladdie righted herself and proceeded. When I told her I had registered for the draft and was going to be examined, she said, "Well, honey, everybody has to die sometime."

I was twenty-eight in 1942, and it looked like to me that I ought to have got my mind settled on some of the major questions. But the war did to my thoughts what a harrow does to crusted ground. I was too old to be lured by visions of adventure and heroism as some of the younger fellows were; I was just normally afraid, for myself and the world. That cloudy fear of what might happen was bad enough. What was worse was trying to reckon with war itself, what caused it, and what justified it. When I was younger, from what I had felt and read and seen in pictures, I had imagined war as a great, blind force like a hard wind at night that trampled and bloodied the ground, leaving behind only loose stones and splinters and bodies torn to pieces. This new war, like the previous one, would be a test of the power of machines against people and places; whatever its causes and justifications, it would make the world worse. This was true of that new war, and it has been true of every new war since. The dark human monstrous thing comes and tramples the little towns and never even knows their names. It would make Port William afraid and shed its blood and grieve its families and damage its hope.

I knew too that this new war was not even new but was only the old one come again. And what caused it? It was caused, I thought, by people failing to love one another, failing to love their enemies. I was glad enough that I had not become a preacher, and so would not have to go through a war pretending that Jesus had not told us to love our enemies.

The thought of loving your enemies is opposite to war. You don't have to *do* it; you don't *have* to love one another. All you have to do is keep the thought in mind and Port William becomes visible, and you see its faces and know what it has to lose. Maybe you don't have to love your enemies. Maybe you just have to act like you do. And maybe you have to start early.

Anyhow, what I couldn't bring together or reconcile in my mind was the thought of Port William and the thought of the war. Port William, I thought, had not caused the war. Port William makes quarrels, and now and again a fight; it does not make war. It takes power, leadership, great talent, perhaps genius, and much money to make a war. In war, as maybe even in politics, Port William has to suffer what it didn't make. I have pondered for years and I still can't connect Port William and war except by death and suffering. No more can I think of Port William and the United States in the same thought. A nation is an idea, and Port William is not. Maybe there is no live connection between a little place and a big idea. I think there is not.

Did I think that the great organizations of the world could love their enemies? I did not. I didn't think great organizations could love anything. Did I think anybody would live longer by loving his enemies? Did I think those who were going to die could stay alive by loving their enemies? I did not.

Was this a good war? I knew that it could not be good. Was it avoidable? I don't know.

I might have become a conscientious objector if I had had more confidence in myself. I certainly did think that "love your enemies" was an improvement over all the other possibilities, but getting to be a conscientious objector required "sincerity of belief in religious teaching." Was "love your enemies" a religious teaching just because Jesus said it? Or did it have to be taught by a church? I was not a Quaker. So far as I knew, I had never even seen a Quaker. And suppose you got to be a conscientious objector: What did you do next? Next, I supposed, you left Port William, whose young men who were not conscientious objectors would be getting hurt and killed. I had a conscientious objection to making an exception of myself. As had happened before, my mind was failing me; I couldn't think my way all the way through. As I saw it, I had two choices: to fight in a war and maybe kill people I wasn't even mad at and who were no more to blame than I was, or take an exemption that I really didn't believe was right either and couldn't believe I was worthy of. I couldn't imagine what lay beyond either choice.

What decided me, I think, was that I could no longer imagine a life for myself beyond Port William. I thought, "I will have to share the fate of this place. Whatever happens to Port William must happen to me." That changed me, and it cleared my head. It didn't make me feel good to be sharing the fate of Port William, for I knew there would be pain and trouble in that, but it made me feel good to have my head clear. Afterward, I slept all night for the first time in weeks.

If I could have found in my mind a plain and simple way to be right, that would have been something. I would have been changed in another way, and my life ever afterward would have been different. But having reached the crisis—the crossroad, so to speak—I failed. I didn't have at all the feeling of being right.

And then it turned out that I had spent all my sleeplessness and agony on a choice that I didn't have to make. One day they loaded a bunch of us into a bus and took us off to be examined. We had to take our clothes off and line up and submit to being looked at and poked and felt of like a pen of slaughter lambs. I hadn't been quite so lost and nameless since my first night at The Good Shepherd.

I said to myself, "Well, here you are, naked and ashamed, at the stockyards at last. After all your efforts to evade another talking-to across the top of a desk, you are coming now to somebody who is going to point at you with the end of his fountain pen and tell you to go and die for your country. And probably you are going to do it."

We would come up to these doctors and stand in front of them, feeling like we had been shorn or skinned, not looking at anybody, and they would tell us whether we were sheep or goats.

I was a goat. This old gray-haired doctor put his stethoscope to my chest and listened and listened, and then cocked his head and listened some more.

"Son," he said, "I don't want to scare you, but you've got a heart murmur, a little valve problem. I'm going to have to disqualify you."

I said, *"What?"* I had gone all of a sudden from feeling humiliated to feeling insulted.

"4-F," he said. "You've got a little fault that's part of your standard equipment."

I said, "What the hell are you talking about? I'm as healthy as a hog!"

He picked up a book and opened it and fingered a page for a moment and then read a sentence that said a man in my condition under the influence of "severe bodily exertion" might become "a pension problem."

The doctor clapped the book shut, said, "I'm sorry, son," and that was it.

I went back to Port William, a free man again, and glad of it, and ashamed to be glad. I felt disgraced by my failure to be able to do what I did not want to do.

One day when Mr. Milo Settle came in for a haircut, he said, "Well, boy, what are we going to do for a barber when you go off to the war? You went to be examined, didn't you?"

"Yes," I said. "And I've been classified."

"What?"

"4-F."

"Why, there ain't a thing wrong with you. You're fit as a fiddle."

"I have a little heart problem. I might not be able to stand severe bodily exertion."

"Boy," said Mr. Settle, "you ain't got a thing to worry about."

After the war started and all the eligible young men and boys had gone away, a new silence came into Port William. The town did not become silent, I don't mean that; Port William always finds a plenty to talk about. The silence I mean was just a general avoidance of what lay heaviest on people's minds: fear. We feared that The News would become all of a sudden *our* news. We feared the news of wounds, deaths, losses; we feared our own grief, which we felt to be waiting. The town continued its conversation about itself, and now also it talked about the war. We all knew which part of the world everybody's son had gone off to, and pretty soon there were some daughters too who had gone away to be nurses, or to serve as Wacs or Waves. There were many new things to be known and talked about, but nobody spoke of fear. And when grief began to come in and replace fear, the grieved, out of consideration for the fearful, did not speak of grief. The nearest anybody came to speaking aloud of these things would be when one of the boys would be shipped overseas to where the fighting was, and his father would have to announce, "Well, he has gone across the waters." Nothing could reduce the strangeness and dreadfulness of that phrase, "gone across the waters."

When Jasper Lathrop had to go into the army, he closed the store, leaving all the town's business in the line of groceries and general merchandise to Milton Burgess. Jasper's father, Frank, and Mat Feltner, who owned the building that Jasper had set up in, sold out the stock and left the shelves and counters empty. In the winters following, until the end of the war, Frank and Mat and Burley and I and various others carried on a rummy game in the little room at the back of Jasper's store, using the meat block as a card table. It surely was one of the oddest card games that ever was, for it wasn't your standard five-hundred rummy. This game did not end. It just stopped when the war stopped.

We had a long piece of butcher paper tacked to the wall with the names of all the players written across the top. When we quit playing for the day, we wrote every player's score under his name. The number of players on any day would vary from two to maybe six or seven. And so far as I know, nobody ever added up the scores; they just accumulated in uneven columns down that long page. Just as the game was a way of waiting for an end that was too long in coming, and as the empty store was a waiting place, so the score sheet was a way of not knowing, as if we would deal and play and take what came, leaving the conclusion to God.

Some coped with their times of fear and worry by becoming awfully quiet. Some would become noisy. Burley Coulter was one who would be noisy. The elder Coulters had died by then and Burley was living alone. After the war started, there would be times when he more or less made my shop his living room. His nephew, Tom, was with a battalion of engineers, first in North Africa and then in Italy. Tom would sometimes have to work under fire, being shot at while he concentrated his mind on something else. I knew that Burley was worrying about Tom when (just two or three times) I saw him fall away from a conversation into thought, and heard him grunt at what he was thinking. Mostly, when he was most worried, he would be working hard to stir up something to laugh about.

He would get up in the midst of the crowded shop, interrupting the conversation, and start outside to relieve himself. "All who can't swim, mount the highest bench," he would cry out, "for the great he-elephant will now make water!"

Or in the latter part of a late-winter Saturday afternoon, his mind turning (as he would not say, but as we knew) to the prospect of a visit to his might-as-well-be wife, Kate Helen Branch, he would stand up and stretch. "Well, boys, I reckon I better get on home and shine, shave, clean up, and sandpaper my tool."

What quieted him was grief. Tom was killed as the invasion fought its way up through the mountains of Italy—somewhere up in the cold and the rocks. For a long time after that, Burley went through the motions, doing about as he had done before, but he made no noise. Tom and Nathan, the sons of Burley's brother Jarrat, had lost their mother when they were little and had come across the hollow to live with their grandparents and Burley. Jarrat, after his wife died, had become a distant, solitary, work-brittle man, and Burley had taken a large share in the raising of the boys. They were his boys as much as their father's, and the raising of them had changed him.

After we got the bad news about Tom Coulter, there was nothing, of course, that anybody could do. Maybe because I wished I could do something and could do nothing, I began to have this feeling that I was watching over Burley. I would be keeping an eye on him, aware of him in a way that I had not been before. The times when he fell away into thought came more often then, and he would have an expression on his face like that of a man who is looking at something he can't quite see. And many a night I sat on with him in the shop, talking of other things, to help him put off going home until he was sure he could sleep. By the time Tom was dead, Nathan had crossed the waters and was in the fighting.

I was learning what I had meant when I decided that I would share the fate of Port William. I had not gone off to war, but the wounds and deaths of Port William boys were happening in Port William. They were happening to me. I was involved; I was being changed. The war years were long because we were always waiting for what we feared and for what we hoped. We felt, I think, that we were failing one another, for we needed to have something we could do for one another and mostly there was nothing. And yet, even in failing one another, even in our silence we kept with one another. People had their ways and kept to them. The crops were planted and harvested; the animals mated and gave birth in the appointed seasons, were fed and watched over; the endless conversation of weather and work went on; memories were kept, stories told, and everything funny treasured up and spread around. The old studied their memories and mused and spoke. We younger ones began to see that we knew things that never had not been known.

New grief, when it came, you could feel filling the air. It took up all the room there was. The place itself, the whole place, became a reminder of the absence of the hurt or the dead or the missing one. I don't believe that grief passes away. It has its time and place forever. More time is added to it; it becomes a story within a story. But grief and griever alike endure.

"What can't be helped must be endured," Mat Feltner said. And he was a man who knew.

When Mat's boy, Virgil, was reported missing in action, and remained missing until "missing" slowly came to mean "dead," things changed between Mat and Burley. Before, they had been friendly acquaintances, as you might say; now they recognized each other and were friends. They were men of two different sorts but they had stepped onto the common ground from which young men they loved were gone.

Mat had the worst of it, maybe. In loyalty to his boy he had to try to believe that "missing" meant *alive somewhere*. And yet lengthening time insisted, like a clock ticking, that it meant *dead*.

Maybe it helped him to have Burley to sit with and talk. Like Burley, he went through the old motions of his life, taking care of what needed caring for, keeping mostly quiet about what was on his mind. But his hard waiting changed him; you could see it in his face.

One night, not long before the war ended, I was sitting in the shop after bedtime. It was a hot night and I had thought I would read a while downstairs to give the upstairs room a chance to cool. There was a pretty good breeze. Nobody had come in, and I sat in the barber chair, which really was the most comfortable chair I had.

I was reading a good book (*The Woodlanders,* by Thomas Hardy, which was in a box of books I had bought for a quarter at an auction), and I stayed on even after I knew it had cooled off upstairs. People went to bed and the town got quiet. For a long time all I could hear were the candle flies fluttering against the screens.

And then I heard footsteps on the walk. It was Mat Feltner. He hesitated, seeing the light, and looked in.

I called to him, "Come in! Come in! Have a seat!"

I knew what he was doing. He was walking away from his thoughts, but his thoughts were staying with him. He was tired but he couldn't sleep.

He seemed glad enough to come in. He sat down, and I closed my book. We talked just aimlessly for a while. We went over all the local goings-on, which neither of us needed to hear about and were not much interested in, but both of us seemed to feel that we needed to be talking.

And then we spoke of the weather, which had been awfully hot. After that, unable to think of anything more to say, we fell into a silence that was troubled and unwelcome.

Trying to end it, I said finally, "Well, we've had a time," speaking of the weather.

And Mat said, "Yes, we've *had* a time," speaking of the war.

We spoke in very general terms, then, of the war and other trials of life in this world.

Mat said, "Everything that will shake has got to be shook."

"That's Scripture," I said, and he nodded.

Thinking to try to comfort him, I said, "Well, along with all else, there's goodness and beauty too. I guess that's the mercy of the world."

Mat said, "The mercy of the world is you don't know what's going to happen."

And then after a pause, speaking on in the same dry, level voice as before, he told me why he had been up walking about so late. He had had a dream. In the dream he had seen Virgil as he had been when he was about five years old: a pretty little boy who hadn't yet thought of anything he would rather do than follow Mat around at work. He looked as real, as much himself, as if the dream were not a dream. But in the dream Mat knew everything that was to come.

He told me this in a voice as steady and even as if it were only another day's news, and then he said, "All I could do was hug him and cry."

And then I could no longer sit in that tall chair. I had to come down. I came down and went over and sat beside Mat.

If he had cried, I would have. We both could have, but we didn't. We sat together for a long time and said not a word.

After a while, though the grief did not go away from us, it grew quiet.

What had seemed a storm wailing through the entire darkness seemed to come in at last and lie down.

Mat got up then and went to the door. "Well. Thanks," he said, not looking at me even then, and went away.

14

For Better, for Worse

Ernest Finley may have been right in saying that in Port William we were more or less a classless society. On the other hand, we may have been a two-class society: Cecelia Overhold, and everybody else. Or maybe we were a three-class society: Cecelia Overhold, and everybody else, and me. I couldn't imagine Cecelia in those early days as well maybe as I can now, but as I have said, she was a good part of the reason for my social ineligibility. She was my enemy.

But she was Port William's enemy too. Cecelia never liked Port William. She was from Hargrave, and she had some of the social smuggery of the Hargrave upper crust. She married Roy Overhold because he was handsome and she was in love with him, I suppose, and then found that Port William was beneath her—and therefore that Roy, who belonged to Port William, was beneath her. What, after all, would a proud and socially ambitious young woman from Hargrave do with a husband who could be fully entertained by talking or playing cards beside some public stove in Port William for half a winter day? She did not like Port William pronunciation, diction, and grammar. She did not like its public loafing and spitting. She did not like its preoccupation with crops, livestock, food, hunting, fishing, and weather. She did not like its taste in church windows. And so on. She remembered all the personal affronts and insults that she had suffered, going back, I think, to about 1928, when she and Roy got married.

Her particular cross (or curse) was her sister Dorothy in Los Angeles, whom she had a few times gone out to visit. California, in Cecelia's mind, was the one Utopia of the world. "Oh," she would say, "it's a real place, a wonderful place. You can see the stars of the picture shows alive. You can step right out your back door and pick an orange from a tree. Everything out there is up-to-date. Dorothy has such lovely friends." This "California" was the stick she used to measure Port William, and to beat it with. And her mythological sister measured us Port Williamites with a foot or so to spare. Cecelia, as with every look and gesture she let us know, was entirely at ease only in the company of her equals—a company that included, besides herself, only her sister. And of course Cecelia held some secret doubts about herself; you can't dislike nearly everybody and be quite certain that you have exempted yourself.

Cecelia was a regular churchgoer. I would say that she was safely within the definition of "a pillar of the church." That, you might have thought, would have helped a little to ease the difficulty between her and Roy, but I don't think it did.

How much the church *meant* to Cecelia I really don't know. (I know it provided her with most of her best occasions for high-hatting me.) So far as I could tell, she was not a forgiving, forbearing Christian, and yet I have wondered if at times the church, to her, didn't stand for some kindness or gentleness that she yearned toward in her heart. But in her practice it seemed to stand merely for gentility and righteousness that, so to speak, justified her in her difference from Roy, who was not a pillar of the church. When he went, he went in a kind of self-embarrassment, utterly failing to see the connection between it and himself, which caused him to sit as far from the pulpit as possible and as near the door.

The church, I would guess, meant little enough to many of the men of Port William, who (if they went) were not comfortable in it and whose chief preoccupation with respect to it was to keep the preacher from finding out how they really talked and thought and lived. Like, I think, most of the people of Port William, Roy lived too hard up against mystery to be without religion. But like many of the men, he was without church religion. Which is to say that, especially in his own eyes, he was without an acceptable religion. And so in her dealings with him Cecelia thrust the church out like a lion tamer's chair. And Roy, who had never claimed to be a lion, would thereupon be discovered to be not on the attack, or even on the defense, but merely not present. Which surely must have been a further disappointment to her, which maybe seemed to her to verify or justify her general disappointment in him. He, anyhow, was out, and she was in, and neither of them ever could quite forget it.

Roy, I guess, was about as ordinary as a man could be. He was ordinary even in his religious discomfort. In all his life he never did anything that surprised Port William. Except for the sometime extremity of his misery, I don't think he ever surprised himself.

By the time I knew him, Roy was showing some wear, and he was a baldy like me. But once he had been handsome, maybe even pretty. He'd had black curly hair and blue eyes as startlingly clear, almost, as the glass eyes of a doll. One time, with a pride that also embarrassed him, he showed me a picture of himself as a young man. In appearance, at least, he must have seemed a fit match for the beautiful young Cecelia, ever stylish, ever slender. Maybe in the time of their courtship he had looked malleable to Cecelia—good raw material, a man she could make something out of.

As it turned out, Roy was not malleable. What he was already was what he was going to be; what he was already was all she got. She couldn't make anything out of him that he hadn't already become by the time she got started on him. She couldn't even reduce him to anything less than he was.

She was disappointed in him. And this wasn't just *her* disappointment, for I think he was disappointed in himself for being a disappointment to her. It was a disappointment like a nail in your shoe. It wasn't completely disabling, but it couldn't be ignored either. It didn't go away. It wore worse.

But I don't think Roy maintained himself as he was by resistance. I don't think he fought with her or made much of an argument in his own favor. When she raised the pressure, he just escaped. He just quietly shifted off into one of the maybe innumerable precincts of Port William or the surrounding outdoors where she disdained to go. (Her invasion of the Grandstand on that fine morning in the spring of 1937 was not usual. It was provoked by I don't know what extremity of grief and rage.) As a rule, when the pressure was on, Roy eased away. He was not by nature a man who was very much in evidence.

If a soft answer turneth away wrath, maybe *no* answer stirreth wrath up. It was something like that. Roy had the aspect of a man who had eased away from trouble he had not got rid of. He was a quiet, smiling man, a humorous man who never laughed aloud—a good man, I always thought, whose only severe critic was his wife.

Cecelia would have liked a husband she would have been proud to display, a man who looked good in a suit, who was affable, talkative, and charming, desirable (but not too desirable) to other women. She would have been an excellent wife, maybe, to a certain kind of doctor, maybe even a preacher. Roy finally failed to measure up to any of her standards. Dressed up, he never looked like he was wearing his own clothes. In social situations, if he could not find one of his own kind to talk with about grass and livestock and the other things his kind talked about, he was little better than deaf and dumb. And he was not desirable to other women—not, at least, to any woman Cecelia could imagine.

The time she took him on a trip to visit her sister in California was (for reasons that Port William saw as clearly as if the whole town had gone along) the *only* time she ever took him. The whole week he wore his Sunday suit, in which he looked like a badly stuffed animal. He smiled at everything and said almost nothing. He walked about, looking for nobody knew what, like some forest or swamp creature newly acquired by a zoo. Or so the talkers in my shop imagined.

When he got home I asked him, "Well, how was it?"

He only smiled and gave one little shake to his head.

When he died, Roy's dead body, in his last ill-fitting Sunday suit, seemed to preserve the integrity of his long discomfort. He looked (unless you deliberately reminded yourself otherwise) as if he would lie there, the center of far more attention than he had ever sought, in mere embarrassment forever.

If Cecelia was my enemy, that was because (as I now believe) she saw me as her enemy. As the town's barber, as the host of that mostly masculine enclosure, the barbershop, and as the town's permanent bachelor, a piece of raw material permanently raw, forever to be unimproved by a woman of her discriminating powers, I must have seemed to her to be the very gatekeeper of that unregulated other world that Roy eased away into whenever he eased away.

15

The Beautiful Shore

In the last spring of the war, Uncle Stanley Gibbs more or less ran aground as Port William's grave digger and church janitor. He could still dig a grave, he said, but was having more and more trouble getting out of it after he dug it. But also he got fired, first as grave digger and then as janitor, for his inability to control his mouth. He had modified the worst of his vocabulary when he assumed the dignity of associating with preachers and undertakers, but vocabulary really was the smallest end of the problem. Uncle Stanley had no more sense of privacy than a fruit jar. He would tell you at length about his manner of coping with the piles, or his plans for bachelorhood in case Miss Pauline died before he did. His plans for bachelorhood rested on the premise that as soon as Miss Pauline breathed her last, he would cease to be rickety and toothless and deaf and would become a tomcat around the women, as he had been once upon a time.

"Well," Uncle Stanley would be saying for the further enlightenment of whomsoever might be listening, "the madam goes around committing virtue left and right. She looks like the last of pea time now, and you would never know it, but me and her fell together after the fashion of hemale and shemale, same as everybody."

And so on.

Anyhow, as his successor Uncle Stanley chose me, because he thought I had both time to spare and the necessary intelligence—for, as he said, "not just anybody can dig a grave."

I accepted because I was going on thirty-one by then and beginning to see that I needed a little something extra to put away for my old age, in case I lived to be old. Digging graves and cleaning the church were not going to put me in a penthouse in Miami, but I thought they might get me into a nice camp house down along the river, where I could fish when I felt like it.

To salve my conscience for taking the old man's jobs, on which he had depended for self-importance as much as money, I hired him to stay on as my supervisor, and thereby learned some things that I needed to know and quite a few that I did not. Uncle Stanley loved to sit on the edge of a grave, dangling his feet in, and instruct me to do what I was already doing, his conversation varying between unspeakable and incredible. But he didn't last long. In the first winter after the war, survived by Miss Pauline and thus forsaking forever his dream of a widower's bachelorhood, he finally got into a grave he could not get out of. And I was the one who covered him up.

Barbering is a social business; it involves conversation just about by necessity. For me, after Uncle Stanley died, grave digging was a solitary business. Just once in a while I would get caught with a grave to dig on one of my busy days at the shop and would have to hire a hand or two, but mostly, up in the graveyard, I worked alone. It was hard work, and often it was sad work, for as a rule I would be digging and filling the grave of somebody I knew; often it would be the grave of somebody I liked or loved.

It was a strange thing to cut out the blocks of sod and then dig my way to the dark layer where the dead lie. I feel a little uneasy in calling them "the dead," for I am as mystified as anybody by the transformation known as death, and the Resurrection is more real to me than most things I have not yet seen. I understand that people's dead bodies are not exactly *them,* and yet as I dug down to where they were, I would be mindful of them, and respectful, and would feel a curious affection for them all. They all had belonged here once, and they were so much more numerous than the living. I thought and thought about them. It was endlessly moving to me to walk among the stones, reading the names of people I had known in my childhood, the names of people I was kin to but had never known, and (pretty soon) the names of people I knew and cared about and had buried myself. Some of the older stones you could no longer read because of weathering and the growth of moss. It was a place of finality and order. The people there had lived their little passage of time in this world, had become what they became, and now could be changed only by forgiveness and mercy. The misled, the disappointed, the sinners of all the sins, the hopeful, the faithful, the loving, the doubtful, the desperate, the grieved and the comforted, the young and the old, the bad and the good—all, sufferers unto death, had lain down there together. Some were there who had served the community better by dying than by living. Why I should have felt tender toward them all was not clear to me, but I did.

There were a lot of graves of little children—most of them from the last century or before—who had died of smallpox, cholera, typhoid fever, diphtheria, or one of the other plagues. You didn't have to know the stories; just the dates and the size of the stones told the heartbreak. But all those who were there, if they had lived past childhood, had twice in this world, first and last, been as helpless as a little child. And you couldn't forget that all the people in Port William, if they lived long, would come there burdened and leave empty-handed many times, and would finally come and stay empty-handed. Seeing them come and go, and come and stay, I began to be moved by a compassion that seemed to come to me from outside. I never said to myself that it was happening. It just came to me, or I came to it. As I buried the dead and walked among them, I wanted to make my heart as big as Heaven to include them all and love them and not be distracted. I couldn't do it, of course, but I wanted to.

That place of the democracy of the dead was sometimes a very social place for the living. People would come to visit the graves, sometimes from far away, or they would come looking for the names and dates of ancestors, and they would meet and talk. Sometimes old friends would meet after a long separation and would have to make themselves known to one another again. I was always learning something.

One of the best days of the year, for me, was Decoration Day, when people would come from near and far with flowers to decorate the graves. Besides being beautiful and fragrant with all the roses and peonies and boughs of mock orange, it was a kind of grace and benediction, and a kind of homecoming. I liked to make a show of being busy in the graveyard so I could watch and listen.

I was doing that one Decoration Day when I saw Hibernia Hopple get out of her car with an armload of the white and pink peonies that she would divide between her mother's family, who were buried at Port William, and her father's at Goforth. This was about 1960. Before she could shut the car door and turn around, Burley Coulter had seen her and come over.

By way of greeting, he said, "Hibernia, I want you to tell me something."

She turned, saw who it was, and said, "What?"

He said, grinning at her, "Ain't you about lost all your ambition?"

She blushed as pink as a peony. There had been something between them. "Burley Coulter," she said with complete affection, "you need to be shot."

I don't know if you would call grave digging "severe bodily exertion." It surely was the hardest work I have ever done, but it didn't kill me before I gave it up a few years ago. I expect I am by nature a lazy person, and so I never went at it with what you would call violence. But you can't dig a grave without working hard. I mean you have to apply yourself. And after I would get about halfway down, well into the yellow clay that would be either hard or sticky, a voice would begin to speak in my mind; it would say, "Deep enough! Deep enough!" And then I would dig on down as deep as I was supposed to go.

I will say this: It made me strong. After I started digging graves, I got healthier and stronger than I had ever been in my life. And it taught me *how* to be a lazy person. I just didn't let reluctance stand in my way.

Taking care of the church was steadier but easier. I didn't have the time to spare on Saturdays, and so I did most of my work at the church on Friday afternoons, going up there usually right after dinner so as not to be caught in the shop.

To go up to clean the church was to go back somewhat into the world of women, in which I had been a welcome guest when I used to go there holding Aunt Cordie's hand, a little boy petted and made over by the old ladies who were the pillars of the faith in their day. I didn't want to suppose that the women would be purposely looking for signs of carelessness in the housekeeping of the former little boy, but I didn't want them to find any, either. And so I didn't "give it a lick and a promise," the way Uncle Stanley often did. Uncle Stanley held that the congregation dusted the pews by sitting in them, but when I cleaned I got into the corners and the cracks and dusted everything.

About that time, I started more or less regularly attending the Sunday morning service, partly because, after I had taken care of the place, I didn't want to appear indifferent to what went on there, and partly (I confess) to receive the women's compliments on my work. They thought I was doing a good job, and I loved to hear them say so.

The sermons, mostly, were preached on the same theme I had heard over and over at The Good Shepherd and Pigeonville: We must lay up treasures in Heaven and not be lured and seduced by this world's pretty and tasty things that do not last but are like the flower that is cut down. The preachers were always young students from the seminary who wore, you might say, the mantle of power but not the mantle of knowledge. They wouldn't stay long enough to know where they were, for one thing. Some were wise and some were foolish, but none, so far as Port William knew, was ever old. They seemed to have come from some Never-Never Land where the professionally devout were forever young. They were not going to school to learn where they were, let alone the pleasures and the pains of being there, or what ought to be said there. You couldn't learn those things in a school. They went to school, apparently, to learn to say over and over again, regardless of where they were, what had already been said too often. They learned to have a very high opinion of God and a very low opinion of His works—although they could tell you that this world had been made by God Himself.

What they didn't see was that it is beautiful, and that some of the greatest beauties are the briefest. They had imagined the church, which is an organization, but not the world, which is an order and a mystery. To them, the church did not exist in the world where people earn their living and have their being, but rather in the world where they fear death and Hell, which is not much of a world. To them, the soul was something dark and musty, stuck away for later. In their brief passage through or over it, most of the young preachers knew Port William only as it theoretically was ("lost") and as it theoretically might be ("saved"). And they wanted us all to do our part to spread this bad news to others who had not heard it—the Catholics, the Hindus, the Muslims, the Buddhists, and the others—or else they (and maybe we) would go to Hell. I did not believe it. They made me see how cut off I was. Even when I was sitting in the church, I was a man outside.

In Port William, more than anyplace else I had been, this religion that scorned the beauty and goodness of this world was a puzzle to me. To begin with, I didn't think *anybody* believed it. I still don't think so. Those world-condemning sermons were preached to people who, on Sunday mornings, would be wearing their prettiest clothes. Even the old widows in their dark dresses would be pleasing to look at. By dressing up on the one day when most of them had leisure to do it, they signified their wish to present themselves to one another and to Heaven looking their best. The people who heard those sermons loved good crops, good gardens, good livestock and work animals and dogs; they loved flowers and the shade of trees, and laughter and music; some of them could make you a fair speech on the pleasures of a good drink of water or a patch of wild raspberries. While the wickedness of the flesh was preached from the pulpit, the young husbands and wives and the courting couples sat thigh to thigh, full of yearning and joy, and the old people thought of the beauty of the children. And when church was over they would go home to Heavenly dinners of fried chicken, it might be, and creamed new potatoes and creamed new peas and hot biscuits and butter and cherry pie and sweet milk and buttermilk. And the preacher and his family would always be invited to eat with somebody and they would always go, and the preacher, having just foresworn on behalf of everybody the joys of the flesh, would eat with unconsecrated relish.

"I declare, Miss Pauline," said Brother Preston, who was having Sunday dinner with the Gibbses, "those certainly are good biscuits. I can't remember how many I've eaten."

"Preacher," said Uncle Stanley, "that'n makes eight."

Having stated the rule, I must honor the exceptions. There were always some in the congregation who didn't like or enjoy much of any-

thing. And a few of those young preachers were bright and could speak—
I mean they could sound as if they were awake, and make you listen—
and they were troubled enough in their own hearts to have something to
say. A few had wakefully read some books. Maybe one or two of these
might even have stayed on in Port William, if they could have lived poor
enough. But they would have a wife and little children, and the economic
winds would blow them past and beyond. And what, maybe, would Port
William have done with them if they had stayed? Port William tends to
prefer to hear what it has heard before.

In general, I weathered even the worst sermons pretty well. They had
the great virtue of causing my mind to wander. Some of the best things
I have ever thought of I have thought of during bad sermons. Or I would
look out the windows. In winter, when the windows were closed, the
church seemed to admit the light strictly on its own terms, as if uneasy
about the frank sunshine of this benighted world. In summer, when the
sashes were raised, I watched with a great, eager pleasure the town and
the fields beyond, the clouds, the trees, the movements of the air—but
then the sermons would seem more improbable. I have always loved a
window, especially an open one.

What I liked least about the service itself was the prayers; what I liked
far better was the singing. Not all of the hymns could move me. I never
liked "Onward, Christian Soldiers" or "The Battle Hymn of the Republic." Jesus' military career has never compelled my belief. I liked the
sound of the people singing together, whatever they sang, but some of
the hymns reached into me all the way to the bone: "Come, Thou Fount
of Every Blessing," "Rock of Ages," "Amazing Grace," "O God, Our
Help in Ages Past." I loved the different voices all singing one song, the
various tones and qualities, the passing lifts of feeling, rising up and
going out forever. Old Man Profet, who was a different man on Sunday,
used to draw out the notes at the ends of verses and refrains so he could
listen to himself, and in fact it sounded pretty. And when the congregation would be singing "We shall see the King some-day (some-day)," Sam
May, who often protracted Saturday night a little too far into Sunday
morning, would sing, "*I* shall see the King some-day (Sam May)."

I thought that some of the hymns bespoke the true religion of the
place. The people didn't really want to be saints of self-deprivation and

hatred of the world. They knew that the world would sooner or later deprive them of all it had given them, but still they liked it. What they came together for was to acknowledge, just by coming, their losses and failures and sorrows, their need for comfort, their faith always needing to be greater, their wish (in spite of all words and acts to the contrary) to love one another and to forgive and be forgiven, their need for one another's help and company and divine gifts, their hope (and experience) of love surpassing death, their gratitude. I loved to hear them sing "The Unclouded Day" and "Sweet By and By":

> *We shall sing on that beautiful shore*
> *The melodious songs of the blest . . .*

And in times of sorrow when they sang "Abide with Me," I could not raise my head.

Other things about my janitorship I liked without qualification. I liked the church when it was empty. When I would go there to do my work and would come in out of the bustle and stir, and would shut the door and the quiet would come around me, and I would see the light falling unbroken on the scarred and carved and much-repainted old pews—well, it was lovely. I would work as quietly as I could so as to be in the quiet without breaking it. Coming there so soon after dinner, I would sometimes get sleepy, and then I would lie down on the floor and take a nap. I would just go dead away for maybe twenty minutes and would wake up in wonder, rested, at one with the quiet, and the light still the same.

My best duty was ringing the bell on Sunday morning. The bell rope came down into the vestibule through a hole bored in the ceiling. The rope was frayed where it had worked back and forth through the hole for a hundred years, and the hole was worn lopsided. Pulling the rope always felt awkward at the start, never the way I expected. You would feel the weight of the bell as it began unresponsively to swing on its creaky bearings up in the steeple. You might have to swing it two or three times before the clapper would strike. And then it struck: "Dong!" And then around the sound of the clapper striking, the sound of the bell bloomed out in all directions over the countryside, into all the woods and hollows.

It was never easy for me to stop ringing the bell, I so delighted in that interval of pure sound between the clapper strokes. The bell, I thought, voiced the best sermon of the day; it included everything, and in a way blessed it.

What gave me the most pleasure of all was just going up there, whatever the occasion, and sitting down with the people. I always wished a little that the church was not a church, set off as it was behind its barriers of doctrine and creed, so that all the people of the town and neighborhood might two or three times a week freely have come there and sat down together—though I knew perfectly well that, in the actual world, any gathering would exclude some, and some would not consent to be gathered, and some (like me) would be outside even when inside.

I liked the naturally occurring silences—the one, for instance, just before the service began and the other, the briefest imaginable, just after the last amen. Occasionally a preacher would come who had a little bias toward silence, and then my attendance would become purposeful. At a certain point in the service the preacher would ask that we "observe a moment of silence." You could hear a little rustle as the people settled down into that deliberate cessation. And then the quiet that was almost the quiet of the empty church would come over us and unite us as we were not united even in singing, and the little sounds (maybe a bird's song) from the world outside would come in to us, and we would completely hear it.

But always too soon the preacher would become abashed (after all, he was being paid to talk) and start a prayer, and the beautiful moment would end. I would think again how I would like for us all just to go there from time to time and sit in silence. Maybe I am a Quaker of sorts, but I am told that the Quakers sometimes speak at their meetings. I would have preferred no talk, no noise at all.

One day when I went up there to work, sleepiness overcame me and I lay down on the floor behind the back pew to take a nap. Waking or sleeping (I couldn't tell which), I saw all the people gathered there who had ever been there. I saw them as I had seen them from the back pew, where I sat with Uncle Othy (who would not come in any farther) while Aunt Cordie sang in the choir, and I saw them as I had seen them (from the back pew) on the Sunday before. I saw them in all the times past and to come, all somehow there in their own time and in all time and in no time: the cheerfully working and singing women, the men quiet or reluctant or shy, the weary, the troubled in spirit, the sick, the lame, the desperate, the dying, the little children tucked into the pews beside their elders, the young married couples full of visions, the old men with their dreams, the parents proud of their children, the grandparents with tears in their eyes, the pairs of young lovers attentive only to each other on the edge of the world, the grieving widows and widowers, the mothers and fathers of children newly dead, the proud, the humble, the attentive, the distracted—I saw them all. I saw the creases crisscrossed on the backs of the men's necks, their work-thickened hands, the Sunday dresses faded with washing. They were just there. They said nothing, and I said nothing. I seemed to love them all with a love that was mine merely because it included me.

When I came to myself again, my face was wet with tears.

16

Rose of San Antone

Back in those days I still wanted to take an active part in the ongoing life of the twentieth century, and so two or three years after the war I bought a car. There had been a lot of public works during the Depression, a lot of new roads had been built, and the country had opened up. Along the river on our side, from Ellville up to Stoneport and beyond, the all-weather roads had gone in, and home dances and moonshine had gone out. Until the 1930s the roads in these parts went to the river; there was not much need for a road *along* the river, which was in its way a road.

In Port William after the war the idea that you could "jump in a car" and drive to Hargrave in only a few minutes was still fairly new. The time had been, and not long back, when people in Port William who wanted to go to Hargrave would walk down to Dawes Landing and take the boat.

The old homemade Saturday nights, when they would carry the furniture out into the yard and roll up the rugs and dance until sunup, were gone and done for. Now especially the young ones wanted to jump into a car on Saturday night and run down to Hargrave where whiskey and beer were legal and there were picture shows and places where you could drink and listen to the jukebox and dance. In fact, you could go and do those things on any night except Sunday. Hargrave was the great world, in a small way. Down there they did distinguish the masses from the classes. There was real money in Hargrave, and real poverty, and public virtue, and semiprivate depravity. There was always something of interest going on that you had to pay to get into. A bachelor barber of limited means in Port William, where most of the entertainment was free, obviously needed to pass downward to Hargrave now and again. And so I bought the car, and with the help of a lot of free advice learned to drive it, and went down to Hargrave and got myself licensed.

The car was an old green Dodge sedan from the age before the war. I bought it, on time, from Mr. Milo Settle, who halfway did not want to sell it to me, for he had so enjoyed having it to sell. He gave me a look and a snort, and said, "Boy, where have *you* got any business going?"

After I had bought it, I was secretly a little horrified by it. When I was not driving it, which was nearly all the time, it sat with a complacent expression in the driveway beside the shop, seeming to be eating and digesting my money. Like certain women I had encountered out in the great world, it would not be available unless paid. It was quite a nice car, except that it needed a new set of rings. When I drove it, a great cloud of blue smoke rose behind it. A number of people told me that from the Grandstand on a clear winter day they could watch my progress all the way to Hargrave, as if I had been driving a steam engine.

I was not quick in making up my mind to get the engine overhauled—that required five years. Otherwise, I took good care of the car, as I did of everything I spent money on. I drove it very little, rarely going any farther than Hargrave. I never drove it over forty miles per hour, and seldom that fast. I did not enjoy being inside a machine that was under any kind of a strain. Though it had never had so much as a dent and I kept it as shiny and new-looking as I could, the sight of it easily reminded me of wreckage. Because the nicer it looked the more fragile it appeared to be, and because I was always a little afraid of it, the old Dodge and I often seemed to be on the verge of becoming junk, flesh and metal beyond the help of money. The thought of that would make me grunt. It seemed to me more than a little hellish to be traveling by fire. And yet there were times when I would see in my mind's eye my shiny and stately car passing down through the river bottoms toward Hargrave, gliding smoothly onward in front of its plume of smoke, its engine madly and almost silently whirling under the hood, and I would be deeply impressed. I called it the Port William Zephyr.

Why did I need to go to Hargrave? For one thing, I needed a haircut every couple of weeks or so. The barber I patronized was a large, clumsy man named Violet Greatlow, whose shop was in the living room of an old brick farmhouse on the edge of town. Violet had married past middle age a woman as large in girth though not so tall as himself, and the floor of the shop was always strewn with the fruit of his loins and various playthings. Violet was always saying, "Honey, sweetheart, watch out of the way now so Daddy don't tramp on your little laigs." I enjoyed the homey atmosphere, and I found Violet a source of endless wonder and delight.

I never told him I was a fellow barber, and if he knew he never said so. He wasn't much of a listener, not a great payer of attention to things outside his head.

When I first went to him, I said, "Do you give discounts to bald customers?"

He said, "Young feller, I don't charge for cutting; I charge for knowing when to stop."

Violet was a semi-drunk, an inventor, a great talker. His purpose in telling his elaborate tales seemed to be to reduce them finally to the lowest platitude. "Well, sir," he would say, concluding, decisively clearing his throat, "you never know, do you?" Or: "It takes all kinds to make a world." Or: "Well, it's a fact, ain't it, that there ain't nothing certain in this world but death and three good meals a day."

Or he would say, out of the midst of one of his rare silences: "I'm telling you what—I don't know what we're going to do about this goddamned government. It's getting bad. Do you know that?"

Violet believed that you couldn't tell he was drunk if he chewed caraway seeds. In truth, it was hard anyhow to tell when he was drinking, he was by nature so stolid and deliberate and firm on his feet. The best evidence that he was drunk was that he pulled out about as much hair as he cut off. When I was his only customer, I would always sit down in one of his waiting chairs as if I had come in to visit. If I smelled the faintest hint of caraway, I would listen to him a while and then leave.

As an inventor, Violet was not quite the Thomas Edison of his time.

During the war, I remember, he invented a tank that was so big it would have to be rafted across the water on two aircraft carriers. It would scarcely ever have to shoot. It could destroy a good-sized town merely by running over it. Like most of Violet's inventions, this one was all in his mind. He had offered his idea to the government in a letter he wrote one day with his bitten pencil, but had received no answer. "Now, I want you to tell me," he said, "can you beat that?"

Violet's greatest true-life adventure was the long afternoon he had spent locked up in jail. He had been, for want of a client, more than half asleep, lounging in the barber chair after he had eaten his dinner, when Loony Riggins, the jailer, came rushing in to get him to cut a prisoner's hair. The prisoner needed to look good for his appearance in court.

"You just as well come on right now," Loony said. "I'll let you in and let you right back out when you're done."

And so Violet (in the spirit strictly of public service, for he did not enjoy these assignments) allowed himself to be transported to the jail and locked into a cell with the needy prisoner. Loony went out with a great clanking of metal doors and clicking and clashing of locks. In the silence that followed, the prisoner sat in a chair and submitted to Violet's cutting and combing, which did greatly improve his looks. The newly barbered prisoner looked, Violet thought, "respectable and maybe even honest."

When the job was done, and five and ten and then fifteen minutes passed without so much as a message from Loony, Violet began to get nervous. He ran out of anything to say to the prisoner whose hair he had cut, and sweat broke out on his face. He tiptoed and leaned this way and that, trying to catch sight of some free man in the outer world who might be called to, but he saw no one.

"*He* ain't going to come back," said the prisoner in the next cell with no attempt to disguise his pleasure. "You might as well make yourself at home."

When Violet turned his sweaty face to look at him, the prisoner in the next cell grinned at him with several golden teeth and said, "It's lucky you didn't bring them scissors of yours. We would cut your wee-wee off."

In fact, Violet had prided himself on his foresight in not bringing his scissors to the jail. Nobody had had to tell him not to. He made out with just his clippers and a comb.

But the prisoner in the next cell had no sooner made his disrespectful remark about Violet's wee-wee than Violet put his hand into his pants pocket and recognized there the shape and heft of his pocketknife, which was sharp.

This complicated his mind. "There I was," he said, "just as much a prisoner as if I had committed a crime and got caught, an innocent man in there with, for all I knew, felons and murderers—in *danger*. And that son of a bitch didn't do a thing but sit there all afternoon *grinning* at me, with them gold teeth! I tell you what, I'm telling you *right* now, I was in a heck of a fix."

Fortunately, there were only two prisoners, the one now honest in appearance and the one with the gold teeth.

Violet found that there was a corner he could stand in with nobody behind him, watching both of the prisoners and also the door of the jail for the return of Loony Riggins, his deliverer. All afternoon as he stood there, pretending not to be worried, his hands were deep in his pants pockets, keeping track of his wee-wee and his knife.

That afternoon lasted a month, maybe a year. By suppertime, Violet said, he had got a lot older, and was hungry too.

"One of them flunkeys brought in supper—as bad a food as ever I eat—and I said, 'I want out of here.'"

"And he said, 'I don't know nothing about you getting out of here. I ain't received no orders to that effect.'"

Loony didn't come back until dark, after Violet had given up all hope, and he came hurrying because he had suddenly remembered that he had forgotten Violet.

"I didn't know whether to kiss him or kill him," Violet said. He thought of doing both, and then he did neither, for it was wonderful to be free.

Of course, a man does not have to buy a car in order to get his hair cut (though there have been worse reasons). That was just an incidental advantage. What I really got the car for was to participate in the night-time social life of Hargrave. I was already participating, but I was getting tired of riding down there on the running boards of cars and in the back ends of trucks, and then maybe having to walk home. And so I squandered some of my savings and some of my wages in the interest of living life more fully and abundantly.

To be plain about it, I was lonesome. I wanted the company of women. The male society of my shop was pretty steadily available, and it provided a great variety of intelligence and amusement. But in Port William, for the reasons I have named, I was pretty much denied the society of women. Oh, at church and other places I would be among women, but I would not be *with* them. Maybe this is not easy to explain. It is not exactly a hardship but it is not a pleasure either to be among women who know you are there but don't look at you, or who speak to you in a distant and resolutely friendly way as if you might be anybody on earth except in particular yourself.

It was longing for the society of women that sent me smoking down to Hargrave, where I would dance the awkward jig of ineligible and undyingly hopeful bachelorhood. I wanted to talk with women while being looked straight at. I wanted to joke and laugh and flirt with women. I wanted to be with women who would let you do something nice for them—take them to the picture show, buy them some supper, hold open the car door while they got in and out, give them a little present of some kind. Whatever rewards might lie beyond would be fine with me, but in those days what I elaborated in my waking dreams were the possible pleasures of the mere society of women.

My situation seemed to call for the society of *bold* women, who would not be put off by my ineligibility, my semi-youth, my rather obscure handsomeness. They did not need to be women of the higher type, or of penetrating intelligence. Like many another man in my position, I rambled among the beer joints and roadhouses, and enjoyed mostly the society of barmaids and waitresses. Because of my duties at the shop, I would often get to Hargrave late. I would park the Zephyr and go into the dim light and the mixed smells of spilled beer and cooking meat and disinfectant and urine and perfume and sweat, as pungent as a fox's den. If I could—if I didn't get hailed by any of my Port William colleagues—I would sit at a booth or table by myself and order a beer.

Sometimes I would just sit there by myself and drink my beer while

Mr. Ernest Tubb, on the jukebox, wished that his blue moon once again would turn to gold. He did not wish it prettily, I thought, but he wished it sincerely. After a couple of beers I would wish it sincerely also.

If it was late enough and business was slow, one of the waitresses might come and sit down with me, and we would visit. These women were bold enough to suit anybody—they were knowing and unsurprised—and the ones that liked me I liked back. Often one or another would go out with me after closing time, or we would arrange a date for the picture show on Sunday night.

Sometimes, at first, my nights in Hargrave would have no social result at all. Or the only social result of a Saturday night would be a date for a picture show on Sunday night, and I would have to bum another ride to Hargrave and maybe walk home after the show. It was completely awkward, and I would have to ask afterward why I had gone to so much trouble for so little pleasure. So you can see why I bought the Zephyr. But even after I got the car, there would be a sort of hangover of vanity and futility—much hankering and trouble in return for satisfactions that were small and fleeting. And then I got together with Clydie.

My favorite sitting and beer-drinking place was the Rosebud Cafe, just a few steps off the courthouse square. It was a friendly, homey place that served generous hamburgers, and excellent fried oysters in the months whose names contained an *r*. After a while (I had just entered the era of the Zephyr), Clydie came to work there. She was Clyda Greatlow—Violet Greatlow's niece, in fact. But whereas the Greatlows tended to be large and lumbering ("swole-gutted," Burley Coulter called them) and dark, Clydie was slender ("a mite on the buxom side of scrawny," she would say), quick on her feet, and a freckled redhead. She had a lot of humor but no nonsense.

I got so I really liked her. And she seemed to like me. When she got a break in her work she would come and sit with me. I would give her a cigarette and light it for her, and she would relax for a few minutes and we would talk. It was a little scrap of homelife we would have then. We would exchange the news about ourselves and tell each other our stories. When we met we both were more or less thirty-four. I was feeling a little shelf-worn, and maybe she was too.

Clydie lived with and, I believe, pretty much supported her widowed mother, Mrs. Sigurnia Greatlow, and her old-maid aunt, Aunt Beulah. Miss Sigurnia and Aunt Beulah were elderly and needed some looking after. Clydie never said so, but I think she might already have married somebody if she had not been caught in obligation to the old ladies. She was Miss Sigurnia's only child and didn't feel she could leave, and it wasn't the sort of household a young woman would feel like bringing a husband into. They lived in a rickety big old white frame house in not the best part of town. Miss Sigurnia was deaf and tended to stay either somewhat behind or out of the running entirely, crocheting an interminable sequence of doilies and listening to "Ma Perkins" and "Our Gal Sunday" and "The Romance of Helen Trent" on the radio turned up to thunderous volume. The roost was ruled by Aunt Beulah, who had her ways from which she deviated no more than a train from the track. Her hearing was as sharp as Miss Sigurnia's was dull. Aunt Beulah could hear the dust motes collide in a sunbeam; she could hear spiders chewing on flies. Aunt Beulah thought the world had done her a long list of disservices, and she kept the list faithfully and knew it by heart and recited it often. She was, in fact, a sort of old-age version of Cecelia Overhold. She felt that the entire population of Hargrave had failed to recognize her innate superiority. "People in Hargrave," she would often say, "don't know whom I am." She was in favor of perfection and hated everything that was not perfect, and for this she had God's permission. I liked hearing Clydie tell stories about Aunt Beulah because they were fairly terrifying, and because Clydie had the grace to think they were funny. Clydie's life was poor and hard enough, but in her stories and her laughter you never felt any suggestion of complaint. You felt strength. She had the courage of a bear.

I was a longish time asking Clydie to go out with me. I was enjoying things as they were, and I was afraid she would turn me down, which would change things. I had seen that she was a woman of penetrating intelligence. Somehow I had learned that she had a boyfriend who came to Hargrave during the tobacco market and who returned from time to time to see her. But I noticed that in her conversations with me, which were getting more familiar, she never mentioned this other fellow, and that made me think the way might be clear.

I couldn't bear to ask her during one of our conversations, because it would have interrupted something I did not want interrupted. But one night when I had ordered a beer and she had brought it, and "San Antonio Rose," a particular favorite of mine, was playing on the jukebox, and the singer sang, "Be-neath the stars all alo-one," I said, "Fair maiden, might I have the inexpressible pleasure of escorting you to the picture show?"

She painted me a brief mustache with the wet rag she was carrying in her hand, and went her way.

In a little while, though, when she got a break she came back and sat down. She looked straight at me, for I was watching her and waiting, and said, "Why, sure. When?"

I would be pleased to say I loved her, but "liked" is probably the better word. I liked her hugely and thoroughly and admired her and was in a way crazy about her, but I did not love her in the way that, later, I would come to love Mattie Chatham. She did not overly occupy my mind when we were apart. Though she gave me much happiness, I did not long for her. I think I took my cue from her in this, and she defined for us the way we would be. We were dear companions, but we were independent. I think she always kept her other beau, the tobacco buyer from somewhere down south, and we both pretended that I didn't know it.

She was no pushover. She interested me enough that I was willing just to come along and wait to see what was going to happen. We sometimes went to the picture show, but what Clydie really liked to do was dance. On her night off, or late, after her shift was finished, we would go out to Riverwood or one of the other roadhouses where there was always a jukebox and sometimes even a band. Clydie liked for us to have a drink or two of whiskey, just enough to "spook us up a little," as she put it, and make us a little dreamy, and then we would dance to slow songs in the semidarkness of one of those old nightspots. I didn't really know how to dance. I did what Clydie called "the walking hug," but she was biased toward the hugging part herself, and we did fine.

It came about that on nights when it suited her, which was pretty often, when we would get back to her house and I would be bringing the Zephyr to a halt, Clydie would say, "Won't you come in for a cup of tea?"

It was some tea. There was an outside stairway that went up to her room at the back of the house, like the one that went up to my own upstairs, and we would go up, Clydie quietly and I silently. The rule was that I *had* to be as silent as if I weren't there. Clydie and I passed our intimate life together inside a little globe of silence that leaked not a murmur of mine into the hearing of Aunt Beulah.

I remember the first night that Clydie invited me in. I said, "I would be delighted, my little Rose of San Antone."

She said, "Jayber, listen. From the time we get out of this car, you have *got* to be quiet."

I was a little whiskey-silly and excited too, and I didn't listen. We got out and I took her arm and said something out loud, carrying on in a big way.

And then she took hold of *my* arm with a strength that was just shocking. She had her ways of clarifying your mind, when she wanted to. She whispered right in my ear, "*Shh!* If you make one more *squeak*, Jayber Crow, I'm going to knock you down and scream my friggin' head off!"

You can imagine that I crept in to my reward even as a field mouse to its nest.

17

Forsaking All Others

Troy Chatham did not go to the war. Like me, he was 4-F. He had a "trick knee," the result of a basketball injury. This had not much interfered with his participation in basketball, but it kept him out of the army. Perhaps it was thought that he could not endure "severe bodily exertion"— although, like me, he proved able to do so. Perhaps it was feared that he might become a "pension problem." Troy called it his "million-dollar wound."

"Trick *knee!*" said Burley Coulter. "What he's got is a trick *head.*"

Troy and Mattie were married in the late fall of 1945, shortly after her twenty-first birthday. The wedding would have taken place three years earlier, when Mattie and Troy graduated from high school, except that Athey and Della Keith would not consent to it. I believe that Athey and Della were right, but being right need not count for much, especially when the proof comes too late. And when the proof comes, what do you have to compare it with, so you know that proof is what it is?

Mattie was an obedient daughter who loved her parents. But they had tried her to the limit and they knew it. They were in a bad fix. Finally, they had to consent to a marriage they did not like—either that or lose the friendship of their only daughter in the same marriage without their consent. Mattie was a grown woman in love, and they had to let her go, with their blessing, enduring what could not be helped. And there was no use in thinking of that fluid, glistening instant that always seems, in looking back, to have come between what might have happened and what happened, when one might have made some little choice that would have changed forever the course of things.

Troy brought nothing to the marriage but himself and an automobile in which he had invested most of his earnings from wage-working and the little tobacco crop he raised with his father. He had sunk down in actual achievement from his days on the basketball team, but he continued to present himself in the manner of a star. He was all show, and he had the conviction, as such people do, that show is the same as substance. He didn't think he was fooling other people; he had fooled himself. He thought he saw what he thought we saw. Sometimes after he left my shop, I would discover that my teeth were clenched.

It would have been easier if I could have thought that Mattie was willfully foolish or silly, in some way deserving of him. But this was impossible for me to think, given any number of things I knew. I had to propose to myself that she had seen something in him that I had not seen, and then I had to wonder what. I thought, and hoped, it was more than his undeniable physical attractiveness, though that might have been enough. I admitted, reluctantly, that he had energy; he was not lazy. With greater reluctance, I required myself to admit that he was not stupid. He had, in fact, plenty of intelligence—plenty more than he ever used, in fact. And then I thought, "Suppose there is somewhere in him, after all, some tenderness that he has shown only to her." And then perhaps I could imagine a little how it was. Suppose you were a young woman, offering yourself to the life of this world, to the use of the life force, as young women do. Suppose this young man, excellently handsome and graceful and strong, out of his unquestioning self-confidence, turned toward you with tenderness, with need, such as he had shown to no one else. Suppose that you could not know that you yourself had made the tenderness in him that you felt. Suppose that within his tenderness you felt rewarded, cherished, and safe. Do you see?

Even yet, when I think of them at that time, newly married in their beauty and their young longing, I feel a shiver go over me, and it is not a shiver of foreboding, of knowing what is to come. It is a shiver of recognition of what the two of them desired, and of what, for a while, they even had.

Not long after they married, they moved into a newly vacated tenant house on the Keith place, for where else would they have gone? Nowhere better. In offering the house, Athey and Della did the obvious and the right thing, and at the same time began the undoing of everything.

It was a pretty good small house in a shady yard, well back in the bottom at the end of a lane. It had a good garden spot and its own outbuildings and barn. The spring of 1946 felt full of promise. The war was over. Prices were good—better, maybe, than they ever have been since. The new crop year was beginning. Troy put in his plant beds and started his plowing. Della walked back across the fields every morning to help Mattie fix up the house, and when he had his own work caught up Athey would come along. For a while, it may even have seemed to the Keiths that the old farm had received its rightful inheritors who would carry it on when the time came.

Athey Keith was one of the best farmers in the Port William neighborhood in his time. He had five hundred acres, nearly all in the river bottom, nearly all arable except for the hollows and the timber patches. Athey raised tobacco and corn, followed by wheat or barley, and then by clover and grass. He had cattle and sheep and hogs. In the long barn behind his house he would have a dozen or so good work mules of various ages. He would buy a few yearlings every fall, and sell a broke team or two in the spring. Everything on the place, including the crops and animals, was well kept and looked good, for Athey would have it no other way.

I can't tell you exactly how Athey managed his farm. My knowledge of farming is mainly from looking and hearsay and my outdated memories of Uncle Othy's little sideline farm at Squires Landing, and so I can't give as many details as you might like. But Athey interested me, and I listened both to him and to whatever was said about him. What I do know is that he used his land conservatively. In any year, by far the greater part of his land would be under grass—for, as he would say, "The land slopes even in the bottoms, and the water runs." He was always studying his fields, thinking of ways to protect them. He was doing what a lot of farmers say they want to do: he was improving his land; he was going to leave it better than he had found it. I know too that his principle was always to maintain a generous margin of surplus between his livestock and the available feed, just as between the fertility of his land and his demands upon it. "Wherever I look," he said, "I want to see more than I need, and have more than I use." And this is a principle very different from what would be the principle of his son-in-law, often voiced in his heyday: "Never let a quarter's worth of equity stand idle. Use it or borrow against it."

I learned a good deal about Athey from men who had been his tenants. In Athey's time, and surely before, there had always been two tenant families on the place, each occupying the small farmstead allotted to it. As far as I ever discovered, Athey dealt generously with them, seeing that they had all the garden space they could use, pasture for their milk cows, grain for their poultry and meat hogs, and firewood from the woodlots and fencerows. He gave them work and paid them fairly when they were not in their crops. His assumption was that if they prospered, he would prosper. Not all of them liked him—not all of his neighbors liked him—for he was strict in his ways, and, though he was not a talkative man, there was never much room between what he said and what he thought. Whether they liked him or not, Athey's tenants tended to prosper. In my time there have been several landowning farmers in the Port William neighborhood who got their start, and a good deal of their knowledge, as Athey's tenants.

The Keith place included seventy-five or eighty acres of very good timber standing around slues and hollows, along the river, and in the sizable corner that lay on the far side of Coulter Branch. Athey logged the woodlands on the main tract only for firewood and the posts and lumber he needed on the place. The woods beyond the branch he never used at all. This was maybe the finest stand of trees in our part of the country, and Athey was proud of it. He protected it from timber buyers by asking considerably more for it than its market value. As long as he could make

a living farming, that patch of timber would always be worth more to
him than to them. He called it the Nest Egg. Whose nest egg it was he
never said.

Coming into my shop one day and finding Athey in the chair, Burley
Coulter hung up his hat and sat down and said nothing, and then said,
"Athey, ain't you going to sell your big woods down by the branch?"

The question was oddly intoned. Burley was trying to sound as if he
thought Athey ought to sell it, in case he was going to. But he was asking
because he was *afraid* Athey was going to, and he was anxious to find
out.

"Oh, I *reckon* not," Athey said.

I knew that Athey knew that Burley was anxious. Athey wouldn't lie
to him, but he didn't want to relieve him too quickly either. He was starting to enjoy himself. "Oh, I *reckon* not" could have meant either that he
wasn't going to sell the timber, or that he was thinking of selling it.

"Well," Burley said, shifting in his chair, "they tell me you been offered
a right smart piece of money for it."

"Why, Burley, it's worth more than that to me just for the squirrels."

Burley said, still doubtful, "You eating them squirrels, Athey, or just
raising them for the market?"

"Oh, I reckon I eat 'em. There's some mighty good eating has come
out of them woods, Burley," Athey said, knowing that Burley knew this
better than he did. He smiled mostly to himself, as if he knew many
other things besides.

Burley, who now saw that Athey had leveled with him about the sale
of the woods, leaned back. "It takes a mighty good rifle to shoot a squirrel out of one of them tall trees."

"I wait for them to come down," Athey said.

That was a fairly long conversation for Athey at that time. He was still
in his power then. When he would come in for a haircut, he would just
be pausing in the midst of a swing; he always had something going on at
home that he wanted to get back to.

Della kept as busy in and about the house as Athey in the fields and
barns—cleaning and washing, cooking, laying up food, feeding hands at

harvesttime. Between them they kept the cellar and smokehouse well stocked and more always coming in from the garden and barnyard and fields.

"Hard work makes for a good appetite," Doc Markman said learnedly in my shop one day.

"What helps *my* appetite," said Athey, "is knowing I got something to *eat*."

They were a sight to see, Della and Athey were, in their vigorous years. They had about them a sort of intimation of abundance, as though, like magicians, they might suddenly fill the room with potatoes, onions, turnips, summer squashes, and ears of corn drawn from their pockets. Their place had about it that quality of bottomless fecundity, its richness both in evidence and in reserve.

It was because of what he had in reserve that most people called Athey "Mr. Keith." Even Uncle Othy called him "Mr. Keith," though he had known him as a boy. When we would pass the Keith place on our longish buggy ride to church on Sunday mornings, Uncle Othy would always say something complimentary: "Well, I see Mr. Keith has got a good crop of corn, as usual"; "I see Mr. Keith has got a fine pair of young mules."

Burley called him "Athey" by the same privilege by which he hunted his woods: Athey liked Burley; they were neighbors. I call him "Athey" because, after he and Della moved into Port William and he began coming almost every day to sit a while with me in my shop, he told me to do so, acknowledging, I think, his decline in the world from host to guest.

For (and, you might say, of course) that is where Athey was going to end up: in town. He and Troy were different, almost opposite, kinds of men.

Athey said, "Wherever I look, I want to see more than I need." Troy said, in effect, "Whatever I see, I want." What he asked of the land was all it had. He had hardly got his first crop in the ground before he began to say things critical of Athey and his ways. "Why, *hell!*" he would say, "it's hard to tell *what* that old place would produce if he would just plow it." Or: "Why the hell would a man plow just forty acres of a farm he could plow all of?" He would say these things leaning back in his chair, his ankle crossed over his knee, his foot twitching. He was speaking as a young man of the modern age coming now into his hour, held back only by the outmoded ways of his elders. This was the substance of his talking at town, where mostly he was looked at and listened to without comment. He was not yet ready to present his case to Athey. So far, he was just propping himself up, asserting his superiority perhaps just by habit; nothing had required him to suspect that the reference point or measure of what he did or said might not be himself.

In coming to the Keith place, he had come into an order that perhaps he did not even recognize. Over a long time, the coming and passing of several generations, the old farm had settled into its patterns and cycles of work—its annual plowing moving from field to field; its animals arriving by birth or purchase, feeding and growing, thriving and departing. Its patterns and cycles were virtually the farm's own understanding of what it was doing, of what it could do without diminishment. This order was not unintelligent or rigid. It tightened and slackened, shifted and changed in response to the markets and the weather. The Depression had changed it somewhat, and so had the war. But through all changes so far, the farm had endured. Its cycles of cropping and grazing, thought and work, were articulations of its wish to cohere and to last. The farm, so to speak, desired all of its lives to flourish.

Athey was not exactly, or not only, what is called a "landowner." He was the farm's farmer, but also its creature and belonging. He lived its life, and it lived his; he knew that, of the two lives, his was meant to be the smaller and the shorter.

Of all this Troy had no idea, not a suspicion. He thought the farm existed to serve and enlarge him. And it seemed that this was the way it was going to be. In that first year of 1946, because of the newness of his situation and Athey's enforcement of the farm's restraints and demands— by working much and spending little, and by Mattie's savings and skills learned from her mother—Troy did well. He contracted little debt, easily paid out of the year's earnings, with a good sum of money left over. All he had to do was learn and keep on, work and be patient.

In the fall of that year, Mattie and Troy had their first child—Della Elizabeth, named for her grandmothers, and called Liddie. Later, just before Christmas, after he had sold his crop, Troy bought a tractor and several implements, using a considerable portion of his year's profit as a down payment and borrowing the rest from the Independent Farmers Bank. In town—but not, or not yet, in Athey's hearing—he said that in the spring we were going to see him "cut loose."

Buying a tractor at that time was not unusual. A lot of people were doing it. The young men who had been in the war were used to motor-driven machinery. The government was teaching a new way of farming in night courses for the veterans. Tractors and other farm machines were all of a sudden available as never before, and farmhands were scarcer than before. And so we began a process of cause-and-effect that is hard to understand clearly, even looking back. Did the machines displace the people from the farms, or were the machines drawn onto the farms because the people already were leaving to take up wage work in factories and the building trades and such? Both, I think.

You couldn't see, back then, that this process would build up and go ever faster, until finally it would ravel out the entire old fabric of family work and exchanges of work among neighbors. The new way of farming was a way of dependence, not on land and creatures and neighbors but on machines and fuel and chemicals of all sorts, *bought* things, and on the sellers of bought things—which made it finally a dependence on credit. The odd thing was, people just assumed that all the purchasing and borrowing would merely make life easier and better on all the little farms. Most people didn't dream, then, that before long a lot of little farmers would buy and borrow their way out of farming, and bigger and bigger farmers would be competing with their neighbors (or with doctors from the city) for the available land. The time was going to come— it is clear enough now—when there would not be enough farmers left and the farms of Port William would be as dependent as the farms of California on the seasonal labor of migrant workers.

It is hard, too, to say that anybody was exactly blamable for this—or anybody in particular.

Old farmers like Athey Keith, who understood or at least *felt* what was happening and what it would cost, were ignored, laughed off by young farmers like Troy Chatham. Young farmers who *ought* to have understood just didn't. People followed their own ideas of their own advantage, and it was clear only later, and too late, that everybody's idea led off in a slightly different direction from everybody else's. After the Depression and the war and the years of work that they were now beginning to think of as slow and too hard, the country people were trying to get away from demanding circumstances. That was why I bought the Zephyr. We couldn't quite see at the time, or didn't want to know, that it was the demanding circumstances that had kept us together.

Troy went into debt and bought his new equipment because he didn't want to be held back by demanding circumstances. He was young and strong and ambitious. He wanted to be a star. The tractor greatly increased the power and speed of work. With it he could work more land. He could work longer. Because it had electric lights and did not get tired, he could work at night.

When it came time to plan for the next year, wishing them to be friends and eventual partners before Athey would die and Troy would become the farm's farmer, Athey walked Troy over the sod ground that was to be broken for row crops, showing him the outlines of the plow-lands and where the backfurrows were to run. And then he led him on to show him the next year's cropland, and then the next year's, laying the pattern before him. None of what I'm telling now is guesswork. Troy talked about himself in town as if he were the subject of a news broadcast. To not know what was going on, I would have had to be deaf and maybe also blind.

Such knowledge ought to have passed from Athey to Troy as a matter of course, in the process of daily work and talk. And it would have, if Troy had been willing to have Athey as a teacher, let alone a friend. But the connection between them was already strained. Troy wanted to go in his own direction—or so he thought, poor fellow. His way, even when he had to work with Athey, was to hold himself a little aside and keep quiet. It was the quietest he ever was, probably. He was protecting himself from knowing what he did not want to know, thinking that his silence signified his superiority. He did his talking in town, and Port William listened, nodded, scratched its ears, grunted, and kept its opinions mostly to itself.

Troy's sole response to that winter afternoon's walk with Athey was: "We need to grow more corn."

This brought Athey to a stop. The law of the farm was in the balance between crops (including hay and pasture) and livestock. The farm would have no more livestock than it could carry without strain. No more land would be plowed for grain crops than could be fertilized with manure from the animals. No more grain would be grown than the animals could eat. Except in case of unexpected surpluses or deficiencies, the farm did not sell or buy livestock feed. "I mean my grain and hay to leave my place *on foot*," Athey liked to say. This was a conserving principle; it strictly limited both the amount of land that would be plowed and the amount of supplies that would have to be bought. Athey did not save money at the expense of his farm or his family, but he looked upon spending it as a last resort; he spent no more than was necessary, and he hated debt. You can see where my sympathies were. He was, in his son-in-law's opinion, "tight" and unwilling to take the necessary risks. "Risk is necessary in this farming game," Troy said. He meant extraordinary financial risk—as if the risk of hail, wind, flood, drouth, pests and diseases, injury and death were not enough. "You've got to spend money to make money."

Troy's demand to grow more corn was a challenge, Athey knew, not only or even mainly to himself but to the farm and its established order; he felt a shudder fall through him, and he knew that he was being changed; he was being pushed toward something he had not imagined, let alone intended. He looked down at his feet and thought, his right wrist caught as usual in his left hand under the tail of his jacket. And then he looked away and thought.

"If you raise more corn," he said, "you'll have to buy fertilizer." He said "you," for he had determined that he himself would not grow the corn or pay for the fertilizer, and he knew that Troy would have to borrow against the crop for the fertilizer.

"Hell, *I* don't mind buying fertilizer!" Troy said.

Athey agreed to let him grow ten extra acres. Which, Troy thought, was not enough. He arranged to grow thirty more acres, on the shares, on a neighboring farm. Pretty soon he would be working away from home, into the night, while Mattie, carrying the baby on her hip, went about doing his barn chores.

And so the farm came under the influence of a new pattern, and this was the pattern of a fundamental disagreement such as it had never seen before. It was a disagreement about time and money and the use of the world. The tractor seemed to have emanated directly from Troy's own mind, his need to go headlong, day or night, and perform heroic feats. But Athey and his tenant and his tenant's boys were still doing their work with teams of mules. Troy liked to climb on the tractor, open the throttle, and just go, whatever the time of day, his mind invested with the machine's indifference to weariness and to features of the landscape. A day, to Athey, was measured by daylight and by the endurance of living bodies; it was divided in two by dinnertime; it ended at suppertime. Athey worked at a gait that in his time some had found to be too swift, but which was now revealed as patient.

The conflicts were inescapable, were just *there* as part and parcel of the farm and what was happening on it. The work of the farm now went on at two different rates of speed and power and endurance. It became hard to cooperate, not because cooperation was impossible but because the tractor and the teams embodied two different kinds of will, almost two different intentions. It was a difference of character and history. At the time all this began, Troy was twenty-three years old and Athey sixty-seven. Athey belonged to that life that had, in fact, ended with the war; he could not imagine the life that was to come. Troy, who could not imagine the older life, was overflowing with the impatience of the new one.

And Troy felt also that he had a lot to prove. As it turned out, he would have more reason every year to feel so.

Year by year, he increased his rented acreage elsewhere, thereby increasing the pressure on Athey to give him more say-so over the Keith place. For Troy would one day farm that farm, and Athey wanted his interest there. Little by little, he began giving way to Troy's wants and ideas, and the old pattern of the farm began to give way.

Judging from what Troy repeated in town, conversations between him and Athey finally degenerated into one-sentence exchanges. Athey would tell what he had done in the last half day or day, and Troy, laughing or in anger, would repeat some version of his final judgment on all things slow and old: "Shit! I could've done that in two hours!" Part of

Troy's resentment came from knowing, without needing to be told, that "the old man" thought his work was too fast and too rough, that he lacked sympathy and was too hard on things. Athey had only to stand by and look and say nothing, and his point was made.

Troy had begun to see Athey and the others as "in the way." He would tell of working with them, for instance, on the same mowing land, and having to slow down until they could pull out at the turns to let him and his tractor go ahead. "By God," he would say, "I just wanted to drive right over the top of 'em!"

I confess that I heard this with a sense of guilt, for by the time Troy began to say such things I had bought the Zephyr and had succumbed to something of the same impatience. My wonderful machine sometimes altered my mind so that I, lately a pedestrian myself, fiercely resented all such impediments on the road. Even at my sedate top speed of forty miles an hour, I *hated* anything that required me to slow down. My mind raged and fumed and I cursed aloud at farmers driving their stock across the road, at indecisive possums, at children on bicycles. Ease of going was translated without pause into a principled unwillingness to stop. Hadn't I been there and didn't I know it? And so, self-accused, having begun by resenting the insult to Athey, I ended by yielding Troy a little laugh and a nod of understanding, which shamed me and did not make me like him any better.

In 1949, Mattie gave birth to their second child, named as if, and perhaps intentionally, for nobody: James William, called Jimmy.

18

Untold

It was impossible to know of the trouble down at the Keith place without supposing that Mattie was caught somewhere in the middle, and isolated. Her mother could only have been torn and troubled by the conflict, but Della was free in the privacy of her own heart to take sides and stand by Athey. Athey, mostly in silence, was entirely on his own side.

But Mattie, I thought, was divided. Though she was in love with her young husband, she was her father's daughter still. Somewhere, sometime, the full force of their difference would have to be suffered—and Mattie would be the one who suffered it. That she was her parents' child meant, as Troy's ambition and his arrogance grew clear, that she would finally have to love him without approving of him. In fact, their marriage settled early upon the pattern it would always have: she was trying to wind up at home the thread that he unraveled elsewhere. He had been seized by a daydream of "farming big," having what he wanted. What he wanted, as time would reveal, was to be a sort of farming businessman, an executive who would "manage" the "operation" from an office with a phone while other people (and machines) did the actual work. He got so far finally as to build and furnish a "farm office," which he never really had time to sit down in. While he connived and contrived and borrowed, and drove day into night, trying (as he learned to put it) to "increase the profit margin by increasing volume," she gardened and canned and tended to her hen flock and milked the cows and did whatever else Troy "didn't have time to do," and of course she took care of the children.

She was taking up the slack. We all knew it. One Saturday afternoon somebody waiting for a haircut said something about Troy Chatham's tractor equipment, for he already had more than anybody around. And Burley Coulter, who had my razor hone on his thigh, sharpening his knife, said without looking up, "The best equipment *he's* got is his wife." Somebody laughed, and somebody said, "Yep," and everybody nodded.

But the remarkable thing was that Mattie Chatham never looked like a woman who was put upon and divided in her loyalties and having a hard time; she didn't look as though she would have welcomed sympathy, or as though she needed it. She was not her parents' child for nothing. She was going about her life, taking her pleasures as she found them, suffering what was hers to suffer, doing what she had to do. She had about her no air of self-pity or complaint. And this could only have been because, in her own heart, she was not pitying herself or complaining. It was as though her very difficulties had confirmed her in her sense of herself and her capabilities.

I knew Mattie Chatham a long time, and I never knew her to falsify or misrepresent herself. Whatever she gave you—a look, a question, an answer—was honest. She didn't tell you everything she knew or thought. She never made reference even by silence to anything she suffered. But in herself she was present. She was present in her dealings with other people. She was right there. She was, to my eye, a good mother who liked and enjoyed her children, leaving them free within limits that both she and they understood. But she was also coming into responsibility for the community.

You don't have to know Port William long before you see that whatever coherence it has is largely owing to certain women. Maybe, since I no longer live *in* Port William, I shouldn't generalize about it, but this is the way it seemed to me then. Art Rowanberry was surely right (mostly right) in saying that "people in Port William don't have their own business." One result is that people know who needs help. In Port William the women, like the men, talk. It is wonderful how secrets, always told secretly, can get around; I have been told the same secret three times in one day, each time with a warning to tell nobody. But some women seem more likely to act on what they know than most men. The men are not uncharitable; they are quick to get together to harvest a crop for a neighbor who gets sick. But it is the women more than the men who see to it that cooked food goes where it is needed, that no house goes without fuel in the winter, that no child goes without toys at Christmas, that the preacher knows where he should go with a word of comfort. This is a charity that includes the church rather than the other way around. Margaret Feltner was one of the women who saw to such things; so was Della Keith; so, as she came into her time, was Mattie Chatham.

Of course, my semipublic participation in the nightlife of Hargrave was known in Port William. I had no more of "my own business" than anybody else. And of course, my reputation as an ineligible bachelor barber, grave digger, and church janitor (known to partake of the manly nightlife of Port William *and* to favor the society of bold women in the nightspots of Hargrave) made me perhaps always a little more hopelessly marginal to the womanhood of Port William.

And yet I was something more than an observer. I was more or less tolerated because of my usefulness, and also, I believe, because of the remote chance that even so black a sheep might yet be washed whiter than snow. I continued to attend the services and other gatherings at the church, just in case I was needed to open or shut the windows or bring in extra chairs, and to make sure all the lights were turned off afterward. And so I was having a good bit to do, in a servantly way, with the women, who often had reason to tell me what needed to be done or what needed getting ready for. Mattie Chatham, as time went on and the older women became less able, had a way of being involved and seeing to things. Her way was quiet and unobtrusive—and effective; she got things done. She was never bossy (as, for instance, Mrs. Pauline Gibbs always was) but was just simply and quietly kind. She certainly made nothing special of me. But when she asked me to do something, she asked clearly knowing that she was putting me to trouble. She would say, "Jayber, would you mind?" And she always thanked me. She was considerate. That was one of the reasons I remained aware of her. Looking back, when the time came to look back, I could see that I was extraordinarily aware of her even then.

She had come into her beauty. This was not the beauty of her youth and freshness, of which she had had a plenty. The beauty that I am speaking of now was that of a woman who has come into knowledge and into strength and who, knowing her hardships, trusts her strength and goes about her work even with a kind of happiness, serene somehow, and secure. It was the beauty she would always have. Her eyes had not changed. They still seemed to exert a power, as if whatever she looked at (including, I thought, me) was brightened.

And then one Friday not long after the summer solstice of 1950 (at the start of another war), the most deciding event of my life took place, and I was not the same ever again. Vacation Bible School was going on at the church. I went up in the early afternoon as usual to clean up and prepare the building for the Sunday services. I finished my work in the sanctuary, and then because classes and "activities" were going on I went outside to putter around until the building would be empty.

It was a pretty afternoon, not too warm. Mattie had brought the littlest children out into the yard to play games, her own Liddie among them. I picked up some trash along the road in front of the church, then began pulling some weeds out of the shrubbery, aware all the time of Mattie and the children, and pausing now and again to watch.

To be plain about it, I didn't think much of Vacation Bible School. As a product of The Good Shepherd, I didn't think much of confinement. If I had ever gone to Vacation Bible School, I thought, I would not have liked it; I would have been too much aware of the invitation of the free and open summer day. It was nevertheless a great pleasure to me to watch Mattie and the children. She was guiding their play and playing with them, not being very insistent about anything, and they all were having a good time.

I knew well the work and worry she had pending at home, and yet in that moment she was as free with the children as if she had been a child herself—as free as a child, but with a generosity and watchfulness that were anything but childish. She was just perfectly there with them in her pleasure.

I was all of a sudden overcome with love for her. It was the strongest moment I had known, violent in its suddenness and completeness, and yet also the quietest. I had been utterly changed, and had not stirred. It was as though she had, in the length of a breath, assumed in my mind a new dimension. I no longer merely saw her as one among the objects of the world but felt in every nerve the heft and touch of her. I felt her take form within my own form. I felt her come into being within me, as in the morning of the world.

This love did not come to me like an arrow piercing my heart. Instead, it was as though Port William and all the world suddenly quietly fell away from me, leaving me standing in the air, alone, with the ache of acrophobia in the soles of my feet and my heart hollowed out with long-ing, in need of what I did not have.

For a time—how long I don't know—I was lost to myself, standing there still as a tree, and I have always wondered if she saw and knew. And then somehow, as uncertain of my contact with the ground as Julep Smallwood drunk, I made my way out of town into the woods, and sat down and put my head in my hands.

Such a thing is maybe one of the liabilities of ineligible bachelorhood. Maybe it is one of the liabilities of manhood. For a long time I did not know what to make of it, and I suffered from my ignorance. What busi-ness had an ineligible bachelor to be in love with a married woman? Had it been only an infatuation, a desire striking and wounding and passing on by, it would have been a waste of pain. And how was I to know that a waste of pain was not what it was? I felt much and knew nothing. I had been touched by power but not by knowledge. There was nothing to do but submit to the trial of it. After a long time, it proved by its own suffer-ing that love itself was what it was, and I am thankful.

My dreams changed. Before, I had rarely dreamed of any woman I had been attracted to in my waking life. I would dream of women I had glimpsed in passing, or of women I had never seen before, who might, for all I knew, have been nymphs or goddesses. Now I dreamed of Mattie Chatham, of her herself.

I told nobody. Nobody knew of it but me. That alone was a revela-tion. I had always made it a rule of thumb that there were no real secrets in Port William, but now I knew that this was not so. It was the secrets *between* people that got out. The secrets that people knew alone were the ones that were kept, the knowledge too painful or too dear to speak of. If so urging a thing as I now knew was known only to me, then what must other people know that they had never told? I felt a strange new respect for the heads I barbered. I knew that the dead carried with them out of this world things they could not give away.

From that moment up in the churchyard, Mattie Chatham became a demand and a trouble on my mind. I began to contrive (usually without success) to be near her. I wanted, as I would say to myself, to be in her *presence,* as if her presence were a fragrance, or a light that was within her and shone around her. And within this influence or power that I called her presence was Mattie herself, her palpable self, ripe and beautiful, unimagining, it seemed, within my fully awakened imagining of her, within my awareness unaware. There were times when my desire stood before me like a spoiled child, insisting that it should be given what it did not have—what it did not know it could not have.

Looking back, I still feel a kind of shame about that passage of my life. I ceased to be solitary (as, in a manner of speaking, I have always been) and became furtive, leading a secret life in my thoughts, which were always as urgent and unrefusable as a knock on the door late at night, and which always led straight to impossibilities that seemed nonetheless possible. I might as well have been back at the orphanage, surrounded by strangers and dreaming of home.

Thinking of Mattie, I began to imagine the intimacy of marriage, which I thought might be a name for admission into presence. In marriage, a man and a woman might come gladly into each other's presence. This was something, I think, that would not have occurred to me in thinking of Clydie, who always consciously reserved something of herself. Clydie was always holding a high card that she wouldn't play—or maybe couldn't play, given her circumstances. But what moved me so toward Mattie was the sense that she withheld nothing; she was not a woman of defenses or devices. Though she might be divided in her affection and loyalty, within herself she was whole and clear. She would be wholly present within her presence.

But thinking of Mattie's marriage, I saw too how a marriage, in bringing two people into each other's presence, must include loneliness and error. I imagined a moment when the husband and wife realize that their marriage includes their faults, that they do not perfect each other, and that in making their marriage they also fail it and must carry to the grave things they cannot give away.

Thinking of Mattie's marriage and of the certainty of pain and loneliness in it gave hope to my desire, which insisted upon itself without reference to anything else. One thing it did was make me think myself desirable. This love had come to stand beside me and it was mine because in certain respects it overruled me and I belonged to it. It wasn't perfect in its mastery. I went on with my workaday life and my pleasures about as I had before. I allowed, I think, no change in appearances that would have been a giveaway. I hadn't been a boy in a long time and was pretty firm in my habits. And yet I was changed.

Clydie saw it. She would say, patting me with her hand as if I were a horse, "Jayber, my poor old boy, where has your mind gone off to?" And she would give me a grin, seeing something, and yet only guessing, and yet hard to fool.

And I would say, "Oh, lovely Clydie, *you* know where my mind goes when it goes off."

And she would say, leaving her question aside, for it was her principle to claim no rights over me as a way of warning me to claim none over her, "Yes, my dear Jayber, I know one place."

But for longer than I wish it had, my longing for Mattie Chatham held its hand over my thoughts and dreams and the visions of my mind, so that I was never satisfied for long and never much at rest.

Another thing it did was make Troy Chatham an object of fascination to me, second only to Mattie herself.

From watching Troy when he was more or less alone and when he was with other people, I knew that he was a lonely man, and I knew this without compassion. He was lonely because he could imagine himself as anything but himself and as anywhere but where he was. His competitiveness and self-centeredness cut him off from any thought of shared life. He wanted to have more because he thought that having more would make him able to live more, and he was lonely because he never thought of the sources, the places, where he was going to get what he wanted to have, or of what his having it might cost others. It was a loneliness that sometimes even he felt; you could see it. A self-praiser has got to accept a big loneliness in order to accept a little credit.

Another thing: Although he would laugh when he thought he should, he was just about completely humorless. He was a man you would rather not tell a sexual joke in front of, because he wouldn't think it was funny; he would think it was interesting. It wouldn't appeal to his sense of humor; it would appeal to his curiosity. He had a dirty mind. He could *tell* a sexual joke without seeing it was funny. He would laugh because he was supposed to, but he really thought he was passing on a piece of inside information, showing off his manhood and his knowledge.

Well, as I've said, I didn't like him. I never had liked him, and now I didn't just not like him; I hated him, and I found it a pleasure.

Of course, according to the freedom and democracy of my shop, I was obliged to serve him as I did all the rest, and I did this with the deference and obligingness that I reserved for the few clients I did not in one way or another enjoy. I didn't wish to appear, even to myself, to be unwilling to do my duty. And yet when he occasionally asked for a shave in addition to a haircut, I could feel the razor's edge tingle and itch with appreciation of the softness of his throat. This, you understand, was not a feeling that I exactly approved of. I felt it because it came to me, and I did my best to cover it up.

Even so, one day when Troy stepped, shorn and shaved and scented, out my door, I heard Burley Coulter say, "What you been doing?"

"Getting my ears lowered," Troy said.

And Burley said, innocently I am sure, but I feared not, "You're lucky you still got both of 'em."

I felt accused and a little guilty, shaken in fact.

Burley came on in. "I need to get my hair cut bad," he said.

And I said, glad of a reason to grin, "Well, that's the way I cut it."

The visions of the mind have a debt to reality that it is hard to get the mind to pay when it is under the influence of its visions. The lower Troy Chatham fell in my estimation, the better I thought of myself. And this was because of my overmastering feeling for Mattie. I was being carried away by a process of reasoning that was entirely invented by me and had nothing to do with anything in this world. I reasoned that if Troy was hateful to me, then he must be at least objectionable to Mattie, and she must want to be shed of him. I thought that if he was objectionable to her, then she might be attracted to me as one who truly loved and appreciated her. My thoughts returned again and again to that afternoon up in the churchyard when my feeling had declared itself to me and for a moment I had not been at myself, when she may have seen and understood. Did she know? I had reached a level of sophistication at which I could know I was fooling myself and still fool myself.

It embarrasses me to confess that such thoughts and their attendant visions possessed my mind for more than a year. It was a mercy when finally my vision grew so reckless and extravagant that even I could maintain it no longer.

This was in the October of the next year when the leaves had brightened to their brightest and had started to fall. Things had reached a sort of culmination of badness down at the Keith place. No differences had ever been resolved between Troy and Athey. Troy's power had only grown as Athey gave way, trying to secure Troy's loyalty to the place at the place's expense and to preserve the possibility of friendship between the two households. Every year the acreage of plowed land had increased. In 1950 there had been a change of tenants, and the new man bought a tractor. In Athey's big feed barn there finally would be only a single team of mules—an old pair that Athey swore would die on the place rather than be sold.

All this, you see, appeared to excuse my supposing (by a logic purely glandular) that Mattie would like to be free of Troy. One evening, alone in the shop, sitting in the barber chair with a book lying open and forgotten on my lap, I all of a sudden saw in my mind a vision of Mattie and me running away together. We were in my old Zephyr and we were putting Port William behind us.

The incompleteness of the vision was the giveaway, and was what finally ruined it. Before we could have wound up running away, for instance, there would have had to be an understanding between us. I had not imagined that, and could not have. Mattie would have had to give me a look, a smile perhaps, of consent—and this, though the thought of it filled me with the pain of longing, I could not imagine. I could not imagine what we might have said to each other. Nor could I imagine where we were going or what we were going to do. There was just some border somewhere ahead of us that we yearned to cross. In my vision the two of us were just running. My old car, having caught our eagerness, was going down the river road very much faster than forty miles an hour, shuddering seemingly with its own excitement, a long plume of blue smoke rising behind. And I suppose that just this escaping, just this speed and this violence of exertion in a car's engine, was the fullest expression of my love as I had understood it so far. As I drove the old car mercilessly toward wherever in the world we might have been going, piling one presumption on the top of another, I was saying to myself, or perhaps praying, "Why can the world not permit two lovers (*any* two) a moment of escape, free of all its claims, to be *in* love, just the two together, each the other's all?"

What destroyed my vision and all such visions, removed me from the chambers of imagery and put me back in the world again, was the assumption (not supportable even by imagination) that Mattie would have consented to such a thing. The proposition that she might have consented was more daunting to me than the certainty that she would not have. It made me *see*.

Supposing she would have consented, I saw that what I would be asking of her would not be just that moment of abandon, the thought of which had so commanded me (imagination had spared me nothing of that), and not even just her love. I would have been asking for her life, for the power to change her into what could not be foreseen. If I destroyed what already existed, what would I replace it with? For something always exists before you get there with your desires and visions, and this simply had not occurred to me before in such a way that I could feel the truth of it. What did I have to offer?

If you love somebody enough, and long enough, finally you must see yourself. What I saw was a barber and grave digger and church janitor making half a living, a bachelor, a man about town, a friendly fellow. And this was perhaps acceptable, perhaps even creditable in its way, but to my newly chastened sight I was nobody's husband.

I realized that my desire was far simpler than its circumstances (as maybe desire always is), and that it proposed things practical and final, not of visions but of this world, and that was where my vision failed. It was as though I had been covered all over for a moment by a beautiful shawl and a cat had caught a raveling and in another moment pulled it all away.

But this was not the end of my love for Mattie Chatham. After the figments of presumption and delusion had all fallen away and I again saw myself as I was and my circumstances as they were, I loved her more, and more clearly, than I did before. I became able to imagine her as she was and not as a subject of a dream. In my thoughts of her, she stood apart from me. I seemed to see her whole. When I realized the futility and absurdity of my old self-begotten desire, that was when the arrow struck. It entered my heart, and I could not pull it out. The hopelessness of my love became the sign of its permanence.

So it is that the life force may take possession of a man—so that in the end he may be possessed by something greater, no longer at all belonging to himself.

The thing I must tell about now I did not see happen, but it is as clear to my mind as anything I ever saw. As soon as I heard of it, I could see (and hear) it happening in my mind. I have not been able to think of it since without seeing it happen. And I am not alone in this.

Mattie loved wildflowers. She loved almost everything that grew out of the ground, but wildflowers especially. She loved just to look at them, and she loved to gather them (the ones that would last) in bouquets to take to church. It was always a pleasure to me to go in on Sunday mornings from spring to fall and see her bouquets in a vase on the communion table in front of the pulpit. No two were ever the same, and yet they all stood for her, as they stood in her eyes for the place itself, its beauty that she recognized and so honored.

On a Saturday afternoon late in the fall of that year, Mattie took Liddie with her and went out to gather asters along the side of the road. There was a place where a thickety fencerow ran along the top of the bank that came steeply down to the road ditch. It was on the inside of a rather sharp curve. The bank there was a wild garden of the tall asters whose blooms are purple with yellow centers. They seem to burn and give light in that time when the year is darkening.

Mattie walked among the dry grass stems and the fallen dry leaves and the smaller white-petaled asters called farewell-to-summer, gathering the long-stemmed purple asters and building a sheaf of them in the crook of her left arm. She would carry them into the church in the morning in a vase, and they would look like a torch. The blooms were going past their prime by then and she was working studiously, taking only the freshest ones.

Liddie was five years old, a big girl in her own estimate. She was carrying on a conversation with her mother in which her mother was not participating. And Liddie, coming along behind at her own whim, was not minding at all her mother's silence. She was carrying on, in a lively and charming way, *half* a conversation, and her mother would remember this.

While she talked she was pulling off one by one the aster blooms and putting them in her hair. She had her mother's hair. She was making herself a sort of hat or crown, though it looked like neither and was not tidy or symmetrical, for she had no mirror and was not particularly concerned anyhow.

After a while, when she would perhaps have wanted to look into a mirror if she had had one, she said, "Look, Momma. I'm beautiful."

When Mattie did not reply or look around, an excitement came over Liddie, for suddenly she knew that she was beautiful and she wanted to be seen. She was seized by a little dance that carried her down off the bank and into the road where her mother could best see her.

"Momma!" she said. "Look how beautiful I am!"

Mattie turned then and saw how beautiful Liddie was, and saw the car that she had not heard or heeded before, and heard within the shriek of braked tires on the blacktop the almost too small impact, and saw Liddie in the air like a tossed doll.

Knowing in that instant that what she saw not only could never be undone but never could be unknown to her ever again in her life, she cried out and ran to Liddie and knelt down. She gathered Liddie into her arms, beautiful indeed with the asters all awry in her hair, and small, and without life.

When I come again to this place in my memory of what I did not see but cannot stop seeing, I must be painstaking in separating the driver from the car. I see him open the door and get out, and I see that he is not a maniac or a demon. He is a boy, maybe twenty, who was not at fault, who was not going too fast, who could not possibly have stopped in time, in the time he had, and yet who knew, getting out and seeing helplessly what he had done, that it could not be undone or ever unknown again as long as he would live.

And that is where my seeing in my mind stops. I see them there as if forever: the stricken boy, the mother on her knees at the roadside holding her dead child, the sun suddenly gone beyond the hilltop, and the chill of the evening coming down.

How that moment ends and shifts or evolves into the next moment I do not know and have never imagined. For always I am the first to move; I must get up out of my chair or out of my bed and walk, until the world, as it always does, provides me something more to do.

19

A Gathering

Mat Feltner was sitting on the pedestal of a large gravestone. A tobacco stick held by both hands was propped against the ground in front of him. He was studying the stick as if reading it. He said: "When I was a boy, I had a stickhorse that gave me a lot of trouble. One day I was riding him down toward your shop there, and he threw me. Skinned both of my knees and one elbow, and I didn't like it atall. When I got on him again, I made him run all the way out to Uncle Dave Coulter's lane. By the time we turned around and headed back, I had him well in hand and he was satisfied to go at a walk."

All the trees were bare by then. The tobacco was cured in the barns and a good bit of the corn had been gathered. It was a fine warm afternoon. Mat was doing what he sooner or later got around to doing every fall. He had come up to take care of his people's graves. Nathan Coulter had come with him and they had brought two or three other hands. Mat had started out in the morning working with the others; in the afternoon, as he tended to do more and more as he got older, he left the work to the younger ones and in the weakened fall sunlight wandered off among the stones, renewing his knowledge of who lay where and of what they had been in their time.

After they had found and mowed and neatened the graves of every known Feltner and Coulter and Catlett and Wheeler and Beechum and other kin, the family lines branching back into the viney older part of the graveyard that nobody much thought about anymore, they righted a leaning stone that belonged to Pvt. Avery Wheeler, C.S.A., who, as he walked back into Port William after Appomattox, was killed by a Union soldier already home. And then Mat led them to the graves of other dead who had awakened again in his thoughts and made their claims upon him:

"Here, boys, let's put in a few licks here. This is old Aunt Ret Overhold. She gave me a many a biscuit with butter and jam."

"Here, boys, this is old Uncle Royal Burgess. When she was just a little bit of a girl, Bess stole a primer out of his store, and I made her take it back and confess, and he gave it to her."

"Over here, boys. Let's do a little something for Elder Johnson. The man was an artist at putting a shoe on a horse."

And so it would go until his homages and his remembered debts were paid.

I was there because I had learned his ways and loved to hear him when he went back into his memories. When I knew he had gone out to the graveyard with his hands, I would get free if I could and go there myself, to be in his company for a while. I would be there, you might say, in the line of business.

I would listen while he talked, and while he talked the mute stones spoke. Or we would sit together and not talk while he smoked his pipe and watched the younger men at work. He was a man you were comfortable in sitting with and not talking. But that day, maybe because of the memory of the young soldier killed in his homecoming, Mat dwelled upon the violence that had been in the town in his own early days. Port William had had three saloons then and, in its isolation, no law to speak of. For a while there had been a town board that hired a marshal, who, when he went to make an arrest, would be much inclined to ask permission of the arrestee. Election days were dangerous, for political arguments would lead to fighting or rock-throwing. Or to shooting, which Mat thought might have been the least dangerous, because often the shooters were too drunk to aim straight—though his own father had been killed by a drunk man with a gun.

One day his mother was sitting on the front porch when a man, badly cut and bleeding, came running up the walk, pursued by several other men. She got up, opened the door into the house, shut it behind the hurt man, and stood in front of it. But the pursuers said, "We're his friends!" And she opened the door to them also, and helped them to wash the man and bind up his wounds.

Having finished his story, Mat fell silent and looked away. I knew his homage then was to his mother.

And then he told about Uncle Ive Rowanberry and his sister Verna.

When the Civil War was starting up, Uncle Ive, then just a big boy whose mother was still calling him, instructively, "Iver William," went off to join the Confederacy. The Rowanberrys, as a matter of fact, owned a family of slaves who, after emancipation, were also Rowanberrys. Still, I don't think Ive Rowanberry was drawn to the Confederacy because of the issue of slavery. I think he went because, as he is said to have said, "Home is home, and I don't want any other son of a bitch telling me what to do."

At about the same time Verna Rowanberry married a boy by the name of Sylvan Shoals, who had already enlisted in the Union Army for reasons not exactly opposite to those of his brother-in-law, but he did believe with religious fervor in the national union and he did not want slaveholders telling him what to do.

Uncle Ive's military career was not heroic. He was captured by the Home Guard on his way to enlist and spent the entire war in a Union prison at Louisville. He believed he would have enjoyed the war, for he had been intending to join the Fourth Kentucky Cavalry and he liked to ride. But he did not enjoy prison, which obliged him for a long time to be pent up indoors with other sons of bitches telling him what to do. He had gone off to enlist as a rather thoughtless and exuberant Confederate. He came out of the prison an embittered and principled one. He was by nature a good-humored and even a happy man, but he held his grudge.

Sylvan Shoals went to the war and fought and came home with a wound that he eventually died of. And the breach never healed between Ive Rowanberry and his sister. With them, as with the country, the war did not end the division but only gave the two sides a high-toned language that kept the differences raw. Although Ive, in fact, never fired a shot in anger in his life, it was to Verna as if he personally had given the death wound to Sylvan Shoals. And although neither Sylvan Shoals nor Verna had even known where Ive was after his departure from home, it was to Ive as though they personally had turned the key that locked the prison door.

Perhaps, after it was all over, Ive and Verna met and had words—Mat didn't know. Anyhow, the breach between them widened. Time, which is supposed to heal, only made them old. Their difference was principled, having to do with two versions of freedom, and so they were free from each other. Uncle Ive settled on a little hillside place on Catlett's Fork and lived his life. Verna married again and passed her days and years over on Willow Run. It was easy enough not to meet, and they didn't see each other (knowingly at least) for fifty years. And then one winter day Verna happened to be at the store at Dawes Landing. She was a widow for the second time by then, dressed in black. As she left, she met Uncle Ive, who was coming in, carrying a sack of shot and gutted rabbits to sell at the store, an old man bent over under his load.

"Howdy," said Uncle Ive, and kept going.

When he got into the store, he swung off his load and asked, "Who was that old woman?"

Presently Nathan and the others finished their work, loaded their tools into the back of Nathan's old pickup, and left, taking Mat with them. And I sat on a while by myself in the quiet. I had been the barber in Port William for fourteen years by then, and the grave digger and church janitor for six years. My mind had begun to sink into the place. This was a feeling. It had grown into me from what I had learned at my work and all I had heard from Mat Feltner and the others who were the community's rememberers, and from what I remembered myself. The feeling was that I could not be extracted from Port William like a pit from a plum, and that it could not be extracted from me; even death could not set it and me apart.

History overflows time. Love overflows the allowance of the world.

All the vessels overflow, and no end or limit stays put. Every shakable thing has got to be shaken. In a sense, nothing that was ever lost in Port William ever has been replaced. In another sense, nothing is ever lost, and we are compacted together forever, even by our failures, our regrets, and our longings.

My vision of the gathered church that had come to me after I became the janitor had been replaced by a vision of the gathered community. What I saw now was the community imperfect and irresolute but held together by the frayed and always fraying, incomplete and yet ever-holding bonds of the various sorts of affection. There had maybe never been anybody who had not been loved by somebody, who had been loved by somebody else, and so on and on. If you could go back into the story of Uncle Ive and Verna Shoals, you would find, certainly before and maybe after, somebody who loved them both. It was a community always disappointed in itself, disappointing its members, always trying to contain its divisions and gentle its meanness, always failing and yet always preserving a sort of will toward goodwill. I knew that, in the midst of all the ignorance and error, this was a membership; it was the membership of Port William and of no other place on earth. My vision gathered the community as it never has been and never will be gathered in this world of time, for the community must always be marred by members who are indifferent to it or against it, who are nonetheless its members and maybe nonetheless essential to it. And yet I saw them all as somehow perfected, beyond time, by one another's love, compassion, and forgiveness, as it is said we may be perfected by grace.

And so there we all were on a little wave of time lifting up to eternity, and none of us ever in time would know what to make of it. How could we? It is a mystery, for we are eternal beings living in time. Did I ever think that anybody would understand it? Yes. Once. I thought once that I would finally understand it.

What I had come to know (by feeling only) was that the place's true being, its presence you might say, was a sort of current, like an underground flow of water, except that the flowing was in all directions and yet did not flow away. When it rose into your heart and throat, you felt joy and sorrow at the same time, and the joining of times and lives. To come into the presence of the place was to know life and death, and to be near in all your thoughts to laughter and to tears. This would come over you and then pass away, as fragile as a moment of light.

With that presence around me in the still evening, I got up and walked from the older part of the graveyard to the newer and back over the crest of the ridge away from the road. The day ending, winter coming, I walked in the spell of knowledge that I knew I could not keep intact for long.

And then I saw what I at first thought was a sack or a large rag that the wind had blown onto the earth of a new grave. And then I knew what it was.

Walking in her grief, she had followed the old path that in her childhood she and the other children had followed, coming up out of the river bottom to school in the days before school buses, and then she had cut across through the Feltner place to the graveyard. She lay on the raw mound of the grave as if trying to shelter it with her body, ever so still and given up and small. Her face was turned away. I could hear her crying. She drew in her breaths as if they were forced upon her, she having not the will either to breathe or not breathe. I knew that in all the world I was the only one who knew where she was.

I knelt beside her, according to my calling in this world.

I said, "Mattie."

And then, after a while, again: "Mattie."

She nodded her head to say that she had heard.

I laid my hand on her shoulder. I said, "You can't stay here."

20

How It Held Together Partly

Anybody would think that by being a bachelor a man could keep clear of trouble with a woman. On the basis of common sense (of which I have always had just short of enough) that is what I would have thought. But my experience has proved otherwise.

Trouble with a woman is not something I ever greatly desired, though at times I have greatly desired women. If you think that is one more serious failure of common sense, you are right. However, the trouble that comes from desiring women is not exactly what I mean by trouble with a woman.

The trouble I mean is in being actively and somewhat joyously disliked by a woman you may not much desire in the way of a man with a maid, but all the same would rather not be disliked by. I see I am going to have to tell you what I am talking about.

Cecelia Overhold forgave her husband Roy now and again as they traveled the broken terrain of their marriage; not often, but now and again, they would arrive at the same place at the same time, and then I think she forgave him, at least temporarily. But she never forgave me. She disliked me perfectly and steadily, so far as I know, for the rest of her life. And this I have always minded. Sometimes I have resented it; mostly I have been sorry.

To mind being disliked by a woman you don't desire and are not married to is yet another serious failure of common sense. So be it. I have always counted being unmarried to Cecelia Overhold as a privilege; it surely is better to be disliked distantly than intimately. It surely is far better to be disliked by somebody you don't love than by somebody you do. Even so, I mind. Even so, failing to love somebody is a failure.

Therefore, of course, I have turned over and over in my thoughts the events of that Sunday morning at the Grandstand so long ago. I ask myself: If I had climbed that tree like the others, would she have liked me better? Was it my passivity in the face of attack that she detested? Did she see it as indifference to her, or disrespect? A gentleman, after all, does not customarily lie supine on the ground in the presence of a lady. Did she think I was lying there in case of an opportunity to look up her skirt? Did she have a natural aversion to bald-headed ineligible bachelors? Was it that I had seen her in her rage? Sometimes the effect seemed so to outweigh the cause that I would have to test the evidence again by touching with my tongue the notch she had made in my grin. Often her dislike of me, when I have had it on my mind, has made me feel unlikable. And so, though I have been unmarried to her, I have not been free of her.

You knew merely by looking at her that Cecelia had a case to make. She thought the human condition was a calculated insult to her personally, the fault of certain people in particular. If she wasn't the president of the United States, or Mrs. Rockefeller, or at least happy, it was somebody else's fault, not hers. Her stinger was always out.

This was generally known, of course. I don't think she would have had to *say* anything to publish her thoughts and feelings. People generally suppose that they don't understand one another very well, and that is true; they don't. But some things they communicate easily and fully. Anger and contempt and hatred leap from one heart to another like fire in dry grass. The revelations of love are never complete or clear, not in this world. Love is slow and accumulating, and no matter how large or high it grows, it falls short. Love comprehends the world, though we don't comprehend it. But hate comes off in slices, clear and whole — self-explanatory, you might say. You can hate people completely and kill them in an instant. Cecelia knew how to deliver the killing look and the killing refusal to look. She could give the tiniest little snub that would cause your soul to fester with self-doubt and self-justification and anger. And these were things she could pass along to you because all of them were festering in *her*.

She knew that I had taken courses at the university and was a reader of books; that I had become by choice a mere barber, grave digger, and church janitor in Port William. Maybe that was what she could not forgive me for. Her favorite way of revenge was to ignore me, and she did this not just by not noticing me but by appearing to be as yet uninformed of my existence. But when I was near at hand, as I often was at church functions and such, she liked also to stand with her back to me and say to another person, for my benefit, bad things about Port William and my friends. She would damage everything in order to triumph over one thing. And I will have to hand it to her: She was a master of contempt. At her whim, I would have to tongue the gap in my teeth to verify my existence, or spend two hours muttering about in my mind, constructing an argument in self-defense.

And so maybe I know something of how it was with Roy. Roy and Cecelia never had the child who might have been a bond and a comfort between them. And was it fate, justice, or mercy that the failure of that child to appear may likewise have become a bond, though not a comfort, between them?

Cecelia thought that whatever she already had was no good, by virtue of the fact that she already had it. The things she desired all were things she didn't have. The failure of the entire population of Port William to live up to Cecelia's expectations brought heavy pressure to bear upon any newcomer or outsider who happened in. She was always latching on to new preachers or schoolteachers—anybody from away who supposably might prove to be as superior to Port William as she was. And they invariably disappointed her, either by liking the commonality of Port William or by regarding her as one of its members. Which, as a matter of fact, was correct. She was one of us. If she suspected as much, that must have been the unkindest cut of all.

The only unbridgeable chasm between Port William and Hargrave or Port William and California was in Cecelia's mind—and this, really, was a chasm between herself and everybody else. Maybe there were times when she knew it. When I think of that, I am sorry for her. She could fill a room with hate just by walking in. That was her impact, the way she made you feel at first. And then, if you were willing, you finally could see through that to the mere human she was. A mere human whose hate came from misery.

Looking back now, after so long a time, the hardest knowledge I have is of the people I have known who have been most lonely: Troy Chatham and Cecelia Overhold, the one made lonely by ambition, the other by anger, and both by pride always clambering upward over its rubble.

The problem, you see, is that Cecelia had some reason on her side; she had an argument. I don't think she could be proved right; on the other hand, you can't prove her wrong. Theoretically, there is always a better place for a person to live, better work to do, a better spouse to wed, better friends to have. But then this person must meet herself coming back: Theoretically, there always is a better inhabitant of this place, a better member of this community, a better worker, spouse, and friend than she is. This surely describes one of the circles of Hell, and who hasn't traveled around it a time or two?

I have got to the age now where I can see how short a time we have to be here. And when I think about it, it can seem strange beyond telling that this particular bunch of us should be here on this little patch of ground in this little patch of time, and I can think of the other times and places I might have lived, the other kinds of man I might have been. But there is something else. There are moments when the heart is generous, and then it knows that for better or worse our lives are woven together here, one with one another and with the place and all the living things.

It seemed strange and accidental to me when Athey and Della moved to town. I had never thought of Athey before without associating him with his place, the Keith place, and I am sure he had never thought of himself so. He and it made each other what they were. And then I had to see him parted from it, and learn to think of him apart from it. It was a little as though he had died and been resurrected in Port William. I ought to have been used to this. I had seen it happen before. It had happened, in fact, to *me* before. Maybe it happens to every one of us every day, and we are so used to it that it seems strange only once in a while, when we have to think about it.

The parting clearly had to come. Troy was magnifying himself with power, and Athey, in the working-out of the time and in the natural course of life, was dwindling away. The farm was big enough to contain and shelter and even use many lives, but two such minds could not live in it together. Athey was coming to know that. And then in September of 1952, he misstepped at the top of the ladder as he was going up to mend the corncrib roof. He took a bad fall that broke his leg and (as he said) made an old man of him. Afterward he was lame.

For several days after his fall, lying in his bed, he was thoughtful and spoke little. And then one day when Della came into the room he reached for her hand and she gave it.

"Della," he said, "we have got to leave this place. It's time and past time."

He spoke quietly the two sentences that had come at the end of all his thoughts. He and Della looked at each other. He squeezed her hand and let it go. She knew him and she knew herself. And that was all.

He had nothing he could do with his life's work now except leave it to a man who thought nothing of it. And yet he remained true to himself and he went on, pretty much without looking back. When he was on his feet again and could see to things, he and Della bought a little homestead of twenty acres such as you used to see fairly commonly on the edges and ends of the country towns. There was pasture for the old team of mules and a Jersey cow, room to fatten a couple of meat hogs and to keep a flock of chickens, a good garden spot, the necessary buildings. It was not a place on which they could live as they had lived, for that was past and they knew it, but it was big enough to permit them still to be as they were, to do for themselves and to recognize themselves.

At about the equinox of the next spring, the old pair of mules, Pete and Mike, stood freshly bedded in strange stalls, and Athey slept the first night of his life away from home. But of course what he did was establish the work of his hands again on that little twenty-acre place. He called it "piddling," but his work was perfect. He and that team of mules had got old together, and they understood one another. The mules seemed to understand even that Athey was lame. He could hang his cane on the fence and take hold of the handles of his breaking plow, and the mules would lean into the collars and just nudge the share into the sod. Athey grunted his instructions to them under his breath, and they listened. He stopped them often—as he would put it, in his quiet way of joking about himself—"so they could rest." Everything they did on that little place was beautiful. And soon it came about that we ceased to think of things as "changed" or "new," and Athey and Della seemed again to belong where they were.

Mattie and Troy had moved into the main house on the good farm in the river bottom, and Troy duly swelled himself. In the early summer of 1953, Mattie gave birth to their third child, Athey Keith Chatham.

That was about when the elder Athey began to happen by my shop on a fairly regular schedule. He would get up in the dark before daylight as he always had, do his barn chores, eat his breakfast, and then work in his garden or his little patch of tobacco or wherever else his work was needed. When the day heated up past midmorning, he would amble through town to my shop, for he would pretty well have spent his strength by then and he didn't like to sit in the house while Della went about her work. I was glad to have him. Old Jack Beechum, who had been for several years one of my regulars and a fine friend, had died at the end of the previous summer, and I missed him. Athey came, you might say, to a place that had been prepared.

Old and lame, carrying himself, he said, "like a hatful of eggs," he would step in through the door and stop and look the place over thoroughly. When he had examined in detail everything and everybody there, with his lips pursed and a look of distant amusement in his eyes as if he knew a great deal more than he was going to say, he would say, "Morning!"

"Well," I would say, "anything exciting going on?"

And he would say, "Well, I reckon not. I ain't excited."

He would then hang up his hat and cane, seat himself, remove his eyeglasses from the bib pocket of his overalls, and go through my newspaper. He didn't read it all, but he read it in parts, sometimes moving his lips as he concentrated, all the way from first to last, making a fairly thorough job of it. He was an alert man and did not want to miss anything, though he grunted in disapproval of much that he read, especially prices. The money that Athey had earned in his life had come hard, and he resented the advertisers' implicit assumption that they might fool him into giving it up.

When he had finished with the paper, refolded it, laid it down, removed his glasses, and put them back into their case, he might exchange a few words with whoever else was there, depending on who it was. But he was not a talkative man. He had a good dry wit and abundant intelligence. Usually, when he had said his few words, enough had been said.

One morning when only Athey and I were in the shop, Brother Wingfare came in. He was on his way to Louisville for his classes at the seminary and was in something of a hurry. He said to Athey, in a way that was a shade too indulgent and a shade too cheerful, as if he expected to hear that all was right with the world, "How're you, Mr. Keith?"

"Well, sir," Athey said, "where I used to be limber I'm stiff and where I used to be stiff I'm limber. Do you know what I'm talking about?"

"Yessir," said Brother Wingfare.

"*Nosir,*" said Athey.

"Nosir," said Brother Wingfare.

My shop was a democracy if ever anyplace was. Whoever came I served and let stay as long as they wanted to. Whatever they said or did while they were there I had either to deal with or put up with. As a gathering place for the manhood of Port William, often open at night, it could have been a lot rougher than it was. The problem of governing the place was right there in front of me when I started in. I knew that if it got rough I couldn't call the police; we didn't have any police in Port William. And so from the beginning I held to pretty correct behavior in my shop. I knew better than to drink on the job or anywhere near it. If anybody offered me a drink in the shop, I knew how to refuse with the proper implications. I minded my mouth the best I could and didn't gossip or use any sort of bad language. Certain things that people would say I would not acknowledge that I had heard. Later, my association with the graveyard and the church gave me a little dignity that I used to advantage. Even so, there would be times when I would have to take a stand. It could get socially delicate, you might say. I did very well as long as I knew what my policy was and had used some foresight and more or less prepared myself. The problem came when events got ahead of policy.

I remember a Saturday afternoon in the winter. It was cold. The shop was crowded, some having come as customers, some just to socialize and keep warm. It was not the sort of circumstances I preferred to do my work in. There was too much talk, and it was not quite possible to be sure who came next. To make matters worse, a man I did not enjoy was occupying the space right in front of the barber chair, swinging his arms and giving mouth to a series of extreme and perfectly knot-headed opinions. He had some liquor in him and would have been pleased to be disagreed with. His name was Hiram Hench. His first name (by the working of the local tongue, but also with justice) was pronounced "Harm."

Athey, who had somehow missed reading the paper that morning, was at the back of the shop in the last of the row of chairs, reading it now with such concentration that he might have been out somewhere by himself. I was keeping mindful of him, needing him to be there as he was.

I don't know what led up to it, but I heard Hiram say (maybe just to anybody who theoretically might have been listening, and generously imputing agreement to the theoretical anybody), "Some niggers looks just like apes. Did you ever think about that?"

He had hardly got that out of his mouth before I knew I had a policy against it. But I was not prepared. I didn't know what to say. It was not a situation in which you would enjoy carrying on a serious argument with an idiot. And, to be honest, I didn't want to see Hiram's big fist as close to me as the end of my nose. I wondered if he would hit me when I had a razor in my hand (which, as it happened, I did).

And then I came aware that Athey had lowered the newspaper and was looking at Hiram over the top of his glasses. And then pretty quickly everybody except Hiram came aware of it. And then Hiram came aware of it. He saw where everybody was looking, and he looked around fast right into Athey's stare.

Athey said, "Some white people do too. Did you ever think about that?"

Athey had what I needed and didn't have: seniority and authority. Prompt, regardless courage too. He was a man of standing.

He wasn't finished, but he held Hiram still just by looking at him for what seemed like two minutes before he said any more. Hiram was still grinning, but only with his teeth.

"It might prove out to be," Athey said, "that if we can't live together we can't live atall. Did you ever think about that?"

21

Don't Send a Boy
to Do a Man's Work

Athey was a storyteller too, as it took me some while to find out, for he never told all of any story at the same time. He told them in odd little bits and pieces, usually in unacknowledged reference to a larger story that he did not tell because (apparently) he assumed you already knew it, and he told the fragment just to remind you of the rest. Sometimes you couldn't even assume that he assumed you were listening; he might have been telling it to himself. With Athey you were always somewhere in the middle of the story. He would just start talking wherever he started remembering.

For instance, he knew the whole life history of Fraz Berlew, most of which, by the connivance or contrivance of Fraz himself, was funny. (Fraz was Fielding Berlew's father. The chair, so to speak, that had been held by Fielding in my time had been held by Fraz in the time before.) But there was, in Athey's telling, no sequence to the story at all. The sequence was in the events that reminded Athey of some part of the story. He would, say, fold the newspaper and put it aside, and tell just this much:

"Fraz Berlew was drunk and wandering. He wandered into a saloon down at Hargrave. The saloonkeeper was out and the place was empty. Fraz just helped himself to a considerable portion of the merchandise, and wandered on.

"When he wandered back again the saloonkeeper was there. He said, 'Fraz, did you come in here and drink up a bunch of my whiskey while I was gone?'

"And Fraz said, 'I can't rightly say. But it *sounds* like me.'"

Athey's best story was a long one that I had to hear in a good many of Athey's fragmentary remembrances before I figured out that it was one story and not at least two. Not having Athey at hand in all the circumstances in which he remembered it, I will try to tell it put together.

Athey never knew his mother—that is its necessary beginning. She died before he was a year old, leaving him to be raised partly by his father and partly by a widowed Negro woman, Aunt Molly Mulwain, once a slave and the mother of the woman who, in a later age, I would know as Aunt Ellie Fewclothes.

Carter Keith was a good father. He kept Athey with him as much as his work and, later, Athey's schooling would allow. The Keith place was always astir with work in those days. Everybody on the place would be up and the men and boys at the barns while the stars still shone, and at work by first light. Carter Keith followed the rules that he handed on to his son: He made use of all the daylight he had and would ask no man to do anything that he would not do himself. His tenants and hands knew this and so respected him, and they worked hard.

In the fall and winter, in addition to his farming, Carter Keith had made a sideline of trading in livestock, tobacco, corn, hay, and other things that his neighbors had to sell. What he bought, together with the produce of his own place, he gathered at his landing, loaded onto the steamboats, and sent down the rivers to Louisville or beyond.

From the time he could follow, Athey went to work with his father. From the time he could straddle a pony, he went with his father on his trading trips through the neighborhood. They might ride eight or ten miles, winding about through the creek valleys and over the ridges, gathering up a bunch of calves, it might be, or a few weanling mules, and driving them back home by dark (if they were lucky). And so early in his life Athey rode with his father over the same country that later he himself would court, dance, hunt, and trade over. In his life Athey had traveled much, though not extensively. He knew more of the history and geography of the country between Bird's Branch and Willow Run than most people know of the United States.

Athey didn't *intend* ever to be separated from his father. "That boy stays as close to me as my conscience," his father would say. By the time he was six, Athey considered that he had found his work in this world. And so his father had to make him go to school. Carter Keith (and this also his son took from him) did not speak much, but he spoke pointedly.

He said, "Well, by God, you're going, and your opinion in the matter is of no consequence."

And then, seeing that Athey was sulking, Carter said: "Moreover. If you get a thrashing up there, you'll get the full brother to it down here. You mind what I tell you."

And so when school was in session, Athey did his morning chores, ate his breakfast, and walked the children's path up through the woods to Port William School, starting alone and arriving finally with an assortment of children, mainly Rowanberrys and Coulters. And when he walked back down again, no matter how he delayed, he found his evening chores waiting for him. His father would light the lantern and hand it to him. "If you come home in the dark," Carter Keith said, "you have got to do your chores in the dark."

When he was twelve Athey was big enough to harness a mule, and his father let him have a little crop of his own. By then, when his father would go away he would tell Athey, "You look after things." Athey thought himself a man, but he was wrong. He said, "I was riding for a fall."

That year his father had an exceptionally nice bunch of shoats, due to be fat and ready by the time the nights turned cold. The word had got out and a number of people had spoken for them—neighbors, people in Port William, some from farther away.

It happened, as hog-killing time came on and the talk went around, that the hog-buyers got together with Carter Keith and made a deal by which they would do the slaughtering and work up the meat down at the Keith place to avoid having to move the live hogs, and Carter in turn would provide scalding box, gam'ling pole, firewood, and other necessities at a small surcharge per head. They were going to kill a full two dozen hogs, which would be a big job, but with all the help they had and some careful management they expected to do everything in two days.

The appointed time, when it came a few days after Thanksgiving, turned out to be more complicated than any man would have expected, let alone a boy. The complications came in stages.

First, Carter Keith had accumulated a shipment of tobacco that he would have to accompany to Louisville on the next boat. Which happened to come so early on the day of the hog-killing that you couldn't even call it "morning." When they first heard the *Falls City* blow it was not a long time after midnight. They dressed and went down with a lantern to hail the boat.

After the hogsheads of tobacco were on board, Carter Keith, standing on the end of the gangplank, shook hands with Athey, who was standing on the shore. "Look after things," he said. "See that they have what they need. They'll know what they're doing."

The boat backed away and headed downstream, its lights soon disappearing around the bend, leaving Athey alone and in charge. This was the first complication, but he wouldn't understand that it was a complication until he had understood the second complication, which was still several hours off.

He returned to the house and got back into bed in his underwear and shirt, hoping for more sleep, but had hardly shut his eyes when the wagons of the hog-killers began arriving. The wagons brought, altogether, ten men: Lute Branch, Dewey Fields, Webster Page, Thad Coulter, Stillman Hayes, John Crop, Miller Quinch, Big Joe and Little Joe Ellis (who were no kin), and a small, stout-built man Athey remembered only as Tomtit. Some had bought hogs; some had come to help.

His father had emptied the barn to give stall room to the visitors. Athey went out with his lantern and showed them where to put their teams. Somebody had brought an extra scalding box, so there were two. He showed them where to dig the trenches for the scalding boxes, one on each side of the long gam'ling pole. They dug the trenches, laid fire in them, set the scalding boxes over the fires, and filled the boxes with water.

While the men stood by the fires, waiting for the water to heat and for the daylight to get strong enough to shoot by, Athey did his morning chores and then rushed to the house to get his breakfast. He did not even take his cap off. He dragged out his chair and sat down in it without drawing it up. "Give me my breakfast!" he said to Aunt Molly, who was bringing it.

She withdrew his plate. "Now," she said, "ain't you something, Mister Man. You take off that cap, and square yourself to that table, and act a nickel's worth civilized."

Whereas his father only ruled him, Aunt Molly owned him outright, at least when he was in the house where she could get at him. He did as she said. She gave him his breakfast. When he had eaten it, she let him go. By the time he got back to the barn lot, two hogs were shot and stuck, ready to scald. He pitched in, determined to do a man's work that day.

The second complication was in the person of Put Woolfork, who left his mother's little farm above Squires Landing before daylight that morning, driving a mule to an old spring wagon with springs relaxed almost to the axles. Only the summer before, Put had acquired a wife to help his mother help him with his farmwork. And he had got wind of the hogkilling.

"He had it planned out," Athey said. "He was a man who believed in thinking if it would get him something for nothing."

If he attended the hog-killing and worked or appeared to work, Put thought, then surely they would give him a couple of heads and maybe a backbone, maybe even a sparerib or two. Maybe the more finicky among them (if anybody could be finicky in that hard time) would make him a present of kidneys or hearts or livers or milts or sweetbreads. At the very least, he would have a day of company and talk and a tub or two of guts to throw out for his chickens and dogs. He had two washtubs for that purpose in his wagon.

On his way downriver along the interconnecting farmtracks that passed for a road in those days, Put stopped at the Billy Landing to see what news of that quarter he might take in trade to the hog-killing. The Billy Landing didn't amount to much. The store there was a rough, nearly empty building where Jim Pete Markman went to appear busy when he got tired of sitting at the house. He and Put understood each other. Jim Pete's actual calling in this world was not storekeeping but whiskeymaking. At that, Athey said, he was the best there ever was: "It was prime stuff, as smooth as a baby's cheek—you could gargle with it—and it had a kick like a three-year-old mule."

When Put had discharged the news from upriver and taken aboard all that Jim Pete could or would contribute, Jim Pete asked him what brought him down that way on so brisk a morning.

"Oh, they're having a monstrous big hog-killing down at the Keith place," Put said. "Fat hogs by the dozen, and I don't know who all."

"Well, where was I?" Jim Pete said. "Nobody told *me* about it." And for a minute he sat and thought.

"Well," he said, "I'll tell you what. Kill one for me and I'll furnish the whiskey."

"Why, sure. That'll be just fine," said Put, who had no entitlement to agree to any such thing.

Put was the Julep Smallwood of his day and age. Above all things he loved the taste of somebody else's whiskey. "Why not?" he said.

"No sooner said than done," Jim Pete said.

He brought out a small keg containing maybe three gallons of his sur-passing product and stood it at Put's feet in the wagon. And Put set forth for the hog-killing, a rich man with his offering.

When he got to Carter Keith's barn lot, he set the keg on a big chop-ping block that had been upended in a handy place. "Boys," he said, "Jim Pete wants you to kill one for him, and he's furnishing the whiskey."

And there that keg sat in the midst of the people, Athey said, like the golden calf.

Mr. Dewey Fields, who was the senior man of them, eyed it as if that was exactly what it was. "We ain't having none of that here," he said.

And not another one of them said a word.

"That," Athey said, "was when I ought to have picked up the axe that was leaning right there and split that keg wide open. I was big enough to do it and I had the right. But that was when I played the boy and not the man. After that, I stayed a boy more or less to the end of it."

Put Woolfork did help some, and Athey of course helped. The visi-tors had brought lunches and they ate in shifts, hardly stopping work. Athey went to the house for his dinner. He submitted himself to the eyes of Aunt Molly like a good boy, hoping to get by, but she accused him as soon as he had drawn up to the table.

"What you got out there on top of that block?"

Embarrassed and trying not to sound like it, Athey said, "That's a keg of red-eye that Jim Pete Markman has sent down here for a hog."

"Red-eye!" she said. "Listen at you!"

Athey felt that whatever was going to go wrong at the barn had already been foreseen and judged at the house. He felt himself to be in the hands of fate. He didn't waste any time getting outside again.

By three o'clock, it may have been, they had twenty-five hogs scraped and gutted and hanging from the gam'ling pole. (Athey himself, sure in his confusion that his father would not want to be indebted to Jim Pete Markman, had insisted that they kill the twenty-fifth to pay for the whiskey.)

There was a letup then, and they felt their weariness. At rest, they felt the coldness of the wind. They had much work still ahead. For hours they had been walking by the exalted keg, leaving an empty space around it, a radius of maybe eight feet, as if from suspicion or respect. Now they looked at it.

Big Joe Ellis wiped his mouth on the shoulder of his ragged jacket. "Boys," he said, "I don't know about you all, but a little warming right now would suit me mighty well."

They were silent after that, all of them looking at the keg, until finally Mr. Fields said, "Well, maybe 'twould."

They sent Athey to the house to bring the water bucket and dipper. When he got back they had drawn the bung. He watched the liquor pour from the keg in little gushes, saying, "Good-good-good-good-good." He felt he had a duty of some kind, but he did not know what it was. Also he would have liked to drink from the dipper as it went around and then around again.

I asked him, "Why didn't you?"

"Aunt Molly," he said. "She would have skinned me alive. Also I knew by then that a boy was what I was. I would have got skinned again when Father got home."

Later he would learn the taste of Jim Pete's whiskey. "If it comes to whiskey," he said, "I would rather have his than some of this government-approved." But that may not have been a comment about the quality of the whiskey. Athey did not approve of government approval.

"Oh my!" said Lute Branch. "But don't that grease the axle of the old world?"

"Boys, let's get back to it now," said Mr. Fields. "We got a long ways to go and a short time to get there in."

They began blocking out the meat, laying the carcasses down on a table improvised of boards and trestles, removing the quarters, carving out the backbones and spareribs, carrying the pieces into the stripping room to be trimmed the next day, when they would also grind and sack the sausage and render the lard.

But as they worked now, they drank. There is an irresistible ease in dipping whiskey out of a water bucket with a dipper. It takes no time or trouble at all. And gradually the considerable skill that every one of them had been using all day became fumbling and unsure.

"Well," they had begun to say in consolation or in gleeful complacency, "what you don't get on one piece you'll get on another'n."

"Well, if it can't be ham, it'll just have to be sausage."

They wielded their axes and knives with something like abandon, though strangely there was never a finger cut. Athey saw Little Joe Ellis draw forth a sparerib with hide and a few bristles on the outside, and presently he saw him pick up a middling with a hole in it that you could look through like a window.

Put Woolfork always walked with his knees bent, as if expecting to have to sit down in a hurry. He had his bottom closer to the ground now than usual. He was walking toward the stripping room, carrying a large ham skin-side-down. He hooked his right toe precisely behind his left ankle and fell, tumbling the ham meat-side-down onto the ground. "Well," he said, "I'll eat it, I reckon, if nobody else will."

Big Joe Ellis held up a gobbet of fat that he had either mistakenly or accidentally sliced from a middling and then dropped on the ground. He said, in excellent good humor, "Now, that there piece there now, would you call that there piece sausage or skin fat? Well, God bless it, I'm a-calling it sausage. The dirt on it looks just like pepper."

Dewey Fields was warming himself by one of the scalding boxes, standing in the ashes. One of his overshoes had caught fire.

"Mr. Fields," Stillman Hayes said, "it looks to me like your overshoes is on fire."

Mr. Fields said, patiently, "These ain't my overshoes, honey. I borrowed these overshoes offen Isham Quail."

They were nowhere near finishing that day's work by chore time.

"I do believe," said Lute Branch, "that the women are going to have to do the milking."

"And after that cook up a little mess of victuals, I hope, I hope," said Miller Quinch.

"A virtuous woman," Dewey Fields said, "is a crown to her husband. Her price is far above rubies."

Pretty soon it was dark.

The third complication of that day came in the several persons of the Regulators. These were a kind of Ku Klux Klan, an imitation Ku Klux Klan maybe, for they wore sheets and hoods but their business (so far as Athey knew) was not Negroes, of which there were not many in the Port William neighborhood even in those days. The great interest of the Regulators was in sins against domestic tranquility. They were very hard on drinkers, sellers, and makers of whiskey (which they called "the demon rum"), with the perfectly logical result that every maker and seller of whiskey within a radius of several miles became a Regulator, and the actions of the Regulators were nearly all against new or outside competitors. They had a fairly free hand, for the law was in Hargrave, the roads scarcely existed for a good part of the year, and river transport was expensive and slow. And of course they caused trouble.

"If the Devil don't exist," Athey said, "how do you explain that some people are a lot worse than they're smart enough to be?"

Though they disguised themselves, and thought or pretended themselves disguised, the Regulators' "secrecy" was a useless glamour. They were no more secret or anonymous than the town dogs of Port William, for they rode upon horses and mules that were known to every boy above the age of five. Peg Shifter went so far as to nail a shoe to the end of his wooden leg before riding out with this local whiskey monopoly (which is really what it was)—but that too was only comedy, for as he rode his sheet worked up, confirming the truth already revealed by his mule.

When the Regulators came filing up the long lane past the house and into the barn lot, carrying torches and lanterns, the hog-killing crew did not try to run or hide. They just quit, each one right in the midst of whatever motion he was making, and stood and looked.

Big Joe Ellis said, "Did you ever see the like? Well, I never seen the like!"

The Regulators encircled them. Every man who did not carry a light held a shotgun or a rifle. Athey knew them all. They were the Hench twins, Felix and Festus, old man Tucker Thobe, Peg Shifter, Noble Crane, Jim Doyle, Gid Lamar, Guiney McGrother, U. S. Jones, and Jim Pete Markman.

I asked Athey, "What was Jim Pete doing there?"

He said, "I couldn't tell you everything even if I was to make some of it up."

"Well, gentlemen," old man Thobe chirped through his hood, "we done found you all in breach of the peace and the public good. I reckon you all know, now, that we can't let this sort of doings go on unmolested. No woman nor child would be safe. We're impounding this liquor, and we're going to put you away in that stripping room while we decide on further measures."

"I need to be getting on home now," said Put Woolfork, who was standing and swaying with his legs apart. "I ain't killing no hogs. I ain't even here. I got my cow to milk."

"Even if you knew how to milk, your women would have already done done it for you," Felix Hench called out from inside his hood.

The hooded men all laughed. So did some of the others.

He knew them all, but Athey never quite got rid of the shiver it gave him to hear those hooded men speaking. Though they spoke in their own voices, they were not speaking for themselves.

They drove the hog-killing crew into the stripping room and latched and propped the door. There were windows above the bench all along the north side. Did the Regulators think of the windows? If they did, they assumed that no man there would break a window belonging to Carter Keith. Maybe, since it was too dark to see the windows, the hog-killers were too drunk to remember them. Athey made no move to go in, and the Regulators did not make him go.

They emptied every stall in the barn, turning the guest mules and horses out into the pasture with those belonging to Carter Keith, making work for somebody besides themselves, and stabled their own.

They brought wood from the woodpile and made a fire.

"What're you all doing?" Athey said.

"What we don't have to tell you," said Festus Hench, looking through eyeholes over the dipper, which already was passing around. He was holding the bottom of his hood above his mouth so he could drink.

They sent Athey to the house for salt and a skillet.

"And just a leetle dab of meal," Peg Shifter called after him. "About a gallon."

"*Two* skillets," Guiney McGrother shouted to him, "and *two* gallon of meal."

Aunt Molly helped him get the things they had asked for. She was furious, though maybe not now at him. He was furious himself.

"They say the bottom rail shall be the rider," Aunt Molly said. "But it's the foam and the filth that biles to the top."

He brought them the skillets and the salt and meal. They began to slice meat from the joints and middlings that had not yet been carried to the stripping room. They took the tenderest cuts—hamstrings, tenderloins, slices of ham and shoulder—and greased the skillets with fat and started frying the meat. They made corn pones and dropped them into the grease.

Although Athey was hungry, he stood away from the fire. But when the good smell of the frying meat came to him he had to holler out: "Why don't you all cut some mouth holes in them things if you aim to eat like mortal humans?"

"Because we ain't got one of them little old mouths that runs like a calf's ass," Felix Hench said.

And Guiney McGrother waved his pistol at Athey and said, "*Get* to the house!"

He made as if to go but went instead and let himself quietly into the corncrib, where he could watch them through the slats.

He could see that somebody in the stripping room was sober enough to have found a match and started a fire in the stove. Otherwise there was no sound from there. They were sleeping.

The Regulators had laid their weapons down and removed their hoods. They feasted on the free pork and drank what to all of them but

Jim Pete Markman was free whiskey. Jim Pete was drinking hard in order to reduce his loss. When they finished eating, they dutifully covered their heads again with their hoods to make themselves official. They talked and laughed, sitting and then leaning and then lying around the fire. It was too big a fire, for the firewood also was free to them. Finally they too quieted down and went to sleep. Athey watched and watched, cold and determined—determined to do what, he did not know. He was no longer a boy who thought himself a man. He was a boy trying unsurely to make up for his failure to be a man when a man was needed. It was the first time he ever was awake all night long.

Now that he was a boy no longer thinking of himself as a man, the spirit of his father seemed to be telling him what a man ought to do. When the fire had died down almost to coals, he slipped out of the crib and went over to where the Regulators were sleeping. He knew how to squirrel hunt, and with what seemed to him in his fear the patience of the moving stars, he took their guns two at a time and buried them in the wheat in the granary. After that, he warmed himself at the coals of the fire, ready to run if anybody moved. It was way into the night by then. Before long it would be morning. And soon the gray of it rose among the eastward stars.

In a while he heard a little tapping from the inside of the stripping room. He went over and leaned to the wall. "What?" he said.

"Athey?" It was Webster Page.

He said, "Yessir."

"Are they asleep?"

"Yessir."

"Where's their guns?"

"I put them away."

"Where?"

"In a place."

"What about Guiney's pistol?" This was Lute Branch.

"I put it away too."

Somebody back in the room groaned and muttered something, and Lute Branch said, "*Damn* your head! Stir yourself!"

"Athey," Webster Page said, "are you listening?"

"Yessir."

"Unfasten this door. Now, wait! Listen! As soon as you do that, let loose all their mules and horses. Run 'em out! Hear?"

"Yessir."

And that was what he did. He unlatched the door and took the props away, and then ran to the barn. He opened every stall and drove the beasts out into the dimness.

Somebody among the Regulators cried "Whoa!" and then he heard a great gibberish of cries and curses as the forces of temperance and family order awoke. Before he was out of the barn again he heard the hooves swerve past the waking sleepers, cross the lot, go through the gate and on out the lane past the house.

When he came out of the barn, he saw the little man called Tomtit square himself in the posture of John L. Sullivan in front of a tall gangly Regulator who was probably Guiney McGrother. In their hoods and apart from their horses and voices, it was harder now to tell which Regulator was which. Tomtit danced and sparred impressively in front of the big Regulator and then made the mistake of trying to get close enough to hit him. Long before Tomtit got the Regulator within his reach, he came within reach of the Regulator, who hit him in the face with great force but also indifferently, as he might have swatted a fly, and Tomtit went down as if he had no bones.

And then Guiney, if that was who it was, wound up like a pitcher and swung at Webster Page, and missed, and Webster Page knocked him down.

And then one of them, maybe U. S. Jones, came running at Mr. Fields and tried to jump over a log two steps before he got to it, and then stumbled over the log—and Mr. Fields, of all people, knocked *him* down.

Given the numbers involved, it really wasn't much of a fight. The hog-killing crew were on average a good deal younger than the Regulators, they were more offended, and they weren't wearing hoods. A hood is far from an ideal garment to wear in a fistfight. Several of the Regulators had trouble aligning their eyes with their eyeholes.

And so the fight didn't take long. On the other hand, it didn't end in a rout as it ought to have done. Nobody felt good enough. The defeated did not feel like running and the victors did not feel like pursuing. Finally the fight just subsided in place like a fire burning out.

The victors were all standing and the others sitting or lying down. Athey heard the *Blue Wing* blow out on the river. Her engine seemed hardly to hesitate as she went by the landing. And then almost too soon Carter Keith had stepped into the barn lot in his black suit and hat, having stayed in Louisville only long enough to receive payment on his shipment of tobacco and catch the next boat home.

Now that he was standing there, they saw the shambles they had made of the place. Carter Keith stopped and stood looking, and he was white around the mouth.

Athey went to face his father. "I ought to busted that keg as soon as it was set down," he said. "It's all my fault."

"I don't believe so," his father said, and he put his arm around Athey.

He said to the Regulators, "You goddamned sackheads get out of here and go home."

He told Athey, "Run yonder and tell Aunt Molly to make some coffee. Tell her to make it strong."

Mr. Fields and Webster Page and the others had begun to stir, trying to get themselves back to work. Athey's father walked among them as if he were wading.

"If there's anything I can't stand," he said, "it's a damned nasty hog-killing."

In the new day Athey ran to the house to tell Aunt Molly to make coffee. She would in a short while fix breakfast for them all, but she grunted as she lifted herself out of her chair at the window where she too had kept awake all night. "Rest me, Jesus!" she said. The Regulators were now filing past the house, carrying their saddles.

The sight of the Regulators had, to Athey, the force of revelation. He saw them now wholly apart from power, seniority, even meanness. They were only men. Peg Shifter, in person, had never been friendly to Athey; as a Regulator, he had seemed terrible. Now he hopped along like a one-legged crow, not keeping up with the others. It occurred to Athey then that it might be possible to feel sorry for Peg Shifter, and in later years he did.

22

Born

As much as you will let it, Port William will trouble your heart.

I remember the McEndry brothers—Pistol and Hamp and Lank and Spiz—who were just more or less grown boys back in the late thirties. They would come walking into town every Saturday night with their hair oiled and combed in waves, their shirtsleeves turned back two turns above their wrists, lighted cigarettes dangling from the corners of their mouths. They always obliged Whacker Spradlin by drinking all of his whiskey they could hold. When they were drunk they always wanted to fight. When they fought they always got whipped. All four of them.

Hamp and Spiz were killed in World War II, and Pistol was wounded. They received medals. They were heroes.

And poor old Focus Fanshaw, unsound in the head and drunk too, one night jumped off the wall in front of Dolph Courtney's store headfirst into the road to demonstrate the proper form of diving. They brought him down to me bleeding and barely conscious. I washed and disinfected his wounds and made him stay until he could walk without help. When he could talk again, he said, "Boys, that ain't a good place to dive. The bottom's too close to the top."

Of course we laughed. And remembered and told again and laughed again. There were always woes enough, and Port William savored its own comedy—which of course had to do more often than not with somebody's woe.

And I remember Roger Roberts, called by everybody according to his own pronunciation "Woger Woberts." Woger was famous for his reply to Burley Coulter, who had suggested that Woger's newly broken crop ground was rich enough to grow maidenheads: "Nope. 'Twon't. Too many woots and wocks."

The big boys used to like to distract Woger while one of them slipped up and locked his arms around him; they wanted to hear him say, "Turn me awoose!"

If they were bothering Woger when Athey Keith passed by, he would say, "Boys, don't do that," and they would stop and stand away. Athey would give them a nod.

Such was Athey's influence when he walked among us. As he got older he seemed to become always more tender. He cared for his mules and his cow and spoke of them as if they were members of his family. He always had something to say to babies and small children. He talked to the dogs he met in his passages through town.

Of a lame hound named Gnats, who belonged sort of to everybody in those days and who got around in a three-legged lope, Athey would say with amusement and respect, "There goes old Gnats, doing his arithmetic, putting down three and carrying one."

He had been a good man always, I think, but this tenderness was new. It was the tenderness of an old man who had been busy all his life but now had time to pay attention to useless things. But it was more than that. It came to Athey, I think, also because of his difference with Troy Chatham and all that it had led to and meant, which was a suffering he neither complained of nor denied. He was (as he did say) a man who had outlived his time, and maybe this gave him the freedom to speak to creatures that could not answer.

When they left the river and moved to Port William, Athey and Della retained title to the farm. About this I know more, probably, than anybody concerned ever intended for me to know. The barbership of Port William was, as I've said before, a privileged position. People sometimes confided in me deliberately; sometimes, almost forgetfully, they handed me puzzle pieces. A man is not to blame, I hope, for mere consciousness. How could I help but notice that some pieces fitted others?

Athey and Della retained title to their farm on the advice of their lawyer, Wheeler Catlett. When Athey raised the question of whether or not to sell the farm to Mattie and Troy at a cheap price and take their note for it, Wheeler said, "Hell, no! You're not dead yet."

This forced Troy to decide (it would have been his decision) whether to stay as a tenant on his in-laws' farm or try to do better—that is, it forced him to admit that he could not do better. Nothing I know causes me to believe that Troy could have financed the purchase of the farm (or any comparable farm) on reasonable terms at that time—or, for that matter, at any time later. Still, you can see that he could find reason to feel affronted by his enforced tenancy on a farm that he wanted to own but that was not for sale to him.

And that wasn't all. At about the same time, Athey and Della made their wills, by which the farm, after both their deaths, would go to Mattie alone. This too was done on the advice, or anyhow with the concurrence, of Wheeler Catlett. I don't know for certain when or how Troy learned of this. What happened not much later (something I am about to tell you) makes me think he learned of it pretty soon. Knowing that, he knew also that unless he exerted himself powerfully (and got much luckier than he had been) he would sooner or later become not his in-laws' tenant but his wife's.

You could argue, if you wanted to, that Athey and Della were ungenerous in this and misused their power. You could propose that if Troy had not, at this time, felt himself chosen against and excluded, he might have done better than he did. You could propose that Wheeler gave bad counsel—that he, who had seen so much of division, ought to have known the danger of dividing husband and wife.

I concede the weightiness of these thoughts, and I acknowledge that I am well acquainted with Wheeler Catlett's prejudice in the matter. Wheeler was no longer a young man by the time he wrote Athey's will. He may not have known yet that he too was a man outliving his time (though such was the case), but he loved Athey and understood exactly what Athey was and what he stood for, and he had no time for Troy, whom he also understood.

The problem with Troy was that he was a dreamer. He was a dreamer in the most demanding practical circumstances, increasingly taking the advice of people who were not in his circumstances. He was a man who, because of his nature and the nature of his circumstances, always had everything at stake. He had no margins. After he had reached a certain extremity of commitment and debt, he had no room to turn around in, even if he had wanted to turn around. And the country had entered a time when it was easier for a man like Troy to "get big" than to save himself, if need be, by getting smaller. Some such men walked a tightrope, balancing debt and equity, to a sort of desperate "success." Others swelled until they burst.

At any rate, leaving the farm to Mattie alone would prove a useless precaution, for it only put her in exactly the same predicament in which her father had been: She would have to secure Troy's loyalty to the farm (and perhaps to herself and their children) by permitting him to abuse the land and put it at risk.

Port William, watching Troy, would be (by turns or all at once) skeptical, impressed, envious, dismissive. Mattie, I think, finally withdrew her approval of his ambitious plunging and wished him to be kinder to things and more careful. Her naming of her third child after her father may have bespoken this. She may have expressed her difference to Troy, but I don't think she would have brought it to a quarrel. She was a woman of patience and steady affection; I doubt that she had qualified, even in her own thoughts, her loyalty to her husband. When you saw them together (which was not all that often) they did not appear to be in any way estranged.

And yet she had ceased to believe in his plans and promises and maybe in him. Troy, knowing this, and knowing, if he did, that she was to be the sole heir of the farm, which he could not buy, must have felt forsaken and therefore (as self-sorrowful married men might wish to think themselves) "free."

You might say that I was pretty "free" myself at that time. My mind had got to where it would return to Clydie and be with her when we were together, which was a relief in its way. It is in fact possible for one man to be strongly attracted to two women at the same time. But according to my experience, two are about enough.

Finally, two would be too many. I was going to have to choose one. As it turned out, I would have to choose the one by whom I could not be chosen.

At about that time, as I remember, I made up a poem about Clydie and quoted it to her one Sunday afternoon as we were taking a walk:

> *Clydie's pretty everywhere—*
> *Lithe and blithe and finely fair.*

And that got me a blush, a hard nudge in the ribs, a very excellent kiss, a straight look, and a laugh.

Well, things went along and went along until we got to the cold downward end of 1954, and pretty soon it was Christmastime. The young people who were away at college all came home. Word got around that there was going to be a big Christmas dance up at Riverwood. Henry Catlett's band was going to play. It was going to be a blowout.

"Oh, we've *got* to go to that, Jayber," Clydie said. "We'll go and watch those young 'uns and do like they do. And then we'll go and do like *we* do."

"Count me in," I said.

The proprietress of Riverwood was Mrs. Doozie FitzGerald (with a capital G). Riverwood had seen better days. NIGHTCLUB and MIXED DRINKS had once blinked alternately on and off in neon out front, and in those days it was open for business from noon to exhaustion. But no more. The locals had never called it a nightclub; they called it a roadhouse. By 1954 it was a roadhouse only now and again. Doozie (or Mrs. Fitz, as she was often called) had lost her liquor license, her old cook had died, and she had got too stingy to meet the wage demands of anybody young. She was living by then on Social Security or dividends or who knew what, and she supplemented her income by opening Riverwood on Saturday nights or "special occasions," charging admission (always a dollar more than advertised) to dance to a band or the jukebox, and selling setups to the customers. Her staff now consisted only of one old waiter and general handyman named Chum.

On the appointed evenings, Mrs. Fitz stood behind a small table at the door, collecting the payments of admission plus the dollar surcharge, which was always expected, routinely protested, and routinely paid. Her dyed-black hair chopped off in bangs at about her eyebrows, her lips painted rosy red, she wore a blue dressing gown and fuzzy blue slippers open at heel and toe.

The night of the Christmas dance was starless. A few snowflakes were floating down out of the dark sky into the aura of electric light in front of Riverwood. I was moved to see the snowflakes melting in Clydie's hair as I helped her out of her coat. She was wearing a light green dress with a full skirt that set off her figure, and I reached around her waist and gave her a little hug.

We protested and paid and went past Mrs. Fitz's table into the darker room. The band already was playing and couples were dancing. Mindful that we were older than most, we took a table a little off to itself and yet where we had a good view of the floor. For a while we just watched. The boys were wearing their good suits. The girls were in party dresses, all dolled up. It was a pretty thing to see them dancing. The room was lighted by rows of shaded electric candles along the walls, an imitation log fire in the fireplace, and (so far) by a few lamps overhead that cast a soft glow onto the dance floor. Everybody (including, of course, me) had brought a pint or a half-pint stuck away in his pocket or in his date's purse. From various places in the room you could hear the young people calling for setups: "Chum! Chum!"

The parents of some of the younger young people may have thought that these Riverwood parties were chaperoned by somebody. In fact, they were chaperoned only by Mrs. Fitz, who (belonging to the laissez-faire school of roadhouse management) went early to bed, and by old Chum who was an impartial witness. Chum was by nature unalert, and not able to see very well even in daylight. He was, moreover, slow and clumsy. To hire him alone to wait on that uproarious and bedazzled crowd was a form of punishment, though Mrs. Fitz evidently had no motive for it except greed.

From start to finish—four or five hours—the boys would be hollering,

"Chum! Chum! Over here, Chum! Where the hell you at, Chum?" And Chum would be desperately ignoring them all until in his good time he got to them, poking his way through the crowd, holding up his tray.

The band was playing a fast number and the floor was full of jitterbuggers when Andy Catlett came in with Nell Gale, who had been recently the sweetheart of his brother, Henry. Henry, seeing them from the bandstand, brought his hand down, stopped the song they were playing right where it was, and started playing "Your Cheatin' Heart." Andy began to dance with the girl, holding her close and whirling round and round. Henry made his saxophone sob and moan as if his heart would break—and then, while the piano player took a solo, reared back and laughed at his brother, so maybe his heart was not too broken, after all. As the song finished Andy made another spin beside our table and dipped low, leaning the girl backward onto his arm, and we could hear her suck in her breath through her teeth. She was quite a girl.

Pretty soon (as usual) somebody turned off the overhead lights, which made it a lot cozier and somehow quieter, and a lot harder on poor old Chum. The music seemed to penetrate better in the dimness. The band was playing "Stardust," and Clydie and I got up to dance.

We danced to the slow songs and sat and watched during the fast ones. We spiked our setups and toasted each other and a number of other things that came to mind. We sat close together. Clydie took my hand and held it in her lap. A wonderful feeling came over us. Outside was the cold, dark, starless night. Inside was warmth and music and mellowness and gaiety. Inside Clydie and me was the good, even, friendly, growing warmth of desire, and our hands held one another in Clydie's lap. It was lovely to dance and watch the young people dancing. Most of the dancers (including, of course, me) began to have the illusion that they were dancing better than they actually were. Still, the young people were fine to watch, and sometimes funny too.

Andy Catlett, ecstatic but less than graceful, picked Nell Gale up in his arms and, whirling round and round, crossed the dance floor and fell down in front of the fireless hearth.

And Alfred Pindle, after he got a few drinks in him, danced just by trotting back and forth in a rhythm having nothing whatever to do with any song that any band had ever played. He trotted along rather quietly, with his eyes filmed over as if he heard an entirely different music far off. Before long, his girl began to have the limply resigned and submitted look of a small animal carried by a cat.

But most of them danced well enough, and there were two couples who danced beautifully. I mean they would have danced beautifully if you had seen them cold sober dancing in broad daylight in the middle of the road.

The band played "Smoke Gets in Your Eyes." They played it slow, slow. It was as if the musicians and the dancers and the whole room were in a trance. Clydie and I swayed to the slow beat, and it seemed that the feeling inside us made us light so that we were floating on the music. We were dancing close, barely moving. Clydie really knew how to put herself against you. She was a snuggler when she wanted to be.

I said right into her ear, "Clydie, my sweet, you feel heavy on the branch and ready to pluck."

She said, "You got it, boy."

When I looked up again, I looked directly into the face of Troy Chatham, who was dancing with a woman whose face I did not see, but her long blond hair could not have been Mattie's.

Troy gave me a wink and a grin, raising his hand to me with the thumb and forefinger joined in a circle.

I stopped dancing. What I felt must have showed in my face, for Clydie pushed away from me and said, "What's the matter with you, Jayber? Are you sick?"

I said, "I am. I'm as sick as a dog."

And I headed for the men's room.

Andy Catlett was there, drying his hands, ready to go out.

He said, "Hey, Jayber!"

I said, "Hey, Andy!"

He said, "Don't go goosing no snowflakes," and went out. As the door opened and shut again, the music sounded distantly in a kind of yawn.

I wasn't, as Clydie thought, sick at my stomach. I was sick at heart, and I don't mean that just as a manner of speaking; I was seriously afflicted. Do you know what picture came flying into my mind when I looked up and saw Troy Chatham looking at me over the head of whichever Other

Woman that was? Not of Mattie at home with the children, wondering where Troy had gone off to and who with. Not that picture (which came to me clearly enough, later), but the memory of Mattie as she had been on that day when I knew I loved her. I had thought many times of her as I had seen her then, with the children so completely admitted into her affection and her presence—as, I thought, a man might be if he wholly loved her, if she wholly trusted him, a man who would come to her as trustful and heart-whole as a little child. I had thought of a flower open-ing among dark foliage, and of a certain butterfly whose wings, closed, looked like brown leaves but, opened, were brilliant and lovely and like nothing but themselves.

But I was thinking too, as Troy winked at me and raised his sign: "We're *not* alike!" And that was what sickened me, because I wasn't sure.

I wasn't sure of anything. I hadn't been particularly aware of being drunk out on the dance floor, but now I was drunk, blinking and unsteady in the harsh light and the stench of that grudging little room. I held on to the washbasin and tried to think. What I was sure of was that I wanted to get out of there and be gone, but I didn't want to go back through the dance hall and the dancers. I didn't want to see Clydie. I was going to be a while understanding what had happened in my mind, but I understood that, whatever it was, it had made me unfit for Clydie. I didn't want to go back to Clydie, after all our loveliness, as a mere drunk to be helped out to the car.

And then I saw the little window rather high up over the toilet. I unhooked the sash and shoved it open. It looked impossibly narrow, but I was maybe no more rational than a penned sheep that lunges at a crack in the wall. I stepped up onto the rim of the toilet and then onto the flush tank, and thrust my right arm and then my head and both shoul-ders through the hole, and made as much of a jump as I could manage. And then I panicked. I had no foothold, my left arm was pinned between my ribs and the window. I began to suppose that some delighted boys were about to come in and see me stuck there with my legs waving about and would pull me back inside again. That thought sobered me some and gave me strength.

The men's room was actually a little lean-to stuck onto the back of the building. I clawed around on the wall until I caught hold of what must have been a vent pipe or a downspout, and then I got my left foot against one of the stanchions of the toilet stall. I gave a mighty push and a pull, feeling the buttons pop one at a time off my jacket and the left sleeve tear loose at the shoulder, and then I tumbled out into the world headfirst, landing amidst a bunch of old tires, several garbage cans, thrown-away car parts, and other junk and trash.

As nearly as I could tell by feel, I was bleeding somewhat from a cut above my right ear and another on the bridge of my nose, and I was shy some skin along my ribs and belly. The rest of me was all right and able to get around, but I knew I had to use some caution now, for I didn't want to be "helped" by anybody. I didn't want to be kept safe from further damage to myself by being locked up in the county jail, either.

I eased around to the Zephyr, where by good luck I had left my hat and coat. I put them on so as to leave no dirt or blood on the upholstery, found a scrap of paper, and wrote a note to Clydie. The note said:

Dear Clydie,
I am taken ill (iller than you think or I can describe) and have got to go. I don't know when we will see each other again. I am changeable, I hope. Here are the keys to the car. I am leaving it to you with thanks for everything. You have been a true friend to one in need.

Love,
Jayber

It shook me to see what I had written and the way I had signed it: "Love." I said earlier that I didn't love her so much as I liked her. I will have to take that back. Love has a scale, and Clydie and I were on it somewhere. It hurt me to be leaving her.

But I had to go. It seemed that my way in this world had all of a sudden opened up again (like a door? a wound?) and was leading me on. I was thinking, "Oh, I have got to change or die. Oh, I have got to give up my life or die."

Maybe I was wanting to get to a place where I could not be mistaken, at least in my own mind, for Troy Chatham. I thought, "I am *not* like him." But that thought didn't detain me long. I was thinking also of Mattie. I was going to have to choose. I was going to have to know what I was going to do.

I was plenty aware of the way I looked. My wrecked suit was mostly hidden by my overcoat, which I buttoned tight all the way up, but a man dressed as I was, drunk, with blood on his face, would surely be of interest to the police and maybe to other people. I pulled my hat low, turned down the brim, turned up my coat collar, and started walking home. I had to go back to Hargrave, through Hargrave, across the bridge at the river mouth, through Ellville, and then up the river road to Port William— twelve miles or better. I didn't know what time it was. It was late.

There wasn't much traffic. I walked on the left-hand side of the road, well off the pavement. When cars approached I stepped behind a tree, if one was handy, or kept walking with my head down. I tried to walk straight and fast to give the impression of sobriety and purpose. It was too cold, anyhow, to loiter.

When I got into Hargrave I turned off the main drag and went through on a darker street. After I got across the bridge, where I had no hiding place, I took care that nobody saw me the rest of the way home. On the Port William road, there was too good a chance that I would be recognized. At that time of night there were not many cars—three, maybe four. When I heard one coming I would get behind a tree or lie down in the weeds. I didn't want a ride. I didn't want help. I didn't want to explain anything or answer any questions.

Once I got beyond the town lights, the night was as dark as the inside of a cow. I couldn't see anything I looked directly at. By not looking at anything, by keeping my eyes focused on the dark in front of me, I could distinguish between the black surface of the road and the whiteness of the snow that, as it got colder, had begun to cling to the grass and weeds along the ditch. I kept to the darker side of the difference, and step by step, with a little surprise every time, felt the road there, solid underfoot. It was cold enough that I had to keep knocking along as fast as I could. I would have been glad to have more between my feet and the road than the soles of my Sunday shoes and a thin pair of socks. That it was snowing I could tell when a stray flake melted on my face, but it was snowing only as it had been earlier—a few big flakes drifting slowly down.

After I got used to the going, and the unseeable road and the cold and the dark and the wandering flakes of snow had become the established world of my journey, the thoughts of my mind began to separate themselves like the unbraiding strands of a cut rope.

I thought of Mattie at home up the river ahead of me, perhaps lying awake. I knew the subject of her thoughts, but I did not know her thoughts. I knew that she knew what her problems were, and that she would deal with them, that she *was* dealing with them, but I did not know *how* she was dealing with them. I did not know what she was saying to herself as she dealt with them. I knew (it never occurred to me to doubt) that, whatever her problems, whatever her thoughts, she was intact and clear within herself. This was what moved me and drew me toward her, though I could not come near her or be in her presence.

I knew also that Troy was incoherent and obscure within himself. He was a wishful thinker. A dreamer. His mere dream had led him into the reality of endless work and struggle, endless borrowing and paying of interest, endless suffering of the weather and weariness and the wear and tear of machines, and yet he was a dreamer still. He was an escapee. He would plunge from the confines of one dream into the confines of another. In the midst of his altogether laborious and wearing and frustrating life, in the middle of a winter's night, he would turn up at a roadhouse dance with the lips of a strange woman on his mind and a grin on his face. Where the hell did he think he was? *What* did he think he was?

What Troy Chatham was was my business—not because I chose to make it my business, but because it was. It was my business because I did not want to be what he was, and that was no sure thing. It was a fearful thing to be like him. But what I saw, walking up that dark road, was that it would also be a fearful thing to be unlike him. I saw that I had to try to become a man unimaginable to Troy Chatham, a man he could not imagine raising his hand to with the thumb and forefinger circled—but to do that I would have to become a man yet unimaginable to myself.

What I needed to know, what I needed to become a man who knew, was that Mattie Chatham did not, by the terms of life in this world, have to have an unfaithful husband—that, by the same terms in the same world, she might have had a faithful one.

On the dark road that night, I might have been anywhere at any time;

I did not know where I was even in the little world I knew; I couldn't have told you the time of night within three hours. And in all that darkness and unknowing, I was trying to say to myself that I knew what I was, that I could not have been just anybody.

In my mind, then, I began to question myself and answer myself. I wanted clarity, I wanted sight, but it seems to me that I did not try to think the thoughts I thought. I did not foresee the thoughts I was going to think.

"You want to believe that Mattie Chatham did not *necessarily* have to have an unfaithful husband."

"Yes. That is right."

"But can you prove that?"

"Maybe not."

"She could prove that she could have a faithful husband only by having one."

"I suppose so."

"So her need, then, you're saying, is to have a faithful husband?"

"Yes, that must be what I'm saying."

"Well, where is she going to get one?"

"Well, I don't know. It seems a stupid question. She already has got a husband."

"But is he not unfaithful?"

"Yes, he is unfaithful."

"And she needs a faithful one."

"Yes, she does."

"But if she never has one, you will never know if the terms of this world might have allowed her to have one."

"I suppose that is right."

"But where could—*how* could—she get one?"

"Well, if she ever is going to have one, I'm sure, of course, it will have to be me."

"Wait, now. Hold on. Do you know what you just said?"

"Yes."

"Do you mean that you love Mattie Chatham enough to say what you just said?"

"Yes. Oh, yes! I do."

"You love her enough to be a faithful husband to her? Think what you're saying, now. You're proposing to be the faithful husband of a woman who is already married to an unfaithful husband?"

"Yes. That's why. If she has an unfaithful husband, then she needs a faithful one."

"A woman already married who must never know that you are her husband? Think. And who will never be your wife?"

"Yes."

"Have you foreseen how this may end? Can you?"

"No."

"Are you ready for this? Think, now."

"Yes. I am ready."

"Do you, then, in love's mystery and fear, give yourself to this woman to be her faithful husband from this day forward, for better for worse, for richer for poorer, in sickness and in health, till death?"

"I do. Yes! That is my vow."

I tremble to say so, but when I had given that assent, it seemed that there were watchers watching in the dark who all of a sudden could see me.

Maybe I had begun my journey drunk and ended it crazy. Probably I am not the one to say. But though I felt the whole world shaken underfoot, though I foresaw nothing and feared everything, I felt strangely steadied in my mind, strangely elated and quiet.

The sky had lightened a little by the time I reached the top of the Port William hill. It was Sunday morning again. I left the road and more or less felt my way home over the fences and through the fields, at considerable further expense to my clothes and shoes. I climbed into my frozen garden, went up the stairs, and let myself into my room. There was still some warmth from the coal fire I had left burning down in the shop. I sat in my chair and let the cold, slow daylight come around me.

Part III

23

The Way of Love

It is a fearful thing to be married and yet live alone, and sleep alone (as I felt in my worst nights) like the dead in the ground. And yet ever after that night of the Christmas dance, I lived under the power of my vow, and I kept it.

Sometimes I knew in all my mind and heart why I had done what I had done, and I welcomed the sacrifice. But there were times too when I lived in a desert and felt no joy and saw no hope and could not remember my old feelings. Then I lived by faith alone, faith without hope.

What good did I get from it? I got to have love in my heart.

Was I fooling myself? I know myself to be a man skilled in self-deception, and so maybe (for the sake of argument, for the sake of whatever truth may be in argument) I ought to suppose that I was fooling myself. If, in addition to my being her husband, Mattie had been my wife and we had lived together, would we not have bickered and battled at times, as other married couples do? Would she not at times have been as incomprehensible and exasperating to me as most men's wives appear to be at times? Would I not have been to her, at times, as thwarting and outrageous as most women's husbands evidently are? Why should I assume that I would have loved her all her life?

All I can answer is that I did love her all her life—from the time before

I ever saw her, it seems, and until she died. I do love her all her life, and still, and always. That is my answer, but in fact love does not answer any argument. It answers all arguments, merely by turning away, leaving them to find what rest they can.

I was married to Mattie Chatham but she was not married to me, which pretty fairly balanced her marriage to Troy, who became always less married to her, though legally (and varyingly in appearance) he remained her husband.

Young lovers see a vision of the world redeemed by love. That is the truest thing they ever see, for without it life is death. I believed that Mattie had seen that vision in the time of her falling in love with Troy Chatham, and that she kept it still and honored it. And so I honored it. But the answering vision, which ought to have been his, was mine. And my marriage to Mattie was validated in a way by Troy's continuing invalidation of his marriage to her.

Only once did that questioning voice of my dark walk return. It said, "Is it *legal* to be married to somebody who is not married to you?"

I said, "I guess it's legal to be married to any number of people as long as they don't know it."

"But there's not any comfort in that."

"No," I said. "No comfort." But I had to laugh.

I had not, you see, arrived at any place of rest. Maybe I had not solved a single problem or come any nearer to the peace which passeth all understanding. But I was changed. I had entered, as I now clearly saw, upon the way of love (it was the way I followed home from Hargrave that snowy night; maybe it was the way I followed back to Port William during the flood), and it changed everything. It was not a way that I found for myself, but only a way that I found myself following. Maybe I had always followed it, blunderingly and uncertainly. But now, though it was still a dark way, I was certainly following it. At first I thought that this great change had come to me during my walk after the dance at Riverwood. Later I knew that it had come the day, up there in the churchyard, when I fell in love with Mattie and my heart cracked open like an egg.

Now that I knew what it was that had led me from the start, I had to reckon with it. I had to look over what I had learned so far of life in this world and see what light my heart's love now shed upon it. What did love have to say to its own repeated failure to transform the world that it might yet redeem? What did it say to our failures to love one another and our enemies? What did it say to hate? What did it say to time? Why doesn't love succeed?

Hate succeeds. This world gives plentiful scope and means to hatred, which always finds its justifications and fulfills itself perfectly in time by destruction of the things of time. That is why war is complete and spares nothing, balks at nothing, justifies itself by all that is sacred, and seeks victory by everything that is profane. Hell itself, the war that is always among us, is the creature of time, unending time, unrelieved by any light or hope.

But love, sooner or later, forces us out of time. It does not accept that limit. Of all that we feel and do, all the virtues and all the sins, love alone crowds us at last over the edge of the world. For love is always more than a little strange here. It is not explainable or even justifiable. It is itself the justifier. We do not make it. If it did not happen to us, we could not imagine it. It includes the world and time as a pregnant woman includes her child whose wrongs she will suffer and forgive. It is in the world but is not altogether of it. It is of eternity. It takes us there when it most holds us here.

Maybe love fails here, I thought, because it cannot be fulfilled here. And then I saw something that a normal life with a normal marriage might never have allowed me to see. I saw that Mattie was not merely desirable, but desirable beyond the power of time to show. Even if she had been my wife, even if I had been in the usual way her husband, she would have remained beyond me. I could not have desired her enough. She was a living soul and could be loved forever. Like every living creature, she carried in her the presence of eternity. That was why, as she grew older, I saw in her always the child she had been, and why, looking at her when she was a child, I felt the influence of the woman she would be. That is why, in marrying one another, we mortals say "till death." We must take love to the limit of time, because time cannot limit it. A life cannot limit it. Maybe to have it in your heart all your life in this world, even while it fails here, is to succeed. Maybe that is enough.

And so there were times when I knew (I knew beyond any proof) that the faith that carried me through the waterless wastes was not wasted.

I began to pray again. I took it up again exactly where I had left off twenty years before, in doubt and hesitation, bewildered and unknowing what to say. "Thy will be done," I said, and seemed to feel my own bones tremble in the grave.

Not a single one of my doubts and troubles about the Scripture had ever left me. They had, in fact, got worse. The more my affections and sympathies had got involved in Port William, the more uneasy I became with certain passages, not just in the letters of St. Paul, that clarifying and exasperating man, but even in the Gospels. When I would read, "Then shall two be in the field; the one shall be taken, and the other left. Two women shall be grinding at the mill; the one shall be taken, and the other left," my heart would be with the ones who were left. And when I read of the division of the sheep from the goats, I couldn't consent to give up on the goats—though, like most people, I had my list of goats, who seemed hopeless enough to me, and I didn't know what to do about them.

What would I do with a son who killed his father merely to inherit his money, and only a little quicker than he would have inherited it anyhow? What would I do with that woman—she lived up in the big bottom at the mouth of Willow Run long ago—who beat a black girl to death for stealing a spoon and then found the spoon? What would I do with somebody who reduced the world in order to live in it, somebody who reduced life by living it? What would I do with a man who wished for the death of his rival? I didn't know. I could see that Hell existed and was daily among us. And yet I didn't want to give up even on the ones in Hell. For the best of reasons, as you might say.

"You don't want to go to Hell, honey," said Miss Gladdie Finn.

"I don't," I said. "But I don't reckon it has enough room for everybody who's eligible."

"Well, I don't know," she said. "A soul is mighty small."

But now I could see something else too—something, I suppose, that old Dr. Ardmire knew I did not see, and knew I would not easily see. My mistake was not in asking the questions that so plagued my mind back there at Pigeonville, for how could I have helped it? I can't help it yet; the questions are with me yet. My mistake was ignoring the verses that say God loves the world.

But now (by a kind of generosity, it seemed) the world had so beaten me about the head, and so favored me with good and beautiful things, that I was able to see. "God loves Port William as it is," I thought. "Why else should He want it to be better than it is?"

All my life I had heard preachers quoting John 3:16: "For God so loved the world, that He gave His only begotten Son, that whosoever believeth in Him should not perish, but have everlasting life." They would preach on the second part of the verse, to show the easiness of being saved ("Only believe"). Where I hung now was the first part. If God loved the world even *before* the event at Bethlehem, that meant He loved it as it was, with all its faults. That would be Hell itself, in part. He would be like a father with a wayward child, whom He can't help and can't forget. But it would be even worse than that, for He would also know the wayward child and the course of its waywardness and its suffering. That His love contains all the world does not show that the world does not matter, or that He and we do not suffer it unto death; it shows that the world is Hell only in part. But His love can contain it only by compassion and mercy, which, if not Hell entirely, would be at least a crucifixion.

From my college courses and my reading I knew the various names that came at the end of a line of questions or were placed as periods to bafflement: the First Cause, the First Mover, the Life Force, the Universal Mind, the First Principle, the Unmoved Mover, even Providence. I too had used those names in arguing with others, and with myself, trying to explain the world to myself. And now I saw that those names explained nothing. They were of no more use than Evolution or Natural Selection or Nature or The Big Bang of these later days. All such names do is catch us within the length and breadth of our own thoughts and our own bewilderment. Though I knew the temptation of simple reason, to know nothing that can't be proved, still I supposed that those were not the right names.

I imagined that the right name might be Father, and I imagined all that that name would imply: the love, the compassion, the taking offense, the disappointment, the anger, the bearing of wounds, the weeping of tears, the forgiveness, the suffering unto death. If love could force my own thoughts over the edge of the world and out of time, then could I not see how even divine omnipotence might by the force of its own love be swayed down into the world? Could I not see how it might, because it could know its creatures only by compassion, put on mortal flesh, become a man, and walk among us, assume our nature and our fate, suffer our faults and our death?

Yes. And I could imagine a Father who is yet like a mother hen spreading her wings before the storm or in the dusk before the dark night for the little ones of Port William to come in under, some of whom do, and some do not. I could imagine Port William riding its humble wave through time under the sky, its little flames of wakefulness lighting and going out, its lives passing through birth, pleasure, suffering, and death. I could imagine God looking down upon it, its lives living by His spirit, breathing by His breath, knowing by His light, but each life living also (inescapably) by its own will—His own body given to be broken.

Once I had imagined those things, there was no longer with me any question of what is called "belief." It was not a "conversion" in the usual sense, as though I had been altogether out and now was altogether in. It was more as though I had been in a house and a storm had blown off the roof; I was more in the light than I had thought. And also, at night, of course, more in the dark. I had changed, and the sign of it was only that my own death now seemed to me by far the least important thing in my life.

What answer can human intelligence make to God's love for the world? What answer, for that matter, can it make to our own love for the world? If a person loved the world—really loved it and forgave its wrongs and so might have his own wrongs forgiven—what would be next?

And so how was a human to pray? I didn't know, and yet I prayed. I prayed the terrible prayer: "Thy will be done." Having so prayed, I prayed for strength. That seemed reasonable and right enough. As did praying for forgiveness and the grace to forgive. I prayed unreasonably, foolishly, hopelessly, that everybody in Port William might be blessed and happy—the ones I loved and the ones I did not. I prayed my gratitude.

The results, perhaps, were no more than expectable. I found, as I had always found, that I had strength, but never quite as much as I needed—or, anyhow, wanted. I felt that I might be partly forgiven, as I was partly forgiving; Port William continued to be partly blessed and happy, as before, and partly not; I was as grateful as I said I was. And so perhaps my prayers were partly answered; some perhaps were answered entirely.

Perhaps all the good that ever has come here has come because people prayed it into the world. How would a person know? How could divine intervention happen, if it happens, without looking like a coincidence or luck? Does the world continue by chance (since it can hardly do so by justice) or by the forgiveness and mercy that some people have continued to pray for?

But why ask? It was not just a matter of cause and effect. Prayers were not tools or money. Sometimes in my mind I would be sitting again in Dr. Ardmire's office, as if I had returned to 1935 out of my later life to give him my report. I finally knew, I told him, why Christ's prayer in the garden could not be granted. He had been seeded and birthed into human flesh. He was one of us. Once He had become mortal, He could not become immortal except by dying. That He prayed that prayer at all showed how human He was. That He knew it could not be granted showed His divinity; that He prayed it anyhow showed His mortality, His mortal love of life that His death made immortal. And I could see Dr. Ardmire looking straight at me with that distant, amused light in his eyes, and I could hear him say, "Well. And now what?"

I had learned a good deal since 1935, I supposed. But did that mean that I could explain much of anything? It did not. Did it mean that my way in the world was now lighted to the very end? It did not.

I prayed like a man walking in a forest at night, feeling his way with his hands, at each step fearing to fall into pure bottomlessness forever.

Prayer is like lying awake at night, afraid, with your head under the cover, hearing only the beating of your own heart. It is like a bird that has blundered down the flue and is caught indoors and flutters at the windowpanes. It is like standing a long time on a cold day, knocking at a shut door.

But sometimes a prayer comes that you have not thought to pray, yet suddenly there it is and you pray it. Sometimes you just trustfully and easily pass into the other world of sleep. Sometimes the bird finds that what looks like an opening is an opening, and it flies away. Sometimes the shut door opens and you go through it into the same world you were in before, in which you belong as you did not before.

If God loves the world, might that not be proved in my own love for it? I prayed to know in my heart His love for the world, and this was my most prideful, foolish, and dangerous prayer. It was my step into the abyss. As soon as I prayed it, I knew that I would die. I knew the old wrong and the death that lay in the world. Just as a good man would not coerce the love of his wife, God does not coerce the love of His human creatures, not for Himself or for the world or for one another. To allow that love to exist fully and freely, He must allow it not to exist at all. His love is suffering. It is our freedom and His sorrow. To love the world as much even as I could love it would be suffering also, for I would fail. And yet all the good I know is in this, that a man might so love this world that it would break his heart.

After that night of the Christmas dance, I never owned a car again. I can see now that this in itself was an important stage of my journey. It was a step backward, maybe. I was no longer progressing. From then on, I didn't often leave the Port William neighborhood. If I went anywhere I either walked or bummed a ride.

The world all at once became bigger, as big almost as I remembered it from my childhood. Hargrave had drawn farther away. If I went there now I had to think ahead and allow time. For me there was no more jumping into a car and running somewhere. Louisville and Lexington, places I had driven to now and again in the Zephyr (for reasons soon hard to remember), I never went to again.

My social life changed. Before, I had yearned for company, especially the company of women, and had gone seeking it. Now I no longer went seeking, but taught myself (not always easily) to make do with the company that came.

I felt older. I felt that I had seen ages of the world come and go. Now, finally, I really had lost all desire for change, every last twinge of the notion that I ought to get somewhere or make something of myself. I was what I was. "I will stand like a tree," I thought, "and be in myself as I am." And the things of Port William seemed to stand around me, in themselves as they were.

I went regularly about my duties, my meals, my lying down and rising. My days and tasks seemed not to be accumulating toward anything. I was making nothing of myself. I was not going anywhere. In the silences of the shop on summer days, I could hear the clock ticking (a sound I love), and the ticks did not seem to add up to minutes or hours, but merely passed. Customers and loafers entered the shop, made their curious mixtures of character and preoccupation, spoke the resulting conversations, and went away. The talk flared, burned brightly, or died down, according to the availability of fuel.

"Woger," said Grover Gibbs one fine day to Roger Roberts, speaking generously in the spirit of an older man advising a younger one, "looks like you and Sassy ought to have some children. Everybody ought to have at least a few."

"Ain't no use in plantin' 'em one night and wootin' 'em up the next," said Roger, causing Grover to slump forward suddenly as if knocked in the head.

"Looord, what is this weather coming to?" said Julep Smallwood, looking out at the rain turning to snow on a bitter north wind.

And Burley Coulter said, "Aw, Julep, it'll all average out to something tolerably comfortable."

"He drinked a fifth of whiskey a day, and smoked hard to tell how many cigarettes," said Grover Gibbs, shaking his head, "and it finally killed him."

"How old was he?" asked Mr. Milo Settle, biting.

"Ninety-two."

One Saturday night, Walter Cotman sat tilted against the wall in a wire-back chair and told in his matter-of-fact way, without ever a smile, about going to Corbin Crane's sale and buying back one by one the tools that he had loaned to Corbin and that Corbin still had when he died. Walter said, "I hated to ask his widow for 'em."

"I always keep springwater in the radiator on my car," Grover Gibbs proclaimed to John T. McCallum.

"Now, why," said John T., already outraged, "would a man ever do any such of a thing as that?"

"Well, did you ever hear of a spring that froze?"

"*And,*" said Grover, "I had an old sow that got out of the pen through a hollow log. It was a crooked log, so I stuck *both* ends under the fence. She run herself to death just going round and round."

John T., looking off through the window into the far distance for relief, said, "Psht!"

Reading in the paper of the death of a beautiful actress, Athey Keith said, "She has passed from the beautician to the mortician."

"What's the matter, old hoss?" said Burley Coulter to Big Ellis, who one evening stepped a little painfully through the door.

"Well, Burley," Big Ellis said, being honest, "my knees is giving me trouble."

"First your knees," Burley said, "and then your ass."

They found a certain wondrous glee in the joke of getting old, and they varied it endlessly.

"Age," said River Bill Thacker toward the end of a conversation to the general effect that time, contrary to expectation, made old men out of young ones. "Age has done more for my morals than Methodism ever did."

"Well," Burley Coulter said, thinking maybe of his mother's years of dying away by bits, "some people live a long time."

Catching his tone, Bill said, "What's the matter with living a long time? It ain't going to kill you."

"No," Burley said. "Not for a long time."

Burley Coulter and Big Ellis were telling the story of how they baked the cake. Both of them were *in* the story and I had heard them tell it maybe a dozen times, but they were telling it again. It was always a good story.

The crops were laid by. Annie May, Big Ellis's wife, had gone to spend a week with her brother. Burley, for some reason, had wandered over to Big Ellis's early in the afternoon, maybe just to pass the time. Big Ellis somehow had on hand a fifth of very good whiskey, of which he generously offered Burley a drink, which Burley then praised and recommended to Big Ellis, who drank and generously offered it again.

Events, and the story too, began to slide a little at that point. Before long, it seemed, Grover Gibbs and Rufus Brightleaf showed up for some reason, and Grover for some reason had three pints of very good whiskey in a minnow bucket in the back end of his truck. And then it seemed that some others showed up. They had a happy, sociable, amusing time all afternoon.

About midway of the latter half of the afternoon they got hungry. Burley suggested that they ought to fry some fish. So they got Big Ellis's seine and went and seined his pond. They caught an excellent mess of fish and two turtles. Some of them started dressing the catch, and Burley and Big Ellis, both of them pretty good cooks, started breading the fish and frying them and making corn pones and a big pot of coffee.

They had a fine feast. But then Rufus Brightleaf said they ought to have some dessert—he was a cake man himself. So Burley and Big Ellis said well, then, they would make a cake.

That put them into new territory. Neither of them had ever made a cake before, so they had to go by Annie May's recipe. It was going to be an angel food cake.

They went strictly by the directions. They separated the egg yolks from the whites, beat the whites, mixed up all the other ingredients, and put the batter into a cake pan. It did not fill the pan—nothing like.

"It ain't enough," Burley said.

"It ain't nothing like enough," said Grover Gibbs, also a pretty good cook, who had come over to criticize. "I could eat that big a cake by myself."

So they got the dishpan and repeated the recipe until the pan was full, making sure they would have plenty for everybody, and using up in the process most of the eggs Annie May had saved up to sell at the store.

When they opened the oven at the end of the prescribed time, they had an angel food cake of exactly the same dimensions as the oven, containing within it the racks of the oven and the dishpan.

That night, by the time they got the oven cleaned and the kitchen set to rights in anticipation of Annie May's homecoming the next morning, Burley and Big Ellis were more sober than they wished to be.

But it was a good cake. Even the dogs and the hogs thought so.

The nation lapsed into peace there for a while, between the Korean War and the one in Vietnam. Or, rather, instead of fighting a war, it was merely getting ready to fight one, and for a while Port William eased along without patriotic deaths. The farmers' economy, which was pretty good at the end of the Second World War, stayed pretty good for a while, though it began a long slant downward in the early fifties. For just a while, it was possible for Port William to think and act as if it had a future as itself, although there were signs, if you were looking for signs, that as itself it was fading away. The blacksmith shop had been closed since Mr. Will Johnson died in 1951. The elder Mixters had died; one of Bill's boys was working in an explosives factory in Indiana, the other in construction in Louisville. The old music had about entirely gone. Television had come. Instead of sitting out and talking from porch to porch on the summer evenings, the people sat inside in rooms filled with the flickering blue light of the greater world.

And yet for a while Port William kept on as pretty much itself. (Maybe something of itself will always be there. Who is to say?) There remained among the men those who, at least in the daytime and some even at night, would rather sit and talk in my shop or the poolroom or the garage or one of the stores than sit at home and watch TV. The rowdy boys still held a sort of loose party way into Saturday night in bearable weather, talking in the sitting places in front of the stores, driving back and forth in their cars, playing the radio loud, smoking, talking, laughing, scuffling, drinking some. Now and then they would build a fire and sit around it. They were noisy enough, but as a general thing in those days they caused no serious trouble. (It had been a longish while since anybody from Port William had been shot in Port William, and it would be a longish while again. Of course, though all things don't come to all men, all things sooner or later come to somebody, and Port William had had and would have its allotment of shooting.) About the time the boys all dwindled off to sleep, Athey Keith and the other old farming men grew tired of their beds and began to stir out to their chores, if they had any, or they came to the sitting-and-talking places to wait for daylight.

I went through the days about as the others did, keeping to my habits, as a rule not overly concerned, not too often surprised. The days came one at a time, filling their length according to the season. People grew hair, came and went through the shop door and the church door, lived and died, assuming that I would do my duties. It was as though the covenant I worked by was not between me and the Port Williamites, but between them and the world, which somehow had agreed to furnish me. I had been granted, it seemed, and I was happy enough to be taken for granted.

My strange marriage (which not a soul on earth knew about but me) seemed to have placed me absolutely. I was where I was, in body and mind and heart too. Though I was divided from the female society of Port William as much as before, I did not feel estranged from it as before. I was involved, a participant. The community I lived in and served by my unillustrious yet needful work was Mattie's community also. I had become eligible to understand it in that way. We were thus joined. I lived as I thought she did: hoping for good, reconciled to the bad, welcoming the little unexpected happinesses that came.

But to be the keeper of a solemn, secret vow is no easier than it sounds. Of course I could say to myself (and I did), "Since you're the only one who knows about it, you don't have to keep it. Who would blame you?" I was no Jephthah, but I knew that what I had done made me, by some standards, a fool.

And yet I could not give it up. I don't know if I can explain. It was not just that I needed my love for Mattie, and needed to feel that I had a right to it, and could not imagine myself without it. My thoughts as I walked through the dark after the Christmas dance remained with me. It seemed to me that, because of my vow, a possibility—of faith, of faithfulness—that I could no longer live without had begun leaking into the world.

My vow was not something I thought much about in the daytime. Then it would be just a presence in the background, steadying and reassuring, even pleasurable. Maybe I won't desecrate it by saying it was a little bit like a bank account: something won, decided, no longer needing to be decided, available in time of need.

At night (not every night, but often enough) was when it shook me. Past a certain hour of the darkness, a certain tick of the clock, the strands of habit, expectation, common sense, and small pleasures that had held me through the day slowly broke apart. It was like watching the V of a goose flock disintegrate as the birds circle down to land. It would be as though I stood off on the edge of my life, watching it being lived by somebody else. I felt no resentment against the man I saw living my life, but he was unimaginable to me, just as he seemed unable to imagine the observer who watched him under cover of darkness. I saw as a bird sees, each eye looking out on its own in a different direction, no two images ever resolving into one. To save myself, I would try to summon up a vision of Mattie, but I could not see her. I could not imagine her. Some nights in the midst of this loneliness I swung among the scattered stars at the end of the thin thread of faith alone.

And then I would wake up and be in awe to see the daylight coming and my old familiar workaday life taking shape again in the dear world. Coherence and clarity returned. I could imagine myself again. I could imagine Mattie Chatham. I could imagine Port William.

24

A Passage of Family Life

From the time he could walk, and maybe before, Jimmy Chatham wanted to be with his grandpa. Mattie and Troy never brought him to town that he didn't beg to stay, and of course it often suited Athey and Della to have him stay. You could probably say that it always suited Athey.

The attraction was not just Athey himself, though I judge that might have been enough. Jimmy loved Athey's place and his ways of working. He loved working with Athey at whatever Athey did. Troy's work was too high-powered, fast, and dangerous by then to permit a small boy to stay along with him, let alone help him. But Athey's ways of working permitted company. Wherever Athey went, Jimmy could go with him. Whatever Athey did, Jimmy could help him do. And Athey didn't just pretend to be helped, either. He gave the boy real jobs to do, and paid him in pennies and nickels for his work. He showed him things that needed to be picked up and carried and put down. He let him gather the eggs, each one perfect, out of the straw of the nests, and put them into a basket. He showed him how to shell corn for the hens. When Athey plowed his little crops or his garden, Jimmy would be on the old mule's back, guiding him between the rows and turning him at the row ends, saving Athey the need to bother with the lines. Athey paid the boy a nickel a hundred to catch bean beetles. He taught him to pull weeds, and later to use a hoe. When Jimmy got big enough to use a pocketknife, Athey bought him a two-bladed one and taught him how to sharpen it. He taught him how to make willow whistles, and popguns out of elder stalks, and corncob pipes to smoke corn silks in.

By the time Jimmy was big enough to go about on his own, the students were being gathered in to Port William School in buses. The children's path, from the river road through the Rowanberry place and up through the woods to town, had been abandoned. Jimmy rewore it, or wore his version of it, tracking back and forth between his house and Athey's. This pleased Mattie, of course, for it pleased her father and her son. To her, that path had been a happiness that she was glad to think had now been handed down.

The problem was that, for Jimmy, it pretty soon became a path of escape. Of necessity, because of the long hours and the hurry of his work, Troy had left to Mattie the worry and care of the children. As long as Jimmy was small, Troy didn't much care where he was, just so he was presumably safe and out of the way. And then Jimmy, who obviously was a capable boy, got big enough to reach the brake and clutch of a tractor with his feet and to be useful to his father in a number of ways.

But by that time Jimmy had become a fair master of the work on Athey's little place. He could milk. He could drive a team. He was learning something of the use of judgment. He was excited by the way his grandfather's art gave beauty to their work and brought it to fruitfulness. Boylike, not quite realizing what he had done, he had made his choice. Between Troy and Athey, he preferred to work with Athey. Between Troy's way of farming and Athey's, he preferred Athey's.

This was not because Athey spoiled him. He treated the boy lovingly but he made him toe the mark too. He didn't settle for fractions.

And it wasn't because Athey was competing, even in his own thoughts, for the son against the father. Athey would not have done that. If Jimmy had not wanted, on his own, to be with Athey, Athey would not have tried to entice him.

It just happened. It happened because Jimmy was attracted to Athey and took to his ways, and because Athey was generous and in need of a boy. And of course the need grew greater. Athey was failing, and Jimmy was coming along just barely in time to take up the slack. Finally, when they would go to work together, it was the boy who was working and the old man who was tagging along, giving instruction now and then, and comforted to find that the instruction was less and less necessary. What should have happened between Athey and Troy had leaped over a generation and happened between Athey and Jimmy, but in a way too late for them both, and certainly too late for the farm down in the river bottom.

Troy must by then have begun to feel, even though he didn't (he wouldn't) know, the disarray that had entered into the world. He was in appearance irritated and in his heart maybe angered by the defection of his son. He complained about it openly in town. "Every time I need him for something he's up here with the old man, fiddle-farting around with a half-dead team of mules."

I remember Jimmy Chatham well from those years. He was the kind you don't forget. He clearly was going to have his father's good looks and physical capabilities. But he was better natured than his father. For one thing, he never complained. He seemed to have no instinct for the making much of oneself that complaining requires. For another, he had a sense of humor. From the time he was just little, he would look straight at you, and he never looked at you without grinning.

He had mischief in him, you could see that. Behind that grin were notions and energies wanting to be let loose. Now and again Athey would have to check him, but all he needed to do was speak. "Nup!" he would say. "Look out, now." Jimmy would look at him to see if he meant it, and then come to heel. Athey always meant it, and Jimmy always looked at him to see if he did.

Athey began to suffer little strokes. No one of them was enough to bring him down. Little by little they whittled him away. It happened slowly, but not so slowly that you couldn't see it happening. A kind of fumbling in both speech and motion grew upon him. It took him longer to make his daily trips to my shop, longer to get through the door. There were more times when he had to stand back from his work and let Jimmy do it alone. It was a blessing that Jimmy was willing and able.

And then for a couple of days I didn't see Athey. It was early March, the weather mean, and I laid it onto that, though I couldn't remember when he had missed a day.

The third morning, Mattie stepped into the shop. That was something unexpected and rare; for a moment I was just sort of caught up by the beauty of it. And then I was afraid. I said, "How's your dad?"

"Not very well."

"I was afraid of that."

"I don't think he's going to be up to the trip," she said. "For a while." I saw the moisture come into her eyes, and she blinked it away. "So, Jayber, we were wondering if you could come to the house to shave him, maybe every couple of days, and cut his hair when he needs it. Would you mind?"

I said, "I'd be glad to do it. You know I would."

"Yes," she said. "I know you would."

And so I knew that Athey had taken another step down. I knew more than that. I knew he was fighting for every scrap of independence he had left, not to be imposing on anybody. If he could no longer shave himself, Della or Mattie either one could have shaved him, and would have been glad to do it. But he didn't want them to do it. He didn't want to require that of them. They understood. If I did it, he could pay me and it would be all right. Also they knew it would do him good to have company. He would be glad to see me.

I did as they asked. Every other day, usually late in the afternoon, I went to Della and Athey's house. Athey sat in a chair in the kitchen and I shaved him. When he needed a haircut, I brought my equipment and cut his hair. Always I tried to come when I didn't need to be in a hurry. When I finished my work, I would pull out a chair and sit down, and Athey and I would talk. Mostly I talked. He was finding it hard. I told him the news; I saved up anything odd or interesting or funny so I could tell him. And he would nod or laugh or make a comment, usually only a word or two.

Della (and Mattie, if she was there, which she often was) would leave the kitchen to Athey and me until I had finished my work and we had had a visit. And then she (or she and Mattie) would come out and offer coffee and maybe cookies or a slice of pie, and then sit with us and we would carry the conversation on a little further. Sometimes they would ask me to stay to supper. Sometimes Mattie and her two boys would stay for supper too, and we would all sit down together.

Sometimes Troy would be there, but not often and never for long. He was coming by dutifully, keeping up appearances. He didn't want to be there. Troy didn't want Athey to matter to him, didn't want to be bound to an old man dying, couldn't bear to be enclosed by a house where death had come as a patient guest. He shrugged it off like an ill-fitting jacket, calling over his shoulder without turning his head as he went out, "Well, if you need anything, let me know."

Jimmy came regularly in the mornings and evenings and did up the barn chores, and hung about at other times when he could. The two of us patched together made Athey a sort of son-in-law-come-lately.

And so for a while there I took part in a little passage of family life, and with the family I would most have chosen if I had had the choice. It was something I might have prayed for, if I had thought of it, but it was not among the possibilities I had foreseen. It was just a good thing that came.

You can imagine maybe what it meant to me to be acting as almost a family member, and to be treated by Mattie as one who had been in a way chosen and who had something of use to offer. To have her feel free to ask me for help was to me freedom itself.

It was strange that Athey's growing weakness should have brought forth so kind a pleasure to me, but it did. That grief should come and bring joy with it was not something I felt able, or even called upon, to sort out or understand. I accepted the grief. I accepted the joy. I accepted that they came to me out of the same world.

Athey became less and less able. For a while, just propping himself with his cane and dragging his feet out to the kitchen was a job that took a long time and a lot of rest afterward. And then he could manage that only with help. And then he couldn't manage it at all. He still insisted on getting up early in the morning and, with help, dressing as he always had in overalls and workshirt, though now he spent most of the day sitting in his chair. On Sundays he wore over his clean overalls and shirt a blue coat that once had belonged to a suit.

He had become in body only a reminder of himself, bent and somehow loosened in form, weak and inexact in motion. His hands had become soft as cushions, the skin on the backs of them papery and pale. The women kept him clean. The room he sat or lay in was neat and bright. I kept him shorn and shaved and looking nice. We preserved his pride.

He never complained. He was stubbornly principled, doing for himself the little, and the less and less, that he could do. And his eyes to the last looked back at you as they always had. I had known him well for twenty-three years. I had seen him change from a vigorous man whose thoughts were all of life to a man who knew he was dying and who still lived willingly and thoughtfully and humorously. As I carried my bits of news to him and did for him what I could, I had already begun to mourn him, as I saw that Della and Mattie had also.

It got to be late April. We'd had some lovely weather. The woodlands were strewn with wildflowers and overhead were making shade. Everybody was busy about the fields and plant beds and gardens. The season had made its claim. And then there came a day of brittle-feeling showers driven over the town by a cold wind that, after the warm days, seemed to come through your clothes in slices.

I went to the back door as I always did and knocked twice, and nobody answered. I opened the door and leaned in. The kitchen was empty. As a kitchen was apt to be at that time of day, it was cool and formal, full of the reduced, mingled smells of seasonings and cold food. A cloth, as always, was spread over the things on the table, the chairs all shoved in at their places. There was a great pressure of silence in all the house.

I called quietly, "Anybody home?"

And even more quietly Della called back, "In here, Jayber."

I laid down my barbering tools and tiptoed, suddenly full of knowledge, to Athey's room. It was the sitting room, where they had moved in a bed for him when he could no longer climb the stairs. I stopped in the door.

Della was standing on the far side of Athey's bed, holding his hand. He had felt poorly after dinner and had wanted to lie down for a nap, something he had resisted doing. She let him sleep a long time and then could not wake him. His eyes were open, but he was staring at nothing. She could not allow herself to leave him even to call Mattie on the phone. She looked at me and shaped silently the words, "He's going." The words tugged at her mouth, but she was not crying. Seeing me hesitate, she smiled and said, "I'm glad you've come."

I went over to the bed then and picked up Athey's other hand. He was breathing, but already he was not there. I could feel a small tremor in the hand I held. There was almost no pulse. We stood a while with him, holding his hands. And then he ceased to breathe.

The eyes have a light. They give a light. I saw it go out in Athey's.

When the light had gone, Della, looking down, gently laid her fingers on his eyelids and closed them. She placed his hands together. She touched his forehead.

When finally she looked up at me, the light of our own eyes seemed to startle and glitter in the air between us.

And then, as her tears started to fall, she smiled and said, "Well."

After my many days of a sort of family membership, it was strange to step back into my mere duty. I dug Athey's grave. I waited, standing aside, as the bearers brought the coffin up among the stones. And then, when the last of the living had gone away, I mended back the ground.

After Athey's death, I never went to his and Della's house again. There was, after that, no want of friendship between Mattie and Della and me. A certain confidence, a certain understanding, had been established and would remain. But our reason to be together had been withdrawn. And so the world changes.

It wasn't until Decoration Day that I talked with Della again. I walked to the graveyard early, the first thing, as I always do on that day, to make sure the place looked good, and also because I liked being there on that day.

Della was already there when I got there. The daylight was just coming. I imagined that she had been lying awake, missing Athey, and had been moved by the thought that it was Decoration Day and was glad to have that day's visit to make, something to do.

She had brought a great vase of white peonies, every blossom with a beautiful stain of red on the center petals, and had stood it in front of the stone that bore the legend:

ATHEY KEITH   DELLA KEITH
    1879–1961   1887–

There was young grass on the grave by then. She was bending over it, her left forearm propped on her left knee, doing what might have been gardening or housekeeping—weeding, tossing away dead leaves and small stones. I made a walk around the place, over the hilltop and out of sight, not wanting to disturb her.

When I came around again to where I could see her, she had begun to walk away, slowly, reading the stones as she went. She saw me and raised her hand, and I went over.

I said, "Hello, Della."

She ignored my greeting, seeming, in speaking to me, just to go on with her thoughts. "Well, Jayber, it's odd the things we do. I know he's not here. Or, anyhow, I don't *feel* that he is. He seems more gone from here than anywhere. And yet I come here, and I think of him. I can't do anything for him where I think he is. I do what I can. Those are pretty peonies, don't you think?"

"They're beautiful," I said.

Her eyes had a glaze of tears that did not fall. I was touched entirely by the look of her and the sound of her voice. I said, "Della, are you all right?"

She said, "There are leftovers, Jayber. There are things I did or said that I wish I hadn't, and things I didn't do or say that I wish I had. When he finally got free of his sickness and awful clumsiness there at the last, I was glad, and yet I was sorry I was glad, and yet I miss him. But am I all right? Yes, I am all right. You know, Jayber, Athey never knew his mother."

She went her way, then, and left me standing there still as a stone, all filled to running over with the force of what she had put into my mind.

It was the thought of Heaven. I thought an unimaginable thought of something I could almost imagine, of a sound I could not imagine but could almost hear: the outcry when a soul shakes off death at last and comes into Heaven. I don't speak of this because I "know" it. What I know is that shout of limitless joy, love unbound at last, our only native tongue.

The Chathams' youngest boy, Athey Keith, or A. K. as they called him, was only seven at the time of his grandfather's death, and I think he was not much affected by it. A. K. was a study—and I speak now from later knowledge. He seemed to be by nature what you might call a good boy. He was a good student. When he got old enough, he was (in a resigned or routine sort of way) useful to his father. But he was also, seemingly by nature, not attracted at all to farming, or to much of anything else that Port William had to offer. He was quiet, as unhumorous as his father, and independent, standoffish. His mind, from the time he was just a little fellow, was elsewhere and he did not pretend otherwise. It was as if he had hardly come to consciousness before he was consciously waiting for a chance to be gone to some other place. And when the chance came he took it; after that he returned as seldom as possible. I never understood him or, to be honest, had much feeling for him. I suppose his mother understood him, if anybody did. I know Troy didn't. But I don't think Troy ever understood anybody, including himself. Of the Chathams' three children, I think A. K. was the most like Troy—though I don't think he particularly *liked* Troy, which may explain him somewhat.

Of all of us who knew Athey, the one who was most affected by his death, the one who was affected forever by it, was the older boy. Athey's death itself was a world's end for Jimmy. It was the loss of a companion and friend, which is what Jimmy thought it was. It was also, as the rest of us could soon see, the loss of a steadying influence. A worse loss may have been the little farm that the two of them had worked together. The place wasn't actually sold until after Della's death, but it was lost to Jimmy when Athey died. By the time it was sold, Jimmy himself was lost.

Della held on to the place, saw to it that the old mules grazed there until they died, as Athey had wanted them to do, and let Jimmy raise the tobacco crop. But no shoats were purchased that spring to be grown out and fattened for slaughter in the fall, the milk cow had been sold, the chickens given away, the garden leveled and sowed in grass. The old household integrity of the place, the put-together picture puzzle of it that Jimmy had loved, had to be given up. It was too much for Della alone.

"But *I'll* do it," he said, shedding a boy's tears for the last time in his life. "*I'll* take care of it."

It was, of course, not possible. He was only another child trying to call back what was forever gone. The little place, as it had been, was not possible. What had held it together and justified it had been Athey, and Athey was gone. Jimmy was a big boy, too old now to be fiddling around. His daddy needed him.

From that time on, Jimmy Chatham was a young man with a calling he could not answer.

Troy did need him. He needed somebody. He needed more help, as usual, than he could afford. It was opportune that his own son had grown strong enough to be of use.

The problem was that Jimmy had grown strong enough also to rebel. He didn't take to working for his father, he didn't like his father's ways or sympathize with his predicament, and he altogether lacked A. K.'s ability to resign himself even temporarily to what he disliked.

Troy was stretched tight in every way, financially, physically, and men-tally—as he had been and was going to be. He was farming too much rented land, doing it badly, spending too much time on the road. His work was always a little (or more than a little) behind, always under the shadow of hopelessness and defeat. He was always exasperated or des-perate. And always, in town, he was bluffing and blustering, acting the part of a man of large concerns, with many irons in the fire, needing to be in a hurry. And he *was* in a hurry. He had worked himself into cir-cumstances of debt and obligation that hurried him even beyond his wish to look like a man in a hurry.

To Jimmy, this meant that they were always toiling in a mess, always facing too much work that they would have to do in too much haste, and with aging, overworked equipment. It meant that Troy always expected too much and was never satisfied.

Troy's dependence on Jimmy, which increased as the boy grew older, gave Jimmy commensurate power to make trouble, which of course he used. The two of them were at war from the start. Jimmy had as yet no way of escape, and he could not or would not willingly obey. Troy could not help hinting and even saying that Jimmy had been misled by his grandfather's influence. Nor could he overlook any fault or error in his son's work. "Did you think you were still up there driving that old team of mules?" "Did you think you could do that while you were asleep?"

Jimmy was quick with sass when he wanted to be. He tried all the effects of deliberate incomprehension and slowness. He could go for days without saying a word to anybody.

Sometimes, in his new sullenness, he helped his mother in her gar-den, or she would send him to care for the chickens. But it was not the same. This work seemed only to impress on him a hopelessness that he felt without knowing. His mother's work and his father's were not parts of the same thing.

They no longer kept a milk cow or slaughtered hogs for their own use. Such things Troy liked to be seen dismissing with a wave of his hand. "I'm not fooling with any damned milk cow." Such enterprises did not conform to his idea of "the business of farming." He believed that he could not afford to fiddle around. He did not do little jobs. The business of farming had to do with "volume." He would say, "There's no money in that," as if it were his bravery to know that many things had to be overlooked or driven through or reached across to get money, of which nevertheless he needed more than he got.

Troy's one aim was to be at work with the greatest available power in the biggest possible field. During the sixties, with Athey gone and Della out of the way, and Mattie resigned or unable to resist, he began tearing out fences, plowing through waterways, bulldozing groves of trees. He didn't want anything in his way. He wanted to be seated on power, driving on and on. His belief (his religion, you might as well say) was that if he went on covering ever more ground with ever greater power, discounting the costs in worry, weariness, and soil erosion, he could finally be a success, a real businessman, with an office he actually sat and worked in. He would have status. People would look at him with envy.

He was a dreamer. He could not imagine himself as he was or where he was. And so he dreamed of himself as he would never be. For a dream he borrowed money, rented land, bought machines, drove them in big fields to the limit of endurance and beyond. It was a dream he could not have escaped even if he had waked up, for he belonged to it by his pledge and signature. His name was on too many dotted lines. The too little he earned by too much work already belonged to other people before he even earned it.

To Jimmy, such work was solitary confinement. It was slavery. He knew it instinctively, without thinking about it. He knew it because he had known his grandfather and was in spirit his grandfather's son. His own father he did not know, really, and never would. And so he could not see a way out. He was, after all, only a boy of twelve and then thirteen and fourteen and fifteen.

He still had his grin, but now it was turned away from the family. Now it was turned to the world. It was a grin of readiness. He was waiting to see what the world might offer. He wanted and expected it to offer something if not better at least different. He wanted to hear its dare. You could still see the mischief in his grin, but you could see trouble too. All he needed was a car.

25
A Period of Disintegration

Athey Keith died in the spring of 1961. As I look back on it now, his death seems to have been the start of a new run of hard times for Port William, and of course for other places like it. Still and always, Port William was contending with The News. The local news was just talk, the result of Port William's never-ceasing observation of its own doings and its listening to itself. The other news, The News of the World, seemed to have to do principally with The War and The Economy.

I know it is somewhat objectionable to capitalize such things and speak of them as if they were freestanding creatures. But The War and The Economy were seeming more and more to be independent operators. The War, I thought, was just the single Hell that is always astir in the world, always going on in modest ways even when it has not broken out in full force. And the nations were always preparing funds of weapons and machines and people to be used up whenever The War did break out in full force, which meant that sooner or later it would.

Also it seemed that The War and The Economy were more and more closely related. They were the Siamese twins of our age, dressed alike, joined head to head, ready at any moment to merge into a single unified Siamese, when the crossed eyes of government should uncross. The War was good for The Economy. There was a certain airy, wordy kind of patriotism that added profit to its virtue. There was money in it, as Troy Chatham would say, who himself was being used by The Economy like lead in a pencil or in a gun. After he was used up, he would not be given a second chance. There is no rebirth in The Economy.

When I say that Port William suffered a new run of hard times in the 1960s, I don't mean that it had to "weather a storm" and come out safe again in the sunshine. I mean that it began to suffer its own death, which it has not yet completed, from which it may or may not revive. And here, talking against the wind, so to speak, I must enter, along with my lamentation, my objection. You may say that I am just another outdated old man complaining about progress and the changes of time. But, you see, I have well considered that possibility myself, and am prepared to submit to correction by anybody who cares about a community, who can show me how the world is improved by that community's dying.

At about the time of Athey's death, Milton Burgess also died, leaving everything to his sister in Dayton. Which is to say that Burgess General Merchandise, Milton's headquarters and profession and hobby and staff of life for nearly sixty years, was (you might as well say) without an inheritor. The sister had a son, but he lived in Denver and of course was not inclined to stop midway in his life's journey and come to Port William to keep store.

The store was put up for sale, and to everybody's surprise nobody wanted it. The old building had swayed a little in the winds that had blown since 1874 and was not quite as handsome or as steady on its feet as it had been in its youth, but it still had some life ahead of it. And it was still pretty fully stocked, ready to go on being a store. It could not have made anybody rich, but there was a living in it.

It was not a living that anybody wanted. Nobody wanted it because having it would have involved irregular hours, irregular pay, full-time responsibility, some worry, and living in Port William. It had about come to the point where nobody wanted to live in Port William who wasn't already in the habit of living there, or who could afford to live anyplace else. The world had become pretty generally Ceceliafied. We had received no young doctor to take the place of Dr. Markman, whose little office had begun to sink back onto its haunches. Nobody wanted to make a little money if making it required them to worry as well as work.

Nobody wanted to have to be responsible after "quitting time." They had the idea of an eight-hour day and a weekly check. So finally Burgess General Merchandise went for whatever it would bring at the court-house door. Braymer Hardy bought it for not much, sold out the merchandise at a profit (though he said not), and turned the building over to his wife to use as an "Antique and Junque" store. She used it mainly as a place to keep things, opening for business only when she felt like it, and pricing her stuff to keep. One night some drunken prophet scrawled COME HOME in a big scripture of green paint on one of the windows. When Josie Hardy died, Braymer held an auction of the contents and gave the building to Billy Gibbs and his boys as the price of tearing it down.

The demise of Burgess General Merchandise gave Jasper Lathrop the monopoly (if you would call it that). Commerce in Port William did not cease—it hasn't ceased yet—but in some ways the slant was getting steeper. Jasper Lathrop, like most country merchants then, bought chickens and eggs and cream from the farmwives. This was a more important prop to the local economy than you might think. It was one of the mainstays of the household economy of the farms, helping the families to preserve their subsistence by making a ready market for the surplus. But also it was a valuable tie between Jasper and his customers. It brought in trade.

But that ended. The household poultry flocks began to dwindle away. So did the little household dairying enterprises of two to maybe half a dozen cows. The farmwives, who once had come to town with produce, bought their groceries, and gone home with money, now went to the store (maybe in some more distant town) with only money and went home with only groceries.

The Economy no longer wanted the people of Port William to produce, for instance, eggs. It wanted them to eat eggs without producing them. Or, more properly speaking, it wanted them to *buy* eggs. It didn't care whether the eggs were eaten or not, so long as they were bought. It didn't care how fresh they were or how good they were, so long as they were bought. Perhaps, so long as they were paid for, The Economy was not much interested even in delivering the eggs.

For The Economy was studying the purpose of The War, which is to purchase and not have. The customers of The War (all of us, that is) purchase life at a great cost and yet lose it.

And The War was just as busily studying the purpose of The Economy, which is to cause people to purchase what they do not need or do not want, and to receive patiently what they did not expect.

Having paid for life, we receive death. By now, in this nineteen hundred and eighty-sixth Year of Our Lord, we all have purchased how many shares in death? How many bombs, shells, mines, guns, grenades, poisons, anonymous murders, nameless sufferings, official secrets? But not the controlling share. Death cannot be marketed in controlling shares.

Also going, soon to be almost entirely gone, were the sheep flocks. Sheep had been always a part of farming in this region of the world. Port William, over the years, had sent thousands and thousands of spring lambs to Louisville. The lambs would be born in January and February and sent to market straight off the ewes in May and June. The wool, it was said, kept and fed the ewes, and the lambs were clear money. And then that dwindled away in only a few years. "Dogs," the farmers would say after they had sold their flocks. "The damned dogs were cleaning me out." But I don't think that altogether explains it. When a lot of people have sheep, after all, stray dogs tend to disappear.

Age, I think, may have had more to do with it. The farmers were getting older. The young people were leaving or, if they stayed, were not interested. Sheep require a lot of work and trouble. People were less willing to be up at night in the winter with lambing ewes. But also once a fabric is torn, it is apt to keep tearing. It was coming apart. The old integrity had been broken.

And the farmers, some of them at least, were worrying. They knew that farming was in decline, losing diversity, losing self-sufficiency, losing production capacity. A sort of communal self-confidence, which must always have existed, had begun to die away.

You could hear it in the talk. Elton Penn, say, would come in on a Saturday night for a haircut, and then another good farmer, Nathan Coulter maybe or Luther Swain, would come in, and then others. Prices and costs would be quoted, news exchanged, comments made, questions asked. It would be a conversation that I could pretty well have written down word for word before it took place. They would talk quietly, humorously, anxiously about what was happening to them. They were feeling their way through facts they could not help but know toward a hopeful prediction they could never make. "If things keep on this way," they were asking, "what is going to become of us?"

Well, they already suspected what I now know. They were going to die, most of them, without being replaced. Some of them would die alone, in houses from which everybody else had gone, to the graveyard or "away." Poor old Luther Swain was dead alone for two days, lying on his face in his barn lot. (To his grandchildren, wherever they were, if they could have known him, he would have been no less strange than Abraham.) But they weren't worrying just about themselves. They were worrying about the fate of their life, what they had lived by and for, their work, their place. They ventured even to worry about the fate of eaters (who were not worried about the fate of farmers). I've heard it a thousand times: "I don't know what people are finally going to do for something to eat."

And one night Elton grinned, I remember, and said, "I've wished sometimes that the sons of bitches would starve. And now I'm getting afraid they actually will."

The others laughed, knowing what he meant. They are dead now, most of them. Most of them kept on farming until they died. They kept on because they had no choice, or because that was what they had always done and was the way they knew themselves, or because they liked it. Or for all of those reasons. And as long as they farmed they worried about farming and what was to become of it. This worry was maybe the main theme of conversation in my shop for a long time. The older men and some of the younger ones returned to it as if dutifully. But it wasn't a duty. It was just a continuation of the pondering and the wondering and the fear and the great sorrow that had been in each of their minds as they went about their often lonely work.

I don't think that such thoughts had ever been in the minds of farming people before. Before, no matter how hard they worked or how little they earned, farmers had always had at least the assurance that they were doing the necessary work of the world, and that before them others (most likely their own parents and grandparents) had done the same work, which still others (most likely their own children and grandchildren) would do when they were gone. In this enduring lineage had been a kind of dignity, the dignity at least of knowing that the work you are doing must be done and that it does not begin and end with yourself. Now the conversation in my shop was burdened with the knowledge that their work might come to an end. A good many of them already knew to a certainty that they did not know who would be next to farm their farms, or if their farms would be farmed at all. All of them knew that neither farming nor the place would continue long as they were. The dignity of continuity had been taken away. Both past and future were disappearing from them, the past because nobody would remember it, the future because nobody could imagine it. What they knew was passing from the world. Before long it would not be known. They were the last of their kind.

Troy Chatham, if he was there, would hold himself outside this conversation. But he could not be too much aloof from it, because he needed to stay close enough to look down on it. He despised their fear and the old-fashioned, nearly lost hope that was the cause and meaning of their fear. To Troy, in his zeal for newfangledness, they and their thoughts were as out-of-date as last year's snow. They were leftovers, obsolete. The world, ever advancing toward better things, was just waiting for them to get out of the way. He never said as much outright, but he made his point by his standing aloof, by his looking down, by his refusal of their hope and their worry. He made his point by not bothering to make it.

He did say, and said often enough, that he had the answer: modernize, mechanize, specialize, grow. They were all involved (unavoidably, as they saw it) in the industrialization of farming, but they didn't believe Troy. A few of them—Elton Penn, for one—returned his contempt. How could you thrive if you were buying everything you needed and your costs were increasing faster than your earnings? If you were losing money or breaking even on growing corn, how could you correct that by growing more corn?

Troy would answer by talking about man-hours, efficiency, economy of scale, and volume. He was attending meetings, listening to experts, and he had their language.

Or one of them would say, "Well, I reckon maybe that's all right, if you don't mind borrowing the money."

Troy had a ready answer to that too. "Debt is just an ordinary business expense," he would say.

And then, knowing they knew he was, by their standard, too much in debt, he would say, "I never expect to be out of debt again in my life. If you've got anything paid for, borrow against it. *Use* it. Never let a quarter's worth of equity stand idle."

Was he talking to persuade himself?

They knew too that he didn't have any equity to speak of, beyond his equipment. But he was going to have some, or Mattie was. So far he had only borrowed increasingly for operating expenses, using as collateral his paid-for equipment and the next year's crops on an ever-larger rented acreage. When Della died and Mattie inherited the Keith place, he would all of a sudden have at least within reach enough idle equity to suit maybe even him.

Troy Chatham was not the only one listening to the experts. In 1964, acting on the certified best advice, the official forces of education closed the Port William School. It was a good, sound building, with swings and seesaws and other playthings on the grounds around it, and they just locked the doors and sent the children in buses down to Hargrave. It was the school board's version of efficiency, economy of scale, and volume. If you can milk forty cows just as efficiently as twenty, why can't you teach forty children just as efficiently as twenty? Or for that matter, a hundred or two hundred?

Having no children of my own, I may have no right to an opinion, but I know that closing the school just knocked the breath out of the community. It did worse than that. It gave the community a never-healing wound.

It was a great personal loss to me, for I had loved seeing the children gathered and let loose, as if the schoolhouse breathed them in and out. I liked hearing the children's voices suddenly set free at the end of the school day. Some of the teachers, of course, had been bad and some good. But how good or bad they were Port William knew, and knew without delay. Whether the parents interfered for good or ill, the school was right there in sight and they at least could interfere. The school was in the town and it was in the town's talk.

When the school closed, the town turned more of its attention away from itself. If people are driving down to Hargrave on school business or for school events, they might as well shop in Hargrave, or get their hair cut there. Port William lost business. I did. I don't want to sound mercenary, but of course a community, to be a community, has to do a certain amount of its business within itself. Did somebody think it could be different?

The old Port William Hotel, with its long front porch that had once accommodated the rocking chairs and summer-evening conversations of drummers and other travelers on the river, had become first a sort of happenso old folks' home, and then a sort of happenso apartment house. And then one night in 1964 it departed from history altogether by burning very quickly to the ground.

Mat Feltner died in 1965. It was late August, the busiest time of the year. His funeral took place just in a little pause in the workday.

When the gathering at the graveside had dispersed and driven off, I was surprised to see that Burley Coulter still hung around. He hung around while the undertaker, Petey Tacker, and his assistant gathered and loaded their equipment. Though the time for my work had come, I stood with Burley making talk.

Digging a grave is one thing. I was always glad for company when I was digging a grave, which can be lonesome and a little depressing. It is a descent that maybe nobody can make altogether willingly.

Filling a grave is another thing altogether. There is something just about unbearably intimate about filling a grave, especially if it matters to you whose grave it is. I would rather do it by myself. I would rather, if I had my rathers, not be seen doing it. It is the very giving of the body to the earth, the sealing over of its absence until the world's end.

But Petey and the assistant went their way and there Burley still was, talking with me on the subjects I managed to bring up and showing no signs of leaving.

So I said, "Well—," and went over to the big stone where I had put my digging tools out of sight.

Ordinarily in Port William usage, when you say "Well—" with a certain intonation, the other person says, "Well, I reckon I better get on home," and then you can get on with your work or close your shop or whatever you need to do.

But when I got back with my spade, Burley had taken off the jacket of the suit he had been keeping to wear to funerals for maybe thirty years. He had rolled his shirt cuffs back three turns, loosened his tie, and tucked it into his shirt. He smiled at me, saying nothing, and took the spade.

I saw the point then, and went to the little toolshed and got another spade and came back and helped him.

We didn't say anything more. We worked until the last little clods had been scraped out of the grass and tossed onto the grave. We tapered and smoothed the mound to Burley's satisfaction.

And then he handed his spade to me, swung his jacket over his sweated shoulder, and walked away.

By that time the interstate highway was boring its way into our valley and across it and out again on the other side. Everything it came to looked smaller than it had looked before. Whatever it came to that was in its way, it destroyed. It was a great stroke of pure geometry cut through the country maybe five miles down the river from Port William—close enough that, now, when the town is quiet, it can hear the sound of more traffic in a few minutes than ever went through it in a month.

The interstate cut through farms. It divided neighbor from neighbor. It made distant what had been close, and close what had been distant. It interrupted the flow of water through the veins of the rock. All the roads that had gone through our part of the country before had been guided at least somewhat by the place—by features of the land, older roads, property boundaries. This one, this great casting away of the earth, respected no presence, no limits. It remembered nothing. Anything that was in its way had to move or be moved, house or hill, barn or field, stream or woods. Big bulldozers cut the land away down to the rock. Power drills bit into the rock. Explosions cracked and shook the rock and the pieces were hauled away. Places where lives had been lived disappeared from the face of the world forever.

The older men of Port William would drive down to look at the machines as they worked and to marvel at the expense and the power and the upheaval. One day a worker whose chainsaw had quit cranked it several times and then in disgust flung it in front of an oncoming bull-dozer, which covered it up. Port William had never before thought of such a possibility.

More even than television, the interstate brought the modern world into Port William. More even than The Economy and The War, it carried the people of Port William into the modern world. It was a thing of unimaginable influence. People in Port William would find it handy to drive to work or to shop in Louisville. And Louisville would find it handy to grow farther out into the countryside. City lots would be carved out of farms, raising of course the price of farmland, so that urban people could enjoy the spaciousness of rural life while looking evening and morning at the rear ends of one another's automobiles.

Port William shrank yet further. The interstate dwarfed it in scale and made light of its needs. Fuel, money, and people gathered to the interstate as water gathers to the river. The time would come when Mr. Milo Settle would be on the phone to the Standard Oil Company. "This is Milo Settle here at Port William," he would say, as if he were calling no farther than Hargrave. "Milo," he would say. "M-i-l-o." The problem was that the company would no longer deliver as much gas as he needed for his customers. They were squeezing him out in favor of the service stations on the interstate. "I've been selling your products for fifty years," he would say, justice and indignation shaking his voice, to some powerless secretary or receptionist in some place that he knew no more about than she knew about Port William. He might as well have been talking to the chairman of the board. "Fifty years!" he would say, unable to believe that so many years could mean nothing.

That great road—moving, it seemed, purely according to its own will—was the mark of an old flaw come newly ordered into the world. Who could doubt that if everything stood in its way, nothing would be left?

26

Finalities

It was late at night, a Saturday in the winter. I heard a light, hesitant tapping on the glass pane of the door, which I thought at first was a dream, and then I heard it again. And then I heard her call quietly, "Jayber?" I knew who it was.

I said, "Yes. Wait a minute."

I felt in the dark for my pants and shirt and put them on, and then turned on the lamp by the bed.

When I opened the door, feeling the cold flow in on my bare feet, she said, "I'm awfully sorry to bother you, Jayber."

I said, "It's all right. Won't you come in?"

She said, "I will just step inside, if you don't mind."

She stepped in like a girl, light over the threshold. She had the lightness of a girl, a woman's gravity in her eyes.

It was cold out, but that was not why she stepped inside. She didn't want to be seen where she was. She had left Troy's old pickup well up the street, he being gone in their car. But she was smiling as if everything was all right, which I knew it could not be.

You might say that this was the ridiculousness that a married ineligible bachelor barber's upstairs room was specifically prepared for.

I dragged my one chair out from the table and turned it toward her. "Would you like to sit down?"

She was fully aware of the social awkwardness and wanted to hurry past it. "No. Thank you, Jayber. Jayber, I need your help."

"Well, you can have it."

"Or *maybe* I do. Maybe you can't help."

"Well, let's see if I can."

She said, "They've arrested Jimmy down at Hargrave."

I could guess why, so I didn't ask.

"Drunk," she said. "He was driving that old car down the sidewalk in front of the courthouse, but this time they're just calling it drunk. I don't want Troy to find out, if I can help it."

There was trouble enough in her eyes and voice, but no appeal for sympathy. She had a problem and had set about solving it.

"Is it bail money you need?"

"Yes. I don't have the cash and I don't want to write a check." She named the amount. She said, "Jayber, if you can, would you mind? I knew I could ask you."

"You were right," I said. "You can ask me."

I had the money. I was using the bank by then, but I had kept my old habit of stashing away a little account on my own. I had maybe three or four hundred dollars stuck between the pages of an old copy of *Paradise Lost*. I was embarrassed to reveal this to Mattie, but it was also the only time in my life when I was sort of grateful and proud to have been so sly.

I handed her the amount she needed.

She said, looking straight at me, "Jayber, thank you. I'll get this back to you before long."

I wanted to say, "Take it. Keep it. It's yours." But of course I couldn't. It would have been like sending her a valentine.

I said, "You're entirely welcome."

She had taken off her gloves to put the money into her purse, and now she was putting them on again.

I said, "Do you want me to go get him?"

She kindly did not ask me how I was going to do that in the middle of the night without a car. She said, her hand on the knob of the door, "No, thank you. I had better be the one to do that."

And then, looking back at me, she said, "Of course I've warned him. And his daddy has."

"I know," I said.

I knew too, and knew that she knew, that Troy's warning had been coal oil on a fire.

For a little while after she was gone her fragrance stayed in the room.

Jimmy Chatham was a problem that couldn't be solved at home. Maybe it couldn't be solved anywhere anytime soon. You could describe the problem easily enough by just adding and subtracting. All there was to it was visible, I mean. Jimmy was not dishonest or shy or sly. He didn't have many secrets, if any. For one reason, everything he did had some reference to his all-out battle with his father. He could make no secret of what he did because what he did was intended in the first place to be an announcement.

Unlike Troy, he was attractive in a way that people didn't envy or resent. Everybody liked him. He was always right into whatever fun was available, and he was not very particular about what he called fun. He was, I can tell you, plenty smart, though not a good student. He might have been a fine athlete, but was as willfully disappointing in that as in other things. He would be ineligible because of bad grades, or he broke the training rules, or he made some kind of mischief. Aside from the work he did grudgingly for his father to earn the little freedom that he made much of, he was what you would have to call a wild boy. He made a few brief token submissions, enough to get by, but in general nobody could do anything with him. He was beyond appeal.

The problem with Jimmy was, he had liked the place he was born in until Athey died; after that, he hadn't liked it. Since then his aim had been to defy that place when he was in it and to get out of it as far as he could whenever he could. As soon as he was sixteen he bought an old car that he was then, as he saw it, enslaved to his father to pay for, and that kept him in the unhappiness of breakdown and repair and new parts and envy of better cars. He was stuck in the momentary life of having fun, enduring work to earn money to have fun, and getting into trouble. When the car was running he would be in Hargrave on Saturday nights and sometimes on other nights.

In Hargrave he turned that big grin of his to the world. The grin said, "Come on, world, show me what you got." And the world understood him perfectly. The world came up with beer, girls, gasoline, dances, boys in need of a fight, and pretty soon marijuana. Jimmy's message home was trouble and a kind of fame. He pretty well won the wildness contest of his generation.

He was having (when he had it) no end of fun, and of course was not making himself happy. A part of the cost of making his father unhappy was the unhappiness of his mother. That by itself was enough to make Jimmy unhappy, for he was not a hard-hearted boy and he loved his mother. He was wild, but he was also bewildered. He was caught (as his father was caught) and he didn't know how to get loose.

People were sort of awestruck by him in a way, and yet worried about him too. He was coming to no good, and nobody wanted that. They hoped that something would settle him down. Maybe even he hoped something would.

Nobody knew when or how he decided to enlist in the army. Nobody knew whether or not he had been sober when he did it. We just heard one day that he had done it, and that he was soon to be gone. He had done it the minute he was old enough. At least he had solved his problem with his father. In Port William people mostly were relieved. They could quit worrying about him if they didn't know what he was doing.

It was not maybe the best time to join the army. The War had broken out again, this time in Vietnam. Everybody hoped Jimmy Chatham would not have to be in a war. He had, it seemed, a fair chance not to be. The army, after all, was scattered over half the world. People thought the army would give Jimmy a look at the world, teach him some things, and help him to settle down. Even I, sad to say, thought it might. I hoped it would.

When I looked at him in his wildness and sadness and bewilderment, ready to leave us, I would think what love had led to. Ever since, remembering him, I have thought of that.

Once Jimmy was gone (as you might have predicted, as maybe Jimmy predicted), Troy realized how much he had depended on him. He missed him, thought better of him, and excused his faults. In town he reported on his travels and bragged on his accomplishments.

Troy also became a fierce partisan of the army and the government's war policy. The war protesters had started making a stir, and the talk in my shop ran pretty much against them. Troy hated them. As his way was, he loved hearing himself say bad things about them.

One Saturday evening, while Troy was waiting his turn in the chair, the subject was started and Troy said—it was about the third thing said— "They ought to round up every one of them sons of bitches and put them right in front of the damned communists, and then whoever killed who, it would be all to the good."

There was a little pause after that. Nobody wanted to try to top it. I thought of Athey's reply to Hiram Hench.

It was hard to do, but I quit cutting hair and looked at Troy. I said, "Love your enemies, bless them that curse you, do good to them that hate you."

Troy jerked his head up and widened his eyes at me. "Where did you get that crap?"

I said, "Jesus Christ."

And Troy said, "Oh."

It would have been a great moment in the history of Christianity, except that I did not love Troy.

Burley Coulter and Big Ellis had come in for a haircut, riding in Big Ellis's car. It was the late winter of 1969. Late February or early March. The sun was shining for the time being, but the ground was too wet to plow. It was the between-times that comes every year. The farmers were still feeding the stock and doing their other wintertime chores. Their minds were still wintery. But now they could feel spring coming. As soon as they could get into their fields, the new crop year would begin.

Burley and Big Ellis were old. They were looking forward to the spring work, but also they were dreading it. Some would have said they were too old to work, but they were still working. For a while they were going to be sore and too tired. Toward the middle of the morning, needing something to do, Burley had wandered over to Big Ellis's. And then they had wandered into town—literally wandered, for Big Ellis tended to drive hither and yon between the ditches.

Both of them had got their hair cut and had sat back down, wearing their hats again. They were in no hurry. I climbed into the chairman's chair and sat down myself.

Big Ellis yawned, took his hat off and rubbed his head, looked out the window at the sky, in which there were again a few clouds. "It would be fine if this weather would get cleared on out of here now. Fellows like me have got to get to work." He giggled a little, knowing that we knew that fellows like him were not overeager to get to work. He put his hat back on.

"Well, it's not going to clear out for a while," Burley said. "It'll rain again by dark."

"Now, I'll just bet you it won't," Big Ellis said.

"How much?"

"One dollar."

"I'll take that bet," Burley said. "I'll give that dollar a good home."

The bet, I knew, meant nothing. Neither of them, if he won, would take the other's money.

"Fair and square, now," Big Ellis said. "No praying."

"No. Even Steven," Burley said. "If you won't, I won't."

About then we heard a car pull in behind Big Ellis's and stop.

Big Ellis leaned to the window and looked out. "Now, who would *that* be? I don't know that car."

We heard the car door open and shut. There were some brisk steps on the walk and then the shop door opened and a man we had never seen before came in, a young man, dressed up, carrying a clipboard with some papers on it. He pushed the door shut, consulting the clipboard, and looked at us.

"Is there a Mr. Crow here?"

"That would be me," I said.

He was (I believe he said) Mr. Mumble Something of the Forces of Health and Sanitation. He put out his hand and I shook it. He did not look again at Burley and Big Ellis.

"I'm here to make an inspection," he said. He propped the clipboard on his belt buckle and began to look at various things and make check marks on a ruled page.

Maybe you are used to this sort of thing and don't mind. Maybe you have inspected inspectors and found them worthy of the highest approval. But I have to admit that I minded.

It was not as though I was running a barbershop in a prison. I was running a freewill operation. Except for the small boys who came in under parental orders, my customers were volunteers, who inspected the property and equipment every time they came in. They could see for themselves. I wasn't barbering in a school for the blind, either.

That I was still charging fifty cents a haircut when most barbers had gone to a dollar might have had something to do with bringing some of them in, but only some of them. Most of my customers, I think, were satisfied enough. But they came to my shop, really, because they had always come, and because they felt at home.

Maybe you can understand why I minded if you recollect that my shop was only partly my place of business. Partly it was my living room. It was Port William's living room, or one of them.

How would you feel if a government inspector, even the most approvable of government inspectors, walked into your living room, ignored your guests, and began looking over your furniture and making check marks on a clipboard?

Burley and Big Ellis were embarrassed. They sat, saying nothing, glancing now and again at the inspector but mostly looking out the windows. Even the inspector seemed to be embarrassed. He didn't look at any of us. He strolled about in the shop as if he were alone, looking at things, making little grunts under his breath, and checking various items on his paper.

For him himself, I sort of felt sorry. But he was not there as himself. He was the man across the desk, the one I had so dreaded to meet again. But this time, I thought, it was not a desk but a whole building full of sub-assistant-secretaries. He did not speak for himself but for a man behind a desk who spoke for a man behind another desk, who also did not speak for himself.

The inspector, or the man inside the inspector, was just a young fellow with black wavy hair and black-rimmed glasses who had got Somewhere and made Something of himself.

"Mr. Crow," he said, as if from quite a distance, his voice echoing up the levels of authority, "I don't see any fixtures. Do you have hot running water?"

I had a big metal urn with a spigot at the bottom. It sat on a little coal-oil stove. I could regulate the burner and keep the water at just the right temperature for shaving.

I didn't say anything. I didn't know what to say, and I didn't want to say anything. I got down from the barber chair, picked up my shaving mug, carried it over to the urn, put it under the spigot, and turned the handle. The water ran. It was hot. The inspector made a check mark.

Actually, I didn't even have cold running water. The town pump across the road no longer pumped, but Mr. Milo Settle had put a pipe into the well to pump water from it into the garage. I carried my water in buckets from a spigot in Mr. Settle's garage.

The young man inside the inspector looked at me and smiled. "Where does your water come from, Mr. Crow?"

I smiled back. I said, "From the heavens."

And then the young man disappeared again. The inspector said that I was in violation of Regulation Number So-and-so, which required that all barbershops should be equipped with hot running water.

I pointed to the urn from which I had just run some hot water.

He said the hot water had to run from a proper faucet at the end of a pipe, not from a spigot on an urn. He signed and dated the sheet with the check marks on it and gave me a copy.

The young man inside the inspector said, "I'm sorry, Mr. Crow."

I said, "Your sorrow is noted and appreciated."

And then Burley, who had not yet paid me, stood up, reaching for his wallet.

"Jayber," he said, "it's fine of you to give all us Port William people free haircuts. But I think a little donation from time to time is only right."

He fumbled in his wallet, finally plucked out a dollar bill, and laid it on my cigar box on the backbar.

"I ain't out anything," Burley explained to the inspector. "That's just the dollar I'm about to win off of Big Ellis here."

Big Ellis, who had paid me, started giggling then, and *he* got out a dollar bill. He got up and put his donation on top of Burley's.

"I ain't out anything," he said. "Same reason."

And just then, from a cloud we had not seen coming, it began to rain.

Wheeler Catlett always came into my shop in a hurry, with momentum. If the latch hadn't opened when he turned the knob, it would have been too bad for the door. Wheeler was my lawyer, you might say, if you don't mind speaking informally. I had never been to his office. If I wanted to know anything in the legal line, I consulted him while I cut his hair.

Wheeler was maybe too familiar with that sort of thing, but also it amused him.

"Suppose," he said, "that you ever actually came to my office as a paying client, and I said, 'Jayber, while you're here, how about giving me a haircut?'"

And I said, "Why, Wheeler, I'd do it, of course, and wouldn't charge you so much as a thin dime. So I reckon we're even."

"I reckon we are," Wheeler said.

The inspector's visit had stayed on my mind. I wasn't mad at the inspector. I wasn't mad, period. I had progressed enough to know there was nobody to be mad *at*. The inspector was a hand in a glove. The hand wasn't responsible, really, and the glove without a hand in it was merely empty. What I felt, properly speaking, was just a sinking or an empty feeling in the pit of my stomach every time I thought about that ruled sheet of paper with the check marks on it. I could feel change coming and I didn't want it to come. I didn't know what it would be. Like, I suppose, every stray dog and cat, I would like a change for the better, but I fear changes made by people with more power than I've got.

And so the first time Wheeler came in after the inspector's visit, which was pretty soon, I brought the subject up.

"Suppose," I said, "that I just ignore it and don't do anything. Just keep on going the way I've always gone. What can they do to me?"

Wheeler snorted, maybe to announce his awareness that he was being solicited yet again for free legal advice, maybe with a certain amusement at the fix I was in. "Well, sir," he said, "I have never defended a barber for neglecting to have hot running water, and so I don't know. They can do something to you, you needn't to worry about that."

He thought a minute and then said, "You can find out what they can do to you. They'll be glad to show you, I imagine. It's just a question of how much you're willing to pay to find out."

"I don't want to pay anything to find out," I said.

Wheeler said, "I didn't think so," still amused. But then he became serious. He could be a friend. "That's the point. You want to stay clear of those people, if you can."

"That's what I want. If they don't bother me, I surely won't bother them."

"I understand. But they're in the business of bothering you. If you don't get into compliance, they'll come back and find it out, or one of your competitors will report you."

"Who would compete for Port William heads?" It was too innocent of me to say that, but I hated to face the truth. I thought of Violet Great-low, and then I thought, "Surely not."

"Hell fire, *anybody!*" Wheeler said. "Any barber in driving distance. So instead of paying to be out of compliance, why don't you pay to get into compliance?"

I said, "Wheeler, you can see what's here. A water line, a water pump, a water heater, faucets and a sink, maybe a cistern—all that would be worth more than the building, and just for a few drops of shaving water a day."

"Well, you could put in a proper bathroom."

"What would a proper bathroom be worth to one bachelor?"

"I don't know," said Wheeler, who of course had one, or maybe two, and was not a bachelor. "Not much, maybe."

I tried one more shot. The donation business had caught on. Burley had been telling people about it. And most people who donated were paying a dollar. I was getting a raise without even asking.

I said, "Well, suppose I just give away haircuts and live off of donations? Go out of business and into charity, so to speak."

"It's just a question of how much you're willing to pay to find out," Wheeler said. "It would be an interesting case. But do you want to be the subject of a case?"

It came clear to me then. I had come to another parting of the ways. I didn't know what the next step would be, but I knew I was going to have to take a step.

I wiped the lather from Wheeler's neck and sideburns, brushed off the loose hair, and whisked away the cloth. "Well, anyhow," I said, "this is one of my free haircuts."

I *meant* to mean that I was trading him a free haircut for free legal advice, but Wheeler said, "I know it," and he laid his donation on the backbar. It was a dollar.

When Jimmy Chatham was killed in Vietnam it was not something anybody could easily believe. The War had come again and we were in it, there was no doubt of that. And yet it had changed. It was not what it had been before. It was not, for instance, World War II. It was smaller and seemed farther away. We at home were less involved. We sent fewer of the young. We made no sacrifices. There was nothing we used less of. People did not try to save gasoline, but drove their vehicles just as much and just as fast as ever. It was easy for people to guess that things were mainly all right.

And then all of a sudden we had among us this dead boy in a coffin— a dead boy who was one of us, whom we had known (and not quite known) for a few years in the time of the world as Jimmy Chatham, the child of Mattie and Troy, grandchild of Della and Athey. And the sun and the moon shone on us as before, as if we had not heard the news.

I dug the grave. I waited while the pallbearers—Jimmy's friends, unbelievably young—bore the flag-covered coffin to the grave and the mourners gathered. When they had assembled, instead of standing well out of the way as I usually did, I took off my hat and stepped in under the edge of the tent.

The preacher spoke his words and prayed his prayer. The salute was fired. The bugler sounded taps: "Day is done, gone the sun—" The flag was folded and handed to Mattie, who received it like a child wrapped in swaddling clothes and shed not a tear. She sat erect. She tossed her head backward slightly once, as if to shake rain from her hair, and that was all. Troy, who had been stoic at the time of Liddie's death, wept with one hand over his face.

Afterward, it seemed for a while that Troy had been almost unmade by his grief, but then, having nobody else to be, he became himself again and continued on. I think he was ashamed that he had been seen in his weakness. He seemed to assert himself again in order to deny that he was weak. He was still young enough to believe in his strength. And, really, he had no choice; his life had been determined by then. Until he died he would have to stay in it and live by its established terms the best he could.

Of course I had no more right to stop and grieve than anybody else. For a while, though, I felt that I too was being unmade by grief. Grief and bewilderment. Jimmy Chatham had been so much alive in my imagination that I could not easily imagine him dead. I could not imagine him dead without grieving, or without imagining his mother's grief, which made me grieve.

Before he died, I wondered, had he imagined that he could die?

Both sides, in making war, agree to these deaths, this dying of young soldiers in their pride. And afterward it becomes possible to pity the suffering of both sides, and to think of the lost, unfinished lives of boys who had grown up under hands laid with affection on their heads.

It seemed, after he was killed and buried, that my own left hand kept the memory of the shape and feel of Jimmy Chatham's head when he was little and I would have to clamp my hand above his ears to keep him from looking around while I cut his hair.

Somewhere underneath of all the politics, the ambition, the harsh talk, the power, the violence, the will to destroy and waste and maim and burn, was this tenderness. Tenderness born into madness, preservable only by suffering, and finally not preservable at all. What can love do? Love waits, if it must, maybe forever.

In any moment when I was quiet, tenderness and madness would come upon me and contend to no purpose, to the making of no sense. I could hardly bear to read the newspaper, which filled me with disloyalty and unbelief. We were, as we said again, making war in order to make peace. We were destroying little towns in order to save them. We were killing children in order that children might sleep peacefully in their beds without fear. We were raping and plundering a foreign land (and our own) for the sake of "love of country." We were carrying into the heavens this cruelty and emptiness of heart. I felt involved in an old sickness of the world. I was sick with that sickness and could see no end. We had waded halfway across a bloody mire and could not get out except by wading halfway again, either forward or back.

For a while again I couldn't pray. I didn't dare to. In the most secret place of my soul I wanted to beg the Lord to reveal Himself in power. I wanted to tell Him that it was time for His coming. If there was anything at all to what He had promised, why didn't He come in glory with angels and lay His hands on the hurt children and awaken the dead soldiers and restore the burned villages and the blasted and poisoned land? Why didn't He cow our arrogance? Lying awake in the night (for again sleep was coming hard) I could imagine the almighty finger writing in stars for all the world to see: GO HOME.

But thinking such things was as dangerous as praying them. I knew who had thought such thoughts before: "Let Christ the King of Israel descend now from the cross, that we may see and believe." Where in my own arrogance was I going to hide?

Where did I get my knack for being a fool? If I could advise God, why didn't I just advise Him (like our great preachers and politicians) to be on our side and give us victory and make sure that Jimmy Chatham had not died in vain? I had to turn around and wade out of the mire myself.

Christ did not descend from the cross except into the grave. And why not otherwise? Wouldn't it have put fine comical expressions on the faces of the scribes and the chief priests and the soldiers if at that moment He had come down in power and glory? Why didn't He do it? Why hasn't He done it at any one of a thousand good times between then and now?

I knew the answer. I knew it a long time before I could admit it, for all the suffering of the world is in it. He didn't, He hasn't, because from the moment He did, He would be the absolute tyrant of the world and we would be His slaves. Even those who hated Him and hated one another and hated their own souls would have to believe in Him then. From that moment the possibility that we might be bound to Him and He to us and us to one another by love forever would be ended.

And so, I thought, He must forebear to reveal His power and glory by presenting Himself as Himself, and must be present only in the ordinary miracle of the existence of His creatures. Those who wish to see Him must see Him in the poor, the hungry, the hurt, the wordless creatures, the groaning and travailing beautiful world.

I would sometimes be horrified in every moment I was alone. I could see no escape. We are too tightly tangled together to be able to separate ourselves from one another either by good or by evil. We all are involved in all and any good, and in all and any evil. For any sin, we all suffer. That is why our suffering is endless. It is why God grieves and Christ's wounds still are bleeding.

But the mercy of the world is time. Time does not stop for love, but it does not stop for death and grief, either. After death and grief that (it seems) ought to have stopped the world, the world goes on. More things happen. And some of the things that happen are good. My life was changing now. It had to change. I am not going to say that it changed for the better. There was good in it as it was. But also there was good in it as it was going to be.

Burley said, "Well, have you seen your buddy lately?" I knew he meant the inspector.

It was late March or early April by then. Burley was waiting out another wet spell.

"No," I said. "I hope not to become any better acquainted with the inspector."

"How're you going to keep from it? You're inspectable, ain't you?"

"Well," I said, a little fearful of what I knew I was about to say, for I had not yet said it even to myself, "I suppose I'm going to have to shut her down."

"What!" Burley said. "You can't do that! Hell fire! What'll we do without a barbershop?"

"Well, barbershops' days are numbered, anyhow. The boys and young men don't want their hair barbered anymore. They're wanting it 'styled.' And I reckon I don't want to learn how to style. I'm not up with the times, and I reckon I'll just stay behind."

"You're just going to *live* here, then?"

"No, I reckon I'm going to leave."

"Leave! Where? I mean where *to?*"

"I don't know. To the river, maybe. I always thought that if I lived on the river, I'd fish. More, I mean, than I have so far." I was listening to myself with some interest, for I certainly had not thought it through.

"*Fish?*" Burley said. He was often enough a fisherman himself, but he knew that to some respectable people fishing was a vice, an addiction of sorts that led to worse things. And so he said "*Fish?*" as though to warn me of what others might think.

"I thought," I said, and I had to clear my throat, for I was going to speak of an old dream that I had not thought of in a long time. The dream came from about the time I became Uncle Stanley's successor as grave digger and janitor. Or maybe it came all the way from my days at The Good Shepherd. "I thought I'd buy me a little patch down by the river, with trees and maybe a garden spot. I'd build me a little house out of secondhand lumber. I'd end my public life and commence a private one. I'd build a little boat."

There it was. That was what I wanted to do. I could see my boat, my green boat, floating light as a leaf by the shady bank at the end of a path coming down from the house.

Burley was grinning. He saw. He knew. But he said, "You don't have to build no house. I *got* a house I'm not using. Lord, I don't expect I've stayed two nights in it since Mam died."

He was talking about his little camp house, where we'd come ashore out of the flood that morning in 1937. I hadn't seen it many times since then, but I knew the look of it. I saw what he saw.

"And you'd be willing to part with it?"

"No need for me to *part* with it. I'll just give you the use of it."

27

A New Life

To feel at home in a place, you have to have some prospect of staying there. The inspector's visit and my talk afterward with Wheeler had forced me to think of leaving and to suffer the thought. My mind didn't really give up on my shop until Burley Coulter offered me his camp house on the river and I imagined my boat floating on the water. I knew for sure then that I was going, because I knew where I was going to go.

It is strange the way your mind withdraws from a place it knows you are going to leave. I didn't plant my garden in town that spring. I leveled it and sowed it in grass. I didn't replenish the coal pile when it ran low. Looking ahead to the possibility of renting the building, I used my spare time in painting the outside, roof and walls, and re-puttying the windows. And so I began my farewell.

I was no sooner convinced that I was going to leave than I became eager to be gone. Staying and thinking of going, for one thing, made me sad. I had lived and worked there, after all, for thirty-two years. I had come when I was twenty-two, hardly more than a boy. And now I was fifty-four, pretty old to be making a new start in life. But also I was looking forward to this new start. That little house down there among the trees by the river had become a new vision of my mind. I longed to go. I began putting things I wasn't using into cardboard boxes.

I know better by now than to try to predict what is to come. But of all the stages of my life—Goforth, Squires Landing, The Good Shepherd, Pigeonville, Lexington, Port William—this one here on the riverbank bids fair to be the last. Unless of course I fall and break something or become an emergency of some other kind, and give up the ghost finally in front of an institutional TV set down at Hargrave. Who knows?

Some of the changes in my life were imposed, and some were chosen—if by "chosen" I may mean that I chose what I seemed already to have been chosen by, desire having obscured the alternatives. And each change has been a birth, each having taken me to a new life from which I could not go back. And I have asked myself, "Would I have known such births if, from Pigeonville or Lexington, I had taken one of the paths by which people get somewhere and make something of themselves?" But of course I have no answer.

The night before I left, I boxed up the last of the things I would take with me, leaving out only what I would need to pass the night and to fix breakfast. The few electrical gadgets I had I put in a clutch beside my little refrigerator to give to whatever ones might rent the place, for I would have no electricity on the river. I put everything in order. And then I went to bed.

And then, unable to sleep, I got up again and stripped the bed, folded the bedclothes, put them in a box, stuffed the pillow in on top, shut the box and tied it with a piece of twine. I tried sitting in my chair by the window then. But I was too stirred up to keep still for long. Thirty-two years had seemed a long time to me when I first thought of leaving. Now that I was ready to go, it seemed that almost no time at all had passed since I had come there and slept the first night cold, having no fuel to make a fire. It seemed all to have been a passing, and I was again what I had been during so many of my younger years, a stranger and a traveler.

I went out. It was late. There was enough moonlight to brighten the trees and the roofs and walls of the houses and throw their bottomless black shadows beyond them. The town, filled with sleep, was just wonderfully quiet. Nobody was out. The young had finally gone to bed. The old had not yet begun to wake up.

Loafing and wakefulness are two of the principal arts of Port William.

Maybe, too, they pass in Port William for public duties. In the business places and the street, people loaf and talk to the point of discomfort and the neglect of other things. They stand in the cold and think of yet more to say until their noses are red and their toes half-frozen. Some carry the conversation on into the night, long after the stores have closed. Some rise early and begin again before daylight.

In its conversation, its consciousness of itself, its sleep and waking, Port William has always been pretty much an unofficial place. It has, really, nothing of its own but itself. It has no newspaper, no resident government, no municipal property. Once it owned and maintained the part of the road that passed through it, two dug wells with pumps, and a stout-walled, windowless jail in which one malefactor had spent one night. These were all of its public domain. For the supervision of these things and the keeping of the peace, there was a town board, a mayor, and a constable. With the revenue from licensing saloons and fining (with their permission) the local troublemakers, they maintained the town properties. Their one great civic feat was causing the first telephone company to whitewash its poles. But all that was a long time ago. Port William would remember bits of it occasionally, but mostly it forgot. Mostly the town's history had become its ways, its habits, its feelings, its familiarity with itself.

In the quiet, in the fall of moonlight upon it that last night of my life there, Port William slept and dreamed the dreams its history had brought it to. In the time of my stay it had suffered its own history, of course, but also the history of the larger world that contained it. In those thirty-two years that now seemed almost no time at all, the town had shrunk and declined. Some of its quiet that night was the quiet of sleep. Some was the quiet of emptiness and absence. The blacksmith shop was long gone. The hotel was gone; the empty lot where it had stood had become (in the way of Port William) a sort of happenso parking place for cars and pickup trucks. Burgess General Merchandise, which would remain standing for a little while yet, was closed, useless, as still as a grave. The poolroom was closed. The school was closed. Mr. Milo Settle and the garage were in decline and soon to be gone. The barbershop would be closed forever. In many of the houses, now, widows and widowers slept alone. Even in the daytime those houses had begun to give off the feeling of vacancy. Their windows had begun to have the look of sightlessness.

If you knew the place, if you had known it for long, you could not look at it without feeling that its life was being irresistibly pulled at by larger places. It was stretching itself farther and farther in order to hold together, traveling farther in order to stay in place. It was like a spider's web that will stretch so far and then break.

I thought, "Here once, forever gone."

But then, in the flimsiness of time, in the moonlight, the presence of the town so strong upon me, I thought, "Now and forever here."

It was a little port for the departure and arrival of souls, and was involved in more than time. It seemed all alight with the ghost that, so to speak, wore it. I walked slowly out of town and past the graveyard and on out to the Grandstand, from where I could see the valley a long way up and down. And then I walked back again. I fixed my breakfast and washed and packed up the dishes and the skillet. Daylight came. Soon Elton Penn was there with his truck. And then Burley and Nathan Coulter came, and Andy Catlett and Martin Rowanberry. We were ready to load up and go.

With so many on hand to help, I was embarrassed at having so little to move. Subtracting the few things I was going to leave, and the things not worth keeping that I had kept only because I was used to them and now had thrown away or burned, I really didn't have very much. There was room to spare in Elton's truck. The only thing that taxed us much was the barber chair, which I was taking because it was comfortable. I had never moved it from its place in all the time I had been there. There was something shocking about taking it away, as though we were loading the chimney. There was something inconsolable about the bare circular print it left on the floor, unpolished by footsteps over fallen hair.

I was touched by a kind of pity when I saw the two rooms emptied at last. The little building that for thirty-two years had been as familiar to me as my own clothes now looked as if neither I nor anybody had ever lived there. Separated from the daily human life that had been lived in it, it looked almost unbearably flimsy and temporary and inadequate and purposeless and poor: "Ye must be born again." I took Barber Horsefield's paper clock whose hands always pointed to 6:30, wrote GONE on the back of it, and hung it up once more in the window.

It was good to have the others there. They made of that momentous

day and my grief only a practical job of work. And I needed all the help
I had in bringing the stuff down through the woods. It was a longish
carry, and steep until we got to the narrow bench where the house stood.

But now the mood had changed. Even mine had. It was a pretty place
and a pretty day. The spring wildflowers were blooming and the birds
were singing all around. The river was up almost to banktop, with considerable current, calling forth thoughts of distance and drifting away as
the risen river always does. Everybody was excited by the thought of
new life beginning in a new place.

The others got to joking about the wild way I was apt to carry on,
away off there by myself. Mart Rowanberry, who knew stories of certain
social events that had occurred in Burley's younger days, jigged his knees
a time or two to make the floor vibrate. "It ain't as stout as it used to be,
Burley."

Burley wagged his thumb at me in comment upon my age and solitary habits. "It won't *need* to be as stout as it used to be."

By midmorning all my furniture was in place, my friends were gone,
and I was unpacking my boxes of clothes, bedclothes, books, and kitchen
things. I had a kettle of water boiling on the stove and was feeling pretty
much at home.

The camp house was built by Ernest Finley, the carpenter and wood-
worker who was Mat Feltner's brother-in-law. He built it on a bench well
above the river on a two-acre patch of land between the river and the
road, bounded on the upriver side by Katy's Branch and on the downriver side by the property known as the Billy Landing, owned in those
days and for a good while afterward by Beriah Easterly, who kept a little
store there that never amounted to much and amounted to less and less
as the years went by.

Ernest built the house in 1916 or thereabouts, when he was scarcely
more than a boy. Even in those days, he was a solitary, quiet sort of fellow who loved to fish the rockbars and slips for bass or bream or new-
lights. At that time, there wasn't a proper road going along the river.
When Ernest went down to camp and fish, he considered himself to be
pretty well beyond the workaday world of Port William.

He set the house on good stout yellow locust posts. He salvaged poplar framing and siding from a tumbledown half-log house on the Feltner place. He bought new pine tongue-and-groove flooring and new galvanized tin roofing, which were delivered to him by boat at the Billy Landing. He built a tight two-room cabin. The part of his work that is under roof is still good to this day.

The smaller of the two rooms is the kitchen, with shelves and cabinets and a table that is hinged so as to fold up against the wall. The larger room is for sleeping and sitting. Both rooms have windows with sliding sashes and screens and heavy outside shutters that can be bolted shut if you go away, which I never have. Not yet. A porch goes along two sides. On the side toward the river, because of the narrowness of the bench, the porch rests on tall stilts. Outside the larger room, the porch is roofed and screened so that in summer you have, really, three rooms. The porch that is open to the weather has been replaced twice, once by Burley, once by me.

In his time Ernest kept the place well-equipped with bedclothes, cooking things, dishes, and other necessities. When he came down for a stay, provided the fish were biting, about all he needed to bring was cornmeal and lard.

When Ernest came home crippled from World War I, he had no further use for the place. He sold it to Burley Coulter, who at the time was pursuing a career as the Coulter family's black sheep, and who therefore needed from time to time a home away from home. Over the years Burley had settled (and aged) into a quieter, more responsible life, and so the house had passed to me.

It is in most ways the best and in every way the most beautiful place I have ever lived in.

Sometime in the 1920s, I think, Burley painted the house with a paint that must at the start have been green. Over the years it had weathered to a flaky grayish blue-green that had something of the character of the lichens and mosses you see on tree trunks. It looked as old as the oldest trees around it. It had become a work of time, fitting the place as no work merely of hands could have done. The grace of the fashion of it was no longer just in its design and construction but also in the marks upon it of time and use and the way the trees around it had grown and shaped themselves during half a century.

For one man and a few sticks of furniture, it is plenty big. Especially in summer, when the doors and windows are open, it seems roomy, airy, and light. And yet I am always surprised, returning to it from the road or looking up at it from the river, to see how small and inconspicuous it is, tucked in against the slope, under the trees. It is a house, but sometimes it has the feeling of a burrow or a den in a hollow tree.

This hillside was cleared and cropped maybe twice or three times, like most of the hillsides around here. And the trees around the house are the ones that are quickest to return to abandoned croplands close to streams where the soil is fairly rich: water maples, elms, sycamores, locusts, box elders, a few cottonwoods and walnuts, a wild cherry or two, and down along the water's edge, of course, the willows.

For the first several years I was here, I kept a sort of yard cleared for some distance around the house, once a year scything down the nettles and wild grasses and elderberry bushes and seedling trees. And I kept open a prospect on the river. This suited me for a while and seemed the proper thing to do. I loved the clarity and neatness my mowing and cutting made. And then one year I stopped, not from laziness (though using a scythe on a hillside will produce sweat enough) but just to give room and welcome to whatever would come. Since then I have mowed mainly my paths down to the river and across to the garden and up to the road and the woodpile and out to the privy. When the trees send their branches too close, I cut them back to keep them from scraping the walls or banging on the roof. The windfalls that are big enough I saw up and split for stovewood. Otherwise I let it be as it will. Now, sitting out on the porch in the summer among the tops of the young trees, I am among the birds. And in the last few years something wonderful has begun to happen. Not just near the house but all along the hillside, the seedlings of the true forest have begun to come to the higher ground: sugar maples and hickories and chinquapin oaks. Now that I am old, I talk to them, I talk to the birds, the way Athey Keith used to talk to the stray dogs and cats in his own exile up in Port William.

Wonders do happen. Another one was that the barber's trade followed me down to the river. I didn't expect that. I didn't suppose it at all.

I hadn't been down here more than two or three days—I was still in the midst of all the little jobs of settling in—when Art and Mart Rowanberry came down the path among the trees. It was a beautiful day with a good, warm, season-changing breeze blowing up the river. I had a pair of carpenter's trestles set up on the porch, was building a new screen door.

"Well, now," Art said, "ain't it a fine day overhead!"

And Mart said, "Well, I don't reckon you're working."

I said, "Oh, a little." And then it came to me: He meant barbering. And I said, "Sure!"

It was a little hard to pretend that I was, in fact, "working." I did not appear to be expecting customers. Books were piled on the seat of the barber chair and clothes were hanging over the back of it. My barbering tools were laid back on the top shelf of a cabinet in the kitchen. The neckcloths I had stuck away at the bottom of a chest in the other room. But I made the pretense. I unloaded the chair and gathered up my equipment in a hurry. Art stepped up and took his seat. Mart backed a sitting chair up to where he could talk to me and look out at the river at the same time.

"Now, you know," I said, "I don't have electricity here and can't use the electric clippers."

"That don't make one bit of difference," Art said. "What you don't cut this time, I reckon you'll cut the next. I reckon they was cutting hair a long time before they had electric."

"Well, you're getting it fixed up mighty nice," Mart said, looking around.

And so the old life of the shop was born again, but this time out on the fringe of society, in the wilderness, you might say.

When I had cut Mart's hair, they sat on, visiting a while, offered their help if ever I should need it, and, leaving, they laid their donations a little self-consciously on the table in the kitchen.

Others came. Mostly now it was the older men. I didn't see much of the young men and the boys. (The young don't come to the river anymore, even to swim or fish. You don't often run into them hunting in the woods. Mainly, they don't go where they can't drive.) Nor did mothers come, bringing their little boys. I didn't see anybody whose hair had got so it required styling. But my other old customers, when they had a little time on their hands, mainly on Saturdays, would come sauntering down the path from the road, sometimes three or four together, to get haircuts, to visit, to sit and talk and look at the river, and then to leave their donations, always dollar bills, somewhat secretly laid down on the kitchen table or on the shelf where the water bucket sits or by the lamp on the stand by the bed.

I was running, you might say, an "underground" barbershop, a guerrilla free enterprise off in the woods, born out of the world into the world again. My clientele you might describe as a nonrenewable resource. I haven't gained many new clients, and the old ones have slowly dwindled away. But the ones who have remained have been faithful. Their coming is made even more an act of faith because in this house on the river I have no mirrors on the walls. Here, I am the sole judge of my work. When they climb into the chair, they have to trust me. They have to be willing beforehand to be satisfied with what I can do with scissors and comb and razor only. I became a barber from before my time, surviving after my time.

I took their donations freely as they were given. It was freedom we were living in, after all, down here on the river, on the edge of things. I had come here to be free (though only, maybe, for as long as possible) of the man across the desk, of the gloved hand of inspection and regulation. My customers (my friends, my guests) and I made a little bootleg society in which we freely came and went, took and gave.

Burley's was the only donation I refused. He would offer and I would hand his money back.

"Much obliged to you, sir," I would say. And I would say, to remind him, "No need for you to *part* with that. I'll just give you the use of it."

The first thing I did, once I was moved in and had my household plunder situated to where I could find things, was plant a garden.

When Beriah Easterly died, Jarrat Coulter had bought the Billy Landing property, which now belonged to Nathan. There was a patch of good bottomland there, maybe four or five acres, well above most floods, that the Coulters always liked to keep in alfalfa, row-cropping it just whenever the alfalfa stand needed renewing. The little field was awkwardly placed for the Coulters, reachable by road from their home places only by a considerable roundabout, but over the years they had taken good care of it.

"Now, Jayber," Burley told me, "You'll want to put your garden over there. That corner next to your house is a good black piece of ground. And it's close enough to you that you can keep the deers and coons out of it—for sure, if you have a dog."

I had never even mentioned a garden, but Burley, as before, was taking satisfaction in seeing me well set up in the world. Though he no longer went there much, he loved this place that he had given me the use of, and he loved the thought of my living there. He was seeing visions, and was full of advice and eager to help.

It surely did suit me to have a garden. The two properties were divided only by a gulley from a culvert under the road, and my first thought in response to Burley's proposal was that I would build a nice footbridge across the gulley. I knew also that I *needed* a garden, for I was going to have to be careful, as always, in my economic arrangements. But it was a new life I was beginning, and I wasn't sure how it was going to work.

"It's in sod, ain't it?" I said. "How'll I plow it?"

"Oh, *I'll* take care of that," Burley said. "It don't need plowing. I'll just disk it up good and loose. You worry about gathering up seeds and stuff and getting ready."

What he did, of course, since he didn't count himself an equipment man and disliked driving machines on the road, was send Nathan to do it. Burley wasn't inclined to put himself forward much. Mostly he left the planning of their work to Nathan. But Burley had seniority, and when he did ask, Nathan would comply.

Burley was right about the ground. Nathan disked it thoroughly and left it level, in nice shape. That evening Burley walked down to hear my compliments. We went over to look. He reached his hand into the ground, raised a fistful, and let it fall through his fingers. "Not a thing wrong with that, is there?"

I said, "Not a thing that I can see."

It was a dark, deep sandy loam that looked almost good enough to eat. By the evening of the next day I had planted potatoes, onions, early greens, carrots, and salad stuff, and had set out a row of cabbages. When the ground had warmed a little more and the danger of frost had entirely passed, I planted corn, yellow summer squash, beans, and other heat-loving things. I set out three dozen tomato plants.

Making the garden completed my departure from Port William. At that season I had naturally regretted giving up my garden in town. I had mourned over it, remembering the way the fresh young plants had looked in the long rows behind the shop. They had been art and music to me. But now I had planted another garden in another place in a different kind of ground, and expectation pulled my mind away.

And Burley was right too in seeing that a gardener in my circumstances needs a dog. I have had a couple of Border collies that Danny Branch picked up for me in his endless tradings. Once they catch on that you don't want the deer and coons and groundhogs eating your garden, those good dogs will make a lifework of driving them out, and a Border collie is not so apt to wander as a hound is.

In those early days on the river I was living one of my happiest times. The visions of my mind filled me from morning to night, and I would go to sleep thinking of what I would do the next day. I had lots of work to do. The house had from time to time been stayed in, but until I came it had never been lived in. It owed its survival to Ernest Finley's good work at the beginning, and to the durability of the wide old yellow poplar boards. But now it required many small repairs. For days and days I was eagerly employed with rule and square and hammer and saw. I patched and repaired and replaced. I added new shelves and cabinets to suit my own notions and needs. None of this was fine work. It was all of used lumber and was crude enough. But it was neat too, all proportioned and placed in a good way. It would be hard to tell you, hard for you to believe, how pleased I was by the new nailheads gleaming in the old boards. I bought lime and a brush and by degrees, moving the furniture here and there, whitewashed the walls inside, which brightened and cheered the place considerably. I built a new privy to replace the one that had floated off in the flood of 1964. I cut back the branches and the saplings that had closed in around the house.

Every little difference I made seemed a significant change in the world. I would finish a piece of work and then I would stand and look and admire the way it fitted in with everything else. Just sweeping the porch seemed to make the tree limbs spread and hover more gracefully above it. Where a falling limb had poked a hole through a screen, I took a fine wire and stitched on a patch, and then sat a while and looked out the window, feeling that my work had improved the view.

Everywhere I looked, the prospect was new and interesting. Nowhere I had lived before had been so intimate with the world. A pair of phoebes were nesting under the eaves above the porch. Owls called at night, sometimes right over the roof. I would hear a fish jump and look up to see the circles widening on the water. Sometimes, just sitting and looking, I would see the fish when it jumped. Birds were nesting and singing all around—all kinds of birds, and I began to learn their names. Every tree seemed to be offering itself to the use of the birds. And there was the river itself, flowing or still, muddy or clear, quiet or windblown, steaming on the colder mornings of winter or frozen over, always changing its mood, never feeling exactly the same way twice.

There was a good dug well at an old house site up by the side of the road, not too long a carry, and so I had a faithful supply of drinking and cooking water. But I also put up a lead trough along the eave at the back of the house, with a downspout and rain barrel at each end. I cut up a fallen locust and made a footbridge so I could get to my garden without climbing down into the gulley and then out again. I made handrails for the bridge, which were unnecessary but made my bridge look, from a distance, like a bridge. For a while, as a sort of tribute to good sense, I had to stop myself from walking across it three times every time I crossed it once. I loved to hear the sound my steps made, passing over it.

With Burley's plentiful help and advice, I built a little johnboat. For lightness and durability I built it out of some excellent poplar boards that Mart Rowanberry found for me stored away in a barn. Burley and I (I mostly) sawed out the pattern with a handsaw, put a nice rake in the bow, flared the gunnels, laid in the ribs and rails and seats, set in the oarlocks. We caulked it and painted it green. One afternoon we slid it down the hillside and down the bank and onto the water. It floated light as a leaf in the dappled shadows. That moment was a height of joy that I have never altogether come down from. I opened a path down the slope and dug a fine flight of steps into the riverbank.

I had learned, once, from Uncle Othy how to fish with a trotline. That had been a long time ago, and now I had to learn again from Burley. From that time until now, when the stage of the river has been at all promising, from early spring until late fall, I have usually had a line or two in the river. The river and the garden have been the foundations of my economy here. Of the two I have liked the river best. It is wonderful to have the duty of being on the river the first and last thing every day. I have loved it even in the rain. Sometimes I have loved it most in the rain.

No matter how much it may be used by towing companies and water companies and commercial fishermen and trappers and the like, the river doesn't belong to the workaday world. And no matter how much it is used by pleasure boaters and water-skiers and the like, it doesn't belong to the vacation world either. It is never *concerned,* if you can see what I mean. Nothing keeps to its own way more than the river does.

Another thing: No matter how corrupt and trashy it necessarily must be at times in this modern world, the river is never apart from beauty. Partly, I suppose, this is because it always keeps to its way.

Sometimes, living right beside it, I forget it. Going about my various tasks, I don't think about it. And then it seems just to flow back into my mind. I stop and look at it. I think of its parallel, never-meeting banks, which yet never part. I think of it lying there in its long hollow, at the foot of all the landscape, a single opening from its springs in the mountains all the way to its mouth. It is a beautiful thought, one of the most beautiful of all thoughts. I think it not in my brain only but in my heart and in all the lengths of my bones.

28

Branch

Danny Branch was Burley Coulter's son by Kate Helen Branch. He had his mother's name because she and Burley never married. Or, you could say, they were married without benefit of church or state. Kate Helen's mother was a Proudfoot, and so I guess Danny and I are cousins, at some remove.

Burley, not being a very official person, saw no reason to make Danny officially his son until Danny was grown and Kate Helen was dead—though he had helped unofficially (and in fact in most of the conventional ways) in the boy's upbringing. It was only after Kate Helen's death that Burley saw reason and, in rather leisurely stages, laid public claim to Danny, brought the young man and his bride, Lyda, to live with him in the old weatherboarded log house where the Coulters had begun, and made him lawful heir to all his worldly possessions.

Danny, by then, was already heir to much of his father's character and knowledge. They were good people, Kate Helen and Burley, and Danny was worthily their son. He also was a son of the Depression. He was born in 1932, right in the bottom of it, and before it ended he had grown into knowledge of it. He got what he thought was the point: national prosperity, and especially the prosperity of the nation's farmers, was not permanent; it was not to be depended on; the predictions and promises of politicians and their experts were not to be depended on; if it all had come to nothing once, it all could come to nothing again. As much as any of the old-timers, he regarded the Depression as not over and done with but merely absent for a while, like Halley's comet. He suspected that the world of the Depression was in fact the real world. And so he became a sort of old-timer himself, more like his father or Art Rowan-berry (or, for that matter, me) than most of his contemporaries, who tended to think that everything was going to get better and better, if not in Port William then surely somewhere else. He pretty much took a stand in the old way of farming he learned as a boy. He never quit work-ing horses or (mainly) mules. And as Burley's tenant and then his heir, he made the old farm produce as much as it could of the things he and his family needed. He had perceived, with the help of some instruction from his elders, that there were people in the world who proposed that he should work hard for his money, and that they would then take it from him easily. He did not consent to this. He was, as a result, said to be "tight," which meant that he never spent any money he didn't have to spend, he rarely bought anything new, and he had a pronounced leaning toward any good thing that he could buy cheap or get free.

His wife, Lyda, was a good match for him, except that she would sometimes oppose his fiscal reluctance when it came to the children. There would now and then be some joking about Danny—to the effect, for instance, that he could mash the face off of a dime between his thumb and forefinger, or that he walked on his heels to save his toes—but he was pretty generally respected too. He and Lyda, in fact, were generous people, good to Burley, to their children, and to their neighbors. They were tight of pocket, you might say, but free of heart.

Danny and Lyda's economy included the woods and the river. They ate a lot of wild game—fish, deer, squirrels, rabbits, and such. When their farmwork wasn't pressing them, Danny and his boys would keep a boat in the river down by my camp house. Their boat would seldom be the same one two years in a row. Occasionally they would have no boat at all. The boat, like a good many things the Branches had, would be one they had made or had come upon and got cheap at a sale or in a trade and had fixed up. Like a good many things they had, it was for sale if the price was right. More often than not, their boat (like mine) would be powered only by oars. But sometimes it would have an outboard motor that they had picked up cheap or dragged out of a junk pile and fixed up and made to run. The Branches seemed uninterested in getting somewhere and making something of themselves. What they liked was making something of nearly nothing.

After a late start, Danny and Lyda had seven children: Will, Royal, Coulter (named Coulter Branch, Danny said, for the stream that ran down off the Coulter ridges), Fount, Reuben, and then ("Finally!" Lyda said) the two girls, Rachel and Rosie. I won't need to make much mention of the children; I name them all together now to give them my blessing. If the world lasts, there are going to be Branches around here for a long time. As the boys grew older, they made do with old cars and old farm equipment as they earlier had made do with old bicycles and outboard motors. This is the way they will survive—by being marginal, using what nobody else wants, doing well the work that nobody else will do. If they aren't destroyed by some scientific solution to all our problems, they will go on though dynasties pass. By this late year of 1986 Danny and Lyda have already got a whole company of grandchildren.

As long as I lived up in town, neither Danny nor his boys ever came to me for a haircut. Lyda did the haircutting in that family. I would see the children and Lyda fairly often, especially while the school lasted, but I never saw much of Danny. He was less sociable than Burley, not a town person at all. He was good-humored, perfectly friendly, but a little standoffish, shut-mouthed until you knew him well, not easy to know. Some of the Coulter in him favored Nathan more than Burley.

After the crops were all laid by, in that first summer of my life here on the river, Danny and Royal and Coulter and Fount turned up one morning with their boat in the back of Danny's ramshackledy old pickup truck. I looked out and the four of them were standing on the hillside by the house, looking at the river. They hadn't knocked or called or maybe even looked at the house. When I came out on the porch, all four of them gave me a grin and raised their chins in greeting.

Danny said, "It wouldn't bother you, I don't reckon, if we put our boat in."

"Why, of course not!" I said. "Put in all the boats you want to."

"Well, if you wouldn't care, we might put it in about where you've got your boat."

"Fine," I said. "Use my cable there to tie up to."

Danny granted my offer the consideration he felt was its due, and then said, "Well. All right."

From then on he came to me for haircuts, though the boys never did. Danny came, I thought at first, because he didn't want to be my neighbor, having his boat in the river here and going by so often, without giving me his trade. But finally I realized it was more than that. He was making common cause with me. A barbershop in town, run in the usual way, did not interest him much. A barbershop in the woods on the riverbank, giving free haircuts in return for which people gave away dollars, a barbershop bootlegging haircuts in defiance of authority, dispensing and receiving lawless charity—that appealed to his fundamental dissidence and contrariness. Pretty soon we got to know each other and were friends. Behind or beyond the smiling reticence with which he maintained his distance from other people's curiosity about him, he was watching this getting-and-spending modern world cautiously and with suspicion, as I understood well enough, but also with an amusement that I liked but couldn't reach on my own.

Oftentimes his amusement rose up to merriment. Watching the pleasure boats swarm in the river on a Sunday afternoon, he said, "One of these days they'll trade them things off for a mess of pottage. I know what I'm going to do with mine, Jayber. What are you going to do with yourn?" And he laughed a laugh that came more from the Proudfoots than the Coulters.

To get my own hair cut, I had continued to go down to Hargrave. When I lived in Port William, this was easy enough to arrange. I would hear that somebody was going and would speak for a ride. From the house on the river, it was not so easy. Sometimes it would come to hitchhiking, which could take half a day. I happened to mention this to Danny.

He said, "Why, Jayber, you don't need to go to Hargrave to get your hair cut. Lyda can cut it."

It was evening. He had finished running his lines and was going home. "Come on," he said.

So we went up to his truck and I rode home with him.

"Lyda," he said, "Jayber here needs to get his hair cut."

She said, "Well, he'll have to eat his supper first. I can't stop now."

I said, "Oh, now, I hate to put you to the trouble."

"One more mouth won't make any difference here," she said.

"Naw, Jayber," Burley called from the porch swing, "it won't be any trouble. Come on up. I'll have supper on the table in a few minutes."

Lyda took a swipe at his shoulder with the rag she had in her hand. "*You'll* have it on the table! *That'll* be a fair fine day in Hell!"

"That's where they've got something cooking all the time," Burley said. "Come on up, Jayber."

By then all the children and dogs knew there was a stranger on the place, and they had come to look. They all crowded around me as if maybe I had my pockets full of candy.

"Get back! Get back!" Danny said. "Give a man room to walk!" He made a parting motion with his hands.

Children and dogs fell back to each side like the waters of the Red Sea, leaving a sort of aisle that Danny and I walked through to the washstand by the rain barrel at the corner of the porch. Danny picked up the wash-pan, smote the surface of the water in the barrel with the bottom of the pan to drive the wigglers down, dipped the pan half full of water, set it down on the washstand, and stepped aside, gesturing welcome with his hand. "There's soap and a towel if you'd like to wash up," he said to me, and then to the children and dogs who had clustered around again, "Get back!"

The children and dogs fell back, never ceasing to watch me. I washed up, threw the water out, dipped the pan for Danny, and made my way amongst the children and dogs up onto the porch. "Sit down, Jayber," Burley said, and I sat down.

When he had washed, Danny refilled the pan and stood there watching while the children washed, the bigger ones seeing to the littler ones, who wanted to splash more than wash. Danny said, "Keep your hands off of them dogs, now, till after supper."

You might think that so many young children would make a consid-erable uproar at a meal, but when Lyda called us in to supper those chil-dren (from Will, who was fourteen, right down to Rosie, who was four) went in and sat down in their places and never made a peep. I thought at first that that probably was because I was there, but in fact it was pretty much according to rule. But this wasn't spiritlessness: It was discipline. Out from under Lyda's gaze, the children were noisy enough. When Reuben and the two girls were little, they talked all the time, all at the same time, in high chirps, like a tree full of sparrows.

When the meal was over, the children scraped and stacked the dishes, which Burley then washed and Will dried and put away.

There was a running joke between Burley and Lyda about Burley's reluctance and incompetence at housework, but of course Burley had lived alone for a long time before Danny and Lyda came, and he could do all the household work, if not to Lyda's taste at least well enough. When they came, since it was his house, he might have treated them as the beneficiaries of his hospitality, but instead he made himself their guest. They responded, as maybe they didn't have to do, by being hospitable to him. He was, I think, a good guest, helping especially Lyda in every way he could. She caught his trick of dealing with this arrangement and their large affection for each other as an endlessly branching joke, in which they said the opposite of what they meant. If Burley complained that he was behind in his housework because she was always underfoot and in the way, he meant that she was anything but in the way and he was thankful to have her there. If Lyda said that it would have been a mercy if she had married one husband instead of two bachelors, that meant that she loved them both more than enough to put up with them. And so on.

While Burley and Will did the dishes and Danny and Royal and Coulter and Fount went out to feed the dogs and do a few last chores (the children having milked and fed before supper), Lyda gave me my haircut. The sight of their mother cutting a stranger's hair was so shocking that Rachel and Rosie whispered and giggled throughout the operation, and Reuben could bear to watch only from under the table.

And so I began what I suppose is my final passage of family life, which has not ended yet. I became what Lyda called her "third bachelor, as if I needed another one."

Lyda, of course, took no money for cutting my hair. That I was not to offer to pay her was something I did not even "understand." I just knew it, you might say, from looking at her. It would have been as big a mistake as offering to pay for my supper.

And I, of course, started watching Danny to see that he didn't lay down a dollar somewhere after I had cut his hair. He offered it once more, I believe, and I refused it, and that was all. We were neighbors after that. We kept no accounts.

Lyda was a good barber. Slow, but good. She'd had, after all, a fair amount of practice. She would cut a few snips and step back and look, or maybe walk all the way around you as if you were a public statue, and then cut a few snips more. Several of the family would usually be watching, and there would be a big conversation going on.

If Lyda was a good barber, and if she cut my hair (what there was of it) and all her children's hair, why didn't she cut Danny's? She just didn't. From the time I came to the river, Danny came to me for his haircuts. Don't try to make too much "sense" of this. It was gift-giving, it was manners, it was visiting. It was (last of all) economic—*somebody* had to do the haircutting—but we weren't trying very hard to make economic sense.

I didn't make too regular a thing of going to Lyda and Danny's to eat. I would go sometimes, but not as often as Danny invited me. When I did go, it was fine. Lyda was a good cook, they always had a lot to eat, and it was a fact that one more mouth didn't make much difference there.

But often I would walk up through the woods along the Coulter Branch hollow when I was done with my own supper, and would get to the Branches' about the time they had washed up the dishes. I would sit till bedtime, talking with Lyda and Danny and Burley and whoever else might be there—sometimes Hannah and Nathan Coulter, sometimes Flora and Andy Catlett. In summer, if the weather was fair, we would sit out in the front yard. In winter we sat in the living room by the stove. On the winter nights we would have popcorn, and sometimes Burley would go to his room and bring out his shoebox full of keepsakes, which he would take out one by one and identify and pass around for everybody to see. The smaller children would be playing around quietly or sitting in laps or lying beside our chairs to listen. They were a pretty tumultuous lot when they were turned out with the dogs and the other pet animals that they always had, but in the house they had to toe the line. I so much loved the quiet of those times of talk, when the children were listening or asleep, and we were all aware of the darkness spread over the ridge-tops and the valley.

Burley continued to be a hunter almost until he died. As he got older he gave up coon hunting but kept on foxhunting, which required less walking. His legs were giving out. So, for that matter, was his hearing. I had run out of interest in night hunting by then, and so I didn't go, but Danny or the Rowanberrys would tell me how it was with Burley. When the hounds were far away he couldn't hear them. When they were close he thought they were far away. Then he would listen and tell the others where the dogs were running, though the dogs were not where he thought they were at all. He believed he heard them running in some-place he hadn't been able to walk to for a long time, and he would describe the course of the hunt that was both real and a sort of dream.

He loved to go. It was his freedom and his comfort. Some nights when I walked up there, Burley and Danny and the older boys would be gone. Some nights, it would be Burley alone who would be gone. Some nights when he might have hunted, company would come early, and he would stay and visit.

"If you all hadn't come, he would be out somewhere with those dogs," Lyda said, pretending to scold but in fact proud of him.

"No, now," Burley said. "I'm too old to go every night."

"Well, you've been *going* every night."

"Well, every other night ain't often enough."

Forty years Burley Coulter was my friend. When he died—or, rather, disappeared clean out of the present world—my life was changed. You will know how much, practically and otherwise, my life in Port William and here at the river had been his gift. In a way, I had been living out a vision that he had seen. I had, after all, lived as a man who'd had his dwelling place and his place of business right together, as he had said at the beginning.

He was a man aboundingly evident, and yet one who belonged in some part to mystery, who lived the life of the place in a way that none of us entirely knew. I felt his absence as an abiding presence that I lived in and learned about, as I lived in and learned about the place, now that he was entirely beyond its knowing.

After Burley was gone, it must have been three weeks before I realized that Danny Branch was now my landlord. He never mentioned it, and so I thought I would mention it. The change seemed to call, maybe, for some kind of recognition.

I said, "Listen, I think I ought to be paying you some rent. Let's get Wheeler to draw us up a lease or a contract or whatever's right. I want to be square with you, now."

Of course we were long past that. I had thought so, but when he looked at me I knew it.

"No," he said, "I'll just give you the use of it." And he looked away.

29

On the Edge

Once I was on the river, it became clear that I had to resign as grave digger. A grave digger, as Uncle Stanley enjoyed pointing out, cannot plan his work. People generally don't die on schedule or at other people's convenience. When I was barbering in Port William, I was findable without too much trouble and in not too long a time. Somebody always knew more or less where I was, or which way I had gone. Part of Port William's business is to have such knowledge.

I was harder to find on the river. It was awkward for everybody, too much to ask, and so I gave up grave digging. (By now, of course, they dig and fill the graves with a backhoe, which is not the right way to do it.) Anyhow, it was a load off my mind to be a load off other people's minds.

I kept on as janitor of the church, which is scheduled work. I still walk up on Fridays to clean, as I have always done, and on Sunday mornings I go up to ring the bell and sit through the service. I don't attend altogether for religious reasons. I feel more religious, in fact, here beside this corrupt and holy stream. I am not sectarian or evangelical. I don't want to argue with anybody about religion. I wouldn't want to argue about it even if I thought it was arguable, or even if I could win. I'm a literal reader of the Scriptures, and so I see the difficulties. And yet every Sunday morning I walk up there, over a cobble of quibbles. I am, I suppose, a difficult man. I am, maybe, the ultimate Protestant, the man at the end of the Protestant road, for as I have read the Gospels over the years, the belief has grown in me that Christ did not come to found an organized religion but came instead to found an unorganized one. He seems to have come to carry religion out of the temples into the fields and sheep pastures, onto the roadsides and the banks of rivers, into the houses of sinners and publicans, into the town and the wilderness, toward the membership of all that is here. Well, you can read and see what you think.

I go up by the old children's path through the woods along the Sand Ripple hollow. Where they hurried or loitered or played, I take my time and stop to rest (as I must) and look around. I go to sit with the living where the dead once sat. I sit where once I sat with Uncle Othy and felt, for a while, quiet and safe.

Really, the most worrisome part of my life on the river has been my rental property in town—that is to say, my old shop. It may be that I would have been better off if I had sold it. But I kept it and rented it on the principle that I needed a regular income that would not involve much work and worry. (I was thinking, as I still am, of the time that may come when I may be unable to look after myself.) But of course I could charge only a small amount. And as for work and worry, there have been times when I have thought of slipping up there in the dark and setting it afire.

The very first people I rented it to were a young couple, from whom I took no money in advance, and who fell into disharmony within two weeks. The husband drove his wife and her boyfriend out of town by beating on the boyfriend's balky automobile with an oak two-by-four, the car lurching wildly as if in pain, finally speeding away. All I got out of that was a mess to clean up, and several remarks on how my departure had improved the social life up at town.

Aside from such distractions, I took to the river life, returning to it after nearly forty-five years as if I had never known life of any other kind. By all my work, all my thousand small acts of settling here and renewing my life, I had come to be at home in a place that was not mine and that I never intended to be mine. Neither Burley nor Danny ever offered to sell it. I never offered to buy it. I was past the time in my life when I might have had territorial desires. And yet I had laid my claim on the place, had made it answerable to my life. Of course, you can't do that and get away free. You can't choose, it seems, without being chosen. For the place, in return, had laid its claim on me and had made my life answerable to it.

And so I came to belong to this place on the river just as I had come to belong to Port William—as in a way, of course, I still do belong to Port William. Being here satisfies me. I have no thought of going away. If I knew for sure that I would die here, I would be glad. And yet definite as all this is, it seems surrounded by the indefinite, like a boat in a fog. I can't look back from where I am now and feel that I have been very much in charge of my life. Certainly I have lived on the edge of the Port William community, and I am farther than ever out on the edge of it now. But I feel that I have lived on the edge even of my own life. I have made plans enough, but I see now that I have never lived by plan. Any more than if I had been a bystander watching me live my life, I don't feel that I ever have been quite sure what was going on. Nearly everything that has happened to me has happened by surprise. *All* the important things have happened by surprise. And whatever has been happening usually has already happened before I have had time to expect it. The world doesn't stop because you are in love or in mourning or in need of time to think. And so when I have thought I was *in* my story or in charge of it, I really have been only on the edge of it, carried along. Is this because we are in an eternal story that is happening partly in time?

Of course, I know well what it is to be in a boat in a fog, and mainly I count it among the pleasures. In the early morning in the fog I can't see the river from the porch. I go down the path, following it step by step as it is revealed, and then down the dug steps in the bank to the river's edge. The boat takes shape at first as though it is floating in the air. And then, coming closer, I see its reflection on the water. I loosen the chain and toss it into the boat with a crash that seems more substantial than anything I can see. The fog drifts on a current of air, usually upstream. I step into the boat and feel its buoyancy. Ripples go out from it. I go to the middle seat, place the oars in the locks, and set the boat out onto the water, free of the shore. I row quietly, close along the bank. The river has only the one visible edge. It could be as wide as the ocean. I come to where the end of the trotline is tied to a stout root. I go to the bow seat then and catch the line and raise it. I work my way out along the line from one snooded hook to the next, taking off fish (if any). Now I can see neither shore. The line rises, dripping, out of the water ahead of me and disappears behind. If a fish is on it, I will feel it, something alive out in the fog, down in the dark. Sometimes, after being bent to my work for a while, I will straighten up and see that the fog has lifted and I am again in the known world.

Back at the house, with the river and its mood still in my mind, I fix breakfast and (if the weather is fine) eat out on the porch. And then I have my shave and set the place to rights. If the fog has cleared, the sunlight, glancing off the river, will be rippling and swaying on the walls and ceiling of my house, so that for a while I seem to be living within the element of living light.

I have, to fill my mind and occupy my hands, the daily and seasonal rounds of my economy. I have food to harvest and preserve in the summer and fall, firewood to gather and saw up and split in the fall and winter, the garden to prepare and plant in the spring. I have clothes and bedclothes to wash, and myself to keep clean and presentable. I have the endless little jobs of housekeeping and repair. I have my duties in town. I have my old customers, grown shaggy, who come down the path and call out, "Anybody home?" or "Jayber? You here?" Sometimes in the afternoons, especially Sunday afternoons, back when I got around better than I do now, I would take long walks up in the woods of the valley sides, or in the late splendid woodland that Athey used to call "the Nest Egg." For relief from much eating of fish, it has often been possible to shoot a young squirrel or groundhog or (in cold weather, when I could hope to keep the meat from spoiling) a yearling deer. I have books to read, and much to sit and watch.

I try not to let good things go by unnoticed. In spring the foliage slowly closes in the prospects from all the windows and the porch. When the trees are in full leaf, this place, close to the road as it is, seems remote and set apart. When the leaves fall, the distances lengthen all around. The river is more visible from the house then, and I can see the pastures and cornfields on the far side, and beyond them the hills. Some days a strong breeze fairly fills the place. Every leaf moves, and the sound is like a long breath. Sometimes there is a breeze that moves the leaves without a sound.

And I have known days when the temperature would not rise above zero, when snow would be deep, ice on the river, the north wind rattling the branches. Then this house is a little cell of warmth, a cold brilliance coming in at the windows, a good fire in the drumstove, a pot of bean soup simmering, the dog asleep on the floor. Nobody comes, only the birds to the suet feeders. And I have nothing to do but read and watch. I seem to be in a room in the wind. I talk to the dog, who raises her head to listen and then goes back to sleep.

In the winter and the spring, of course, we who live by the river are ever mindful of the possibility of flood, which is both a dread and an excitement. When the river rises and the currents quicken, it is hard to watch with a quiet mind. When it starts out of its banks, you watch with uneasiness and a wonderful alertness and curiosity. It is like being in a small stall with a big horse. The risen river is large, alive, dangerous, not of your mind, and closer to you than it has been before. You watch.

You watch for what it may do and for what it may bring. You fear what it may do. You feel a little tug to get in your boat and drift away with it. You wonder if you may find, coming down among the rafts of drift, the debris of woodlands and fields and the trash out of human dumps, something that may be of use. Once I caught a pretty good canoe, and once an extra-nice privy that I tied to a tree over by the garden and remodeled into a toolshed.

If the river comes high enough to be a convincing danger (and I can't forget that the water was up to the eaves here in thirty-seven), then I will have it on my mind even when I think I am not thinking about it. I will wake up in the night, listening already before I'm awake for the suck of the current or slap-slap of windwaves against the porch posts.

My first thought always is of my boat. When the river is rising or falling, the boat must be kept free, drawn up or pushed off so that it rises and falls with the river. There is a strange pleasure, when the river is rising, in seeing the boat always drawn up in a new place, floating where maybe the day before I walked. And there is relief, though not much pleasure, in seeing the banks and slopes, slick and shining with mud, appearing again above the falling waters. You kick footholds into the mud as you shove the boat out again and again into the river, keeping it afloat. Eventually, of course, you have to clear the driftwood off the garden and pick up the stranded cans and bottles and pieces of plastic.

But when you have made everything as safe as you can and are reasonably assured that you won't have to load up your stuff and go, floodtime will repay you just to sit and watch. The river seems to be holding itself up before you like a page opened to be read. There is no knowing how the currents move. They shift and boil and eddy. They are swifter in some places than in others. To think of "a place" on the flowing surface soon baffles your mind, for the "places" are ever changing and moving. The current in all its various motions and speeds flows along, and that flowing may be stirred again at the surface by the wind in all its various motions. Who can think of it? Maybe the ducks have mastered it, and the little grebes who are as much at home underneath as on top and who ride the currents for pleasure.

The risen river always leaves something that sooner or later it comes back to get. If it leaves ice, Art Rowanberry used to say, the river is apt to come back in the same season, looking for it—and that often proves to be true. What the river leaves, including ice, is usually more or less a nuisance. Most cans and bottles, once used, are useless. You'll not easily find a use for big clots of plastic foam. The driftwood is often too rotten for anything, but occasionally I find a good board, or a tree sound enough to make firewood.

I am always on the lookout for firewood. I gather every burnable scrap of driftwood, saw up every windfall within carrying distance, gladly accept any loads of poles, old fenceposts, or scrap lumber that anybody wants to give away or trade for haircuts or fish.

Water is a bigger problem here than fire—water, I mean, for drinking, cooking, washing, and bathing. "Why, Jayber, you've *got* a whole riverful of water," somebody is always telling me, and that is probably the joke I'm the tiredest of. In the summer, when it is dry, my rain barrels are soon empty. I must carry all my household water, then, from the well. And also in the winter, when the rain barrels can't be used because they would freeze and burst. If the river is clear enough in the summer, I can do some of my laundry off the end of the boat, but it's hard to get the white things white enough in the river. I have to admit I am finicky about this. Things that are clean ought to *look* clean. There is a great pleasure in being clean yourself in a clean house.

When it is warm enough I bathe in the river. I have been often advised that bathing in the river is using dirty water to get clean (that is another joke I am tired of). But in warm weather it is far easier for me to go to the water than to bring the water to me, far more promising to jump into the river than into the well. To get clean you must use what you are given. Summer afternoons down here on the riverbank can be as steamy and airless as the inside of a kettle. I go about my work then with my clothes sweated through and sticking to me. Thoughts of anything freshening hang about in the mind. I wait until all the work of the day is done, supper finished, and the dishes put away. And then I take clean clothes, soap, and a towel and go down to the water. I lay the clean clothes and the towel on the bow of the boat and strip off my sweaty things. Carrying the soap, I wade out until the water is up to my chin. I soap my head and face. As I wade back toward the shore, I soap the rest of my body as it emerges. I sit on the gunnel of the boat and soap my feet. Then I put down the soap, stand up, take two steps, dive, and swim down into the dark to the limit of breath. When I wade out again, I am cool and clean, delighted as a risen soul.

If the mosquitoes will leave me alone, I love to sit or lie out on the porch and watch the dark come. Past sundown, the light is charmed, the way it is in the early morning. First there will be the swallows circling and dipping over the river. Maybe a kingfisher will come rattling by, skimming close above the surface of the water. Maybe I will see herons flying to roost. And then the bats begin to flicker in and out of sight, and the fireflies rise up out of the weeds, lighting their little lights, and the stars come out. Past a certain time, the darkness and quietness are present all around, the night creatures begin their calls, and you can feel something of the inward life of the world.

In late winter the owls begin to mate and I hear the paired ones calling to each other, back and forth. The wood ducks begin to pair off. I see them sitting together in the trees near the house, and hear the hen ducks crying as they fly. I know spring is coming when, one morning, I hear a phoebe calling, and the woodpeckers drum on hollow trees and the tin roof of my house. Spring has certainly come when I hear the little yellow-throated warbler that sings in the tops of the tallest sycamores. In the summer dusk there is always a pewee calling his name from a dead branch somewhere on the edge of an opening. The Carolina wren sings the whole year round. I hear the frogs and toads at night, starting with the peepers in early spring, and later the crickets and katydids. Something wild is always blooming, from twinleaf and bloodroot early in spring to beeweed in late fall, things of intricate, limitless beauty. Often I fear that I am not paying enough attention.

And how many hours have I spent in watching the reflections on the water? When the air is still, then so is the surface of the river. Then it holds a perfectly silent image of the world that seems not to exist in this world. Where, I have asked myself, *is* this reflection? It is not on the top of the water, for if there is a little current the river can slide frictionlessly and freely beneath the reflection and the reflection does not move. Nor can you think of it as resting on the bottom of the air. The reflection itself seems a plane of no substance, neither water nor air. It rests, I think, upon quietness. Things may rise from the water or fall from the air, and, without touching the reflection, break it. It disappears. Without going anywhere, it disappears.

Here on the river I have known peace and beauty such as I never knew in any other place. There is always work here that I need to be doing and I have many worries, for life *on* the edge seems always threatening to go *over* the edge. But I am always surprised, when I look back on times here that I know to have been laborious or worrisome or sad, to discover that they were never out of the presence of peace and beauty, for here I have been always in the world itself.

You may think, then, that I had arrived, by so simple a movement as that between Port William and the river, at the perfect solution to my problems. But that would be a mistake. It was a good solution, good sometimes beyond praise, but it was far from perfect. Because (to start with) I was far from perfect. However interesting and lovely my days were,

I could get from one day to the next only by passing through a night. I have, it is true, known lovely nights here: nights of sound sleep and good dreams, and nights made wakeful by happy thoughts. But I have not always been a good sleeper, and my thoughts at night have sometimes been far from happy.

Maybe there is a kind of justice that says you must pay for good days with bad nights. And maybe my debt is paid now, for lately I sleep well. But my bad nights continued for a long time after I came to the river. They got worse, in fact. To be alone here in the daytime often doubles the pleasure. But to be alone at night is sometimes only to be defenseless against the oncoming knowledge of incompleteness and imperfection, mine and the world's. Why is hate so easy and love so difficult?

In the daytime, going about my work, I would often make up little rhymes and repeat them to myself. If, say, I was weeding my beans, I would get a rhyme going in my head, and it would say,

> *Beans*
> *Is the means*
> *That redeems,*
> *It seems.*
> *And what*
> *Do beans redeem?*
> *The dream*
> *Of being fat*
> *When times are lean.*

And I would repeat it in my mind, dissatisfied with the part about being fat, which I had never been at any time, and trying to find a better word than *lean* to rhyme with *dream*. Or I would be splitting firewood, a good straight-grained block of ash, say, and I would be sort of exclaiming to myself,

> *I hit*
> *six licks*
> *and split*
> *six sticks!*

Or, after a bad storm, I would say,

> *They fell,*
> *They blew,*
> *They fled,*
> *They flew.*

But of my bad nights I made only one rhyme and it repeated itself to me time and again:

> *Mortality*
> *And error,*
> *Partiality,*
> *And terror.*

It is not a terrible thing to love the world, knowing that the world is always passing and irrecoverable, to be known only in loss. To love anything good, at any cost, is a bargain. It is a terrible thing to love the world, knowing that you are a human and therefore joined by kind to all that hates the world and hurries its passing—the violence and greed and falsehood that overcome the world that is meant to be overcome by love.

On such nights I fell from mere sleep into bad dreams. I would be in a place without memories, wholly cut away from history and the known world. It was a city without trees or birds, with no named streets. The days over it were darkened and the nights lighted. I would be hurrying through it in panic and despair toward a destination I did not know. And around me in the nameless streets in the dimness of day or night, anonymous people were killing one another with stones and fire.

I kept dreaming these dreams after I had waked up. I could not stop dreaming them. I would lie with my eyes wide open, awake and dreaming, the dark room as bedeviled as if the Old Scratch himself stood breathing beside my bed.

The trouble with many of my dreams was that they were perfectly rational, or they came from perfectly rational fears. They came from The Economy and The War—that is to say from The News. It really didn't make any difference whether I was asleep or awake. All I needed was to be alone and quiet and in the dark, so that my mind could concentrate itself on fearful things, and it could not be unconcentrated sometimes until daylight.

Lying in my bed in the dark, asleep or awake, I would know for a certainty that at the headwaters of the river heavy machines were cutting their way along the mountainsides. I could see the trees falling, the roots tearing out of the ground, the ground being shoved aside. I could hear the bedrock shudder and crumble.

I would know that cars and trucks were speeding in narrow lanes day and night along the roads of the world. I would marvel that all of them did not crash into one another, and would flinch in my soul at the certainty that some of them *would* crash. Out of the general blur of haste, one place suddenly would assert itself: a patch of pavement, roadside weeds, crumpled metal, oil and blood, throbbing lights, and then calls going out into the dark distance, people waking up already afraid in a world utterly changed.

And I would know that across the world always, always were wars and rumors of wars. Boys like Forrest Finn and Tom Coulter and Virgil Feltner and Jimmy Chatham were going out to be killed. Boys who had never seen one another, let alone harmed one another, were being taught to kill one another. And the wars grew always worse, as for their own reasons they had to, and the world grew always smaller and more frail.

For a long time then I seemed to live by a slender thread of faith, spun out from within me. From this single thread I spun strands that joined me to the good things of the world. And then I spun more threads that joined all the strands together, making a life. When it was complete, or nearly so, it was shapely and beautiful in the light of day. It endured through the nights, but sometimes it only barely did. It would be tattered and set awry by things that fell or blew or fled or flew. Many of the strands would be broken. Those I would have to spin and weave again in the morning.

But of course the story of my life is not finished yet. I will not live to tell the end of it.

My life, though, has been something (as only now at last I am able to see), but it is something that it has made of itself, not something that I have made of it. All I seem to have done is avoid wherever I could (so far) the man across the desk—for (so far) the world has afforded a little room for a few of us, lucky or blessed, to go around him. And now I wonder if I can die quickly enough and secretly enough to make the final evasion.

"No, Jayber," Lyda said, "you are not going to end up in any damned nursing home."

She is always sending Reuben down to me with a hot meal. "She says she cooked a good deal too much," he'll say, or, "She says you need to taste of this. It's good."

That evening she had sent him to bring me up to supper, as now she often does. We were talking afterward, sitting at the table. I meant to make a joke, realizing only after it was too late to stop that it could be no joke. It was fear, and I should have bitten my tongue. I said, "That was mighty good, my dear Lyda. Something to remember when I'm peeing on myself and watching TV down at the Fair Haven."

The others laughed, to grant my joke and ease my embarrassment. But Lyda didn't laugh. "No, sir!" she said. "Not if the Lord spares *me!*"

Bless her.

But she has not yet thought of everything that I have thought of.

If my bad night dreams needed daytime confirmation, I have not needed to leave the river to find it. It might seem to you that living in the woods on a riverbank would remove you from the modern world. But not if the river is navigable, as ours is. On pretty weekends in the summer, this riverbank is the very verge of the modern world. It is a seat in the front row, you might say. On those weekends, the river is disquieted from morning to night by people resting from their work.

This resting involves traveling at great speed, first on the road and then on the river. The people are in an emergency to relax. They long for the peace and quiet of the great outdoors. Their eyes are hungry for the scenes of nature. They go very fast in their boats. They stir the river like a spoon in a cup of coffee. They play their radios loud enough to hear above the noise of their motors. They look neither left nor right. They don't slow down for—or maybe even see—an old man in a rowboat raising his lines.

The fishermen have the fastest boats of all. Their boats scarcely touch the water. They have much equipment, thousands of dollars worth. They can't fish in one place for fear that there are more fish in another place. For rest they have a perfect restlessness.

I watch and I wonder and I think. I think of the old slavery, and of the way The Economy has now improved upon it. The new slavery has improved upon the old by giving the new slaves the illusion that they are free. The Economy does not take people's freedom by force, which would be against its principles, for it is very humane. It *buys* their freedom, pays for it, and then persuades its money back again with shoddy goods and the promise of freedom. "Buy a car," it says, "and be free. Buy a boat and be free. Buy a beer and be free." Is this not the raw material of bad dreams? Or is it maybe the very nightmare itself?

But wait. Also there were times when good dreams came to me. They *still* come.

Not so long ago I had dreamed, I thought, all night such dreams as I have told. I was exhausted. I thought, "Won't morning ever come?"

And then, asleep or awake, I looked out and saw the stars, and a deep, peaceful sleep came upon me.

The phone rang, which was strange because I have never owned a telephone in my life. I let it ring a long time because, as I told myself, "*My* phone couldn't be ringing because I don't *have* a phone."

When I answered it, it was Athey Keith. He said, "Jayber, if you haven't already done something too silly, come on up to Art Rowanberry's and sit with us for a while."

"All right," I said, and hung up.

I thought, "What's Athey doing calling me up? Athey's dead. And Art Rowanberry. He's been dead two years."

But I got up and put on my clothes. It was still night and the air, when I opened the door and stepped out, was damp and fresh.

I walked along the river road to the Sand Ripple road and walked up into the smaller valley. It was day by then, perfectly cloudless and bright. I crossed the creek on the little swinging footbridge.

As I went along the lane below the house, I looked up and saw Athey Keith and Art Rowanberry sitting on the porch. Elton Penn was there.

Burley Coulter was there. They were smiling, lifting their hands to me, glad to be together, glad to see me.

"Howdy, Howdy!" Art called. "Come up!"

Elton was sitting beside him in the swing. I had sat there with the four of them many a Sunday afternoon, resting and talking. I went up and sat below them on the top step. To be there seemed strange, but it was all right.

"Well, ain't it a fine day overhead," Art said, as he always used to do. And Elton picked up Art's hand and kissed it. There were tears of joy in his eyes.

I sat with them a long time, listening to them talk of the things they had always talked about before. But I didn't know the time. The sun seemed to be standing still. I knew that Uncle Othy's old silver watch was in my pocket, but I knew also that it was not running.

Finally I realized where I was.

30

The Keith Place in
the Way of the World

Della Keith lived to be eighty-four years old. She died in 1971, and the whole Keith estate then passed to Mattie Chatham, who was the only heir. The family name of Keith survived in Port William then only in the given name of Mattie and Troy Chatham's one surviving child, Athey Keith Chatham, known as A. K. And A. K. by then was only technically countable as a citizen of Port William. In the fall of 1971, A. K. enrolled in the college of commerce at the university in Lexington. Within a few years he would realize his father's ambition. He would become a real businessman, sitting at a desk, with other people working for him. By then he would be a long way from home.

When Mattie Chatham inherited the Keith place (and also, of course, the little place in town), she became her husband's landlady. That may partly explain Troy's progress through the years afterward. Mattie was all of a sudden, and merely by inheritance, the owner of a five-hundred-acre farm. Troy, who had been going all-out for twenty-six years, had nothing to show for it but a continuous debt that he claimed to be reconciled to, his status (mostly with himself) as a big operator, and the goad and burden of unquenched ambition. So he must have felt himself, from then on, to be engaged in a contest with fortune, or whatever you might call that power that distributes the goods of the world, giving more to some, who rarely feel that they deserve less, and less to others, who usually feel that they deserve more.

But Troy's life was not determined entirely by fortune. He had in his pride, as a matter of fact, chosen against his father-in-law and his ways. In doing so he had left out of account the possibility that Athey might choose against him, which Athey (and Della) did when they left everything to Mattie alone. In making this choice, Athey and Della (and also Wheeler Catlett, their lawyer) obviously thought that they were protecting Mattie against Troy's haste and his bad judgment. What they failed to consider (or did consider, and couldn't help) was something that I believe all of them knew: that Mattie could not be protected from Troy's haste and bad judgment. By dividing Mattie's fortune from Troy's, they made Troy, in effect, her enemy. He would have to make her party to his bad judgment.

In describing the course of Troy's life after Della Keith's death, I am supposing a little, but not much. More than likely I would not be speaking from knowledge if the barbering trade had not followed me to the river. But talk, as I have said, draws to a barber as water draws to low ground. My customers would park on the side of the road and walk down the path to the house, bringing always their small donations to leave in return for my small service (also donated), and always also they brought a small burden of talk, which they would want to be lightened of before they climbed the path back up to the road again. The times were changing, nobody could doubt that. And in the minds of the older Port Williamites, Troy Chatham seemed to signify what the times were changing to. They pondered over their knowledge of him because they (or most of them) were skeptical and uneasy about change of any kind, and they were uncertain what to think about Troy. They were not sure they got the point that he was so sure he had got. He had simply outdistanced them all, not only in the scale and speed of what he called his "operation," but also in his fearlessness of debt. It is a fact that nearly all the farmers of Port William who were born as late as the 1930s were brought up to distrust debt at the very least, and some of them greatly feared it. To owe what you had not yet earned, to have to work to earn what you had already spent, was a personal diminishment, an insult to nature and common sense. Most of them knew this from experience.

But Troy did not fear debt. He preferred to see himself as a man ahead of his time. He had got so he liked to speak of his creditors as his "business partners." And this was true enough, for he always owed them so much that they could not easily afford to let him fail. The bank continued his loans, and even increased them, to keep him afloat. By owing them he came, in a manner of speaking, to own his creditors. In his applications for credit, he was holding them for ransom. In this way, by having a net worth of probably less than nothing, he had become a man of power.

I know what I know of this partly because Troy was one of my faithful customers who followed me from town to the river. He lacked almost completely the inclination, which was otherwise pretty general in Port William, to keep private business private. In Port William, people usually prefer to talk about *other* people's business. Troy preferred to talk about his own. He had at least the virtue of not being a gossip. He talked to anybody who was on hand about his financial affairs, apparently without the least suspicion that his hearers were not respectful or even envious of the magnitude of his debts. He would talk in this way to (for instance) Nathan Coulter, who never said more than a little about himself or anybody else, and who probably could have paid for all of Troy's assets and some of his liabilities too without borrowing a cent.

If nobody else was available to talk to about his "operation" and his finances, he talked to me, without suspecting in the least that I did not concur in his high opinion of himself. Except for quoting Scripture to him occasionally to heap coals of fire on his head, I acted toward him with tolerance and politeness, and he assumed that I liked him. Maybe he thought that since he liked himself everybody liked him. But, really, I don't think he liked himself. If he did, why would he have worked and suffered so to be something he wasn't—to make "something" of himself? Maybe he disliked himself but thought he was smart enough to convince everybody that he was likable. Maybe he thought he liked himself because he thought he was that smart. Because I never openly disagreed with his financial pronouncements, he assumed that I agreed and was impressed. Why would anybody living as I did not secretly want to be like him?

In fact, of all the trials I have experienced, he was the hardest. He was the trial that convicted me over and over again. I did not like him. I *could* not like him. Maybe I didn't need to like him, but I needed at least not to *dis*like him, and I did thoroughly dislike him. I also enjoyed disliking him. In his presence I was in the perfect absence, the night shadow, of the charity that I sought for and longed for. I had got far enough that I could see how, in this hard and sorrowful and sometimes terrible world, charity could light and ease the way, if a person could be capable of it. I could see how it could show an opening that a man like me might, after all, squeeze through. And in the presence of Troy Chatham, which was getting to be about the only place where I really needed that charity and really suffered for the want of it, I didn't have it.

When Mattie inherited her parents' estate, she used the moneys from the estate and the sale of the property in town to clear the Keith place of the inheritance taxes and all outstanding debts. And then here is what Troy could have done. He could have made it safe in Mattie's keeping. He could have seen that, safe in her keeping, it would have made both of them safe for the rest of their lives. If he had to keep on in his debt-driven plunge toward whatever grandeur he thought would satisfy him, then he could have left her and her inheritance clear of it. But that is not what he did. He followed the way of "business," not of farming or family or marriage. When the apple fell from the tree at last, he was there waiting, with his own hands cupped to receive it.

What he did was persuade her to mortgage the whole thing, first to build a grade-A dairy (milking parlor, loafing shed, silo, Holstein cows, and equipment), and then to "leverage" the purchase of more land. By the time the estate was settled, we were in the bigtime, big-farmer, land-buying jamboree of the 1970s. Men of power were saying again, "Get big or get out." The talk was all of leverage. Land prices were going up, which meant that farmers of ambition could borrow more and more on the land they owned in order to own more and more land.

It was at about that time, I believe, that Troy began to call himself an "agribusinessman." He would quote a great official of the government who had said, "Adapt or die," meaning that a farmer should adapt to the breakneck economic program of the corporations, not to his farm. Troy was sure that he was an adapter and would not die. He loved that word *leverage*. And I remember that one day, when he was talking of this, Nathan Coulter said, "A lever has got two ends. Where is the fulcrum going to go?"

So far as I remember, that was Nathan's only comment on the economics of Troy Chatham. As it turned out, he was right. It turned out that Troy, who proposed to be the lifter, was lifted.

Troy miscalculated the movement of the fulcrum, but that wasn't what was really wrong. If he couldn't control the movement of the fulcrum, why should he have allowed everything to depend on the position of it in the first place? What was wrong was not the movement of somebody else's fulcrum, but Troy's own point of reference. He never knew where he was.

At first, his point of reference was himself, his own wants and his ambition. There is nothing surprising or unforgivable about that, maybe, in a young man. But Troy never outgrew it. I don't think he ever caught on, despite what it cost him, that one of his reference points might have been and ought to have been Mattie. His vanity and pride and self-assurance (pretended or not) obscured her to him from the start. You can imagine that early in their marriage some awareness of her wishes and her sense of things might have distracted him a little from himself and given him a power of thinking that apart from her he didn't have and could never have. But that didn't happen. Maybe Troy's contempt for Athey caused him to ignore what really was the best opportunity of his life, which was to love, honor, and cherish Athey's daughter. Or maybe Troy was, in the ways that counted most, just an incurable chucklehead.

He enlarged his pride by investing it (as well as a lot of money, usually borrowed money) in equipment. And so then the equipment, the power to do things mechanically, became his point of reference. His question was what his equipment could do, not what the farm could stand. The farm, in a way, became his mirror. The farm never at any time was his reference point, and this was his bewilderment and his (and its) ruin. This was why he was reduced by everything he did to enlarge himself; it was why his life was all spending and no gain.

Finally, of course, his debt became his point of reference. What he did, finally, he *had* to do to get the money to pay his creditors. He, his equipment, the farm, and all were just dragged along by debt. He had to keep going because his creditors were on his heels. He had worked like a slave, and he was one.

All the way along—from his first adventures into the postwar mechanization, to the installation of the dairy, to the installation of the confinement hog-raising barn that replaced the dairy, to the final wrack and ruin—he was under the influence of expert advice, first in the form of magazine articles and leaflets and pamphlets, and then in the persons of the writers of the articles and leaflets and pamphlets, who instructed him, gave him their language and point of view, took photographs of the results, spoke of him in public talks as an innovator and a man of the new age of agribusiness, and who had simply nothing to say when their recommendations only drew him deeper and deeper into debt.

Over the years, I pretty much made a point of staying away from the Keith place. I remembered it from way back. Just from what I could see from the road, I knew that it was going down, and I really didn't want to see the rest of it. Besides, I wanted both to spare myself Troy's company and to avoid any appearance of desiring Mattie's.

But one winter day not long before Christmas (this was a year or two before Mattie fell ill), I did go down there. There was a good big slue on the Keith place well back near the river. The wild ducks were gathering there and I proposed to myself to drop down close to the slue in my boat to see if I couldn't maybe shoot me the makings of a good supper.

I rowed down the river into a stout wind that I hoped would last long enough to help me row home against the current. I tied up at a place where the bank was not too steep, clawed my way to the top, and crept across the bottom to the slue. After a long sneak through the standing corn and the tall weeds and the trees, making never a sudden move, never a sound, I came into sight of the slue and found it (as you often do in that kind of hunting) perfectly empty. I found a sitting place on a log in a weed patch and sat there a long time, but nothing came.

Finally I had to move. The cold had got into my clothes, and my hips and knees were so stiff I could hardly stand up. Now that my hunt was over, I began to look around. I told myself that I might kick up a rabbit and have a good supper out of my efforts, after all. But I wasn't really hunting anymore. It had struck me, walking in, that the still unharvested corn crop that I was walking through was poor for the year, and so overgrown with Johnsongrass that you could hardly see the rows. As I looked now, paying more attention, I could see that the soil was pale and hard, lifeless, and in places deeply gullied. I thought of Athey. "The land slopes even in the bottoms, and water runs."

Troy had bulldozed every tree from along the drains and watercourses where Athey had allowed them to stand and get old. He had bulldozed every tree from every foot of ground where you could drive a tractor. The fences were gone from the whole place. Troy was a hog farmer now. Hogs were the only livestock on the farm, and they were all inside pens in the large hog barn that I could smell a long time before I could see it. Except for the larger ones where machines were stored, the other farm buildings looked abandoned—paintless and useless, going down. The buildings in use looked only a little less abandoned. It was no longer a place you could see anybody's pride or pleasure in. In front of the farm buildings, toward the road, the house and yard and garden looked neatly kept—an entirely different kind of presence and feeling there. Behind the barn lots was what I had heard Troy, in his devil-may-care way, call his "parts department." This was a patch of two or three acres completely covered with old or broken or worn-out machines. And here a kind of reforestation was taking place: Weeds and vines and sapling trees of various kinds were growing up all around and even through the machines.

I got to where I could see that and stopped. I didn't go any farther. Every scrap of land that a tractor could stand on had been plowed and cropped in corn or soybeans or tobacco. And yet, in spite of this complete and relentless putting to use, the whole place, from the house and garden all the way back to the river, looked deserted. It did not look like a place where anybody had ever wanted to be. It and the farming on it looked like an afterthought. It looked like what Troy had thought about last, after thinking about himself, his status, his machinery, and his debts.

All of a sudden I felt ashamed, as if I had walked without thinking into some total and embarrassing privacy. I had been, until then, sort of fascinatedly eager to see, and then I realized that I did not at all want to be seen seeing. I crept back to my boat even more stealthily than I had crept up on the absent ducks.

Mattie Chatham was the true child of her parents and their ways. As Mat Feltner used to say, "You can't beat out of the flesh what's bred in the bone." She *belonged* to the good farm that Troy was turning into paper. And she was a true child of the revelation of the 1930s. She seemed always in some way mindful of the Depression, when the Keiths had held life together by living from the place. She knew what the place had meant to Athey and Della, and what they had meant to it. Through all the time and the troubles of her marriage to Troy, she held as well as she could to the old ways. She never let the economies of her household sink down. She was a woman of great energy, whose movements always had a certain force and momentum and resolution, as well as grace. She kept house, kept a flock of chickens, gardened, canned and preserved food, made clothes, practiced every sort of ingenuity and frugality.

Troy depended on her. Surely he knew he did. For a long time, he took her work and his dependence for granted. And then he got embarrassed. He began to feel that she (and, therefore, he) was degraded by the part she played. He was, after all, following the line of what was supposed to be a "success story"—how a smart and talented country boy started out with nothing and finally gained a big acreage of land and made something of himself. And here he was, gaining nothing, and his wife was working to raise the food they ate, which he ought to be able to buy for her. And she would be milking the cows or, later, feeding the hogs, when he had nobody else to do it, when he ought to be able to hire somebody to do it in her place.

She became in a way the sign of his torment, of the failure that he felt but couldn't bear to see, and he began doing something he had never done before. He had always, in his humorless humor, made jokes about women and wives. But now he began to make jokes that were disparaging directly of her. "I'm going home," he would say. "If the woman don't have dinner ready I'm going to raise hell, and if she does I ain't going to eat it." So far as I know, he *was* joking, or trying to. But it was the wrong kind of joke.

Anger is not a sin for no reason. I think I can say truly that I am a man slow to anger. I don't like anger in myself any more than I like it in other people. But when anger comes to me, it comes full force; I remember Elton Penn saying, "Hell flew into me in a minute!" My skin seems to get all of a sudden tighter, my vision gets bad, as if I'm looking through a little hole, and I feel light and joyful and careless. When Troy would let out one of those remarks, I would have to stop and take hold of the chairback with both hands. A barber, you know, is often holding a deadly weapon.

Sometimes if I was alone after he had left, I would seem to wake up from a dream in which I was imagining how I could nick his throat with the razor and make it look like an accident.

Why didn't I do it? I wish I was sure why. Pacifist that I was and am, I am not sure. There were times when, without benefit of any conscious thought whatsoever, I wanted to wreck him in one neat stroke of perfect violence. Was I so good, so deeply convinced of the wrong of killing, that I refrained from doing it without benefit of thought? Was I a coward? Was I afraid of the man across the desk and the clash of the jailhouse door? Or was I too finicky to want him bleeding on my floor? Waking up from a dream of violence is much the same as waking up from a dream of love. You must go on living your life.

I did not love Troy Chatham. I was no longer capable of the effort of will it took to understand why Mattie did. Which would sooner or later remind me that I could not understand why God did. That was my sanity.

Did Mattie, in fact, love Troy? I think she did. I have lived some time beyond my hatred of Troy Chatham by now, and I think she loved him. I think she loved him to the end, and pitied his struggle even as she suffered it. I think so because she was not downbeaten. However she may have submitted herself and her place to what Troy was, and to what he meant to other things that she loved, what she was remained intact. If she had not loved Troy that could not have been so. But she loved him, however at odds with him she may have been, for however long. She remembered and kept treasured up her old feeling for him. She treasured up the knowledge that, though she was not happy, happiness existed. And so as Troy's character wore lower and more awry, her own grew straighter and brighter.

Why did she stay with him and stay loyal to him so many years until death, through so much sorrow and trouble and damage? There were two reasons, I think: She was married to him, which she took as seriously as, after all, I would have had her take it; and she understood, not just his ambition and his foolishness, his selfishness and lack of judgment, but also his fragility. She sacrificed everything to hold him together—maybe wrongly, but I lack the intelligence (or maybe the will) to see how she might have done otherwise, once she was married to him. After all, it wasn't just Troy himself that she was dealing with but the way of the world in her time. It would be hard to argue that one woman ought to have found a way to stand up against a whole drove of experts and their salesmen, who spoke for the way of the world and were certain that there was no other possible way.

And so she was defeated, a good woman who had too early made one bad mistake. And yet she persevered with dignity and good humor, and with a kind of loveliness that was her own. How do I know? I know because from time to time during those years we would be together.

31

The Nest Egg

The Nest Egg was the fifty or so acres of big timber that Athey Keith kept and protected "in case of need," until finally just having and holding it came to mean a great deal more to him than any possibility of need. It lay on the upriver side of Coulter Branch, cut off from the rest of the Keith place and made inconvenient to get to by the branch and its rough hollow, and therefore never even fenced and pastured in the memory of man. Whether or not it was an absolutely "virgin" woods is another question. There were some double-trunked white oaks, big ones, and so there must have been some cutting in there, a long time ago, but only in a few spots. Other places, I thought, had never been touched. Trees were standing in the Nest Egg that had been there when D. Boone and the others came hunting through, and when the first old Keiths and Coulters and Rowanberrys came in and settled: oaks and walnuts and tulip poplars that you couldn't reach halfway around with both arms and that went way up without a limb. It took, as Burley Coulter said, a mighty good rifle (and a mighty good eye) to shoot a squirrel out of the top of one of them. Where the wind had blown one over and its roots had come up, there would be a hollow in the ground bigger than a grave.

One of the happinesses and finally the greatest joy of my life on the river was my nearness to the Nest Egg. It was only half a mile or so away. I would go downriver along the road and then turn in to the Coulter Branch hollow by a lane so little used as to be almost invisible. It really was just a footpath kept worn by occasional hunters or trespassers (like me) and the wild creatures. The path went along between a low wooded slope and a little patch of bottom that had been cropped occasionally in Athey's time but was now covered with thicket. There was a dense patch of the bamboo that we call "cane," about six or eight feet high, which once stood in huge brakes and fed the buffalo before the time of the white people. For some distance in the cane the path was almost a burrow. And then you stepped out of that confinement into a swale wooded with big water maples and ashes and walnuts and sycamores, a sort of entrance hall, spacious and airy. Backwater from the floods often stood there, and the floor was covered with pieces of drift, which in turn were covered in the growing season with a solid stand of nettles. In spring when their foliage was new, these nettles seemed a rich and perfect carpet, though they stood taller than your knees and stung like fire if they touched your skin.

From this place of entrance, being always careful of the nettles, you could make your way up a low, steep slope into the drier woods, untroubled by flooding, where the dark trunks went up so tall, and among them you would see here and there the silver of beeches or, along the hollows, the sudden whiteness of sycamores. This was a many-storied place, starting under the ground with the dark forest of roots and the creatures of the dark. And then there were the dead leaves and the brilliant mosses and the mushrooms in their season. And next were the wildflowers and the ferns in their appointed places and times, and then the spice bushes and buckthorns and devil's clubs and the patches of cane. And next were the low trees: ironwood, hornbeam, dogwood, and (in openings made by fallen big trees) redbud. Above those, the big trees and the vines went up to the crown of foliage at the top. And at all these aboveground stories there was a moving and singing foliage of birds. Everywhere there were dens and holes and hollows and secret nests. When you were there you could be sure that you were being seen, and that you more than likely would not see what was seeing you.

Everything there seemed to belong where it was. That was why I went there. And I went to feel the change that that place always made in me. Always, as soon as I came in under the big trees, I began to go slowly and quietly. This was not because I was hunting (I hunted in other places), but because in a place where everything belongs where it is, you do not want to disturb anything. I went slowly and quietly. I watched where I put my feet. I went for solace and comfort, for a certain quietness of mind that came to me in no other place. Even the nettles and the mosquitoes comforted me, for they belonged where they were.

There were, in the hot, muggy summer days, sure enough a great plenty of mosquitoes. Big ones. And hungry. They could smell your blood beneath your skin at a distance of a hundred yards, and they came whining to the feast, so ecstatic with appetite that they didn't even look up to see if you were watching. You could swat them several at a lick and they didn't seem to mind. They were outlandish big. Burley Coulter used to say that they could stand flatfooted and deflower a turkey. If you went there in good mosquito weather, you were inclined to keep walking; you never thought of sitting down. In general it was best, after the weather heated up, to go to the Nest Egg only on the cooler, drier, breezier days.

On a warm day, a bright day in late April, a Sunday afternoon, I passed right on through the swale where the nettles were and went up that first low, steep slope. From there the woods went back on a sort of platform or terrace that was broken by slue hollows where backwater was still puddled from the late rises. In those places the mosquitoes about added up to a mean dog; you could fairly hear their guts growling. I kept to the high ground and went on to where the slope of the valleyside began to rise. At that point Coulter Branch ceases to be a sluggish, mud-banked stream and becomes a steep, rocky one, coming down in a series of little falls and pools like a stairway. Well up the slope I turned away from the stream and walked out along the face of the bluff to a sort of point near the upper boundary of the Keith land. The woods opened up in that place and, as I expected, there was a fine breeze. I sat down and leaned my back against a big red oak. As I often did, I had brought a book to read.

But I didn't read much, or long. Because of the breeze, the place was full of the motions of shadows and lights. The day was still warming up, and I was not far past a pretty good dinner. A woodpecker was halfheartedly pecking on a hollow limb as if he were neither feeding nor sending a message but just idly whittling or talking to himself. My book slipped out of my hands and woke me up. I stretched out on my back on the dry leaves, then, and went to sleep in earnest.

One of the best things you can do in this world is take a nap in the woods. I slept soundly and without moving for half an hour. As often happens at such times, my mind woke up before my body did. My eyes opened right out of sleep, and I was looking up at the gently stirring treetops and the bright sky, with no other thought on my mind, and my body still deeply resting. It was delicious and I did not want to move.

The woodpecker stopped his drowsy pecking and flew. I raised my head and looked around. Mattie Chatham was coming along the slope about the same way I had come. She was just idly wandering along, looking at everything as she went. She had picked a little bouquet of violets, both the blossoms and the pretty leaves, and was carrying it as she might have done when she was a girl, pleased to have their beauty with her. She seemed surrounded by almost a singing of her sense of rest.

You can maybe imagine my astonishment at waking to the sight of her there, and also my discomfort, for she had not yet seen me. It was a moment of great social awkwardness. I felt it a shame to intrude on her. I knew in an instant that, like me, she had come there for solace and comfort. I could feel, as later I would know, that she was a familiar of the place. Coming there, she stepped over a threshold where her troubles, if they did not quite go away, at least stopped and waited. And so I could hardly assume that this was an offhand encounter, as if we had met in the post office in Port William. I thought of just lying still and letting her go by, or even pretending to be asleep. But I didn't want her to think, if she came nearer and saw me, that I had been slyly watching her. When she turned her head away, I sat up. When she looked back in my direction, I raised my hand and gave a small, noncommittal wave.

She said, "Oh!" in surprise, and not exactly with pleasure. And then, as if we *were* in the post office in Port William, she gave me her good general-purpose smile and said, "Hello, Jayber. How're you?"

"I'm fine," I said. "It's a good day."

"It's beautiful," she said.

She came on, not to where I was but nearby, and sat down.

She said, "I thought I would find a breeze here."

She hadn't looked at me when she spoke. Fearing she had spoken just to be polite, I didn't reply. I didn't know whether she had sat down in friendship, or because she was feeling socially awkward herself, or because she was tired.

And then she did look at me and smiled again, seeming to endow our encounter with a sort of permission. She gestured with her bouquet toward the treetops, through which the sky sent down upon us a network of gently shifting lights. "Lovely," she said.

"Yes," I said. "It is."

We sat there, thus apart and together, for a long time.

After a while she stood up, brushed the leaf chaff from her clothes, and said, "Well, I guess we ought to be going."

She said "we." What did she know? We never spoke of such things. This was in 1970, the year after I moved to the river. She was forty-six years old that year. I had loved her, had belonged to her, then, for a long time. When I think of her now, I am sometimes persuaded that she already knew that. Is this because any man believes, or fears, that a beloved woman not only knows more about him than he knows himself but also knows it sooner than he can hope to know it? Or did she really know?

She said "we," and I stood and followed her by another way back to the path through the cane and on to the road, where she went her way and I mine.

After that, from time to time we would meet, as you might say by accident, somewhere in that patch of woods that her father had named the Nest Egg. It is of the utmost importance that you should understand that these meetings were not trysts. They were not planned—just as, I imagine, such meetings within an ordinary marriage are not—because they could not be. They were not, until they happened, even intended. They happened only because Mattie and I were alive in the same little world of Port William at the same time, and because both of us loved the Nest Egg. From that first day, I knew that these meetings must not be planned, expected, depended on, or looked forward to. They were a hope seen afar, that must be with patience waited for. And in fact a strange unforeseeing patience had come over me, a patience until death. Though I remembered a time when it seemed to me I would gladly have died even just to touch the back of her hand, now I was not disturbed.

At first I would ask myself, "Can this be?" Later, I knew it could.

We would not see each other maybe for many days. When I went to the Nest Egg, I went only to be there, to see what was there, to grow quiet enough to hear its sounds and voices. And then one day again she would be there. Our paths would cross and we would go along a ways together while the season warmed and the leaves unfolded overhead, while the leaves fell or the snow. We walked always in beauty, it seemed to me. We walked and looked about, or stood and looked. Sometimes, less often, we would sit down. We did not often speak. The place spoke for us and was a kind of speech. We spoke to each other in the things we saw. As we went along, ways would open before us, alleys and aisles and winding paths, leading to patches of maidenhair ferns or to a tree where pileated woodpeckers nested or to a place where a barred owl gazed down at us backward over his tail. The woods showed us its small brakes of cane (especially lovely when their green foliage was laden with snow), its ascending vines, its lichens and mosses and ferns, its nests and burrows. We saw warblers, wood ducks, thrushes, deer. Around us always were the passing graces of moving air, lights and shadows, bird flight, songs, calls, drummings. Each of us knew what the other saw and heard. There was no need to ask, no need to say.

We went from paths into pathlessness. The woods has many doors going in and out. It is full of rooms opening into one another, shaped by direction and viewpoint. Many of these rooms are findable only once, from a certain direction on a certain day, in a certain light, at a certain time. They could not be returned to either now, after years, or then, after an hour. Windows opened in the foliage, through which, maybe, we would see a hawk soaring or a distant treetop suddenly shaken by a gust of wind. Sometimes these walks and rooms and vistas seemed arranged for us, for our pleasure, as in a human garden. But these, of course, do not constitute the woods, which is not a garden and is not understandable or foretellable even so much as a garden is.

We would come sometimes into a place of such loveliness that it stopped us still and held us until some changing of the light seemed to bless us and let us go.

We came in April to a slope covered with bluebells, and knelt to smell their cool perfume, so fresh and delicate and unrememberable as to seem to have come from another world.

One afternoon in the spring when we were standing still and silent by the side of Coulter Branch where the water fell with a hundred voices down steps and glides among the rocks from pool to pool, where the mosses were bright green on the rocks and the tree roots and the stonecrop was in bloom, we saw a red fox step out of the undergrowth into a shaft of sunlight where he paused a moment, glowing, and disappeared like a flame put out.

It was a winter afternoon and the snow was falling without wind, straight down. The snow was gathering like blossoms on the green leaves of the cane. In the woods beyond us, we could hear woodpeckers calling. We had not said much. We were standing as still as the trees. The only thing we saw that was moving was the snow.

I said, "It's like time falling, and we and the trees are standing up in it."

"No," she said. "Look. It's like we and the woods and the world are flying upward through the snow. See?"

We stood without saying any more for a long time, flying higher and higher to meet the feathery big flakes as they fell. The evening began to darken. I looked and saw that she had gone, her tracks leading away through the deepening snow. And then I too went away.

These meetings happened from time to time over a period of fourteen or fifteen years. I don't know how many there were—fewer than you would think, perhaps, seeing that they made up so important a part of my life. Since none was ever planned, each one was different, surprising in its way. And yet the terms never changed. Mattie always preserved a certain discretion, not in anything she said, but in the way she was, the way she carried herself and looked. She was with me, but not for me, if you can see what I mean. There was a veil between us. We both kept her vow, as I alone kept mine. I knew there was a smile of hers that I had never seen. And that was well. That was all right.

I dreamed that I was Mattie Chatham.

At first it made me happy to be dreaming that I was her, and then I just was her.

I was walking in a field of October flowers. I was gathering them and laying them in the crook of my left arm. The sun was shining.

Among the drying stems and grasses and the fallen leaves, I saw scattered some whitened bones.

I laid down my bouquet and began picking up the bones that still had the reek of death about them.

As I gathered them up, the bones hurt me. I wept and my tears fell on them.

I thought I would die of the pain of them, but I picked them up, one by one.

From my tears the bones took life and flesh. They became a little girl in a pretty dress, lying asleep in my arms.

My tears fell on her and she woke. She looked up at me and smiled.

And then the light changed, and the vegetation of the ground. It was April and the freshest flowers of the year were blooming under the trees. The little girl was Liddie.

I set her down and she ran about among the flowers, picking the blossoms and putting them in her hair.

She looked at me and laughed.

She said, "Momma! Look how beautiful I am!"

This is a book about Heaven. I know it now. It floats among us like a cloud and is the realest thing we know and the least to be captured, the least to be possessed by anybody for himself. It is like a grain of mustard seed, which you cannot see among the crumbs of earth where it lies. It is like the reflection of the trees on the water.

One afternoon when I had been to the Nest Egg, and Mattie and I had walked together and had parted, I was thirsty and I stopped at the well by the road to draw a drink. It was late in the fall and all the leaves were down. It had been a gray day, November in the world and in the soul. I filled the cup and lifted it. As I did so, I saw something glowing on the horizon. It was one of the hilltops across the river where a patch of sunlight had broken through the overcast. The hilltop was bright, and the valley where I watched was nearly filled with shadow. And then I saw that two nearer ridgetops on the far side of the Katy's Branch valley were also glowing, just the woods at the very top, perfectly golden. And then I saw the shaft of a rainbow dimly to my left across the river. As I watched, the whole arc came gradually visible and grew brilliant over the glowing ridgetops, and I could see just the ghost of the second arc. The sky within the bow was bright, and outside it was dark, the difference increasing and then diminishing as the light left the ridges and the rainbow faded.

When Mattie became ill, she did not tell me. She left it to Port William to tell me, knowing it would. Port William told me, of course, but that (as she also knew) did not grant me permission to speak of her illness to her. We seemed, in fact, to have less and less need to speak of anything. Knowing what we knew, knowing in common much that we knew, not speaking, we preserved the common kindness of those meetings that, never foreseen, seemed yet to have been appointed to us from before the time of the world.

We would meet, walk or stand together a little while, and part—while she suffered the course of her illness, the course of hope and renewed hope, and loss of hope. Finally, as her sickness grew upon her, she came no more.

And, of course, Port William told me the rest—except for the last thing left to tell (which I am going to tell you shortly) that so far is known only to me.

In the days after she died, the world seemed filled with a harsh, caustic, almost shadowless light that it hurt to see.

I am an old man now and oftentimes I whisper to myself. I have heard myself whispering things that I didn't know I had ever thought. "Forty years" or "Fifty years" or "Sixty years," I hear myself whispering. My life lengthens. History grows shorter. I remember old men who remembered the Civil War. I have in my mind word-of-mouth memories more than a hundred years old. It is only twenty hundred years since the birth of Christ. Fifteen or twenty memories such as mine would reach all the way back to the halo-light in the manger at Bethlehem. So few rememberers could sit down together in a small room. They could loaf together in the old poolroom up in Port William and talk all of a Saturday night of war and rumors of war.

I whisper over to myself the way of loss, the names of the dead. One by one, we lose our loved ones, our friends, our powers of work and pleasure, our landmarks, the days of our allotted time. One by one, the way we lose them, they return to us and are treasured up in our hearts. Grief affirms them, preserves them, sets the cost. Finally a man stands up alone, scoured and charred like a burnt tree, having lost everything and (at the cost only of its loss) found everything, and is ready to go. Now I am ready.

32
Seen Afar

This is not an exactly true account of my life. The necessity of telling it has caused me to divide it into strands. Things that happened at the same time, different and even opposite feelings and thoughts that came all at once, have had to be strung out to be told. In fact, many things have always been happening all at the same time. Some of the funniest things have happened on some of the saddest days. Sometimes I have been happy in the midst of sorrow, or sorrowful in the midst of happiness. Sometimes too I have been perfectly content, in the amazing state of ignorance, not yet knowing that I was already in the presence of loss.

This is, as I said and believe, a book about Heaven, but I must say too that it has been a close call. For I have wondered sometimes if it would not finally turn out to be a book about Hell—where we fail to love one another, where we hate and destroy one another for reasons abundantly provided or for righteousness' sake or for pleasure, where we destroy the things we need the most, where we see no hope and have no faith, where we are needy and alone, where things that ought to stay together fall apart, where there is such a groaning travail of selfishness in all its forms, where we love one another and die, where we must lose everything to know what we have had.

But the earth speaks to us of Heaven, or why would we want to go there? If we knew nothing of Hell, how would we delight in Heaven should we get there?

There is Hell enough, maybe, just in the knowledge of what you might call the leftovers of my life: things I might once have done that are now undoable, old wrongs, responsibilities unmet, ineradicable failures—things of time, which is always revealing the remedies it has already carried us beyond.

What became of Clydie Greatlow? I know only a little. After her mother died, Clydie tore loose from her fierce old Aunt Beulah, married the tobacco buyer, and went to live in Georgia. But what happened to her after that? I know I made that none of my business. And yet I wonder. I would like to know.

When Roy died, Cecelia Overhold sold the farm for more money probably than Roy had ever thought of and went to California without so much as a look back. Her sister in that paradise was dead also by then, but there was a nephew, the hero of Cecelia's last will and testament, from whom she anticipated a joyous welcome. The nephew welcomed her by enrolling her into an old folks' home where, forsaken, she did not live long. All Cecelia accomplished in her latter days, really, was to transfer from Port William to Los Angeles the pretty penny she got for the Overhold place. A long time ago, when I had grown up a little, I forgave her easily enough for her dislike of me—though, of course, she never asked me to do so. To forgive her for her own principled misery, her contempt for all available satisfactions on the grounds merely that they were available—that was harder and took longer.

Maybe you think it was a hard thing (I think it was) that Cecelia and Roy endured and suffered through so many years of their trial by marriage. But here is maybe a harder thing that I have thought of at last: What if they endured and suffered through so many years because, even failing each other, they loved each other?

As for Troy Chatham, whose enemy I was for so many years, even against my will, though he never knew it, or cared, if he did know it—I have forgiven him too, even him, even if I cannot say yet that the thought of him gladdens me. Of Troy I will have a little more to say. For now, it is enough to tell that he lost the Keith place, and with it his own life's hard work, which finally amounted to nothing.

I am a man who has hoped, in time, that his life, when poured out at the end, would say, "Good-good-good-good-good!" like a gallon jug of the prime local spirit. I am a man of losses, regrets, and griefs. I am an old man full of love. I am a man of faith.

But faith is not necessarily, or not soon, a resting place. Faith puts you out on a wide river in a little boat, in the fog, in the dark. Even a man of faith knows that (as Burley Coulter used to say) we've all got to go through enough to kill us. As a man of faith, I've thought a considerable amount about a friend of mine (imagined, but also real) I call the Man in the Well.

The now wooded, or rewooded, slopes and hollows hereabouts are strewn with abandoned homesteads, the remains of another kind of world. Most of them by now have no buildings left. Everything about them that would rot has rotted. What you find now in those places when you come upon them are the things that were built of stone: foundations, cellars, chimneys, wells. Sometimes the wells are deep, dug to the bedrock and beyond, and walled with rock laid up without mortar. Virtually every rock in a structure like that, if it is built right, is a keystone; it can't move in or out. Those walls, laid underground where there is no freezing and thawing, will last, I guess, almost forever.

Sometimes the well is the only structure remaining, and there will be no visible sign of it. It will be covered with old boards in some stage of decay, green with moss or covered with leaves. It is a perfect trap, and now and then you find that rabbits and groundhogs have blundered in and drowned. A man too could blunder into one.

Imagine a hunter, somebody from a city some distance away, who has a job he doesn't like, and who has come alone out into the country to hunt on a Saturday. It is a beautiful, perfect fall day, and the Man feels free. He has left all his constraints and worries and fears behind. Nobody knows where he is. Anybody who wanted to complain or accuse or collect a debt could not find him. The morning that started frosty has grown warm. The sky seems to give its luster to everything in the world. The Man feels strong and fine. His gun lies ready in the crook of his arm, though he really doesn't care whether he finds game or not. He has a sandwich and a candy bar in his coat pocket. And then, not looking where he is going, which is easy enough on such a day, he steps onto the rotten boards that cover one of those old wells, and down he goes.

He disappears suddenly out of the lighted world. He falls so quickly that he doesn't have time even to ask what is happening. He hits water, goes under, comes up, swims, or clings to the wall, inserting his fingers between the rocks. And now, I think, you cannot help imagining the way it would be with him. He looks up and sees how far down he has come. The sky that was so large and reassuring only seconds ago is now just a small blue picture of itself, far away. His first thought is that he is alone, that nobody knows where he is; these two great pleasures that were his freedom have now become his prison, perhaps his tomb. He calls out (for might not somebody chance to be nearby, just as he chanced to fall into the well?) and he hears himself enclosed within the sound of his own calling voice.

How does this story end? Does he save himself? Is he athletic enough, maybe, to get his boots off and climb out, clawing with fingers and toes into the grudging holds between the rocks of the wall? Does he climb up and fall back? Does somebody, in fact, for a wonder, chance to pass nearby and hear him? Does he despair, give up, and drown? Does he, despairing, pray finally the first true prayer of his life?

Listen. There is a light that includes our darkness, a day that shines down even on the clouds. A man of faith believes that the Man in the Well is not lost. He does not believe this easily or without pain, but he believes it. His belief is a kind of knowledge beyond any way of knowing. He believes that the child in the womb is not lost, nor is the man whose work has come to nothing, nor is the old woman forsaken in a nursing home in California. He believes that those who make their bed in Hell are not lost, or those who dwell in the uttermost parts of the sea, or the lame man at Bethesda Pool, or Lazarus in the grave, or those who pray, *"Eli, Eli, lama sabachthani."*

Have mercy.

The rest of what I have to tell begins in the amazing state of ignorance. It was a fairly ordinary late summer day, a Monday. I ran my lines the first thing, as usual, and had my breakfast and my shave. I did up my housework, gathered the things that needed washing (which is how I remember that it was Monday), and washed them. Provided I am not short of water, I like washing. I do it on a scrubbing board in a galvanized tub set on two chairs, and I have two other tubs for rinsing. It is pleasant to work a while in the smell of soap, and then to have the smell of the clean wet things drying on the line. Nobody came for a haircut that day, and so I was never interrupted. When I had the washing hung out, I fixed a bite to eat, and ate, and took a nap, and then I went down to hit a few licks in the garden.

I did have a trouble or two on my mind. I knew that Mattie was in the hospital down at Hargrave. Some said she was dying. Some said, well, you never know, for a person can be mighty sick and still linger for a long time. Nobody was saying any more, not even for politeness' sake, that she might get well. You will imagine that I felt powerfully drawn to go to see her, to offer in her presence, as people do, the useless wish that I could do something to help. But I had not gone. I was not going to go. If I didn't go, I knew I would be sorry. But not a soul, including me, had ever acknowledged that I had any concern in the matter. If I went and was seen there, I would embarrass her. I would embarrass myself too. I did think of that.

Troubled or not, grieved or not, you have got to live. And the facts of the case are even harder than that, for however troubled and grieved you may be, you will often find, looking back, that you were not living without enjoyment. That day had a trouble in it that would overwhelm its pleasure, though I did not yet know it.

I was putting off knowing it. All that day there had been a crashing in the wind, the sound of a chainsaw and that of a much heavier engine. But the sounds seemed somehow undemanding. The wind that day was stirring in the nearer trees, and as I went about my work I raised a certain amount of commotion around myself. I made excuses for the crashings and the engine sounds. In this valley, after all, some form of pandemonium is no rare thing. A highway crew will be at work somewhere; the heavy gravel trucks will be running; a towboat or a convoy of pleasure boats will be passing on the river; a crew will be clearing right-of-way under a power line; the forces of the air will be practicing what I suppose to be bombing runs low over the ridgetops; The Economy and The War are everywhere, making their noises.

"Something of Great Importance is going on," I thought to myself, brushing it aside. "Surely The News is happening someplace nearby."

And so it wasn't until I had commenced work in the garden that I all of a sudden stopped, knowing that I knew what it was, and an awful coldness of knowledge went over me from head to foot. I put my hoe away and started for the Nest Egg. It was a painful walk, for I was still hoping to be proved wrong, but every step I took confirmed that I was right.

The thickety little strip of bottomland along the lower end of Coulter Branch had been cleared off with a bulldozer, and that was where they were yarding up the logs. Tremendous logs were lying there, side by side. They made me think of beached whales, great living creatures heaved out of their element at last. But all the logs were not big. Troy Chatham had sold every marketable stick, every tree big enough to make two two-by-fours.

Troy himself was standing among the big logs, looking about. Beyond, off in the woods, the chainsaw ran hard and then more easily and then idled, sputtering, as a tree fell, breaking its way through other trees to the ground. And then you could hear only the engine of the bulldozer that they were dragging the logs with. Presently the dozer burst out through the fringe of cane. It dragged a big log into place beside the other logs and hurried out of sight again, making nothing of whatever saplings were in the way.

Troy saw me then and waved me over. I went obediently, feeling a sort of embarrassment, as if the occasion called for an etiquette that I had not learned. He was grinning his big in-the-know grin. He began talking before I got within hearing.

I said, *"What?"*

He said, "You've got to see it to believe it, don't you?"

I could say nothing. For me, seeing it made it harder to believe. I couldn't quite imagine the world in which it would be believable. Something fundamental seemed to be ending. Athey's Nest Egg now looked small. Now, even in my memory of it, it looked small.

Troy said, "Lord Almighty, the power they've got! And these boys know how to use it! You wouldn't think it, would you?"

"No," I said.

"And look at these logs," he said. "Who'd have thought such trees could have grown here?"

The day was hot and he was sweating. We both were.

He was grinning, wanting to talk. Beyond his need for money, he was needing to be proud. I had begun to feel the world whirling; I wanted to lie down for fear of being flung off.

I knew the story. I knew what had happened. All that "leverage" he had bragged about: The fulcrum had shifted. The price of land had dropped. He no longer had the equity to support his debts. He was about to lose everything that he had believed he owned by courtesy of relentless work and endless debt. In his desperation to salvage something, even just a little dab of pride, he had had to look on Mattie's illness as providential. He had come to that. As soon as she had gone into the hospital (for the last time, I knew now; she was gone from this place forever), he had sold the timber. So I knew too that she had been its protector.

I heard in my mind the voices of how many outraged old men of Port William: "The damned fool! They ought to penitencher the son of a bitch!"

At the clap of that condemnation in my thoughts, what had happened to him seemed to happen to me, and for the first time I saw him apart from my contempt for him. I saw him clear-eyed.

I saw us both as if from a great distance off in time: two small, craving, suffering creatures, soon to be gone. Troy was a beaten man and knew it, and was trying not to know it. You could see it in his eyes. Now at last he was about to inherit a farm that he had worn out, that he had so encumbered with debt that he could not keep it, that I knew would now be dragged into the suck of speculation and development to be subdivided under some such name as Paradise Estates. This was Troy's last play in what he had sometimes liked to call "the game of farming." What did he have left? Another cutting of timber, maybe, if he could wait another hundred or two hundred years.

So there he was, a man who had been given everything and did not know it, who had lost it all and now knew it, and who was boasting and grinning only to pretend for a few hours longer that he did not know it. He was an exhausted man on the way back, not to the nothing that he had when he started out, but to the nothing that everything had been created from—and so, I pray, to mercy.

And there I was, a man losing what I was never given, a man yet rich with love, a man whose knees were weakening against gravity, who needed to go somewhere and lie down. I stood facing that man I had hated for forty years, and I did not hate him. If he had acknowledged then what he finally would not be able to avoid acknowledging, I would have hugged him. If I could have done it, I would have liked to pick him up like a child and carry him to some place of safety and calm.

The time would come (and this was my deliverance, my Nunc Dimittis) when I would be, in the small ways that were possible, his friend. It was a friend, finally, that he would need. I would listen to him and talk to him, ignoring his self-pity and his lapses into grandeur and meanness, giving him a good welcome and a pat on the shoulder, because I wanted to. For finally he was redeemed, in my eyes, by Mattie's long-abiding love for him, as I myself had been by my love for her.

But that day I couldn't stay with him any longer. I needed to leave him and his desperate merchandise and that woods of once-upon-a-time. I needed to go and find a place to lie down. That urge was in me like a natural force. Like a woman or an animal in labor, I longed to lie down, for I was heavy, not with new life but with much dying, many deaths. I had in me the shaking of the fall of all things. I wanted to get as low as I could, as I thought I would want to do had I been in the top of a windblown tree or in a little boat in a storm.

I didn't go home. Anything of the familiar world would have been more than I could bear. I went in amongst the trees between the river and the road. There was a driftlog in an elderberry patch well up the slope. I made my way into that covert and lay down beside the log on the dry leaves. Nobody would find me there, and I needed not to be found.

I fell into a dreadful sleep that maybe was my death itself. I became one with the earth and was anything but at peace. I heard the motors speeding along the pavements and the rivers, the tractors in the fields, the airplanes in the sky, and always, always that chainsaw in the woods. I heard the big trees tearing and breaking their way to the ground, and the thumps of little creatures run over on the road.

It could have been three hours or three weeks that I suffered that dream, but I knew when I woke that it was more than three hours and less than three weeks, for it was early morning and the time of year was the same. I was bewildered, having been changed by my bitter sleep more than I yet could know.

In the darkness a large black-and-yellow spider had woven a perfect web right above me, guying it to the log, several elderberry stems, and my shirt. I eased out from under it as carefully as I could, but not without damaging it. In my bewilderment I spent several perfectly crazy minutes trying to fix it. But of course a man can't make a spider's web, any more than he can make a world. Finally I said, "Pardon me, old friend, I have got to go."

After that I was purposeful. I went like a stranger back to my strange little house. I did my morning chores, ate my breakfast, and then bathed and shaved and put on my best clothes.

Danny Branch's boat happened at that time to be once again in the era of modern transportation. The boys had got hold of another old outboard motor that they maintained at a level of respectability slightly above that of scrap metal. It was a battered, greasy old thing, much scratched and dented. From having observed the Branches, I knew roughly how to run it. I filled the tank, checked everything, and started it. I was on my way down the river to Hargrave before it occurred to me that I had done something fairly remarkable, that the motor might not have started. My only thought had been to get to Hargrave without going by road. I did not want to see anybody or talk to anybody. And I was in too much of a hurry to walk.

The day was already hot. I went humming right down the middle of the river, driving the V of my wake into the quietness. The old motor coughed occasionally as if contemplating a change of mind, but it did not stop. I did not pay it the courtesy even of looking at it.

I tied up to the bank not far above the lock at Hargrave, taking care to leave the boat where it would not call attention to itself.

When I went in out of the hot light, the hospital was so dim and cool that I had to stand still to get used to it.

A lady at a desk said, "May I help you?"

I said, "Mrs. Chatham's room, if you please."

She gave me the number and pointed.

I felt clear and free. Later, it seemed to me that I had given no thought at all to what I was doing, that from the moment I rose from sleep I merely had known.

Her door was open. I started to give a little knock, but then I saw that she was sleeping and I just tiptoed in, to be out of the hallway.

There were tubes and machines all around her. The tubes carried liquids to needles in the veins of her arms. Her hands, which had been strong and capable, were frail. Her face was almost as white as the pillow. She was thin and small. Looking at her at other times, I had been reminded of Athey or Della. A slant of light or a movement would show some passing resemblance. But there, in her diminishment, she seemed to resemble only herself, as if suffering finally had singled her out.

Maybe, as a person sometimes does, she felt me watching. She opened her eyes.

When she saw it was me, she said, "Jayber. Oh, he's cutting the woods." And so she knew.

Her eyes filled with tears, but she said quietly, "I could die in peace, I think, if the world was beautiful. To know it's being ruined is hard."

Then, in the loss of all the world, when I might have said the words I had so long wanted to say, I could not say them. I saw that I was not going to be able to talk without crying, and so I cried. I said, "But what about this other thing?"

She looked at me then. "Yes," she said. She held out her hand to me. She gave me the smile that I had never seen and will not see again in this world, and it covered me all over with light.